EX LIBRIS

VINTAGE CLASSICS

HAPPY MOSCOW

Andrey Platonovich Platonov (1899-1951) was the son of a railway-worker and worked as a land reclamation expert. His most politically controversial works of the late 1920s and early 1930s, including *The Foundation Pit* and *Chevengur*, remained unpublished in Russia until the late 1980s. Other stories were published but subjected to vicious criticism. Platonov worked as a war correspondent and managed to publish several volumes of stories; after the war, however, he was again almost unable to publish. He died in 1951, of tuberculosis caught from his son whom Platonov had nursed on his return from the gulag. *Happy Moscow*, one of his finest short novels, was first published in 1991; a complete text of *Soul* was first published only in 1999.

Robert Chandler's translations from Russian include Vasily Grossman's *Life and Fate*, *Everything Flows* and *The Road*, Leskov's *Lady Macbeth of Mtsensk* and Alexander Pushkin's *Dubrovsky* and *The Captain's Daughter*. He has also translated Sappho and Guillaume Apollinaire. His translation of Hamid Ismailov's *The Railway* and his co-translations of works by Andrey Platonov have won prizes in the UK and in the USA. He is the editor of *Russian Short Stories from Pushkin to Buida* and the author of *Alexander Pushkin*. He teaches part-time at Queen Mary, University of London.

Elizabeth Chandler is a co-translator, with her husband, of Pushkin's *The Captain's Daughter* and of several volumes by Andrey Platonov: *The Return*, *The Portable Platonov*, *Happy Moscow* and *Soul*.

ALSO BY ANDREY PLATONOV

The Return and Other Stories
The Foundation Pit
Soul and Other Stories

ANDREY PLATONOV

Happy Moscow

TRANSLATED FROM THE RUSSIAN BY
Robert and Elizabeth Chandler

VINTAGE BOOKS
London

Published by Vintage 2013

2 4 6 8 10 9 7 5 3 1

This selection and revised translations first published
by The New York Review of Books in 2012

Happy Moscow first published in Russian in *Strana Filosofov* in
1999
Soul first published in Great Britain by The Harvill Press in 2001

Vintage
Random House, 20 Vauxhall Bridge Road,
London SW1V 2SA

www.vintage-classics.info

Addresses for companies within The Random House Group Limited
can be found at: www.randomhouse.co.uk/offices.htm

The Random House Group Limited Reg. No. 954009

A CIP catalogue record for this book
is available from the British Library
ISBN 9780099577256

The Random House Group Limited supports the Forest Stewardship
Council® (FSC®), the leading international forest-certification
organisation. Our books carrying the FSC label are printed on
FSC®-certified paper. FSC is the only forest-certification scheme
supported by the leading environmental organisations, including
Greenpeace. Our paper procurement policy can be found at:
www.randomhouse.co.uk/environment

Printed and bound in Great Britain by
Clays Ltd, St Ives PLC

CONTENTS

CONTENTS

None of this can be told, it can only be played on a fiddle.

—ANDREY PLATONOV
notebook entry, 1932

We have translated the text of *Happy Moscow* as published in *Strana Filosofov*, volume 3 (Moscow: IMLI, 1999). For "The Moscow Violin" we have followed the text published in *Tvorchestvo Andreya Platonova*, volume 2 (Petersburg: Nauka, 2000). The remaining works are translated from the texts included in the *Collected Works* published by *Vremya* in 2009–2011. Copyright in the original works belongs in all cases to the Estate of A. P. Platonov. An earlier version of our translation of *Happy Moscow* was published by Harvill in 2001.

INTRODUCTION
TO *HAPPY MOSCOW*

ANDREY Platonov is not a showy writer, his work is often considered bleak, and he is best known for works set in the depths of the Russian countryside. No one, however, has so vividly evoked the allure of the fairy-tale new Communist capital of the 1930s as Platonov in the dazzling novel he worked on for several years at the midpoint of his literary career: *Happy Moscow*.

In 1935, the fifteen-year-old Wolfgang Leonhard (later to become a well-known political historian) emigrated to Moscow with his German Communist mother. Many years later, he wrote memorably about how hard it had been, during their first weeks in Moscow, to find their way around.[1] The only available maps were of past and future Moscows. It was possible to obtain maps published in 1924, but many buildings had been pulled down since then and many streets renamed. Wolfgang and his mother were excited when new maps suddenly appeared in the shops, but these turned out to portray Moscow as it was intended to be in ten years time—after the completion of a much-trumpeted General Reconstruction Plan. The Moscow of Platonov's novel is equally disorienting, equally lost between a dark past and an impossibly bright future.

The novel's variety of tone and subject matter is extraordinary. A brief picture of a dreary orphanage is followed by a touching chapter about an idealistic Esperantist, a bizarre story of a parachuting accident, and a poetic account of a dinner for members of the new scientific and cultural elite; Platonov evokes their hope of creating "a country of the blessed" with his characteristic fusion of irony and sympathy. Other chapters are devoted to an account of the surgical removal of a tumor from the brain of a small boy; the surgeon's eloquent explanation of how he hopes to discover, in corpses, a "moisture" that will guarantee immortality; a long, detailed description of a Moscow market; a blackly comic account of an adult who imagines he can simply will himself to die; and an oddly brief mention of a child who "patiently, clumsily hanged himself." The chapter about the market is Gogolian in its accumulation of grotesque physical detail; the chapter about the man who imagines he is committing suicide is Beckettian, though written long before any of Beckett's major works. *Happy Moscow* also includes a surprising number of references to shit; the surgeon asserts that the soul is located in the intestines, between the excrement and the food yet to be digested.

Happy Moscow is full of sounds of every kind: repeated shots, the rustle of silk, the strangely resonant heartbeat of Moscow Chestnova (the novel's overwhelmingly beautiful eponymous heroine), a young women's choir, a lonely old man playing Beethoven on a violin, Beethoven's Choral Symphony played from memory on a piano, a "European" jazz orchestra, the cries of market traders, and the noise of machines of every kind—the "din of the new world" that reaches the sixth-floor room of the Esperantist "in the form of a symphonic composition." Yet in the background, there is always a sense that silence may take over. One of the novel's heroes shudders on hearing of the child's suicide, "as if, there in front of him, a weak howl had sounded amid universal silence." And to Moscow Chestnova, as she listens to the old violinist, it seems that "a harsh, dark force was acting with such fury that it was itself falling into despair and crying with a human, emaciated voice on the edge of its own silence."

A conventional view of Russian history sees the 1917 Revolution as a moment of utopian promise and the mid-1930s as a time of fear-shackled, conventional thinking in every area of life. In many respects, however, it was the other way around. For several years from late 1917 the Bolsheviks were trying simply to cling to power, most people were trying simply to survive, and only a tiny—though vocal—artistic avant-garde was proposing utopian plans for the restructuring of both the world and the human psyche. By the mid-

1930s, however, it was the State itself that was claiming to make utopian dreams into a reality. Stalin's slave-labor projects can be seen as grand experiments on humanity and the material world, carried out with a panache that makes the Futurists seem like timid children. The new Moscow metro, with its palatial, marble-columned stations, would have been a truly utopian city, except that no one— as the scholar Irina Paperno has observed—"actually lived there."[2] And the foundation in 1934 of the Union of Soviet Writers was followed by an official declaration that writers were "engineers of the human soul"; a writer's duty was now nothing less than to create a new species of Man.

Meanwhile, research was being carried out in all seriousness into the possibility of human immortality. The historian Katerina Clark writes, "One is struck in looking at *Pravda* and other Moscow newspapers of the 1930s [...] by the recurrent appearance of articles claiming that some miracle cure, some elixir, mental or chemical (one might almost say alchemical), has been invented for overcoming mortality, reversing time's arrow and prolonging or restoring youth, a task particularly charged to an institution with the curious title Institute of the Second Life."[3] The belief in the possibility of overcoming death seems to have expressed itself in a variety of forms —from bizarre medical experiments to the embalming of Lenin's corpse. Platonov himself was only one of many great artists and scientists influenced by the nineteenth-century religious philosopher Nikolay Fyodorov, who believed that our most important task is to resurrect our dead ancestors by gathering their dispersed molecules and stitching them together.[4] A great deal of Platonov's work can be seen as a dialogue with Fyodorov; in his mature work, Platonov treats Fyodorov's ideas with irony, but this irony is tinged with longing—as if Platonov wished that he could still believe in them.

Though his stance is often described as "anti-utopian," Platonov is by no means hostile to the hope and promise embodied in the work of the young scientists, doctors, and engineers who appear in *Happy Moscow*. His thinking can perhaps best be understood from his 1937 article "Pushkin—Our Comrade." In it he discusses the two conflicting principles in Pushkin's poem "The Bronze Horseman": the values of love and everyday life embodied by Yevgeny, the "little man" who loses his mind after his fiancée is drowned, and the seemingly higher values embodied by Tsar Peter the Great. Without Peter there would be no progress; without Yevgeny—Platonov writes memorably—humanity would be left with "nothing but bronze [...] and the Admiralty spire would turn into a candlestick beside the coffin of the dead (or destroyed) poetic human soul."[5] The clash between these two principles was, in Platonov's view, irreconcilable; it would have been impossible for Pushkin to bring his poem to a happy ending. But Platonov continues: "And Pushkin resolved the true themes of 'The Bronze Horseman' [...] not by means of logic or plot but by means of 'a second meaning,' where resolution is achieved not through the action of the poem's characters but through the poem's entire music and organization—through a supplementary power that creates in the reader something extra—the image of the author as the work's main hero."[6]

The same could be said of *Happy Moscow*. Platonov's equivalent of Peter the Great is the newly constructed Institute of Experimental Medicine; his equivalent of Yevgeny is a down-at-heel housing cooperative next door to this institute. The fence that divides these two worlds appears—at least from the viewpoint of the institute—to be merely "a poor fence" that had "wilted completely" and was "child-scale." The surgeon on one occasion steps onto it, and the old fiddler's music can be heard on either side of it. Platonov seems to be suggesting that the world of progress and the world of everyday life are not as separate as they at first appear. Nevertheless, they are in conflict, and this conflict can no more be resolved in Platonov's era than in Pushkin's. Only at the level of art—through the novel's "music and organization" and through "the image of the author"—can the conflict, temporarily, be resolved.[7] Platonov understands the beauty (and horror) of both the old and the new Moscow; in his soul, as in that of the old violinist who appears several times in the novel, there still drifts "a last imagination about a heroic world."

Both the artistic avant-garde and the Bolsheviks had dreamed of creating a new world, liberated from the burden of the past. Platonov, however, understood the importance of memory. Even though his work is full of up-to-the-minute detail, he sees the world around him through a prism composed not only of classical literature but also of folklore and myth. A myth to which he returns many times is that of the battle between the Snake or Dragon and the Thunder God (Perun in Slavic mythology, Elijah or Saint George in the semi-Christianized Russian folk tradition). Moscow Chestnova is an embodiment of the wife of the Thunder God, punished for her adultery with the Snake by being cast out from heaven and down into the underworld. Platonov alludes to this myth throughout the novel, but most clearly of all in the scene when Moscow's parachute catches fire and she blazes across the sky like a streak—or snake—of lightning. Later, she descends into the underworld of the Moscow metro, then under construction; Platonov's silence with regard to her experiences there indicates that it is not so much a real underground (which he could have described) as a mythical underworld (about which nothing can be said). In this mythical underworld she loses her leg and thus herself becomes snakelike. And then she hides away from her friends and colleagues to live with a man whom she has previously described as being like a reptile, hiding away in its hole.[8]

No Russian writer has engaged as profoundly as Platonov with the Soviet world, both with its physical reality and with the distorted language that did so much to create it. At the same time, no Soviet writer is less limited by his era. Not only is his work deeply informed by the past but, like all truly great art, it speaks as much to our age as to his own. The conflict between scientific progress and everyday human values now seems greater than ever. Thanks to advances in both medical and information technology, the question of what makes us human—the nature of consciousness or what Platonov's characters call "the soul"—seems ever more pressing. And the constant likelihood of ever greater ecological catastrophe makes Platonov's assertion—in the voice of Sartorius the young engineer—of the necessity of socialism both poignant and terrifying:

But now!—now it was essential to understand everything, because either socialism would succeed in getting right into the most secret recess of a man's insides and cleaning out the pus capitalism had accumulated drop by drop in every century or else nothing new would happen and each inhabitant of the earth would go off to live separately, keeping this terrible secret place of the soul safe and warm inside them, so as to sink their teeth into each other once again in voluptuous despair and transform the earth's surface into a lonely desert with one last weeping human being.

Happy Moscow begins with a promise of transformation. Each of its thirteen chapters, however, is longer, and more mired in the details of a bleak and complex reality, than the preceding chapter. In much of the last half of the novel, and in the article and the two stories in the second half of this volume, Platonov writes as if he himself were that last weeping human being in a desert.

—ROBERT CHANDLER

HAPPY MOSCOW

I

A DARK man with a burning torch was running down the street into a boring night of late autumn. The little girl saw him through a window of her home as she woke from a boring dream. Then she heard the powerful shot of a rifle and a poor, sad cry—the man running with the torch had probably been killed. Soon after this came many distant shots and a din of people in the neighboring prison ... The little girl went to sleep and forgot everything she saw later in other days: she was too small, and the memory and mind of early childhood were overgrown in her body forever by subsequent life. But until her late years a nameless man would unexpectedly and sadly rise up in her and run—in the pale light of memory—and perish once again in the dark of the past, in the heart of a grown-up child. Amid hunger and sleep, at a moment of love or some young joy—suddenly the sad cry of the dead man was there again in the distance, in the depth of her body, and the young woman would immediately change her life: if she was dancing, she would interrupt the dance; if she was laboring, she would work more surely, with more concentration; if she was alone, she would cover her face with her hands. It was on that rainy night of late autumn that the October Revolution had begun—in the city where Moscow Ivanovna Chestnova was then living.

Her father died from typhoid; the hungry, orphaned girl went out of the house and never went back there again. Remembering neither people nor space, her soul gone to sleep, for several years she walked and ate up and down her motherland, as if in an emptiness, until she came to herself in a children's home and at school. She was sitting at a desk by a window, in the city of Moscow. The trees on the boulevard had stopped growing; leaves were falling from them without any wind, covering the now silent earth for its long sleep to come. It was the end of September, and the year when wars all ended and the transport system began to function again.

Moscow Chestnova had been in the children's home for two years. It was here she had been given a name, a surname, and even a patronymic, since the little girl remembered her own name and early childhood only very indefinitely. She thought her father had called her Olya, but she had not been sure of this and had kept silent, like someone nameless, like that nighttime man who had perished. So she had been given a first name in honor of Moscow;[1] a patronymic in memory of Ivan, an ordinary Red Army soldier who had fallen in battle; and a surname in recognition of the honesty of her heart[2]—which had not had time to become dishonest, in spite of long unhappiness.

Moscow Chestnova's clear and ascending life began on that autumn day; sitting by the window, already in the second class, she was looking into the death of the leaves on the boulevard when she read with interest a sign on the building opposite: A. V. KOLTSOV WORKERS' AND PEASANTS' LIBRARY AND READING ROOM.[3] Before the last lesson the children had each, for the first time in their lives, been given a white roll with a meat patty and some potato, and they were told what patties are made out of: cows. At the same time they were instructed to write a composition for the next day about a cow—if they had ever seen one—and also about their own future life. In the evening Moscow Chestnova, now full of white bread and dense patty, was writing her composition at the communal table; her girlfriends had all gone to sleep and a little electric light was burning weakly. "Story of a Little Girl with No Father or Mother About Her Future Life: Now we are being taught mind, but a mind is in a head, there is nothing on the outside. We must, to be honest, live with labor. I want to live a future life, let there be biscuits and jam and sweets and let me always be able to walk in the fields past trees. Or else I won't live, I won't feel like it. I want to live in an ordinary way with happiness. There's nothing to say in addition."[4]

Subsequently, Moscow ran away from school. She was brought back after a year and was held up to shame at a communal assembly: How could she, a daughter of the Revolution, behave in such an unethical and undisciplined manner?

"I'm not a daughter, I'm an orphan!" Moscow answered—and once again began studying diligently, as though she had not been in absence anywhere at all.

What she liked most in nature were the wind and the sun. She liked to lie somewhere in the grass; to listen to what the wind, like someone unseen and full of yearning, was noising about in the thick of the bushes; and to see the summer clouds float by high above all the unknown countries and peoples. Observation of clouds and space made Moscow's heart beat more rapidly in her chest, as if her body had been raised to a great height and left there on its own. Then she would wander through fields, over simple, poor land, looking carefully and keenly all around her, still getting used to living in the world, and feeling glad that everything in it was fitting for her—for her body, heart, and freedom.[5]

After completing her nine years of school, Moscow, like every young person, began unconsciously looking for a path into her future, into a happy closeness of people; her hands longed for activity, her heart sought pride and heroism, and in her mind some still-mysterious but elevated fate was already triumphing. The seventeen-year-old Moscow could not enter anywhere on her own; she was waiting for an invitation, as if she valued in herself the gift of youth and now grown-up strength. And so, for a time, she became lonely and strange. Then a chance man got to know Moscow and conquered her with his feelings and pleasing manner, and she married him, immediately and forever spoiling her body and her youth. Her large hands, fit for bold activity, were taken up with embraces; her heart, which had sought heroism, began to love just one sly man who kept a tight grip on her, as if she were his inalienable asset. But one morning Moscow began to feel such an aching shame of her own life, not quite knowing exactly why, that she kissed her sleeping husband on the forehead by way of farewell and left the room, not even taking a change of clothes with her. Until evening she wandered along the boulevards and the bank of the Moscow River, sensing only the petty drizzle and wind of September and not thinking anything, being empty and tired.

She wanted, as she had done in her wandering childhood, to find some kind of box or vacant food stall to sleep in, but she noticed she had long grown too big and that there was nowhere she could squeeze into unnoticeably. She sat down on a bench in the darkness of the late boulevard and dozed off, listening to the mutterings of the thieves and homeless toughs who were wandering about nearby.

At midnight an insignificant man sat down on the same bench, with the secret and conscientious hope that this woman might suddenly fall in love with him, since the meekness of his own powers made him unable to seek out love with any persistence. He was not, in essence, looking for beauty of face or charm of figure—he would agree to anything and to the highest sacrifice on his own part if only someone would respond to him with true feeling.

"What do you want?" asked Moscow, who had woken up.

"Nothing," this man answered. "I just—"

"I want to sleep," said Moscow, "and there isn't anywhere."

The man immediately informed her that he had a room. To avoid suspicion of his intentions, however, he suggested she take a room in a hotel and sleep there in a clean bed, curled up in a blanket. Moscow agreed and they set off. On the way Moscow told her companion to get her registered in some place of study, with food and a communal hostel.

"What do you love most of all?" he asked.

"I love the wind in the air and a few other things," said the exhausted Moscow.

"Then it's got to be the school of aeronautics—that and nothing else!" determined Moscow's companion. "I'll do my best."

He found a room for her in the Minin House, paid for three

nights in advance, gave Moscow thirty rubles for food, and set off home, carrying away within him his own consolation.

Five days later, thanks to his efforts, Moscow entered the aeronautics school and moved to the communal hostel.

2

In the center of the capital, on the sixth floor, lived a thirty-year-old man, Viktor Vasilievich Bozhko.[6] He lived in a small room lit by a single window; the din of the new world reached the height of such a dwelling like a symphonic composition—the falsehood of low and mistaken sounds died out no higher than the third floor. The room's furnishings were poor and austere—not because of poverty but because of dreaminess. There was an iron bed as in an epidemic ward, with a greasy blanket impregnated through and through with humanity; a naked table fit for great concentration; a mass-produced chair salvaged from somewhere or other; homemade shelves against the wall, with the best books of socialism and of the nineteenth century; and three portraits above the table—Lenin, Stalin, and Dr. Zamenhof, the inventor of the international language of Esperanto.[7] Below these portraits, in four rows, hung small photographs of nameless people; and in the photographs were not only white faces but also Negroes, Chinese, and inhabitants of countries of every kind.

Until late into the evening this room stays empty; tired, saddened sounds gradually die away in it, bored substance sometimes gives little creaks; a quadrilateral of sunlight, shaped by the window, slowly wanders across the floor and fades into night on the wall. Everything comes to an end, only objects pine in the dark.

Then the man who lives there arrives and ignites the technological light of electricity. As usual, the tenant is happy and calm, because his life is not passing in vain; his body is tired from the day, his eyes have gone white, but his heart is beating steadily and his mind shines as clearly as in the morning. Bozhko, a geometrician and town planner, has that day completed the meticulous plan of a new residential street, calculating the places of greenery, children's playgrounds, and a district stadium. Anticipating a future now close at hand, he works with the heartbeat of happiness, though he looks upon himself, as a man born under capitalism, with the indifference of equanimity.

Bozhko took out a file of the personal letters he received almost every day at his office and, at the empty table, began to concentrate all his thoughts into them. He received letters from Melbourne, Cape Town, Hong Kong, and Shanghai, from small islands hiding away in the watery desert of the Pacific Ocean, from Egypt, from a village in Megara, at the foot of the Greek Olympus—and from countless other points in Europe. Clerks and factory workers, far-off men pinned to the ground by eternal exploitation, had learned Esperanto and so conquered the silence between peoples; drained by labor, too poor for travel, they communicated with one another through shared thought.

Among the letters were several money orders: a Negro from the Congo had sent one franc, a Syrian from Jerusalem had sent four American dollars, a Pole called Studziński sent ten zloty every three months. They were building a workers' motherland for themselves in advance, so they would have somewhere to shelter in their old age, and so their children could eventually escape and find refuge in a cold country now warmed by friendship and labor.

Bozhko punctiliously invested this money in State bonds, sending the certificates by recorded delivery to their invisible owners.

After studying his correspondence, Bozhko would answer each letter, sensing his own pride, and his privilege as a representative of the USSR. But in what he wrote there was no pride at all, only modesty and compassion:

Dear, distant friend,

I received your letter, everything here is going from strength to strength, the communal good of the laboring people multiplies day by day, and the world's proletariat is accumulating a vast inheritance in the form of socialism. Every day fresh gardens are growing, new housing is being occupied, and invented machines are working fast. Different, splendid people are appearing too—I alone remain as before, because I was born long ago and have not been able to lose the habit of being myself. In five or six years we shall have vast quantities of cereals and all kinds of cultured comforts, and the workers from the other five-sixths of the earth,[8] a whole billion of them, can come and live with us forever, bringing their families—and as for capitalism, let it remain empty, unless a revolution sets in there. Pay attention to the Great Ocean, you live on its shore. Sometimes you'll see Soviet ships sailing about—that's us.

Greetings

The Negro Arratau was informing Bozhko that his wife had died; Bozhko responded with sympathy but advised him not to despair: the earth has no one else, no one to be on it but us, and so we must save ourselves for the future. Best of all, why didn't Arratau come straightaway to the USSR? Here, among comrades, he could live more happily than in a family.

At dawn Bozhko went to sleep with the sweetness of useful exhaustion. In his sleep he dreamed he was a child. His mother was alive, it was summer in the world, there was no wind, and great groves of trees had sprung up.

Bozhko was renowned at his workplace as the best shock worker of all.[9] In addition to his official line of work as a geometrician, he was secretary of the wall newspaper[10] and organizer of the local branches of the Osoaviakhim[11] and the International Organization of Aid for the Fighters of the Revolution,[12] as well as being responsible for the factory's allotments and financially supporting a young woman he little knew, paying for her to study in the school of aeronautics and thus diminishing, if only by a little, the State's expenses.

Once a month this young woman came to see Bozhko. He would treat her to some sweets and give her money for her food, along with his pass for the general store, and the young woman would then leave shyly. She was not quite nineteen and her name was Moscow Ivanovna Chestnova. He had met her once on an autumn boulevard, during a moment of his own elemental sadness, and since then he had been unable to forget her.

After her visits Bozhko usually lay facedown on the bed and yearned from sorrow, even though universal joy alone was the reason of his life. After moping for a while, he would sit down to write letters to India, Madagascar, and Portugal, summoning people to participation in socialism and to sympathy with the laborers on the whole of this excruciating earth, and the lamp would shine on his balding head that was filled with a dream and patience.

One day Moscow Chestnova arrived, as usual, and did not leave straightaway. Bozhko had known her for two years, but he had been shy of gazing closely into her face, not hoping for anything.

Moscow was laughing; she had finished the pilot school and had brought with her some delicacies, at her own expense. Bozhko began to eat and drink with the young Moscow, but his heart was being beaten by terror, because it had begun to sense the love long confined in it.

When late night set in, Bozhko opened the window into dark space, and into the room flew moths and mosquitoes, but it was so quiet everywhere that Bozhko could hear the beating of Moscow Ivanovna's heart in her large chest; this beating was so even, resilient, and true that, had it been possible to unite the whole world to it, her heart could have regulated the course of events—even the mosquitoes and moths that settled on the front of Moscow's blouse immediately flew away again, frightened by the din of life in her warm and mighty body. Moscow's cheeks, enduring the pressure of her heart, had acquired a ruddiness that would last her whole life, her eyes shone with the clarity of happiness, her hair had been burnished by the fierce heat above her head, and her body had taken on the roundness of late youth, finding itself already on the eve of that womanly humanity that allows one human being, almost inadvertently, to begin life inside another.

Inseparably, until the new bright morning, Bozhko went on

looking at Moscow—when the young woman had long ago fallen asleep in his room—and a drowsy, happy freshness, like health, evening, and childhood, was entering this tired man.

The next day Moscow invited Bozhko to the aerodrome to look at the work of the new parachutes.

A small airplane took Moscow into its own self and flew high into the eternal deserted sky. At the zenith, the airplane cut its engine, dipped forward, and ejected from its underbelly a small, bright lump that began to drop without breath into the abyss. At the same time, flying slowly and quite close to the earth, another airplane had throttled back its three engines and was wanting to land. Not far above this three-motored gliding plane the solitary little airborne body hurtled defenselessly down with increasing acceleration, opened out into a flower, then filled with air and began to swing from side to side. The plane immediately started all three engines so as to move away from the parachute, but the parachute was too close, it might have been sucked into the whirling streams near the propellers, and the clever pilot once again cut the engines, giving the parachute freedom of orientation. The parachute landed on the surface of a wing and curled up; after a few moments a small figure walked slowly and without fright along the inclined wing and disappeared inside the machine.

Bozhko knew it was Moscow who had flown down from the air. Yesterday he had heard her steady, resonant heart; now he stood crying with happiness on behalf of the whole of bold humanity, regretting that for two years he had given Moscow Chestnova a hundred rubles a month and not one hundred and fifty.[13]

That night, as usual, Bozhko wrote to his world of unseen correspondents, excitedly describing the body and heart of the new human being who was overcoming the deadly space of height.

But at dawn, his letters to humanity completed, Bozhko began to weep; it saddened him that Moscow's heart could fly about through the element of air but was unable to love him. He dozed off and lost himself in sleep until evening, forgetting about his work.

In the evening there was a knock at the door and Moscow came in, looking as happy as always and with the same loud heart as before. Timidly, impelled by the extreme need of his own feelings, Bozhko embraced Moscow, and she began to kiss him in response. A hidden, excruciating strength seethed up in Bozhko's emaciated throat and he forgot himself as he came to know, for all of life, the only happiness of the warmth of a human being.

3

Every morning, when she woke up, Moscow Chestnova looked for a long time at the sunlight in the window, said in her own mind, "It's future time setting in," and got up in a carefree happiness that probably depended less on consciousness than on health and the power of her heart. Next, Moscow would wash, marveling at the chemistry of nature that turned ordinary, scant food (and what filth had she not eaten in her life!) into the rosy purity and blossoming expanses of her body. Even while being her own self, Moscow Chestnova could look at herself as if she were another and admire her own torso during a morning wash. She knew, of course, that this was no achievement of hers but rather the outcome of the precise work of nature and of times past. And later, as she chewed her breakfast, Moscow dreamed something about nature: how it flowed with water and blew with wind, constantly tossing and turning its vast, patient substance, as if in the delirium of an illness ... Nature certainly deserved compassion—it had labored so hard for the creation of man. Nature was like a destitute woman who had given birth to many children and was now stumbling about in exhaustion.

On graduating from the aeronautics school, Moscow had been appointed a junior instructor there. Now she was teaching a group of parachutists[14] how to jump with equanimity out of a plane and to retain this calm during their descent through resonant space.

Moscow herself flew with no particular sense of tension or courage; she would merely, as in her childhood, calculate the precise whereabouts of the "limit"—where it was that technology ended and catastrophe began—and then avoid pushing herself to this limit. But the limit was a great deal further than people thought, and Moscow was all the time moving it still further.

Once she was taking part in the trial of some new parachutes which had been impregnated with a lacquer that repelled atmospheric moisture and would make jumps possible even during rain. Chestnova was equipped with two parachutes, the second one as reserve. She was taken up to two thousand meters and asked to throw herself at the earth's surface, through an evening mist that had developed after long rain.

Moscow opened the door of the airplane and did her step into emptiness; a fierce vortex struck into her from below, as if the earth were the muzzle of a mighty blast engine inside which air is compressed to hardness and stands erect, like a solid column;[15] Moscow felt she was an empty tube, being blown straight through and through, and she kept her mouth constantly open so she would have time to breathe out this wild wind piercing point-blank into her. All about her was dim from mist; the earth still lay far distant. Moscow began to swing from side to side, invisible to everyone because of the gloom—alone and free. She took out a cigarette and some matches, wanting to light up and have a smoke, but the match went out; then Moscow curled up to form a quiet, cozy space by her own bosom and immediately exploded all the matches in the box; carried by the pull of the vortex, flames at once seized the combustible lacquer impregnating the silk straps that linked the burden of the human being to the canopy of the parachute; these straps burnt away in less than a moment, immediately turning white-hot and scattering into ash.[16] What happened to the canopy Moscow was unable to make out—the wind was now burning the skin on her face, as a result of the fierce, ever more blazing speed of her fall downward.

She flew, her cheeks red and burning,[17] and the air tore harshly at her body, as if it were not the wind of celestial space but a heavy, dead substance—it was impossible to imagine that the earth could be harder and still more merciless. "So, world, this is what you're really like!" Moscow Chestnova thought inadvertently as she disappeared down through the half dark of the mist. "You're soft only so long as we don't touch you!" She pulled the ring of the reserve parachute, saw the ground of the aerodrome in its signal lights, and let out a cry of sudden torment—the opening parachute had jerked her body upward with such force that Moscow's bones suddenly all felt like aching teeth all the way through. Two minutes later she was sitting on the grass, covered by the parachute, and she began to crawl out from under it, wiping away the tears beaten out of her by the wind.

The first person to reach Moscow Chestnova was Arkanov, a famous pilot who in ten years of work had not bent so much as one tail flap, who had never known failure or accident.[18]

Moscow crawled out from under the parachute into All-Union celebrity. Arkanov and another pilot supported her from both sides and took her to the common room, welcoming her to earth as they went along. By way of farewell Arkanov said to Moscow, "We shall be sorry to lose you, but then we seem to have lost you already. You don't understand anything at all about the air force, Moscow Ivanovna! The air force is modesty—and you're luxury! I wish you every happiness!"

Two days later Moscow Chestnova was freed for two years from flying work, since the atmosphere is not a circus for letting off fireworks from parachutes.[19]

For some time newspapers and journals wrote about Moscow Chestnova's happy young courage. Even the foreign press reported in full on her leap with a burning parachute and printed a beautiful photograph of the "Celestial Young Communist," but all this stopped and Moscow never really understood her own fame: What was it about?

She was now living on the fourth floor of a new building, in two small rooms. This building was a home to pilots, aircraft designers, engineers of all kinds, philosophers, economic theorists, and other professions. The windows of Chestnova's apartment looked out over the surrounding Moscow roofs while far off, in the faint, dying end of space, could be seen some kind of dense forests and enigmatic watchtowers; at sunset an unknown disk would shine alone there, reflecting the last light onto the clouds and the sky. It was around ten or fifteen kilometers to this alluring country but, were she to go down onto the street, Moscow would not find her way there . . . Now that she had been freed from the air force, she spent her evenings alone; she no longer went to call on Bozhko and she didn't ask her friends over. She would lean out, her stomach against the window-sill, her hair hanging down, and listen to the noise of the universal city in all its triumphant energy, and to the occasional human voice that rose up from the dense and sonorous mass of mechanisms in motion; raising her head, Moscow would see the empty, destitute moon rising up into the extinguished sky and she would feel inside her a warming current of life. Her imagination was continually at work and had never yet tired—in her mind she could sense the origin of matters of every kind and she took part mentally in their existence; in her solitude she filled the whole world with her attention, watching over the flames of streetlamps so they would go on shining, listening to the resounding thuds of the steam pile drivers on the Moscow River so the piles would go securely down into the depths, thinking about the machines that exerted their power day and night so light would burn in darkness, so the reading of books would continue, so rye could be milled by electric motors in time for the morning bake, and so water could be pumped through pipes into the warm showers of dance halls and the conception of a better life could take place in people's ardent and firm embraces—in the dark, in privacy, face-to-face, in the pure emotion of a conjoined, doubled happiness. What Moscow Chestnova wanted was not so much to experience this life as to safeguard it; she wanted to stand day and night by the brake lever of a locomotive taking people to meet one another; she wanted to repair water mains, to weigh out on pharmaceutical scales medicines for patients, to be a lamp that goes out just at the right moment, as others kiss, taking into itself the warmth that a moment before had been light. She was not, however, denying her own needs—she too wanted somewhere to put her large body; she was simply postponing these needs to a more distant future. She was patient and knew how to wait.

When Moscow hung out of her window during these evenings of solitude, passersby would shout greetings to her from down below, calling her to come out and share the summer dusk with them, promising to show her all the new attractions of the Park of Culture and Rest and to buy her flowers and toffee creams.[20] Moscow laughed in reply, but said nothing and did not go. Later, from above, Moscow would see the roofs of the old houses in the neighborhood begin to be populated; whole families would make their way through attics onto these metal roofs, spreading out blankets and then lying down to sleep in the fresh air, mothers and fathers placing their children between them; courting couples would go off on their own into the ravines between roofs, somewhere between the chimney and the fire escape, and, located beneath the stars yet above the multitude of humanity, would not close their eyes until morning.

After midnight almost all the windows in sight would stop shining—the day's shock labor required deep oblivion in sleep—and late cars would whisper by, not disturbing anyone by sounding their horns. Only occasionally would these extinguished windows briefly light up again; night-shift workers were coming home, having something to eat without waking the sleepers, and then going straight to bed, while workers who had already had all their sleep—turbine operators and engine drivers, radio technicians, scientific researchers, aircraft mechanics manning early flights, and others who had been resting—were getting up to leave for work.

Moscow Chestnova would often forget to close the door into her apartment. Once she found a stranger lying on the floor, asleep on his coat. Moscow waited for her tired guest to awake. He awoke and said he was going to live right there in the corner—there wasn't anywhere else. Moscow looked at the man; he was about forty, on his face lay the hardened scars of past wars, his skin had the brown, windbeaten color of robust health and a kind heart, while a reddish mustache grew meekly over his exhausted mouth.

"I wouldn't have come in without asking, my shaggy beauty," said her unknown guest, "but a body needs to be given rest, and there isn't anywhere ... I shan't harm you—you can look on me as a nothing, something like a spare table. There won't be nor sound nor smell of me."

Moscow asked him who he was, and her guest explained in detail everything about himself, producing his documents.

"What do you expect?" said the man who had moved in. "I'm an ordinary man, everything about me is in order."

He turned out to be from Yelets and his job was weighing firewood in a warehouse. And Moscow Chestnova could not bring herself to push communism into the distance because of the paucity of housing and her own right to additional living space; she said nothing and gave her lodger a pillow and a blanket. The lodger settled in; at night he would get up, then tiptoe to the bed of the sleeping Moscow in order to pull her blanket back over her because she used to toss and turn, throwing the bedclothes off and getting cold. In the morning he never used the toilet in the apartment, not wanting to burden it with his own filth and make a noise with the water; he would go instead to the public toilet in the yard below. After a few days of life in Chestnova's apartment, this weigher of wood was already reinforcing the heels on Moscow's worn-out shoes, secretly brushing off bits of dirt that had stuck to her autumn coat, and heating water for tea in joyous anticipation of his landlady's awakening. At first Moscow scolded the weigher for his servility, but after a while, to put an end to such slavery, she introduced a regime of socialist self-sufficiency, darning her lodger's socks and even shaving his stubble with a safety razor.

Soon after this the Komsomol organization[21] allocated Moscow a temporary job in the district military enlistment office; her task would be to liquidate registration irregularities.

4

One day a pale thin man, a reservist,[22] was standing in the corridor of the enlistment office, his military registration book in his hand. It seemed to him that the office had the same smell as places of prolonged confinement—the lifeless smell of a pining human body that consciously acts modestly and thriftily, so as not to awaken within it the fading attraction toward a now distant life and then vainly torture itself with the ache of despair. The insignificance of the staff, the ideological equanimity of the furnishings, provided out of a meager State budget—all this promised the visitor the unfeeling treatment that comes from a poor or cruel heart.

The reservist waited by one of the windows for the clerk to finish reading a poem in her book; he believed that poems make everyone kinder—in the youth of his life he too had read books until midnight, and afterward had felt sad and of no concern. The clerk finished the poem and began to re-register the reservist, expressing her astonishment that, according to his registration form, this man had served in neither the White nor the Red Army, had not undergone the universal military training, had never reported to any recruitment centers, had never been a member of any territorial units or taken part in Osoaviakhim marches,[23] and was now three years late in coming to be re-registered. It was unclear how and in what kind of silence the given reservist, with his old-style military registration book, had managed to hide from the vigilance of the house management committees.

The military clerk looked at the reservist. Before her, behind the partition that kept the calm of the institution separate from people, stood a man whose face, long emaciated, was covered by the lines of a life of dreariness and by bleak traces of weakness and suffering; the clothes on the reservist were as worn as the skin on his face and they kept the man warm only by means of long-enduring filths that had eaten into the decrepitude of the cloth. He was watching the clerk with a timid slyness, not expecting compassion, and often looking down and closing his eyes completely so as to see darkness rather than life; for a moment he would imagine to himself clouds in the sky—he loved them because they had nothing to do with him and he was a stranger to them.

Happening to look into the distance of the enlistment office, the reservist gave a start of surprise; two clear eyes, overhung by concentrated eyebrows, were watching him, not in any way threatening him. Somewhere or other the reservist had often seen such eyes—eyes that were attentive and pure—and he had always blinked against their gaze. "This is the real Red Army!" he thought with sad shame. "Lord! Why have I let my whole life pass in vain, for the sake of maintenance of my own self?" The reservist had never expected anything from institutions but horror, exhaustion, and long-suffering dreariness, but now he saw in the distance a human being who was thinking about him with compassion.

The "Red Army" got to its feet, proving to be a woman, and approached the reservist. He felt frightened by the charm and power of her face, but out of pity for his own heart, which might start vainly aching with love, he turned away from this clerk. Having walked up to him, Moscow Chestnova took his registration book and fined him fifty rubles for infringement of the registration law.

"I haven't got any money," said the reservist. "I'd rather pay in some kind or other."

"What do you mean?" asked Moscow.

"I don't know," the reservist pronounced quietly. "I don't live very well."

Moscow took him by the hand and led him to her desk.

"Why don't you live very well?" she asked. "Is there anything you want?"

The reservist was unable to answer; this Red Army woman smelt to him of soap and sweat, and also of some kind of sweet life that was strange to his heart, which was accustomed to hiding away in its own solitude, in its weak shouldering warmth. His own pitiful position made him bow his head and begin to cry; Moscow Chestnova let go his hand in bewilderment. The reservist stood there for a while and then, glad that he was not being detained, disappeared to his unknown dwelling, to exist somehow or other until the grave, without registration or danger.

But Chestnova found his address on the re-registration form and, some time later, went to call on the reservist.

She wandered for a long time in the depths of the Bauman district before she found the small housing cooperative that was the

reservist's abode.[24] This was a building with an incompetent management committee, and with accounts that were in deficit; the
walls had not seen fresh paint for several years, and the unwelcoming, empty yard, where even the stones had been worn down by children's play, had long been demanding proper care for itself.

Moscow walked with sorrow past the walls, then down the murk-
ily lit corridors of the building; it was as if someone had hurt her or
as if she herself were to blame for the careless, unhappy lives of strangers. When she emerged on the other side of the building, which faced
a blank, uninterrupted fence, she saw a stone porch with an iron
awning and an electric lamp shining above it. She listened closely to
the noise in the surrounding air: behind the fence, planks of wood
were being thrown to the ground and there was the sound of spades
cutting into the earth; near the iron awning, bald and unprotected,
a man was playing a mazurka on the fiddle in solitude. Lying on a
stone slab was the musician's hat; it had lived, on his head, through
all his long misfortunes; once it had covered a youthful head of hair,
and now it was collecting money for the sustenance of old age, for
the support of a feeble consciousness in a bare, decrepit head.

Chestnova put a ruble in this hat and asked the man to play her
some Beethoven. Without saying any word, the musician played on
till the end of the mazurka and only then began Beethoven. Moscow
stood opposite the fiddler like a peasant woman, her feet wide apart
and her face full of grief from the yearning now being agitated
around her heart. The whole world around her suddenly became
abrupt and intransigent—it was composed entirely of hard heavy
objects, and a harsh, dark force was acting with such fury that it was
itself falling into despair and crying with a human, emaciated voice
on the edge of its own silence. And once again this force was rising
up out of its own iron arena and, with the speed of a howl, was routing some cold and faceless enemy of its own that occupied all infinity with its dead torso. And yet this music, losing all melody and
turning into a strident howl of attack, still possessed the rhythm of
an ordinary human heart and was simple, like labor beyond one's
strength performed out of vital need.

The musician looked at Moscow with equanimity and without attention, not attracted by any of her charm—as an artist, he always felt within his own soul a still better and more manly charm that drew his will on ahead, past ordinary delight, and he preferred this charm to everything visible. Toward the end of his playing, tears came out of the fiddler's eyes. He was exhausted by life and, above all, he had not lived his own self in accord with the music; instead of meeting early death beneath the walls of an insuperable enemy, he was standing in the deserted yard of a housing cooperative, old, poor, and alive, with an exhausted mind through which, low down, was still drifting a last imagination about a heroic world. Opposite him, on the other side of the fence, they were building a medical institute for the research of longevity and immortality, but the old musician could not understand that this construction was continuing the music of Beethoven, while Moscow Chestnova did not know what was being built there. Any music, if it was great and human, reminded Moscow about the proletariat, about the dark man with the burning torch who had run into the night of the Revolution, and of her own self, and she listened to it as though it were the speech of the leader and her own word, which she was always meaning yet never saying aloud.

On the main door hung a plywood board with the inscription HOUSING COOPERATIVE ADMINISTRATION AND HOUSE MANAGEMENT COMMITTEE. Chestnova went inside, to find out the number of the reservist's room—on the registration form he had given only the number of the building.

The cooperative's office was down a wooden corridor. On each side, no doubt, lived families with many children, and these children were now crying out in hurt and frustration as they divided between them the food for supper. Inside the wooden corridor tenants were standing and chatting about every theme in the world: food supplies, repairs to the toilet in the yard, the coming war, share accumulation, the stratosphere, and the death of the local laundrywoman, who had been deaf and insane. On the walls of the corridor hung posters of the Savings Bank Board and the International Organization of Aid for the Fighters of the Revolution, the rules of baby care, a man in the shape of the letter Я, abbreviated in one leg as the result of a road accident, and other pictures of life, welfare, and calamities. Around five o'clock in the evening, straight after work, many people would come to this wooden corridor and stand about on their feet, thinking and chatting, right up until midnight, only occasionally needing some letter of reference from the house management committee. Moscow Chestnova was astonished; she could not understand why people clung to the cooperative, to the office, to letters of reference, to the local needs of a small happiness, to exhausting themselves in empty trivialities, when the city had world-class theaters and there were still eternal enigmas of suffering to be resolved in life, and when, no farther than the main door, a fiddler, unheard by anyone, was playing splendid music.

The elderly house manager, who was working in the noise of people, amid smoke and all kinds of questions, gave Chestnova precise details about the entire reservist: he lived in the first-floor corridor system, in room number four, he was a category-three pensioner,[25] the housing cooperative volunteer activists had visited him many times and tried to persuade him of the urgent necessity of his re-registering himself and formally clarifying his military status—but for several years now the reservist had been promising to do all this, saying he would start the next morning and expend the entire day on necessary formalities, yet he had failed ever to carry out these promises for a senseless reason. About six months ago the house manager had visited the reservist to discuss these matters in person; he had exhorted the reservist for three hours, comparing this condition of his to melancholy, boredom, and bodily uncleanliness—it was as if he didn't wash or brush his teeth and was generally bringing shame on himself, with the aim of denigrating Soviet man.

"I really don't know what to do with him," said the house manager. "There's no one else like him in the entire cooperative."

"What does he actually do?" asked Moscow.

"I've already told you—he's a category-three pensioner, he gets forty-five rubles a month. Oh yes, and he's also a member of the volunteer militia, he goes and stands at a tram stop, spends a little while fining the public, and then goes back to his room."

Saddened by the life of such a man, Moscow said, "How wrong it all is!"

The house manager entirely agreed. "There's nothing about him that isn't wrong! In summer he often goes to the Park of Culture—but goodness knows why! He never listens to the band or goes for a walk past the new spectacles—he just sits himself down by the militia post and spends the whole day there. Sometimes he'll talk a little, sometimes they'll send him off on some errand. He likes administrative work—he's a good volunteer."

"Is he married?" asked Moscow.

"No, he's undefined . . . In formal terms he's a bachelor, but for years on end now he's been silently spending all his nights with women. Really this is his own matter of principle, the housing cooperative takes no stand. But the trouble is the women who present themselves to him are without any culture, they're worthless—there's never been anyone like you before. I don't advise it—he's a wretch of a man."

Moscow left the management office. As before, the musician was standing by the entrance, but he was not playing anything; he himself was listening silently to something from out of the night. A distant glow was trembling above the center of the city, rippling through the quick storm clouds; and the enormous sky, packed with darkness, was suddenly yet repeatedly being opened up by a momentary and sharp light that flashed from the tram wires. A choir of young women was singing in a nearby local transport workers club, carrying their own lives away, through the power of inspiration, into distant lands of the future. Chestnova went into this club, and sang and danced there until the master of ceremonies extinguished the lights out of concern that youth should rest. Moscow then went to sleep on a plywood prop somewhere behind the stage; out of girlish habit she was hugging her temporary friend, a young woman as tired and happy as she was herself.

5

Untidy and unclean because of the economy of his time, Sambikin felt the world's external matter like an irritation of his own skin. Day and night he followed the worldwide current of events, and his mind lived in the terror of his own responsibility for the entire mindless fate of physical substance.[26]

At night Sambikin took a long time to fall asleep because of the imagination of labor, now illuminated by electricity, on Soviet land. He saw structures, densely rigged with scaffolding, where unsleeping people came and went as they fastened down young boards made from fresh timber so that they themselves could remain up there, on the height where the wind blows, and from where night, in the form of the remnant of the evening glow, can be seen moving along the edge of the world. Sambikin would clasp his hands from impatience and joy, then suddenly fall into thought in the darkness, forgetting to blink for half an hour at a time. He knew that thousands of young engineers, who had just finished their shifts, were also not sleeping now but restlessly tossing and turning in hostels and new buildings all over the flat plains of the country, while others, who had only that moment lain down to rest, were already muttering to themselves and gradually pulling their clothes back on again, in order to go back out to the building site because their minds were being tormented by some detail, forgotten during the day, which threatened a nocturnal accident.[27]

Sambikin would get out of bed, turn on the light, and walk about in agitation, wanting to undertake something straightaway. He would switch on the radio and hear that music was no longer playing but space was humming in its own alarm, like a deserted road you wanted to walk away along. Then Sambikin would phone the institute clinic: Were there any urgent operations he could assist with? He was told that there was one. A little boy had been brought in with a tumor on his head; it was growing with minute-by-minute speed, and the boy's consciousness was darkening.[28]

Sambikin ran out onto the Moscow street; the trams were no longer running, and the high heels of women on their way back from theaters and laboratories, or from visiting people they loved, were knocking resonantly against the asphalt pavements. Working his long legs, Sambikin ran quickly to the Bauman district, where a special-purpose experimental medical institute was being constructed. The institute had not yet been finally equipped, and only two departments—surgery and electrical treatment—were functioning. The institute yard was heaped with boards, pipes, trolleys, and crates of scientific instruments; the child-scale fence, which separated the construction from some kind of apartment block, had wilted completely and was leaning over.

In this yard Sambikin suddenly heard a pitiful music that touched his heart not so much through its melody as through an unclear memory of something lived through and left behind in oblivion. He listened intently for a minute; the music was playing on the other side of the poor fence. Sambikin got up onto this fence and saw a bald, aged fiddler playing in the absence of people, at two o'clock in the morning. Sambikin read the sign over the main door of the building outside which the musician was playing: HOUSING COOPERATIVEADMINISTRATIONANDHOUSEMANAGEMENT COMMITTEE. Sambikin took out a ruble and wanted to give it to the musician for his work, but the fiddler refused it. He said he was playing for himself now, because he was feeling melancholy and could not sleep until dawn—but that was a long way off...

Outside the smaller of the operating theaters were already hanging two oxygen bags, and a senior nurse was standing on duty. At the end of the corridor, in a separate cubicle whose front wall was made entirely of glass, the sick child was being prepared for the operation; two nurses were rapidly shaving his head. Behind the boy's left ear was a sphere, half the size of his head and filled with hot brown pus and blood, and this sphere seemed like a second wild head that was sucking out the child's failing life. The child was awake and sitting up in bed: he was about seven years old. He was staring with emptied, sleeping eyes, and lifting his hands in the air a little when his heart gasped with pain; he was in torment and did not expect mercy.

With exact sensation, the child's illness at once appeared in Sambikin's quick consciousness, and he rubbed behind his left ear, looking for a spherical swelling, a second mindless head packed with deadly pus. He went to get ready for the operation. Changing his clothes and thinking, he heard a noise in his left ear—it was the pus in the boy's head, chemically eroding and corroding the last plate of bone that protected his brain. Misty death was already drifting through the boy's mind, life was still clinging on behind the shelter of a bony film, but there remained in this film only a fraction of a millimeter of thickness and the weakening bone was vibrating beneath the pressure of the pus.

"What is he seeing in his own consciousness?" Sambikin was now questioning himself. "He's seeing dreams that protect him from horror. He sees his two mothers washing him in the bath when really it's two nurses shaving his hair. And the only thing that frightens him is: Why two mothers? He sees his favorite cat, that lives in his room with him, and now this cat's sunk its claws into his head."

In came the old surgeon, whom Sambikin was to assist. The old man was ready, and he beckoned to his assistant. Sambikin was not yet allowed to operate on his own; he was twenty-seven years old and this was only his second year of working as an assistant surgeon.

All the sounds in the surgical clinic were scrupulously annihilated, and communication was now effected through colored light. Three lamps of different colors lit up in the room of the doctor on duty, and a number of actions were then performed almost noiselessly: a low trolley moved on rubber wheels down the cork floor of the corridor and took the patient away to the operating theater; the electrician switched the electrical light over to the institute's own storage batteries, so that light would not depend upon the chances of the city grid, and then turned on a machine that pumped ozone-enriched air into the theater; the theater door opened without a sound, and a cool, fragrant breeze blew from a special apparatus into the sick child's face. This brought the boy sedation and he smiled, freed from the last traces of suffering.

"Mama, I'm ever so ill. They're going to cut me now, but I'm not hurting at all!" he said, and then became helpless and alien to his own self. Life as if absented itself from him and concentrated itself in the distant and sad imagination of dreams. He saw objects—the entire sum of his own impressions. The objects hurtled past him and he recognized them: here was a forgotten nail he had held in his hands long ago, now the nail had rusted and grown old; here a black little dog, once he had played with it in the yard, now it was lying dead in the rubbish, with a broken glass jar on its head; here an iron roof on a low shed, he had used to climb up onto it so he could look down from a height, now the roof was empty and the iron was missing him but he hadn't been there for a long time; it was summer, his mother's shadow lay on the ground, militia were going by, but their band was playing too softly to be heard ...

The old surgeon suggested Sambikin carry out the operation—he himself would assist.

"Let's start!" said the old man, in the theater's bright silence.

Sambikin took an abrupt and gleaming instrument and entered with it into the essence of every matter—the human body. A sharp, instantaneous arrow left the boy's mind, just behind his eyes, ran through his body—he was following the arrow with his imagination—and struck the boy in the heart; the boy shuddered, all the objects that had known him began to weep for him, and the dream of his memories vanished. Life sank even lower, shouldering with a simple dark warmth in patient expectation. With his hands Sambikin could feel the boy's body growing still hotter, and he hurried. He was draining pus from the now wide-open integuments of the head and penetrating into the bone, searching for the primary seats of infection.

"Gently, slow down!" the old surgeon was saying. Then he turned to the nurse and asked, "Pulse?"

"Arrhythmic, doctor," said the nurse. "Sometimes it disappears completely."

"Never mind—the momentum of the heart is always great. It'll right itself."

"Hold his head," Sambikin ordered the nurses. He was now

starting to clean out the areas of bone in whose pores the pus was concealed.

His instruments clinked, as if he were working cold metal. Stroke by stroke—deeper here, more shallow there—Sambikin was feeling his way, guided by the precise sense of art. His big eyes had gone glassy from lack of moisture—there was no time to blink—and his pale cheeks were now swarthy from the force of the blood coming to his aid from the depth of his heart. As he extracted the sections of bone, Sambikin examined them in the light of the mirror; he sniffed them and squeezed them for better acquaintance with them, and then handed them to the senior surgeon, who threw them with equanimity into a dish.

The brain was getting closer; as he removed pieces of bone from the skull, Sambikin was now studying them under a microscope and still finding nests of streptococci. In some places of the child's head Sambikin had already reached the last membrane of bone guarding the brain, and he began to clean the deathly gray bloom from its surface. His hands acted as if thinking for themselves, calculating each possibility of movement. As he went on removing the streptococci, their numbers decreased, but Sambikin then moved over to extremely powerful microscopes which showed that the pus-generating bodies, though rapidly growing fewer, were still not disappearing entirely. He remembered the famous mathematical equation expressing the distribution of heat along a bar of infinite length, and stopped the operation.

"Pack the wound and bandage it!" he ordered, for the complete destruction of the streptococci would entail slashing to pieces not only the whole of the patient's head but also his whole body right down to his toenails.

It was clear to Sambikin that the patient's body, hot, defenseless, and wide-open, with its thousands of split-open, sucking blood vessels, was greedily absorbing streptococci from everywhere—from the air and, above all, from his own instruments, which it was impossible to sterilize absolutely. They should have changed long ago to an electrical surgery that entered body and bones with the pure and instantaneous deep-blue flame of a voltaic arc—then everything that brought death would itself be killed, and any new streptococci that penetrated a wound would find a burnt-out desert, not an environment that would nourish them.[29]

"Finished!" said Sambikin.

The nurses were already bandaging the patient's head. They turned him over, his face toward the doctors.

The warmth of life, beating out from within, was passing in pink bands across the child's pale face and quickly being washed away; then it would reappear and fade again. His eyes were almost open and had dried up so much that dryness had slightly wrinkled the retinal substance.

"He's dead!" said the old doctor.

"Not yet," Sambikin answered, and kissed the child on his faded lips. "He's going to live. Give him a little oxygen. And nothing to drink until morning."

On his way out from the clinic, Sambikin met a trembling, convulsive woman—the child's mother. She had not been allowed in because of the rules and it being late at night. Sambikin bowed to her and ordered her to be admitted to her son.

Morning was brightening. Sambikin looked across the fence to the neighboring housing cooperative; everything was empty, the fiddler had gone away to sleep. A man of modest appearance came out of the door, along with a wrinkled woman who had been worn out by years and hardship. Her companion was eloquently confessing his love; Sambikin found himself listening with inadvertent attention—in the man's voice he could hear a dark, chesty sorrow, and this made it touching, even though what he was saying was stupid and trite.

"But if there's a war, you'll drop me," the woman was timidly objecting.

"Me? Certainly not! I'm last category, a reservist, I'm almost nothing... Let's go and lie down a bit behind the shed—my soul's aching again."

"Didn't you get enough of loving me when we were in the room?" the woman asked in happy surprise.

"Not quite enough," said the reservist lover. "My heart's still aching, it hasn't cooled down."

"A right young Hamlet!" the woman said with a smile. "Nothing stops him!"

She now felt proud that men liked her and were attracted by her. Hunched from the morning chill beneath his worn-out, tired coat, the reservist hurried off arm in arm with the woman, evidently eager to get shot of everything as soon as he possibly could.

Sambikin set off through Moscow. It was strange and even sad to see the empty tram stops and the deserted black route numbers on their white signs—along with the pavements, the tramway poles, and the electric clock on the square, they were yearning for crowds of people.

As was his way, Sambikin began to ponder the life of substance—the life of his own self; he related himself as if to a laboratory animal, the part of the world he had been allocated so that he could research everything as a whole in all its unclarity.

He thought constantly and without interruption; if Sambikin stopped thinking, his soul at once began to ache—and he would work once again on the imagination of the world in his head, for the sake of the world's transformation. At night he dreamed of his destroyed thoughts, but he would toss and turn in bed to no avail, struggling to recall their daytime order. This tormented him and he would awake, delighting in the morning light and his restored clarity of mind. His long, dried-up, kind, and big body always lived and breathed noisily, as if this man were avid; he wanted constantly to eat and drink, and his huge face had the look of a saddened animal, except that the nose was so great, so alien even to this huge face, that it brought meekness to the entire expression of his character.

When Sambikin got back home, the time was already light; a great summer morning was burning above the earth so mightily that its light seemed to Sambikin to be thundering. He phoned the institute and was told that the child he had operated on was sleeping soundly, that his temperature was falling, and that his mother had gone to sleep too, on another bed. After thinking through everything to do with the operation and all the routine problems, Sambikin began to sense his anguished, now empty heart—once more he needed to act, in order to acquire a task for contemplation and thus silence the unclear and avid cry of conscience in his soul. He slept little—and best of all after long work, in gratitude for which his dreams would leave him alone. Now, though, he had been acting too little; his reason had not been able to tire itself out in his head and it wanted to go on working, rejecting sleep. After rushing helplessly about the room for a while, Sambikin went into the bathroom; he undressed there and examined with astonishment his own young man's body, then muttered something and got into the cold water. The water pacified him, but he immediately realized how much a human being is still a feebly constructed, homespun being—no more than a vague embryo and blueprint of something more authentic—and how much work must be done to unfurl from this embryo the flying, higher image buried in our dream.

6

That evening, in the district Komsomol Club, there was a gathering of young scientists, engineers, pilots, doctors, teachers, performing artists, musicians, and workers from the new factories. No one was over the age of twenty-seven, yet each was already known throughout the new world of their motherland—and this early fame made them all feel a slight shame, which got in the way of living. The men and women who worked at the club, who were older and who had wasted their lives and talent during the unhappy bourgeois times, let out secret sighs of inner impoverishment as they arranged the furnishings in the two halls, setting up one for a formal meeting and the other for conversation and dining.

Among the first to arrive were Selin, a twenty-four-year-old engineer, and Kuzmina, a pianist and Komsomol member who was constantly lost in thought from the imagination of music.

"Let's go fill our faces!" said Selin.

"Yes, let's!" Kuzmina agreed.

They went over to the bar. Selin, a pink-cheeked and powerful eater, immediately consumed eight pieces of bread and sausage, while Kuzmina took only two pastries; what she lived for was play, not the digestion of food.

"Selin, why do you eat such a lot?" asked Kuzmina. "Maybe it's good, but looking at you makes me ashamed!"

Selin ate with indignation; he chewed as he had plowed, with insistent labor, with zeal in both his trusty jaws.

After a while, ten more people arrived together: Golovach the explorer; the mechanical engineer Semyon Sartorius; two girls who were friends, both of them hydraulic engineers; Levchenko the composer; Sitsylin the astronomer; Vechkin the aviation meteorologist; Muldbauer the designer of high-altitude aircraft;[30] and the electrical engineer Gunkin, with his wife. Then came the sound of other voices, and some more people arrived. They all knew one another— through work, through meeting socially, or through hearsay.

While they waited for the meeting to begin, they each devoted themselves to their particular pleasure: to friendship, to food, to questions about unresolved tasks, or to music and dancing. Kuzmina found a small room with a new grand piano, and with delight began playing Beethoven's Ninth Symphony—all the movements, one after another, from memory.[31] Her heart was wrung by the music's deep freedom and inspired thought, as well as by egotistical sorrow that she herself could not compose like that. Gunkin the electrical engineer listened to Kuzmina and thought about the high frequencies of electricity shooting right through the universe, about the emptiness of the high, terrible world sucking human consciousness into itself. Muldbauer saw in the music a representation of the distant and weightless countries of the air, where the black sky is located and amid it hangs an unflickering sun with a dead incandescence of light, and where, far from the warm and dimly green earth, the real, serious cosmos starts: mute space, lit up now and again by stars signaling that the path to them has long been open and free. Yes, better to put an end straightaway to the bothersome conflicts of the earth;

let Stalin himself, let wise old Stalin, direct the velocity and thrust of human history beyond the bounds of the earth's gravity—to the great edification of the earth, to the great edification of reason itself through the courage of an act it has long been destined to perform.

Soon afterward Moscow Chestnova arrived too, smiling quietly from the joy of seeing her comrades and hearing music that excited her life toward the fulfillment of a higher fate.

Last of all appeared the surgeon Sambikin; he had just been in the institute clinic, and he himself had been changing the bandages on the boy he had operated on. He arrived crushed by the sorrow of the construction of the human body, which squeezes between its own bones far more suffering and death than life and movement. And it was strange to Sambikin to be feeling well now, in the tension of his concern and responsibility. His whole mind was filled with thought, his heart was beating calmly and truly, he had no need of a better happiness—yet, at the same time, consciousness of his secret delight was beginning to make him feel shame. He was already wanting to leave the club, to go to the institute and do some work during the night on his own research into death, but suddenly he saw Moscow Chestnova passing. The unclear charm of her outward appearance surprised Sambikin; concealed behind the modesty and even timidity of her face, he could see power and luminous inspiration.

A bell rang for the start of the meeting. Everyone left the room where Sambikin was standing; only Chestnova stayed behind, adjusting one of her stockings. When she had finished with the stocking, she saw Sambikin alone, looking at her. Out of awkwardness and embarrassment—that they should live in the same world, be working for the same cause, yet not be acquainted—she nodded to him. Sambikin walked over to her, and together they went through to listen to the meeting.

They sat down side by side and, amid speeches, amid glory and congratulations, Sambikin clearly heard the pulsation of Moscow's heart in her breast. Whispering into her ear, he asked, "Why is your heart knocking like that? I can hear it!"

"It wants to fly, it's beating its wings," Moscow whispered back to Sambikin with a smile. "I'm a parachutist!"

"In long-ago, now perished millennia, the human body did fly," thought Sambikin. "The human rib cage represents folded wings."

He touched his head, which felt warm; there too something was beating, wanting to fly out from the cell of a dark, lonely confinement.

After the meeting came the time of the communal dinner and entertainments. But first, before sitting together at the shared table, the young guests dispersed through the many rooms.

Sartorius the mechanical engineer invited Moscow Chestnova to dance, and she went off to whirl about with him, studying with curiosity the great round face of this famous inventor in the field of precision industry, this engineer and designer of worldwide significance. Sartorius held Moscow firmly, danced heavily, and smiled timidly, betraying his compressed attraction toward her. Moscow, for her part, looked at him as if she were in love—she was quick to give herself to her feelings and did not play the feminine policy of equanimity. She liked this uninteresting man who was shorter than her, whose face was kind and morose, and who, unable to endure his own heart, had undertaken what was for him an act of extreme boldness: he had gone close to a woman and invited her to dance. Soon, however, he got bored; his hands had grown used to the warmth of Moscow's body, which was hot beneath her light dress, and he began to mutter something. Hearing this, Moscow immediately took offense.

"He takes me in his arms, he dances with me, and then he thinks about something completely different!" she said.

"I just—" answered Sartorius.

"You just what? You can tell me right now!" Moscow said with a frown, and stopped dancing.

Sambikin hurtled past them, with a wind; he too was dancing, having paired up with some Komsomol girl of great prettiness. Moscow smiled at him. "You're dancing too! How come? You are a strange one!"

"One should live from every angle!" Sambikin informed her without pausing.[32]

"And is that what you want?" Moscow shouted after him.

"No, I'm pretending!" Sambikin answered. "I was speaking theoretically."

The Komsomol girl took offense and immediately left Sambikin, and he began to laugh.

"Well go on then! Tell me!" Moscow addressed Sartorius, with deliberate seriousness.

"Is she stupid?" thought Sartorius. "What a pity!" At this moment Vechkin the meteorologist came up to him, followed by Sambikin, and Sartorius was unable to say anything to Moscow in reply. An hour passed before they met again at the communal table.

The large table had been laid for fifty people. Every half meter there were flowers, looking pensive because of their delayed death and giving off a posthumous fragrance. The wives of the designers, and the young women engineers, were dressed in the best silk of the Republic—the government liked to adorn its best people. Moscow Chestnova was wearing a tea-rose dress, which weighed only ten grams and had been sewn with such skill that even the pulsing of her blood vessels was revealed by the rippling of her silk. All the men, even the untidy Sambikin and the unkempt, melancholy Vechkin, had come in suits that were simple but expensive, made from fine material; to dress badly and dirtily would have been to reproach with poverty the country that had nourished everyone present and dressed them with her choicest goods, herself thriving on this youth's strength and compression, on its labor and talent.

Outside the open door, on the balcony, a small Komsomol orchestra was playing short pieces. The night's spacious air was coming through the balcony door and into the hall, and the flowers on the long table breathed and gave off a stronger smell, feeling they were alive in the earth they had lost. The ancient city was full of clamor and light, like a construction site; now and again the voice and laughter of a transient passerby would be carried up from the street, and Moscow Chestnova would feel like going outside and inviting everybody to join them for supper: after all, socialism was setting in! At times she felt so good that she wanted somehow to leave herself behind, to leave her body and its dress, and become someone else—Gunkin's wife, Sambikin, the reservist, Sartorius, or a woman working on a collective farm in the Ukraine.

Chandeliers from the ElectroDevice factory covered the people and the rich furnishings with a pale and tender energy; preliminary light snacks stood on the table while the main supper was still being kept warm far off on the kitchen ranges.

The guests who had gathered, all of them beautiful either from nature or from animation and unfinished youth, took a long time to sit down at the table, looking for the best people to sit beside, though what they really wanted was to sit next to everyone at once.

And when at last they sat down, all thirty of them, their inner resources of life were excited by one another's company and began to multiply, and among them was born the shared genius of vital sincerity and of happy rivalry in intellectual friendship. But their finely tuned sense of relationship, acquired in a difficult, technological culture where victory is not to be won through ambiguous play—this sense of right conduct allowed no place for stupidity, sentimentality, or conceit. Those present all knew, or guessed at, the sullen dimensions of nature, the extensiveness of history, the length of future time, and the true scale of their own powers; they were rational and practical people, not to be seduced toward empty delusion.

Moscow Chestnova was wilder and more impatient than the others. Without waiting for anyone else, she had drunk a glass of wine, and now she was flushed—from joy and from being unaccustomed. Sartorius noticed this and smiled at her with his broad, inexact face like some place or other in the country. His father's surname was not Sartorius but Chewbeard, and his peasant mother had carried him in her innards beside warm, well-chewed rye bread.[33]

Sambikin was also observing Chestnova, and puzzling over her: Should he love her or not? All in all, she was pretty and belonged to nobody, but how much thought and feeling would he need to drive out of his own body and heart so as to make room there for devotion to this woman? And anyway Chestnova would not be faithful to him; never could she exchange all the noise of life for the whisper of a single human being.

"No!" Sambikin decided once and for all. "I won't love her—and I can't! All the more so since I'd have to somehow spoil her body, which would be a pity. And lie, day and night, about how splendid I am. I don't want to, it's too difficult!" He forgot himself in the flow of his thought, no longer remembering anyone present ... Those present, although the dishes before them were both plentiful and tasty, were all eating little and slowly, feeling sorry for the precious food that the workers on the collective farms had won for them, through labor and patience, in the calamities of the struggle with nature and the class enemy. Only Moscow Chestnova forgot herself, eating and drinking like some predatory creature. She said all kinds of foolish things, teased Sartorius and felt shame stealing into her heart from her lying, vulgar mind that was sadly aware of its shameful state. Nobody stopped Chestnova or said anything rude to her, until finally she exhausted her strength and fell silent of her own accord. Sambikin knew that foolishness was a natural expression of wandering feelings that have yet to find their goal and passion, while Sartorius took delight in Moscow independently of her behavior; he already loved her as the living truth, and through his joy he saw her unclearly and untruly.

At the time of late evening and a hubbub of people, Viktor Vasilievich Bozhko quietly entered the hall and sat down on a couch by the wall, not wanting to be noticed. He caught sight of Moscow Chestnova, red and merry, and trembled from fear of her. Some learned young man went over to her and sang:

You've drunk too deep,
You're pale all over,
So dear and sweet
A faithful lover.

Hearing this, Moscow covered her face with her hands—it was unclear whether she had begun to weep or was feeling suddenly ashamed of herself. Sartorius was at that moment arguing with Vechkin and Muldbauer; Sartorius was asserting that proletarian man would be followed by an impassioned and technological being who in a practical way, through his own labor, would sense the entire world. The ancient people who first began history were also technological beings; the cities, ports, and labyrinths of Greece, even Mount Olympus itself, had been constructed by Cyclopes, one-eyed workers—each of them had had one pupil gouged out by the ancient aristocrats to indicate that they were the proletariat, condemned to build countries, dwellings of gods, and ships of the seas, and that there is no escape for the one-eyed.[34] Three or four thousand years had gone by—a hundred generations—and the descendants of these Cyclopes had emerged from the dark of the historical labyrinth into the light of nature; they had retained for themselves one-sixth of the earth, and all the remaining earth lived solely in expectation of their coming. Even the god Zeus, probably, had been the last Cyclops; his work had been to heap up the hill of Olympus, and he had lived in a hut up above and had survived in the memory of the archaic aristocratic tribe. For the bourgeoisie of those frail times had not been stupid; it had translated great workers who died to the category of gods. Being unable to understand creativity without delight, it was secretly astonished that those who had perished could quietly have possessed the highest power of all—the capacity for labor and the soul of labor: technology.

Sartorius rose to his feet and held up a cup of wine. A short man, carried away by intellectual imagination, and with an ordinary face that was warmed by life, he was happy and attractive. Moscow Chestnova gazed at him and decided that one day they must kiss. In the midst of his now silent comrades he pronounced: "Let us drink to the nameless Cyclopes, to the memory of all our exhausted fathers who have perished, and to technology—the true soul of mankind!"

They all drank together. The musicians played an old song, a setting of some lines of Yazykov:

Beyond the wall of stormy weather,
Lies a country that is blessed,
Where the heavens never darken,
Where all is quietness and rest.[35]

Bozhko was sitting submissively and inconspicuously. He was feeling more joy than those taking part in the evening; he knew that the stormy weather was passing and that the country of the blessed lay outside the window, lit by stars and electricity. His love for this country was silent and miserly; he picked up every crumb of good that fell from it, in order that the country should survive in its entirety.[36]

A lavish main course was brought in. Cherishingly the guests began to taste it, but Semyon Sartorius could no longer eat or drink anything. The torment of love for Moscow Chestnova had now taken hold in all his body and heart, and he had to open his mouth and make an effort to breathe, as if he felt tight in the chest. Enigmatically and from far away, Moscow was smiling at him; her mysterious life was reaching Sartorius in the form of warmth and alarm, while her far-seeing eyes were looking at him inattentively, as at a commonplace fact. "Oh what a bitch physics is!" Sartorius said to himself, as he began to understand his own position. "What's left for me now except stupidity and personal happiness?"

The city night shone bright in the outer darkness, sustained by the tension of distant machines; the excited air, warmed by millions of people, was penetrating Sartorius's heart in the form of anguish. He went out onto the balcony, looked at the stars, and whispered old words he had heard and remembered: "My God!"

Sambikin was still sitting at the table, not touching the food; his own thoughts had led him far beyond the next morning and he was attempting, as if through a sea fog, to make out the immortality to come. He wanted to obtain a long power of life, maybe an eternity of it, from the corpses of beings who had fallen. A few years back, while digging about in people's dead bodies, he had taken fine sections from their hearts, brains, and organs of sexual secretion. Sambikin had studied these sections under the microscope and had noticed on them some faint traces of an unknown substance. Later, testing these almost extinguished traces for chemical reactivity, electrical conductivity, and photosensitivity, he had discovered that this unknown substance was endowed with a pungent energy of life, even though it was to be found only inside the dead. There was none of it in the living: on the contrary, patches of death were accumulating in the living long before they perished. Sambikin then fell into perplexity for whole years, and this perplexity had still not left him: How was it that a corpse, even if only for a short time, could be a reservoir of the most abrupt, thrusting life? Investigating more precisely, speculating almost uninterruptedly, Sambikin was coming to suppose that at the moment of death some kind of mysterious sluice opens in the human body,[37] and that from this sluice there flows through the organism a special moisture which poisons the pus of death and washes away the ash of exhaustion, and which is carefully preserved all through life, up until the supreme danger. But where in the darkness, in the bodily ravines of a human being, is this sluice that faithfully and miserlily preserves the last charge of life? Only death, when it rushes through the body, can break the seal on that reserve of clenched life—and then, like an unsuccessful shot, this life resounds inside a person for the last time and leaves unclear traces on his dead heart ...[38] A fresh corpse was permeated through and through with traces of this mysterious, now motionless substance, and every part of a dead person preserved in it a creative strength for those who survived to go on living. Sambikin's intention was to transform the dead into a force that would nourish the longevity and health of the living. He had understood the chastity and might of that infantile moisture that bathes a person's insides at the moment of his last breath; this moisture, added to someone alive but wilting, was able to render that person upright, steadfast, and happy.

Sartorius stood on the balcony for a long time; for him, everything was now undecided and irrelevant. People strange to him were going down the street in a tram. Traffic sounds and spoken words reached his ears as if from far away; he listened to them without interest or curiosity, as if he were sick and alone. What he wanted now was to go straight home, to lie down under a blanket and warm this sudden pain of his, so it would leave him by morning, when he would have to get going again.

Behind his back, his contemporaries were delighting in the consciousness of their own success and of the future technological dream.[39] Muldbauer was speaking about a stratum of the atmosphere, at an altitude of somewhere between fifty and a hundred kilometers, where the light, temperature, and electromagnetic conditions were such that any living organism will neither tire nor die but be capable of eternal existence amid violet space. This was the "Heaven" of the ancients and the happy land of the people of the future; beyond that far distance of stormy weather drifting about low down, there was indeed located a blessed country. Muldbauer was predicting the imminent conquest of the stratosphere and a further penetration into the deep blue height of peace where lay the airy country of immortality; man would then become winged, while the earth would be inherited by the animals and would once again, and forever, be covered over by the dense forests of its own old virginity. "And the animals foresense this!" Muldbauer was saying with conviction. "When I look into their eyes, they seem to be thinking, 'When will all this come to an end? When will you finally leave us?' The animals are thinking, 'When will people leave us alone to follow our own fate?'"

Sartorius smiled a bored smile; he would have liked to remain now in the very lowest place of the earth, or even to find himself a place in an empty grave and, inseparably from Moscow Chestnova, live out his life there until death. But it would be a pity to leave unanswered these night stars that had been looking at him since childhood, a pity to play no part in a universal life now filled by labor and a sense of closeness between people; and he was afraid of walking through the city mutely, his head bowed, with the concentrated, solitary thought of love, and he had no wish to feel mere equanimity toward his own desk—heaped with the drafts and plans of his ideas—to the iron bed he had lain on for so long, or to his desk lamp, his patient witness in the dark and silence of working nights ... Beneath his shirt Sartorius stroked his chest as he said to himself, "Go away! Leave me on my own again, vile element! I'm a straightforward engineer and a rationalist, and I reject you as woman and as love. I'd do better to worship the electron and the dust of atoms!" But the world drifting before his eyes as fire and noise was already dying away in its own sounds; it had crossed beyond the dark threshold of his heart and left behind it only a single living being—the most touching creature on earth. Could he truly renounce this being in order to devote himself to the atom—to a mere particle of dust and ash?

Moscow Chestnova joined Sartorius on the balcony, and said to him with a smile, "Why are you so sad? Do you love me or not?"

She was breathing on him with the warmth of her smiling mouth and her dress was rustling. Seized by the tedium of malice and bravado, Sartorius replied, "No, I'm admiring another Moscow—the city."

"All right then," said Chestnova, readily making peace. "Let's go and eat. Comrade Selin is eating more than anyone. He's really stuffed himself, he's sitting there all red, but his eyes look sad all the time. You don't know why, do you?"

"No," Sartorius replied quietly. "I'm sad too."

Moscow peered through the dark at his disproportionate face; his eyes were open and tears were running down his cheeks.

"There's no need to cry," said Moscow. "I love you too."

"You're lying," doubted Sartorius.

"No, it's true, it's really true," exclaimed Moscow. "Come on, let's go somewhere straightaway!"

As they walked arm in arm amid their celebrating friends, Sambikin watched them through eyes that had forgotten to blink and that thought had carried away to a place the far side of personal happiness. Near the way out, Bozhko suddenly appeared before Moscow's breast and, respectfully, pronounced his patient request. Chestnova was so pleased to see him that she snatched a piece of cake off the table and immediately offered it to Bozhko.

Viktor Vasilievich Bozhko was now working at the Weights and Measures Industry Trust[40] and was entirely engrossed by his concern for weights and measures. He asked Moscow Ivanovna to introduce him to this famous engineer, someone who might be able to invent simple and accurate scales that could be manufactured cheaply for all the collective and State farms and for the whole of Soviet commerce. Not seeing Sartorius's sadness, Bozhko immediately began to speak about the great and unnoticeable calamities of the national economy: the additional difficulties of socialism on the collective farms; the reduced payments to collective farmers; kulak policies that exploited the inaccuracy of weights, scales, and balances; and the massive, if involuntary, defrauding of the worker-consumer in cooperatives and distribution centers . . . None of which would occur if it were not for the dilapidated condition of the State's stock of scales and balances, the antiquated design of the scales, and the shortage of metal and wood for the fabrication of new weighing machines.

"You must excuse me," said Bozhko, "I came here in spite of myself. I know I'm being boring. People here have been talking—and I have heard them—about how man will soon be flying and happy. I will always listen to this with pleasure, but what we need for the time being is very little. We need to be able to weigh flour and grain in the collective farms with accuracy."

Moscow smiled at him with the meekness of her transient disposition. "You're splendid, you're a true Soviet man! Sartorius, go along to their institute tomorrow and design them the cheapest and simplest of scales—and make sure they're accurate!"

Sartorius fell into thought. "That's difficult," he admitted. "It's easier to perfect a steam engine than a pair of scales. Scales have been working for thousands of years. It would be like inventing a new bucket for water. But I'll come to your institute and help you as best I can."

Bozhko gave him the address of his institute and returned with happiness to his room, where he was awaited by his usual labor of worldwide correspondence.

7

They reached the outskirts of the city on almost the last tram, and there was no going back. The horizon reflected a distant electrical glow back onto the earth, and the poorest of lights reached as far as the fields and lay on the ears of rye like an early, faithless dawn. But it was still the middle of the night.

Moscow Chestnova took off her shoes and began to walk barefoot over the softness of the fields. Sartorius followed her in fear and joy; there was nothing she could do now that did not bring trembling into his heart, and he was afraid of the alarming and dangerous life that was unfolding there. He followed after her, all the time lagging inadvertently behind her, thinking about her monotonously but with such tenderness that if Moscow had squatted down to pee, Sartorius would have begun to weep.

Chestnova gave him her shoes to carry. Imperceptibly, he sniffed them and even touched them with his tongue; now neither Moscow Chestnova herself, nor anything about her, however unclean, could have evoked the least squeamishness in Sartorius, and he could have looked at waste products from her with extreme curiosity, since they too would not long ago have formed part of a splendid person.

"Comrade Sartorius, what are we going to do now?" asked Moscow. "It's still night, soon dew will be lying on the ground."

"I don't know," Sartorius answered morosely. "Probably I'll have to love you."

"There's a collective farm asleep in that hollow over there," said Moscow, pointing into the distance. "There'll be a smell of bread, and little children snuffling away in the barns. And cows are lying somewhere in the pasture, and a dawn mist is beginning above them. How I love seeing all this and being alive!"

No cows or little children snuffling in their sleep held any interest for Sartorius now. He even wanted the earth to become deserted, so that Moscow would not divert attention anywhere else but would concentrate wholly on him.

Toward dawn Moscow and Sartorius sat down in a boundary-mark pit;[41] it was overgrown with tall warm weeds that had taken refuge there from the cultured fields like kulaks hiding away in their farmsteads.

Sartorius took Chestnova by the hand. All of nature—everything that moved in the mind as a flow of thought, that drove the heart forward and was revealed to the gaze, always in an unfamiliar and primordial guise, as overgrown grass, as the unique days of life, as the vast sky, as the close faces of people—all of this nature was for Sartorius now enclosed in one body and ended at the border of her dress, at the ends of her bare feet.

Sartorius had spent all his youth in the study of physics and mechanics; he had labored over the computation of infinity as a body, trying to find an economical principle of its action. He had wanted to discover, in the very flow of human consciousness, a thought that worked in resonance with nature and so—even if only by chance, by virtue of living chance—reflected the whole of nature's truth; and he had hoped to secure this thought forever through some calculable formula. But now he was not conscious of any thought at all because his heart had risen up into his head and was beating there above his eyes. Sartorius stroked Moscow's hand, which was firm and full, like a reservoir of sparing, tightly compressed feeling.

"Tell me, Semyon, what is it you want from me?" Moscow asked submissively, ready for kindness.

"I want to marry you," said Sartorius. "More than that, I don't know what to want."

Moscow fell into thought and ate a blade of long grass with her young, avid mouth.

"Yes, it's true—there's nothing else to want when you're in love. But people say that's stupid."

"Let them," Sartorius pronounced gloomily. "All they do is say things—probably they've never loved...What's to be done? Without you I just pine."

"Embrace me then, and I'll embrace you."

Sartorius embraced her.

"Well, has your pining got any easier now?"

"No, it's just the same," Sartorius answered.

"Then we'll have to get married," Moscow agreed.

When an innocent, everyday morning lit up the local collective farms and the outskirts of the huge city, Chestnova and Sartorius were still to be found in the boundary-mark pit. Having known the whole of Moscow in full—all the warmth, devotion, and happiness of her body—Sartorius sensed with surprise and horror that his love had not exhausted itself but had grown, and that essentially he had achieved nothing but remained as unhappy as before. Which meant that this was not the way to attain another person and truly share life with them. How then should one be? Sartorius knew nothing.

Moscow Chestnova was lying on her back. At first the sky above her was watery; then it became deep blue and stonelike; then it turned into something golden and glimmering, as if blooming with colors—behind the Urals the sun had now risen, and it was drawing closer.

Moscow clambered out of the pit, straightened her dress, put her shoes on, and began to walk toward the city alone. She told Sartorius that she would be his wife later; for the time being he should work at the trust for weights and measures, along with Bozhko—she would find him when it was right.

Helpless and insignificant, Sartorius came out after her. He stood alone in the dawn, in the emptiness of the still-unripe fields, stained and melancholy, like a surviving warrior on a now silent battleground.

"But why are you going, Moscow? I love you more than ever!"

Moscow turned to face him. "I'm not leaving you, Semyon. I've already told you I'll be back. I love you too."

"Then why are you leaving me? Come back here again."

Chestnova was standing in bewilderment about ten yards away.

"I'm sorry, Semyon."

"What are you sorry about?"

"I'm sorry about something... No matter how much I live, life never turns out like I want it to."

Moscow frowned and stood in hurt on the border of the tall rye. The sun was gleaming on the silk of her dress, and the last drops of morning moisture, gathered from the tall grass, were drying on her hair. A light breeze was blowing from the low basin of the Moscow River, and the rye was muttering something unclear through its swollen spikes; sunlight, like a thought and a smile, had filled the whole locality. Only Moscow was not merry, and her beautiful dress and her body, both made from this same glittering nature, did not correspond to her sad face. Sartorius led Moscow back to their sheltering grass and could not understand what was making them both feel so bleak.

"Leave me alone!" said Moscow, suddenly moving away from Sartorius. "I've done everything, I've flown in the air and I've had husbands—you're not the first, my sad one, my dear one!"

Chestnova turned away and lay facedown on the ground. The sight of her large, incomprehensible body, warmed under the skin by hidden blood, compelled Sartorius to embrace Moscow and once again, silently and hurriedly, expend with her a part of his own life. Maybe this was something poor and unnecessary, and maybe, far from resolving love, it only exhausted a man—but there was nothing else he could do. And then, without even enduring Sartorius's embraces to the end, Moscow turned her face toward him and smiled mockingly—somehow she was deceiving the man she loved.

Sartorius got back onto his feet again, as if nothing were the matter. He was perplexed: the weeping force of feeling that pulled him toward her had not received any consolation—his heart still ached for Moscow, as vainly as though she had died or were beyond his reach.

"You probably don't love me!" he said, trying to guess her secret.

"No, I do, I really like you," Moscow tried to convince him. "It's hard for me too."

Somewhere in the distance collective-farm carts were already moving over the earth; it was time to go to work in the city, for the two of them to divert themselves and part.

Moscow was sitting in hurt on the grass. As for Sartorius, he had now made peace with his love for her; it would be enough to live with Moscow in marriage, to admire her, perhaps to have children—

and then the pain of his feelings would quieten, his heart would wear itself out and die down forever for the sake of calm and fertile activity of mind.

"When I was a child," Moscow informed him, "I saw a man running down the street at night with fire on a stick, with a torch. He was running to the people in the prison, to set it on fire."

"There was a lot of that sort of thing," pronounced Sartorius.

"I feel sorry for him all the time. He was killed."

"What's so special about that?" asked Sartorius in surprise. "A lot of dead people are lying in the earth; there'll probably never be a heart that will remember all the dead at once and weep for them. What use would that be?"

Moscow went quiet for a while; she was looking at everything with faded eyes, as though she were ill.

"You know what, Semyon? It would be better if you stopped loving me. I've loved a lot of men already, but for you I'm the first! You're a maiden, and I'm a woman!"

Sartorius said nothing. Moscow put one arm around him.

"Really, Semyon—stop loving me! Do you know how much thinking and feeling I've done? It's terrible. And nothing's come of it."

"What hasn't come of it?" asked Sartorius.

"Life hasn't come of it. I'm afraid it never will, and I'm in a hurry now...I saw a woman once, she was pressing her face to the wall and weeping. She was weeping from grief—she was thirty-four years old, and grieving so deeply for her own past time that I thought she had lost a hundred rubles or more."

"No, Moscow, I love you," said Sartorius gloomily. "I'll feel good living with you."

"But I won't feel good living with you," said Moscow. "And you won't feel good either—so why lie and say that you will? I've wanted so many times to share my life with someone, and that's what I still do want—I've never been sparing with my own life and I never will be! What use is my life to me without people, without the whole of the USSR? If I'm a Komsomol member, it's not just because I was once a poor little girl..."

Chestnova was speaking with bitterness, with seriousness, like an experienced old woman who has lived life all the way through. And she withered then and there—because of the weakness of her heart, now clenched inside her breast as if this were somewhere dark and unknown.

"To make you believe me, I'm going to kiss you!"

Moscow kissed Sartorius, who had gone mute from sorrow. He could only watch with terror the sudden aging of her evident beauty, yet this became more powerful still for his love.

"I've just worked it out—why it is that people's lives together are so bad. It's because it's impossible to unite through love. I've tried so many times, but nothing ever comes of it—nothing but some kind of mere delight. You were with me just now—and what did you feel? Something astonishing? Something wonderful? Or nothing much?"

"Nothing much," agreed Semyon Sartorius.

"My skin always feels cold afterward," pronounced Moscow. "Love cannot be communism. I've thought and thought and I've seen that it just can't. One probably should love—and I will love. But it's like eating food—it's just a necessity, it's not the main life."

Sartorius was hurt that his love, gathered during the course of a whole life, should perish unanswered the very first time. But he understood Moscow's excruciating thought: that the very best of feelings lies in the cultivation of another human being, in sharing the burden and happiness of a second, unknown life, and that the love which comes with embraces brings only a childlike, blissful joy, and does nothing to solve the task of drawing people into the mystery of a mutual existence.

"How are you and I to be now?" asked Sartorius.

"We'll keep on being for a long time yet," Moscow said with a smile. "Wait for me, and work with Bozhko at the weights and scales factory—I'll come to you again. But now I'm going away."

"Where to?" said Sartorius. "Sit with me a bit longer."

"No, I really must," said Moscow, and got up from the ground.

The sun had already grown smaller in the sky and was giving off a concentrated incandescence. Locomotives were humming on the spur lines of a nearby construction site, petty airplanes were flying about the sky on training flights, and five-ton trucks were dragging logs behind them, grinding the soil to dust—heat and work had been spreading across the world since dawn.

Putting her arms around his head, Moscow said goodbye to Sartorius. She was happy again, she wanted to go away into the incalculable life that had long tormented her heart with a premonition of an unknown delight—into the darkness of tightly packed people, so as to live out with them the mystery of her own existence.

She went away content, keeping her satisfaction in check; she felt like throwing her dress off and running straight ahead, as if on the shore of a southern sea.

Sartorius was left on his own. He wanted Chestnova to return to him, and for them to become husband and wife trustingly and forever. Sartorius could feel his body being entered by a sad equanimity with regard to the interests of life—troubled and excruciating forces had arisen within him and eclipsed his entire mind, all healthy action toward a further aim. But Sartorius was willing to exhaust in Moscow's embraces everything tender, strange, and human that had appeared in him—anything to make his sense of himself less difficult, to be able to give himself once again to the clear movement of thought and to daily, long labor in the ranks of his patient comrades. He wanted to insure himself against all present or future convulsions of his own life by means of a simple, beloved wife, and so he decided to wait for Moscow's return.

8

The institute was located on the eve of liquidation. Only some time later did Sartorius understand that what is destined for liquidation can sometimes prove not only most durable of all but even to be doomed to eternal existence. This institute was located in the Old Merchant Arcade, in a gallery that had once been a storage place for goods not proof against damp. A staircase went down from the institute into the stone arcade that surrounded the whole of the old merchant courtyard. On the main door was a metal plate: THE MEASURE OF LABOR: THE REPUBLIC TRUST FOR SCALES, WEIGHTS, AND MEASURES OF LENGTH.[42]

The management office of this poor and half-forgotten branch of heavy industry was a single large and gloomy room with a low ceiling like that of an underground vault; where it met the walls, the ceiling came down so low that the employees sitting there almost touched it with their heads. There were a number of desks in the room, with one or two people at each of them, either writing or counting on abacuses. There were only around thirty employees, or not more than forty, but with the noise of their work, with their movement, questions, and exclamations, they created the impression of a huge institution of first-rate importance.

Sartorius was immediately taken on as engineer responsible for the design of new weighing apparatus, and he sat down at a table opposite Viktor Vasilievich Bozhko.

And the days of his new life began. In the course of a few nights Sartorius finished his last project from his previous workplace, the Institute of Experimental Mechanical Engineering, and began to focus his attention on the most ancient machine in the world—the balance. Nothing has changed so little in the course of the last five thousand years of history as the balance. At the time of the Cyclopes, in archaic Greece and Carthage, in great Persia that was felled by the blows of Alexander the Great—everywhere, in all times and spaces, the most universal and indispensable machine has been the balance. Balances are as old as weapons, and it may be that they are one and the same—what is a balance but a sword from the battle, laid across the crest of a rock, for the just division of the booty between the victors?

Bozhko, who was unable to work unless he felt love, in both mind and heart, for the object of the labor entrusted to him, expatiated at length to Sartorius on the decisive importance of the balance in the life of humanity. "The late Dmitry Ivanovich Mendeleyev himself," he said, "loved scales more highly than anything in the world. Even his own periodic table of the elements—even that he loved less. And that's hardly surprising. After all, the whole thing is based on the balance. Atomic weight—that's all there is to it!"

Bozhko also knew why a weighing apparatus is the most unnoticeable and meager of objects. People look keenly only at what lies on the balance; they see the sausage or the bread but don't notice what's beneath them. Beneath the sausage or bread, however, is located the balance, the instrument of honor and justice, a simple pauper of a machine that counts and cherishes the sacred good of socialism, measuring out the nourishment of both factory and collective-farm workers according to their creative labor and the principles of accounting.

And with zeal, with miserliness toward the crumbs of bread that are lost thanks to the inaccuracy of balances, Sartorius immersed himself in his work. Hidden from everyone, two feelings had met and combined together inside him—love for Moscow Chestnova and expectation of socialism. His unclear imagination held out a picture of summer: tall rye, the voices of millions of people who, for the first time, were organizing themselves on earth without the gravitational pull of need and sadness, and Moscow Chestnova, coming toward him from the distance to be his wife. She had gone the rounds of life; along with countless others she had lived life through and had left the years of endurance and feeling in the darkness of her past youth; she was returning the same as ever, only barefoot, in a poor dress, with hands grown bigger from work—yet merrier and clearer than before; she had now found satisfaction for her wandering heart.[43]

The wandering heart! For a long time the heart quakes in foreboding, squeezed by bones and by the misery of everyday life—and at last it rushes forward, losing its warmth on roads that are cold and chilly.

Bent over his desk at the institute, Sartorius worked as fast as he could on improving the construction of the balance. The director of the trust informed him of the danger of weight riots on the collective farms, like the salt riots of old, since a shortage of balances means either a short measure of bread in payment for work, or else— if too much bread is issued—a defrauding of the State. Moreover, the platform of a platform balance—if the balance is inaccurate— can become an arena for kulak politics and class struggle. Another problem fraught with potential danger was the shortage of weights. In many weighing stations, instead of using officially stamped weights, they had been placing all kinds of crazy piffle on the balances: bricks, pig iron, and there had even been cases of pregnant women being sat on a balance and being paid, as if for a day's work, for hiring out their torsos. All this must lead inevitably to the loss of billions of kilos of grain.

Grieving for Chestnova, afraid of living alone in his room, Sartorius would sometimes stay in the institute all night long. At ten o'clock in the evening the night watchman would take a preliminary nap on a chair by the entrance; a little later he would retire into the director's plywood cubicle and settle down in the soft armchair. Time went on passing on the big official clock; the empty desks evoked a yearning for the other members of staff; sometimes mice would appear and look at Sartorius with meek eyes.

He sat alone, working at the same task that Archimedes had once thought about, and Mendeleyev after him. Sartorius could find no solution: the balance was all right as it was—but there was a need for something different and better, something that would require less metal to manufacture. He covered sheet after sheet of paper with calculations of prisms, levers, deformation tensions, costs of materials, and other data. All of a sudden, quite independently, tears would come out of his eyes and flow down his face, making Sartorius feel astonished at this phenomenon: something was living in the depths of his body, like a separate animal, and it was weeping silently, taking no interest in the manufacture of balances. After midnight, when the smell of distant plants and fresh open spaces passed over the entire city and entered through the ventilation pane, Sartorius would lay his head down on the desk, losing precision of thought. This was how, close beside him, Chestnova had once smelled—of nature and kindness. He no longer felt jealous: let her eat good food and plenty of it, let her not fall ill, let her feel joy, let her love passersby and then sleep somewhere in warmth and not remembering any unhappiness.

Once or twice a night the telephone would suddenly ring, and Sartorius would hurriedly listen to the receiver, but nobody was calling him; it was a wrong number and the other person would apologize and disappear forever in speechlessness. Not one of his many friends knew what had happened to Sartorius: he had—for an indefinite time to come—abandoned the high road of technology and forgotten his own fame as a mechanical engineer, which could have become worldwide.

One day Sambikin called on him at home. The surgeon told Sartorius that the spinal cord of a human being is endowed with a certain capacity of rational thought, that it is not only the mind in the head that can think; he had recently checked this hypothesis on a child on whom he was performing a second trepanning—he had had to remove [...][44]

"What of it?" Sartorius asked without joy.

"It's the fundamental secret of life. More particularly it's the secret of the entire human being," Sambikin said thoughtfully. "In the past it was held that the spinal cord works only for the sake of the heart and purely organic functions, and that the brain is the higher coordinating center. That's not true: the spinal cord can think—and the brain takes part in the simplest, most instinctive processes."

This discovery of Sambikin's had made him happy. He still believed it was possible to ascend in one bound to a peak from which all times and spaces will become visible to the ordinary gray gaze of man. Sartorius smiled a little at Sambikin's naïveté: nature was too difficult, by his own reckoning, for such an instant victory, and could not be confined within a single law.

"Well, go on!" said Sartorius.

Sambikin's insides began to gurgle from the noise of his higher feelings.

"Well... this needs to be confirmed experimentally a thousand times. But it may well turn out that the secret of life lies in man's dual consciousness. We always think two thoughts at once, we can't think just one! We have two organs for one object! They think from opposite directions, but they think about the same theme ... Do you realize this could be the foundation of a truly scientific, dialectical psychology such as the world has never known? The fact that a human being is capable of thinking doubly about every subject is what has made him the finest animal on earth."

"What about the other animals?" asked Sartorius. "They've got heads and spines too."

"True. But there's a difference—a trifling difference that has decided world history. It was necessary to get used to coordinating two thoughts, to uniting in a single impulse one thought that rises from out of the earth itself, from the depths of the bones, and another that descends from the height of the skull. It was necessary that these thoughts should always meet at a single moment, that their waves should coincide and resonate. Animals are a little different: they too have two thoughts arising against each impression, but their two thoughts wander off in different directions and don't join in a single impact. That's the mystery of human evolution, that's why man has left all the other animals behind! What allowed him to carry it off was something almost trifling: he was able to train two feelings, two dark currents, to meet and measure their strength against each other ... And meeting, they are transformed into human thought. Clearly, none of this is perceptible ... Animals can experience these states too, but only occasionally and by chance. But man has been nurtured by this same chance, he has become a dual being. And sometimes, in illness, in unhappiness, in love, in a terrible dream, at any moment, in fact, that's far removed from the normal, we clearly sense that there are two of us—that I am one person but there's someone else inside me as well. This someone, this mysterious 'he,' often mutters and sometimes weeps, he wants to get out from inside you and go somewhere far away, he gets bored, he gets frightened ... We can see there are two of us and that we've had enough of each other. We imagine the lightness, the freedom, the senseless paradise of an animal, when our consciousness was not dual but lonely. Only a moment separates us from the animals when we lose the duality of our consciousness, and very often we live in archaic times without understanding what that means ... But then our two consciousnesses couple together again, we once again become human beings in the embrace of our 'two-edged' thought, and nature, organized according to the principle of an impoverished singleness, grits her teeth and curls herself up to escape the activity of these terrible dual structures that she never engendered, that originated inside their own selves ... I find it terrifying now to be on my own! These two passions eternally copulating and warming my head ..."

Sambikin, who had evidently not eaten or slept for a long time, ran out of strength and sat down in despair.

Sartorius gave him some tinned food and some vodka. Gradually the two of them yielded to tiredness and lay down to sleep without undressing, with the electricity still burning, while their hearts and minds went on stirring mutedly inside them, hurrying to process both ordinary feelings and world-historical tasks in the time allotted.

It was a long time since midnight had chimed from the Spassky Tower and the music of "The Internationale" had fallen silent;[45] soon it would be dawn and, in anticipation of this, the tenderest birds, those who stayed only a short time, began to stir in the bushes and gardens; then they rose up and flew away, leaving a country where summer had already begun to cool.

When day dawned and the streetlamps went yellow, the tall Sambikin and the short Sartorius were still asleep on the one settee, breathing noisily as if they had hollow bodies. Though inhibited by sleep, their concern for a definitive structuring of the world still gnawed at their consciences, and from time to time they muttered words, to drive anxiety out of themselves. Where was Moscow Chestnova? Where was she sleeping now? What summer of life was she seeking at the beginning of autumn, leaving her friends in expectation?

Near the end of his sleep, Sartorius smiled. Meek by nature, he felt that he had been buried dead in the earth, in its deep warmth, while up above, on the daytime surface of the grave, only Moscow Chestnova was left to weep for him. There was no one else; he had died nameless, as a man who had truly carried out all his tasks. The Republic was now sated—glutted—with platform balances, and the entire arithmetical computation of future historical time had been worked out, so that fate should become free of danger and never come point-blank against despair.

He woke up satisfied, resolved to construct and bring to perfection a complete technological apparatus that would automatically pump the fundamental everyday power of food out of nature and into the human body.[46] But, early as it was, his eyes had turned pale from remembering about Moscow; moved by fear of suffering, he woke Sambikin.

"Sambikin! You're a doctor, you know the whole reason of life ... Why does life go on for so long, and how can it be comforted or made joyful forever?"

"Sartorius!" Sambikin answered jokingly. "You're an engineer, you know what a vacuum is—"

"Well, yes. An emptiness into which something is sucked."

"An emptiness," said Sambikin. "Come with me, I'll show you the reason of all life."

They went out and got on a tram. Sartorius looked out of the window and met about a hundred thousand people, but nowhere did he notice the face of Moscow Chestnova. She might even have died—after all, time moves on and chance events happen.

They arrived at the surgical clinic of the Institute of Experimental Medicine. "I'm dissecting four corpses today," Sambikin announced. "There are three of us here working on one problem: how to obtain a certain mysterious substance, traces of which are present in every fresh corpse. This substance possesses the most powerful vivifying power for living, tired organisms. What this substance is—we don't know! But we're trying to understand."[47]

Sambikin prepared himself as usual, then led Sartorius to the dissecting room. This was a large, cold room where four dead human beings were lying in boxes that had ice between their double walls.

Sambikin's two assistants took the body of a young woman from one of these boxes and laid it out before the surgeon on an inclined table similar to an enlarged music stand. The woman lay there with clear, open eyes; the substance of these eyes had such equanimity that it could go on shining even after life, so long as it did not decompose. Sartorius felt ill. He decided to run quickly out of the institute and back to the trust, appear before the trade-union committee there, and ask for some kind of comradely protection against the terror of his own yearning heart.

"All right," said Sambikin, now ready for work. And he gave Sartorius an explanation: "At the moment of death there opens in the human body a last sluice, one we have not yet brought to light. Behind that sluice, in some dark ravine of the organism, a last charge of life is faithfully and miserlily preserved. Nothing but death can open up that spring, that reservoir—it remains tightly sealed until the very end. But I shall find that cistern of immortality."

"I see," pronounced Sartorius.

Sambikin cut the left breast off the woman, then removed all the bars of the rib cage and, with extreme caution, made his way to the heart. Together with his assistants he removed the heart and, with his instruments, carefully placed it in a glass cylinder for further investigation; this cylinder was then taken off to the laboratory.

"This heart too bears traces of the unknown secretion I was telling you about," Sambikin informed his friend. "Death, when it rushes through the body, breaks the seal on that clenched life lying in reserve—and then, like an unsuccessful shot, life resounds inside a person for the last time and leaves unclear traces on his dead heart. But that substance, in terms of its energy, is supremely precious. It's very strange—what's most vital of all appears at the moment of the last breath. Nature guards her procedures carefully!"

Then Sambikin began to roll the dead young woman from side to side, as if to demonstrate to Sartorius her plumpness and chastity.

"She's good-looking," the surgeon pronounced vaguely; the thought went through his mind that he could marry this dead woman—who was more beautiful, faithful, and lonely than many of the living—and he carefully bandaged up her destroyed chest. "And now," he went on, "we shall see the general reason of life."

Sambikin opened up the fatty envelope of the stomach, and then guided his knife down the intestine, revealing its contents: inside lay an unbroken column of food that had not yet been processed, but soon this food came to an end and the intestine became empty. Sambikin slowly passed over the section of emptiness and came to the beginning of the excrement, where he stopped altogether.

"You see!" said Sambikin, making a better opening down the empty section between the food and the excrement. "This emptiness in the intestines sucks all humanity into itself and moves world history. Here's the soul—have a sniff!"[48]

Sartorius had a sniff. "All right," he said. "We shall fill this emptiness. Then some other thing will become the soul."

"But what other thing?" smiled Sambikin.

"I don't know," said Sartorius, feeling a pitiful humiliation. "First people must be fed properly, so they won't be drawn into the emptiness of the intestines—"

"If you don't have a soul, it's impossible either to feed anyone else or to eat one's own fill," Sambikin retorted with boredom. "Nothing's possible."[49]

Sartorius bent down toward the corpse's innards, toward the place in the intestines where man's empty soul was located. He touched the remnants of excrement and food with his fingers, conscientiously examined the cramped, destitute structure of the entire body, and said, "This really is the very best, ordinary soul. There's no other soul anywhere."

The engineer turned toward the way out from the department of corpses. He stooped down and left, sensing behind him the smile of Sambikin. He was saddened by the sorrow and poverty of life, saddened that life is so helpless that it must almost uninterruptedly distract itself through illusion from an awareness of its own true situation. Even Sambikin was seeking illusions in his own thoughts and discoveries—he too was carried away by the complexity and great essence of the world in his imagination. But Sartorius could see that the world consisted primarily of destitute substance, which it was almost impossible to love but essential to understand.

9

Moscow Chestnova did not know what to do with herself after deciding not to return to her apartment and not to love Sartorius anymore. For long hours she traveled about the city, walking or taking buses and trams; no one approached her or asked her anything. The whole of life rushed by around her, so petty and rubbishy that to Moscow it seemed that people were not united by anything at all and that the space between them was occupied by bewilderment.

Toward evening she went to the housing cooperative where the reservist lived. The fiddler was tuning his fiddle by the entrance to the house management office; from the other side of the fence, where the medical institute was being constructed, came the whine of a circular saw; and the inhabitants of the housing cooperative were gathering in the corridor for their usual conversation.

Reservist Komyagin was lying on an iron bed in his own little room. He had been looking vainly inside himself for some thought or other, for some feeling or state of mind, but he could see there was nothing there. Trying to think about something, he would lose interest in the object of his reflection before he had even started, and so would abandon his wish to think. But if some enigma did inadvertently appear in his consciousness, he would still be unable to resolve it, and it would ache away in his brain until he physically annihilated it by means of, for example, intensified life with women and long sleep. Then he would wake up empty and calm again, with no recollection of any inner distress. Sometimes suffering or irritation would get going inside him, like tall weeds on waste ground, but Komyagin soon transformed them into empty equanimity by means of these measures of his.

But in recent years he had grown tired of struggling against what was human in him, and sometimes he cried in the darkness, covering his face with a blanket that had not been washed since the day of its manufacture.

A long time before, however, Komyagin had lived an unusual life. The walls of his room were still hung with unfinished oil paintings depicting Rome, landscapes, various peasant huts, and rye growing above ravines. These were Komyagin's work, but he had not managed to complete even one picture, even though at least ten years of time had gone by since he had begun them; and so the little huts had remained ruined and without roofs, the rye had never come into ear, and Rome looked like some provincial town. Somewhere under the bed, among the outlived objects, lay an exercise book with poems begun in his youth and a whole diary, also without any conclusion, broken off in mid-word as if someone had struck Komyagin and he had dropped his pen forever. About three years ago Komyagin had wanted to compile an inventory of his things and objects, but this too he had been unable to complete, managing to enter only four items: his own self, the bed, the blanket, and the chair. The remaining items were expecting to be taken stock of in some future, better time.

Recently Komyagin had been looking everywhere for a button and had found the exercise book with the poems he had once begun. They were taken from village life. He had read the beginning of one poem:

In that night, O in that night, the sleep of field and farm
    was light;
Paths called out to them in silence, stretching out toward
    a star,
And the steppe in languor breathing, bare of body, quiet
    of heart,
Seemed to stand in fear upon a trembling bridge that
    floated far.

The poem had no ending. The one and only chair could not stand on its legs and was in need of urgent repair—Komyagin had once even acquired two nails for this business but had still not got down to work.

Sometimes Komyagin would suppose to himself: "In a month or two I shall begin a new life—I'll finish the paintings and poems, I'll entirely rethink my world outlook, I'll get my documents in order, I'll find myself a solid job, I'll become an exemplary shock worker, I'll fall in love with a woman and she'll be a wife and a friend to me." It was his hope that in a month or two something special would happen within time itself, that time would stop for a moment and take him up into its own movement, but the years passed by his window without any pause or happy chance. And so he would get up from his bed and go out, as a member of the volunteer militia, to exact fines from the public at its places of congregation.

And now it was August of one of these current years. Evening was passing, spreading across the sky a long sad sound that receded into the distance and caused regret and a brooding melancholy to penetrate every heart that was open. And that evening, Moscow Chestnova knocked on Komyagin's door. Without getting up from the bed, he threw the hook off the door with his left hand and invited his guest inside. She went in to him, strange and familiar, in her expensive dress, and she looked around as though this room were her customary dwelling. The reservist decided to surrender immediately: his documents were in disorder and there was no excuse. But Chestnova merely asked him how his life was going, and wasn't it sad to be so alone and useless?

"I'm all right," said Komyagin. "After all, I'm not living—life's just something I got caught up in. Somehow I've got entangled in all this, but I wish I hadn't."

"Why?" asked Moscow.

"I can't be bothered," said Komyagin. "You have to keep puffing yourself up all the time—you have to think, speak, go somewhere or other, do this and that. But I can't be bothered with any of it. I keep forgetting that I'm alive—and when I remember, it scares me."

Moscow decided to stay a bit longer, astonished at the way of life of this man who had been begun so long ago and was still unfinished. Komyagin warmed up some kasha for her, then showed her his favorite painting from a time Chestnova had never known. He found the painting among the junk sheltering under the bed; the painting was not completely finished, but its thought was expressed with clarity.

"If the State didn't object, I should live like that too," said Komyagin.

The picture showed a peasant or merchant—a man who was not poor but was unclean and barefoot. He was standing on a broken wooden porch and, from this height, was peeing downward. His shirt was billowing in the wind, litter and straw could be found in his petty little beard, which was dense with life, and he was looking with equanimity into an unwelcoming world where a pale sun might have been rising or might have been setting. Behind the man was a large forlorn-looking house; inside it, most likely, were stored pies and pots of jam—and there was a wooden bed, equipped almost for eternal sleep. An aging peasant woman was sitting in a glass-covered balcony—all that could be seen was her head—and looking, with the expression of a fool, into an empty place in the yard. Her man had just woken from sleep, and so now he had gone out to relieve himself and check whether anything in particular had chanced to happen—but everything remained constant, the wind was blowing from across ragged, unloved fields, and in a moment the man would return to his rest, to sleep and dream no dreams, so as to live through life all the more quickly and without memory.

Later, Komyagin's old, divorced wife came around, a worn-down woman who had been exhausted since distant times. She very seldom visited Komyagin, and evidently still touched his feelings through a memory of their former affection. Komyagin put out some food for his guests, but the former wife just drank up her tea in silence and got ready to leave, so as not to hinder her husband from remaining alone with this plump new tart of his—as she summed up Chestnova. In her eyes everyone else was plump, and she herself was the only woman in whom no one was interested. Komyagin, however, took Moscow out into the corridor and asked her to go outside for a little walk and then come back again if she needed to.

"I get all weak if I don't live a little with a woman," Komyagin confessed. "I don't know what to do with myself, there's just nothing that interests me. And forgive me—but you and I are never going to know each other."

"Yes, we are!" said Moscow, embarrassed by Komyagin's grief. "But go on now, go to her."

Komyagin, however, stood in the corridor with her for a little longer.

"Don't take offense—"

"I'm not taking offense," Chestnova answered. "I quite like you."

In spite of this, Komyagin felt distressed and bowed his head.

"She used to be my wife, you see. She didn't smell good. She bore my children—and the children died. In bed we were unclean. She became like a brother to me, now she's growing thin and ugly. Our love has been transformed into something better—into a poverty she and I share, into our kinship and sorrow in each other's arms."

"I understand," Moscow quietly agreed. "You're like some foul little reptile, living in its own little hole in the ground. I used to see them as a child, when I lay facedown in a field."

"I quite understand," Komyagin agreed readily. "I'm a nothing."

Moscow frowned, thinking: "Why, why does he exist in the world? It only takes one of him to make all humanity seem like scum—and the only thing then is to beat the likes of him to death with whatever you can lay your hands on!"

"One day I'll come to you and be your wife," Moscow said.

"I shall wait for you," Komyagin agreed.

But Moscow, still a fickle and malleable being, quickly thought better of this. "No," she said, "don't wait for me! I shall never come inside this house again—you're a pitiful corpse!"

She became irritated and unhappy, and she leaned her head against the wall. Out of economy, the light went out in the corridor. Komyagin went back into his room, and for a long time, through the makeshift wall, there came the sounds of long exhausted love and the breathing of human exhaustion. Moscow Chestnova pressed her chest against the cold sewage pipe that came down from the floor above; shame and fear had stilled her, while her heart was beating more terribly than Komyagin's behind the partition. But when she herself had done what he was now doing, she had not known that a bystander feels just as sad, and without knowing why.

No, not here would she find life's high road into the distance— not in poor love, or in the intestines, or in Sartorius's zeal for the comprehension of precise trifles.

She went outside. It was already night. Huge clouds, lit only by their own weak light, were lying close to the surface of the city roofs and being carried away into the dark of the fields, into the mown spaces of an empty, shameless earth.

Moscow set off toward the center, looking into every brightly lit window she passed and stopping for a while outside several of them. Inside their rooms, people were drinking tea with their families or with guests; charming young women were playing the piano; operas and dances resounded from the speakers of wirelesses; young men were arguing about questions of the Arctic and the stratosphere; mothers were bathing children; and two or three counterrevolutionaries were whispering together, having placed a primus stove on a chair near the door, the wick turned up so that the neighbors wouldn't be able to hear their words. Moscow was so interested by all that was happening in the world that she stood on tiptoe on the ledges above the buildings' foundations and gazed inside the apartments until passersby began to laugh at her.

She spent several hours in observation of this kind, noticing joy or contentment almost everywhere yet feeling ever sadder herself. Everyone was occupied solely by mutual egotism with their friends, by their favorite ideas, by the warmth of new apartments and the comfortable feeling of their own satisfaction. Moscow did not know what she could attach herself to, where she could enter, in order to live happily and in an ordinary way. There was no joy for her in homes, she could see no peace in the warmth of stoves and in the light of table lamps. She loved the fire that came from logs in stoves, and she loved electricity, but she loved them as though she herself were not a human being but that very same fire or electricity, the excitation of a force that serves peace and happiness on earth.

Moscow had been wanting to eat for a long time, and so she entered a night restaurant.[50] She had no money at all, but she sat down and got herself supper. All the time, the band was playing some insane European music that contained centrifugal forces;[51] after dancing to this music you wanted to curl your body up into warmth and lie down for a long time in a cramped, secluded coffin. Paying no attention to this, Moscow joined in the dances in the middle of the hall; almost every man present asked her to dance, finding in her something that had been lost in his own self. Soon some of them were crying, burying their faces in Moscow's dress, because they had drunk too much wine, while others immediately began baring their souls to her with precision of detail. The spherical hall of the restaurant, deafened by the music and the howls of people, and filled by the excruciating smoke of cigarettes and the gas of compressed passions, seemed to revolve; every voice in it sounded twice, and suffering kept on being repeated. There was no way here for anyone to break free from the habitual—from the round sphere of his own head, where thoughts rolled on along tracks laid down long before, from the bag of the heart, where old feelings thrashed about as if netted, not letting in anything new, not letting go of the customary—and brief oblivion in music, or in love for an oncoming woman, ended either in irritation or in tears of despair. The later time got and the more the merriment thickened, the quicker the restaurant's spherical hall began to revolve, and many of the guests forgot where the door was and whirled around in terror on the spot, somewhere in the middle, thinking that they were dancing. A man of uncertain age, long silent and with a dark light in his eyes, was treating Moscow to food with delight and sadism, as if introducing inside her not some sweet dish but his own kind heart. But Chestnova was remembering other evenings, spent with her peers; what she had seen then, beyond the open summer windows, was ordinary steppe, opening

into the flat expanse of infinity, and there had been no such spherical thought revolving in the breasts of her comrades, eternally re-
peating itself until it came to its own despair—instead there had
been the arrow of action and hope, tensed for irrevocable movement
into the distance, into space that was straight and severe.

Night was yielding to morning. Somewhere Komyagin was sleeping with the thin woman, somewhere Sartorius was working at the
resolution of all and every problem, while the band went on playing
variations on one and the same rhythm, as if rolling it around the
inner surface of a hollow sphere from which there is no way out.
Moscow's partner was muttering an age-old thought about his own
love and sadness, and about loneliness, as he pressed his lips to the
pure skin close to Moscow's elbow. Chestnova said nothing. After
drinking a little wine for the sake of a pause, her new acquaintance
went back to telling her of his affection, of future possible happiness
if Moscow would return his love.

"Your wheels are spinning round and round, but you're not moving," Moscow answered. "If you love me, then stop."

Moscow's companion did not agree. "We are born and we die on
the breast of woman," he said with a slight smile. "So it is decreed by
the plot of our fate, by the whole circle of happiness."

"Well, you keep your life on a straight line then, without plots
and circles," Moscow advised him. She brushed her index finger
across her breasts. "Look! You'll find it difficult dying on me. I'm
not soft."

A powerful, kind light appeared in the dark of the eyes of this
sudden comrade of Chestnova's. He gazed at her two breasts and
said, "You're right, my dear. You're still very rigid, yes, I can see no
one's been crushing you to death in his embraces. Even your nipples
look straight ahead like the tips of two metal punches. Seeing this is
strange and difficult for me!"

He turned his head away in anguish; it was clear that his love for
Moscow was growing stronger with every novelty he remarked in
her, even the color of her stockings. This was how Sartorius had
loved her, and probably Sambikin too. Moscow looked at her friend

with equanimity; she had no wish to meet, in a new face, someone she had already left behind. If the man sitting in front of her were another Sartorius, then she would do better to return to the first Sartorius and never leave him again.

Before dawn the band began to play their most energetic fox-trot, one that acted even on the digestion. Moscow got up to dance with her new friend, and they danced almost alone amid a hall devastated by long merriment as if by a cataclysm. Many of those present were already dozing; others, surfeited with food and supposed passions, looked on as if dead.

The music revolved fast, like anguish in a bony and round head from which there is no way out. But the hidden energy of the melody was so great that it promised in time to wear a hole through the inert bones of loneliness or to escape through the eyes, if only as tears. Chestnova understood the nonsense she was now doing with her arms and legs, but there were many things she liked even though they were not necessary.

Beyond the window of the restaurant's spherical hall, dawn was breaking. A tree grew outside; it could be seen now in the dawn light. Its branches grew straight up or out to the sides, not circling or turning back on themselves, and the tree ended abruptly, all at once, where it lacked the strength or resources to go any higher. Moscow looked at it and said to herself, "This is me! Good! Now I'll leave here forever!"

She said goodbye to her cavalier, but he began grieving for her.

"Where are you going? There's no need to hurry. Let's go on somewhere else. Just wait a moment while I pay!"

Moscow said nothing. The man made a further suggestion: "Let's go somewhere out into the country—in front of us there'll be nothing at all, only some wind or other blowing out of the dark! And it's always good in the dark."

He was smiling a strained smile, trying to hide his distress as he counted the last seconds before their parting.

"I'm afraid not," said Moscow merrily. "What a fool you are! Goodbye, and thank you."

"Where may I kiss you, on the cheek or the hand?"

"Cheeks and hands are forbidden," laughed Moscow. "Lips are allowed. But let me do the kissing!"

She kissed him and left. The man was left to settle up without her, astonished at the heartlessness of the young generation, who kiss passionately, as if they love, when really they're saying goodbye for eternity.

Chestnova walked through the capital alone in the dawn. Her walk was so self-important and jaunty that the yardmen all turned their hoses away, and not one drop of water fell on Moscow's dress.[52]

Her life was still long, what stretched out ahead of her was almost immortality. Nothing scared her heart, and somewhere in the distance, ready to defend her youth and freedom, cannons were dozing, the way a thunderstorm lies dormant in the clouds during winter. Moscow looked at the sky; she could see how the wind was walking like a living being, stirring the murky mist that humanity had breathed up during the night.

In Kalanchev Square, behind the plank fence surrounding the excavations, the compressors of the Metropolitan Railway were breathing heavily. A placard hung by the workers' entrance: KOMSOMOLETS, KOMSOMOLKA! HELP BUILD THE METRO! YOUR FUTURE WORLD NEEDS A GREAT RAILWAY![53]

Moscow Chestnova believed and entered through the gates; she wished to be a participant everywhere and she was filled by that indeterminacy of life which is just as happy as its definitive resolution.

10

Sartorius had solved the problem of scales for the collective farms. He had thought up a method of weighing grain on a piece of quartz. The stone was quite small, only a few grams. Under compression from load bearing, it emitted a weak electric charge; this charge, amplified by radio valves, then moved a needle that registered the weight on a dial. There were radios everywhere—at grain-collection stations, in the homes of collective-farm workers, and in clubs—and so the new scales consisted simply of a wooden platform, a piece of quartz, and a dial, thus being three times cheaper than the old scales and requiring no iron.

Sartorius was now converting to electricity the whole of the Republic's stock of scales. He wanted to replace the world's passive constant (the earth's gravity) with an active constant—the energy of an electrical field. This would give the machines a sharp sense of accuracy as well as making them cheaper.[54]

Summer came to an end and the rains began, as long and as dismal as in early childhood in the days of capitalism. Sartorius seldom went home; he was afraid of being alone with the yearning he felt for his beloved, vanished Moscow. And so he worked at his plans with zealous concentration, and his heart began to calm down, aware of the benefit, both to the State and to the collective-farm workers, of the millions of rubles that would be saved by the technical improvement of the State's stock of scales.

Here, in the Old Merchant Arcade, in an institute linked to an impoverished and half-forgotten industry, Sartorius found not only recognition for his labor but also human consolation in his sorrow.

Viktor Vasilievich Bozhko, the chairman of the trade-union committee of the weights trust, had learned Sartorius's secret. Sartorius had, as usual, been working late into the evening. There was no one left at the trust except an accountant, who was drawing up the quarterly balance, and Bozhko, who was some way away, putting up a new edition of the wall newspaper. Sartorius was staring out of the window: whole crowds of people were traveling by in trams, on their way home from theaters and being guests. They felt merry in one another's company and could count on their lives getting better, though the technology beneath them was straining—the springs of the tramcars were buckling and the motors were throbbing exhaustedly.

Sartorius bent over his work with still greater concern. There was not only the problem of balances to resolve but also railway transport and the passage of ships through the Arctic Ocean, and he must try to discover the inner mechanical law in a human being that brings about happiness, suffering, and death. Sambikin had been wrong to locate the soul of a dead citizen in the emptiness of the intestines, between the excrement and the new intake of food. The intestines were like the brain; their sucking feeling was entirely rational, and it yielded to satisfaction. If the passion of life were concentrated entirely in the darkness of the intestines, world history would not have been so long and all but fruitless; universal existence, were it founded even on nothing higher than the law of the stomach, would long ago have become splendid. No, it was not only the intestinal empty darkness that had governed the entire world during past millennia but something different and worse, something more hidden and shameful, in comparison with which all the howls of the stomach are touching and justified, like the sorrow of a child. But this other thing had never made its way into the mind and so it had never before been possible to understand it: only what was similar to consciousness, only something resembling thought itself, could ever find a way into consciousness. But now!—now it was essential to understand everything, because either socialism would succeed in getting right into the most secret recess of a man's insides and cleaning out the pus capitalism had accumulated drop by drop in every century or else nothing new would happen and each inhabitant of the earth would go off to live separately, keeping this terrible secret place of the soul safe and warm inside them, so as to sink their teeth into each other once again in voluptuous despair and transform the earth's surface into a lonely desert with one last weeping human being.[55]

"What a lot of work there is to do!" Sartorius said out loud. "Don't come, Moscow, I haven't got time now."

At midnight Bozhko boiled some water with an electric element and courteously offered a glass of tea to Sartorius. He sincerely respected the hardworking young engineer who had willingly come to work for an unknown industry of little importance, turning his back on the glories of aviation, superfast transport, and the decomposition of the atom. They drank tea and talked about how to eliminate defects from the manufacture of weights, about article 21 in the regulations for the verification of measuring instruments, and other such apparently boring matters. But behind all this was hidden the passion of Bozhko's entire heart, since precise weights brought with them a measure of well-being for the collective-farm family; they helped the dawn of socialism and, in the end, brought hope to the souls of all the destitute of the globe. A weight, of course, was hardly a matter of great consequence, but then Bozhko did not see himself as of any great consequence either, and so there was always enough raw material for his happiness.

The capital was going to sleep. There was only the far-off tapping of a typewriter in some late office and the sound of steam being let off from the chimneys of the Central Power Station. Most people were now lying down, in rest or in someone's arms; or else, in the darkness of their rooms, they were feeding on the secrets and secretions of their hidden souls, on the dark ideas of egotism and false bliss.

"It's late," said Sartorius, finishing his tea. "Everyone in Moscow's already asleep. It's probably only scum who are still awake—lusting and pining."[56]

"Who do you mean, Semyon Alekseyevich?" asked Bozhko.

"People who have a soul."

Bozhko wanted to answer, out of politeness, but he said nothing, not knowing what to say.[57]

"But everyone has a soul," Sartorius pronounced sullenly. In weariness, he laid his head on the desk. Everything seemed dreary and hateful to him. Night went on, as exhausting as the monotonous knocking of a heart in an unhappy chest.

"Has it really been established with precision that the soul exists universally?" asked Bozhko.

"No, not with precision," Sartorius explained. "The soul is still unknown."

Sartorius fell silent; his thought had tensed in the struggle against his own narrow, poverty-stricken feelings and their uninterrupted love for Moscow Chestnova, and the rest of the varied world was now present for him only in a weak light of consciousness.

"Can't we hurry up and find out what the soul really is?" asked

Bozhko. "After all, it's true: we can remake the whole world and everything will seem good. But think how much filth has seeped into humanity during the thousands of years we've been like animals! Something's got to be done with it all. Even our body's not the way it should be—it's full of dirt."

"It certainly is," said Sartorius.

"When I was young," Bozhko informed him, "I often wanted everyone to die all at once and I'd wake up in the morning all alone. But everything else was going to stay the same: the food, and all the buildings—and one lonely, beautiful young woman who wouldn't die either, and she and I would meet inseparably."

Sartorius looked at him with sorrow: how alike we all are—one and the same pus flows in all our bodies!

"That's what I thought too, when there was a woman I loved."

"Who was that, Semyon Alekseyevich?"

"Moscow Chestnova," Sartorius answered.

"Ah, her!" Bozhko mouthed soundlessly.

"Did you know her too?"

"Only obliquely, Semyon Alekseyevich, only vaguely. I was neither here nor there."

"It doesn't matter," said Sartorius, remembering himself. "Now we're going to intervene in what lies inside a man, we're going to find his poor, terrible soul."[58]

"It's time we did, Semyon Alekseyevich," said Bozhko. "I've had enough of being the old kind of natural man all the time. My heart's bored to death of it. Mother History's made monsters of the lot of us!"

Bozhko made a bed for Sartorius in the director's armchair, and himself lay down to sleep on the desk. He was now even more content: the very best engineers had now taken on the task of refashioning the inner soul.[59] For a long time he had secretly feared for communism: Might it not be defiled by the alien spirit rising every minute from the lowest depths of the human organism? After all, ancient, long evil had eaten deep into the flesh of life, even the human body itself was probably just one consolidated, enduring ulcer—or else some downright fraud that had deliberately cut itself off from the entire world in order to conquer it and devour it in solitude.

In the morning, when he woke up, Bozhko saw that Sartorius had not lain down at all. He had prepared a whole file of diagrams and calculations for the provision, throughout the Soviet Union, of electrical scales; yet there were dried-up traces of tears on his face, as well as the lines left by his struggle against the obsessive despair of yearning feelings.[60]

Bozhko arranged that the presidium of the trade-union committee should meet that evening. He tactfully informed them of the personal grief of engineer Sartorius and outlined measures for the reduction of his suffering. "Our usual practice is to intervene only in broad and general matters," he said, "but we must also try to be of help in matters that are deep and personal. Think about it, comrades, as Soviet citizens and as human beings! You remember how Stalin carried the urn with the ashes of engineer Fedoseyenko.[61] Although comrade Sartorius's grief is not ordinary, thanks to the depth of his feeling, it must be comforted by ordinary measures, since in life, as I have observed—though perhaps inaccurately—it is ordinary things that are most powerful of all. That, at least, is how it seems to me."

Liza the typist, a member of the trade-union committee, secretly began to love Sartorius, with credulous willingness. Then, however, she felt ashamed. She was a tender and indecisive woman; her face nearly always had a pink flush from the conscientious tension she felt with other people. A virgin, she was filling out early, her dark hair was growing thicker and thicker, and she had come to look so attractive that many men were paying attention and thinking of Liza as their personal happiness. Sartorius alone supposed nothing about her and noticed her only obliquely.

Two days later Bozhko advised Sartorius to take a look at Liza. "She's very sweet and kind," he said, "but her modesty makes her unhappy."

In further time, thanks to shared office work, Sartorius got to know Liza more closely; and once, in perplexity, not knowing what to say, he stroked her hand as it lay on the typing table. Liza left her hand where it was, and said nothing. It was evening; quick as time itself, the moon was climbing into the sky behind the institute walls, as if registering how, minute by minute, youth was draining away.

Liza and Sartorius went out together onto the street, which had been taken over by such a dense toing and froing of people that one might have thought it was here that society reproduced and multiplied. They rode in a tram to the outskirts of the city. It was already late autumn there and a cold dryness stood over the tussocky fields; the rye that had once been growing, lit by the dawn of Moscow's midnight glow, had now been harvested, and the place lay deserted. Filled with terror by what he recalled, Sartorius embraced Liza, looking out into the solitary dark of the night around him; Liza clung to him in response, warming herself and appropriating him with her hands, like a sensible housewife.

After this, Sartorius found in the institute the consolation of his soul, and his dreary ache for Moscow Chestnova was transformed into a sad memory of her, as though she had perished. He received a great deal of money for the quartz scales, and with this money he dressed Liza in luxury. For some time he lived lightly, even merrily, devoting himself to love, theatergoing, and current pleasures of the moment. Liza was faithful to him and happy, her only fear being that Sartorius might leave her; and so, as he slept, she would look long at his face, wondering if there were some way she could painlessly and imperceptibly spoil his appearance, even though he was already far from handsome—he would then be so very hideous that no other woman would love him and he would live with her until death itself. But Liza couldn't think of anything; she didn't know what to do to make Sartorius loathsome for the entire world—and when he smiled in his sleep at some unknown light dream, the grief of jealousy and gathering fury brought tears to her eyes.

Sartorius's mind calmed down. In it, like seed in a seed plot, thoughts and fantasies were once again appearing of their own accord, and he would wake up filled with discoveries and far-flung ideas. He would imagine the impoverished provinces of southern, soviet China, or Malmgren the Swedish scientist, who had frozen to death in the northern ice, already forgotten by the entire world. And, with anxiety from the responsibility of his own life, terrified by its speed, frivolity, and supposed fulfillment, Sartorius worked with increasing haste, afraid of dying or falling in love with Moscow Chestnova again and then feeling torment.

Winter set in. Often Sartorius worked all night long in the institute, while Liza typed away in a far corner. He came up with a project for electrical scales that would weigh the stars at a distance, as they first appeared over the horizon of the east, and for this he received a kiss from the Deputy People's Commissar for Heavy Industry. Gradually, however, Sartorius was losing interest in both scales and stars: he felt inside him a confused agitation that could not be explained by his happy youth, and the mystery of human life was unclear for him. He felt as if no one had ever lived before him and he himself would have to suffer every suffering, to experience everything from the very beginning, in order to find for every body of a human being a great life that did not yet exist. In yearning that was more than he could bear, just to exhaust himself and change his thoughts, he would kiss his Liza, and she would accept his feelings as real. But afterward he would sleep for a long time, his heart drained, and he would wake up in despair. Moscow Chestnova had been right: love was not communism, and passion was sad.

11

That winter, after an alarm signal at two o'clock in the morning, the lift was put into operation in shaft number 18 of the Moscow Metropolitan Construction Project; a young female worker was brought to the surface and an ambulance was summoned.

The young woman's leg had been crushed—the full, upper part of her right leg, above the knee.

"Are you in a lot of pain or not?" asked the foreman, gray from exhaustion and fear, and bending down over her.

"Of course I am, but it's nothing terrible!" the young excavations worker replied sensibly. "Maybe I'll be able to stand up in a moment."

And she really did get up from the stretcher; she walked a few steps, and fell down in the snow. Blood came out of her; on the snow, which was illuminated by a searchlight, the blood seemed yellow, as if exhausted while still in her body, but the fallen woman's face was looking up with shining eyes, and her lips were red from good health or from a high temperature.

"How on earth did this happen to you?" Helping her back onto the stretcher, the foreman kept on with his questioning.

"I can't remember," answered the wounded woman. "Some trucks jumped out at me and forced me into a dead end.[62] But go away now—I want to sleep, I don't want to feel this pain."

The foreman left, ready to tear off one of his own legs, if only this young woman could survive in her entirety. An ambulance came and took the now sleeping worker to the surgical clinic.

Sambikin was the doctor on night duty in the experimental clinic. No urgent cases had been brought in, so he was sitting alone with some dead matter, trying to extract from it the little-known, merry substance stored up for a long life that had not chanced to happen.

Before Sambikin, on the experiment table, lay the boy he had operated on. The boy had lain ill in the hospital for a long time but had died the previous day, and for a short time before his death he had been demented: pus had appeared in the bony cavities of his head, where the operation had been performed, and this pus had instantly, quick as fire, poisoned his consciousness. The nurse told Sambikin how, before the little patient momentarily closed his eyes, they had been calm and well filled; but when he opened his eyes again, it was as if something had pierced right through them—they were bored and empty.

In long solitude Sambikin had stroked the naked body of the dead child—the most sacred property of socialism—and grief had warmed up inside him, a deserted grief that could not be salved by anyone.

Toward midnight, with his instruments, he had dug out the heart in the late boy's chest; then he had removed a gland from the area of the throat and begun to investigate these two organs with his devices and preparations, trying to discover where the unspent charge of living energy was being stored. Sambikin was convinced that life is only one of the rare peculiarities of eternally dead matter, and that this peculiarity is concealed where physical substance is most durably structured; this was why the dead needed as little, to return to life, as they had previously needed in order to die. More than that, the vital tension of someone being consumed by death was so great that a sick person is sometimes stronger than a healthy one, while the dead may have more potential for life than the living.

Sambikin had decided to use the dead to revive the dead,[63] but then he was called to a woman who was wounded but alive.

The woman from the shaft had been laid on the dressing station, her face covered by a double layer of muslin. She was asleep.

Sambikin examined her leg. Blood was bursting out under pressure. It was slightly foaming; the bone was shattered along its whole length and various filths had penetrated into the wound. But the surrounding intact body looked gentle and swarthy, and the curves of late innocence were so fresh and full that this worker surely deserved immortality; even the strong smell of sweat given off by her skin brought with it a charm and excitement of life, reminiscent of bread and of broad expanses of grass.

Sambikin gave orders for the mutilated woman to be prepared for an operation the following day.

In the morning Sambikin saw that it was Moscow Chestnova on the operating table; she was conscious and she greeted him, but her leg had gone dark and the veins, overfilled with dead blood, had swollen up as if she were a sclerotic old woman. Moscow had been washed, and the hair in her groin had been shaved.

"Well, goodbye for now!" said Sambikin, rubbing his large hands together.

"Goodbye!" Moscow replied—and her eyes began to wander, because she had inhaled a sleeping substance given to her by the nurse.

She lost consciousness and began to move her rustling lips in the thirst of a hot body.

"She's asleep," said the nurse, laying bare all of Moscow.

Sambikin worked on the leg for a long time, eventually taking it clean off in order to save the organism from gangrene.[64] Moscow lay there peacefully. A sad, indefinite dream was floating in her consciousness. She was running down a street where animals and people were living. The animals were tearing off pieces of her body and eating them; the people were clawing at her and trying to hold her back, but she went on running farther away from them, downward, toward an empty sea where someone was weeping for her. Her torso was growing smaller by the minute and people had long ago torn off her clothes; in the end there remained only protruding bones, then even these bones were being broken off by children on her path, but Moscow, sensing that she was thin and ever diminishing, patiently kept running farther—anything not to return to the terrible places left behind her, anything to remain whole, even if only as a worthless creature composed of a few dry bones.[65] She fell against harsh stones, and all the people and animals that had been tearing at her and eating her in her flight—all of them piled onto her with heaviness.

Moscow woke up. Sambikin was leaning over her and hugging her, smearing her breasts, her neck, and her belly with blood.

"Water!" said Moscow.

There was no one else in the operating theater. Sambikin had long ago sent away the nurses who had been assisting. From some distant corner came the hissing of a gas burner.

"Now I'm lame," said Chestnova.

"Yes," said Sambikin, not leaving her. "But it makes no difference. I don't know what to say to you . . ."

He kissed her on the mouth. From her mouth came a suffocating smell of chloroform, but he could now breathe in anything at all, if it was breathed out by Moscow.

"Wait," Moscow begged. "I'm ill!"

"I'm sorry," said Sambikin, moving away from her. "There are things that destroy everything—and that everyone destroys. It's like that with you. When I saw you, I forgot how to think. I thought I would die."

"All right," Moscow smiled unclearly. "Show me my leg."

"It's not here. I've had it sent to my home."

"Why? I'm not a leg."

"Who are you then?"

"I'm not a leg, not breasts, not a belly, not eyes—I don't know who I am. Take me away to sleep."

The next day Moscow's health weakened; she became feverish and there was blood in her urine. Sambikin banged himself on the head—to bring himself back from love to his senses—and analyzed his own state both physiologically and psychologically. He laughed, exaggeratedly creasing his face, but he could achieve nothing. The bustle and tension of work forsook him; he wandered like an idler down distant streets, in solitude, occupied by the boring, immobile thought of love. Sometimes he leaned his head against a tree on a nighttime boulevard, feeling unbearable grief; occasional tears made their way down his face and, feeling ashamed, he would gather them from around his mouth with his tongue and swallow them.

During the second night Sambikin took the dead boy's heart and the gland from his neck, prepared a mysterious suspension from them, and injected this into Chestnova's body. Now hardly able to sleep at all, he roamed about the city until dawn. In the morning he found the mother of the dead boy in the clinic; she had come to take her son to be buried. Sambikin set off with her, to help her through the necessary formalities—and that afternoon he found himself walking beside a thin, trembling woman, following a cart where a boy with an empty chest lay in a coffin. An unknown, strange life opened out before him, a life of grief and the heart, of memories, of the need for comfort and affection. This life was as great as the life of the mind and of zealous work, but more mute.

Moscow Chestnova took a long time to recover; she turned sallow, and her arms withered from lack of movement. But through the window she could see the bare, thin branches of some hospital yard tree. All through the long March nights these branches scraped against the windowpane, shivering and yearning, sensing that it was time for warmth to set in. Moscow listened to the movement of the moist wind and the branches, tapped her finger against the glass in answer, and refused to believe there was anything poor and unhappy in the world—it just wasn't possible! "Soon I'll come and join you!" she whispered out to them, pressing her mouth to the glass.

One April evening, when it was already time to go to bed in the clinic, Moscow heard in the distance the play of a fiddle. She listened more closely and recognized the music—it was the fiddler playing in the nearby housing cooperative where Komyagin lived. Time, life, and the weather all change; spring was setting in, and the cooperative musician was playing even better than before. Moscow listened, and pictured to herself the nocturnal gullies out in the fields, and birds in their need flying forward through the cold dark.

In the afternoons Moscow was often visited by friends from her former work in the earth. After the operation, the Metropolitan Works Triangle[66] had twice been to see her, bringing her cakes in boxes—at the trade union's expense.

"When I get better, I'll marry Komyagin," Moscow would think at night, listening to the old fiddler's music as it spread itself out in the vast air. "I'm lame now—I'm a lame old woman!"

She was discharged at the end of April. Sambikin brought her some sturdy new crutches—for all the long path of her remaining life. But there was nowhere for Moscow to go to; before the hospital she had lived in Metro Works Hostel number 45, but now the hostel had been moved and Moscow did not know where to.

Sambikin opened the car door and waited for an address to take her to, but Moscow smiled and said nothing. Then Sambikin took her to his own home.

A few days later, without waiting for the wound on Moscow's leg to heal completely, Sambikin set off with her to the Caucasus, to a sanatorium beside the Black Sea.

Every morning, after breakfast, Sambikin would accompany Moscow to the shore of the noisy sea and Moscow would look for hours into irrevocable space. "I'll go away, I'll go away somewhere," she would keep whispering. Sambikin would remain silent beside her, his guts aching as if they were slowly rotting, while inside his now empty head languished one and the same beggarly thought—of love for Moscow's impoverished, one-legged body. Sambikin was ashamed of his life being so pitiful. In the dead hours after lunch he would walk to a little wood in the hills and there he would mutter to himself, break off branches, sing, beg the whole of nature to leave him alone and finally grant him peace and the ability to work; and he would lie down on the earth and sense how uninteresting this all was.

When he came back in the evening, Sambikin was often unable even to get near Chestnova, so surrounded was she by the attentions, care, and persistence of men who were filling out during their holiday. Moscow's mutilation was now little noticeable; a prosthesis had been brought for her from Tuapse and she was walking without crutches, just with a stick—on which her admirers had already carved their names and the date, along with symbols of noble passions. When she examined her stick, Moscow would think that, if these etchings were sincerely meant, she would have to go and hang herself, for her acquaintances were, in essence, indicating only one thing: how much they wanted to beget children out of her.

Once, Moscow had a desire for grapes, but grapes don't grow in spring. Sambikin went around the nearby collective farms, but the grapes everywhere had long ago been transformed into wine. Moscow felt very upset; since the loss of her leg and her illness she had been seized by all kinds of whims, getting impatient over empty trifles. She washed her hair every day, for example, because she constantly felt there was dirt in it, and she would even cry from distress, because the dirt just wouldn't let up.[67] One evening, when Moscow was in the garden, washing her hair over a bowl as usual, an elderly man from the mountains came up to the fence and silently began to watch.

"Grandpa, go and fetch me some grapes!" Moscow asked him. "Or haven't you got any?"

"I haven't," replied the mountain man. "Where would I get grapes from at this time of year?"

"Well, don't look at me then!" said Chestnova. "Have you really not got a single grape? Can't you see—I'm lame!"

The man from the mountains went off without an answer, but

Moscow saw him again the following morning. He waited for Moscow to come out onto the porch and then gave her a new basket; beneath fresh leaves lay carefully selected grapes, more than a pood[68] of them. Then the man gave Moscow something very small, a scrap of colored cloth. Moscow unwrapped it and found a human nail, from a big toe. She did not understand.

"Take it, my Russian daughter," the old peasant explained. "I'm sixty years old, that's why I'm giving you my nail. If I became forty, I'd be bringing you my toe, and if I were thirty, I'd also have torn off my own leg, the leg you don't have."[69]

Moscow frowned, so as to keep her own joy calmly in check, but then turned around to run away, and fell, striking the lifeless wood of her leg against the stone of the threshold.

The man from the mountains did not want to know everything about someone but only what was best, so he went straight back to his dwelling and never appeared again.

The time of rest and healing came to an end. Moscow had recovered once and for all and had mastered her wooden leg as though it were a living one. As before, Sambikin was accompanying her every day to the shore, then leaving her there on her own.

The movement of water in space reminded Moscow Chestnova of the great destiny of her life: the world really was without end and nowhere would its ends ever meet—a human being is irrevocable.

By the day of their journey back, Sambikin's love for Moscow had been transformed for him into such an intellectual riddle that he began to devote the whole of himself to its resolution, forgetting the sense of suffering in his heart.

12

Sartorius was no longer an engineer of All-Soviet renown; he was now entirely devoted to the affairs of a little-noticeable institute, and both former comrades and more famous organizations had gradually lost sight of him. He went home less and less often in the evenings, staying all night in his workplace instead; as a result, in accordance with the rules of residency, his name was struck off the house register and his belongings were taken to a cell in the local police station. Swallowed up by his mute life, Sartorius collected his things, then threw them down in the corner where the trust's watchman usually dozed in his struggle against the possible theft of property. From then on the institute well and truly became Sartorius's family, refuge, and new world. He lived there with his faithful young Liza and had many friends among his colleagues; and the trade-union committee, headed by Bozhko, protected him from every grief and unhappiness.

In the daytime Sartorius was nearly always happy, and satisfied by his current work, but during the nights, as he lay on his back on heaps of old files, an anguished yearning was being born inside him, growing up from beneath the bones of his chest like the tree that climbed toward the vaulted ceiling of the Old Merchant Arcade and rustled its black leaves there. As Sartorius hardly knew how to dream, all he could do was suffer and observe what suffering was like.

His mind was growing poorer and poorer, his back was growing weak from his work, but Sartorius patiently put up with himself; only now and then did his heart ache—insistently and for a long time, in the distant wilderness of his body, crying out there like a dark voice. Then he would retire behind the cupboard with stacks of old matters and stand there for a while in the gap between items, waiting for the aching bleakness of his feelings to pass away in solitude and monotony.

At night Sartorius slept little. He would pay visits to the family of Liza the typist, drink tea with her and her little old mother—who loved to talk about contemporary literature, and especially about the paths of development of the visual arts—and smile meekly out of despair. Sometimes Viktor Vasilievich Bozhko would come too. Once, before Sartorius, Liza had been seen as Bozhko's intended; Bozhko, however, carried away as he was by institute matters and everyday life with all of his colleagues, had seen no acute need yet to isolate himself in an apartment through marriage and had himself prompted Liza to console Sartorius. For Bozhko, service to a colleague, and this colleague's happiness, eclipsed the elemental passions of the heart, and the hearth that warmed his personal soul was the trust of weights and measures. When he found Sartorius and Liza visiting the little old woman they all shared, Bozhko would apply himself zealously to bringing about their betrothal; it charmed him to see young people who were in love remaining in the same institute and trade union, never leaving the small but close-knit system of the weights and measures industry.

If Sartorius did not visit Liza, he would walk for many miles around the city, spend a long time observing bread and vegetables being weighed in shops on electrical scales of his own design, and sigh because of the dreary process of unchanging existence pressing within him. Later, as the empty night trams hurtled by on their last journeys, Sartorius would stare for a long time into the strange, incomprehensible faces of the few passengers. Somewhere or other he was expecting to see Moscow Chestnova, her sweet hair hanging down through a wide-open window while her head lay on the sill and slept in the wind of movement.

He loved her constantly. Her voice was always sounding for him, in the very closest air; he needed only to recall a single word of Moscow's and he would immediately see in his memory her familiar mouth, her loyal, frowning eyes, and the warmth of her meek lips. Sometimes she would appear to Sartorius in his dreams—pitiful, or already deceased, lying in poverty on the eve of her burial. Sartorius would wake up in grief and cruelty and immediately busy himself with some useful task in his institute, to eclipse this thought inside him that was so sad and incorrect. Usually, though, Sartorius did not dream at all, not possessing the capacity for empty experience.

Time passed almost identically, with only small changes, over the course of many months. The women had long been wearing their warm hats, the skating rinks had opened, the trees on the boulevards had gone to sleep, preserving the snow on their branches until spring, the power stations were working under more and more tension, lighting up the growing darkness, but Moscow Chestnova was nowhere:

neither in the world outside nor in answers to inquiries at the Bureau of Addresses.

In the middle of one winter day Sartorius visited Dr. Sambikin. Sambikin had come back from night work in the clinic and was sitting there quite still, observing the flow of a routine enigma in his own mind.

Strangely, after their separation, the two friends met without joy, although Sambikin, in his usual way, saw Sartorius's visit as a phenomenon of great significance. It even perplexed him.

Then it became clear that Sambikin had loved Moscow insanely and had consciously distanced himself from her, so that he could stand aside and resolve the whole problem of love in its entirety: love was too serious a task, it was inadmissible to fling oneself headfirst into something so unknown. Only afterward, after clarification of the question of his own feelings, did Sambikin intend to meet Moscow again, in order to live out with her the remnant of time until death and cremation.

"She's lame now," Sambikin went on, "and she lives in the room of comrade Komyagin, a member of the volunteer militia. And her surname is no longer Chestnova."

"Why did you leave her lame and alone?" asked Sartorius. "I thought you loved her!"

Sambikin expressed extreme surprise. "It would be strange if I were to love one woman in the world when there are a whole billion of them and among them is sure to exist some still higher charm. Before we go any further, this question requires a clear answer. Here we have an evident misunderstanding of the human heart—and nothing more."

After asking for Moscow's address, Sartorius left Sambikin on his own. The doctor did not show Sartorius to the door and went on sitting there, entirely taken up by thoughts about all of humanity's most important tasks, wishing for universal clarity and agreement with regard to every aspect of happiness and suffering.

In the evening Semyon Sartorius went to the Bauman district and into the yard of the housing cooperative where Komyagin lived.

On the other side of the fence the Institute of Experimental Medicine had been completed and was now illuminated by the clean fire of electricity. By the entrance to the house management committee sat an old beggar with a bald head; his hat lay on the ground, emptiness upward, and across it had been placed the bow of his fiddle. Sartorius put some money in the hat and asked the beggar why his bow was lying idle.

"It's my sign," said the old man. "It's not alms I'm collecting, but my pension. All my life I've played here in Moscow, with ecstasy. All generations of the population have listened to me with pleasure. Now let them give me money for food—till it's time for my death!"

"But why beg?" said Sartorius. "You could be playing your fiddle."

"I can't," said the old man. "My hands tremble from the agitation of weakness. And that's no good for art. I can be a beggar—but I can't be a botcher!"

The long corridor of the old building still smelled of the enduring remnants of iodine and bleach. During the Civil War the building had probably been a hospital, with Red Army soldiers lying in it. Now it was occupied by tenants.

Sartorius went up to Komyagin's door. Behind it he could hear the quiet voice of Moscow Chestnova. She was probably lying in bed, talking to the man she now lived with.

"Remember what I told you—how when I was a child I saw a dark man with a burning torch? He was running down the street in the night. It was a dark autumn and the sky was so low there was nowhere you could breathe."

"Yes, I do remember," came a man's voice. "I've already instructed you about this—I was running to confront the enemy. It was me!"

"It was an old man," Moscow doubted sadly.

"So what? When you're living in the form of a little girl, a sixteen-year-old can seem elderly."

"That's true," Moscow admitted. Her voice was a little sly, a little sad, as if she were a woman in her forties and all this were happening in the nineteenth century, in a large apartment. "And now you're all burned out and charred."

"You're quite right, Musya," said Komyagin, abbreviating her name. "I'm vanishing. I'm an old song. My itinerary's nearing its end. Soon I shall collapse into the ravine of personal death."

Musya was silent for a while, and then said, "And the bird that sang your song flew away long ago to warmer lands. Somehow you're pathetic all over—a mere has-been of a man!"

"I'm all worn out," replied Komyagin. "I understand. I no longer love anything—only a bit of law and order in our Republic."

Musya laughed meekly, in her characteristic way. "Second-class reserve rank and file! How did I find you among such a vast quantity?"

"The world's not so very big," Komyagin explained. "This is something I've given special thought to, and on two occasions. If you look at a globe or a map, there seems to be a lot, but there isn't really. And everything's been taken stock of and noted down. In half an hour you can run your eyes down the entire inventory of territory and population—names, patronymics, surnames, and main biographical data!"

The light went out in the corridor thanks to the advent of some maximal time of night and the economical supervision of the comrade responsible for power consumption. Sartorius leaned his head against the cold sewage pipe that Moscow had once embraced and heard in it the intermittent flows of filth of the upper floors.

"And it's even a good thing that the earth's not so big. You can live a quiet life on it!" Komyagin went on.

Musya-Moscow said nothing. Then came the knock of her wooden leg. Sartorius realized she had sat up.

"Komyagin, were you really a Bolshevik?" she asked.

"Never! Certainly not! What makes you think that?"

"Then why were you running with a torch in 1917, when I was still only growing?"

"I had to," said Komyagin. "There was no militia at that time—and certainly no volunteer militia. People had to be their own self-defense against every enemy."

"But where we lived—and you too—nearly everyone was begging

or starving. My father had three rubles' worth of property—and even that you'd have had to tear off his back and out from his belly. What were you guarding, you fools? Why were you running with a torch?"

"I was an inspector of self-defense. I was running to check the guard posts. When there's very little of everything, that means poverty. And poverty needs all the more protection—it's what's most precious of all. A wooden spoon turns into a silver spoon. It really does!"

"But who fired that shot and all that shouting of voices began in the prison? Don't lie to me!"

"What do you mean—lie? The truth is worse. The man who fired the shot was a mysterious hooligan. And what was going on in the prison was a meeting—they were electing a constituent assembly.[70] People were well fed in there and no one wanted to go out and be free. They had to be driven out into freedom by force. I used to have cabbage soup there myself—I knew one of the warders."

Moscow took a long time to undress, breathing heavily and shuffling her wooden leg. She was probably settling down for the night.

Sartorius waited in terror of a further end. Now and again tenants would go down the corridor to the communal toilet, but they paid no particular attention to the unknown human being in the darkness, as if already accustomed to every kind of incomprehensible phenomenon.

"Blind man in the nettles!" said Moscow behind the door. "Don't you lie down with me, you reptile!"

"Creak away, peg leg!" Komyagin patiently instructed her. "What can you know of the life of a man like me?"

"More than enough! You should be done away with—that's all anyone needs to know of your life."

"Wait a minute! I haven't worked through a single task yet. I haven't thought through my most important thoughts."

"You never will. You're getting old. What are you hoping for?"

Komyagin modestly informed her that he was hoping to win several thousand rubles through the State loan scheme. Then he'd think better of all his thinking and complete all of the tasks he had begun.

"But that may not be for a long time," said Moscow sadly.

"Even if it's only an hour before my death, that'll still give me all the time I need!" Komyagin determined. "Anyway, even if I don't win, even if I don't make my life into something normal, I've made up my mind! As soon as I start to feel my natural doom, I'll get down to all my tasks. I'll sort through all my thoughts and complete everything. Just twenty-four hours or so—that's all I need. Even in a single hour you can cope with all of life's tasks! Life's nothing so very special—I've given particular thought to it and I know what I'm saying. It's not true you need to live a hundred years and that you might not complete all your tasks even then. It's not true at all! You can live emptily for forty years—but if you get down to work an hour before the coffin, you can fulfill everything in good order—everything you were born for!"

They did not talk any more. Komyagin—judging by the sounds—lay down on the floor and sighed for a long time, from disappointment that time went on passing yet his affairs stood still. Sartorius stood there in despondency, lacking any decision. He heard the last human being lock the way out onto the street and retire to their own room to sleep. But Sartorius was not afraid of being all night in the darkness of the corridor. He was waiting: maybe Komyagin would die soon—then he would be able to go into the room himself and remain there with Moscow. He stayed awake in expectation, observing in the dark silence how a nighttime full of events was gradually passing by. From behind the third door after the sewage pipe there began regular sounds of copulation; the cistern on the wall of the empty toilet hissed with air, sometimes more strongly, sometimes more weakly, testifying to the work of the mighty water main; far away, at the end of the corridor, a solitary tenant began several times to shout out in the horror of a dream, but there was no one to comfort him and he calmed himself all on his own; in the room opposite Komyagin's door someone had woken on purpose and was praying to God in a whisper: "Remember me, Lord, in thy kingdom, after all

I do keep remembering you. And grant me something factual—I beg you please!" The other rooms along the corridor also had their events taking place in them—events that were petty but uninterrupted and indispensable, so that the night was charged with life and activity as powerfully as the day. Sartorius listened and understood how poor he was to possess only a single torso that was closed in from all sides. Moscow and Komyagin were sleeping behind the door; their heart was beating subduedly, and along the corridor could be heard communal, peaceful breathing, as if in the breast of every person there were nothing but kindness.

Sartorius felt weary. He knocked cautiously on the door, in order for someone to awake and something to happen. Moscow was sleeping lightly; she turned over and called Komyagin. He replied in irritation: What could she be wanting from him at night when he was of no use to anyone even in the day?

"Check your State bonds," said Moscow. "Turn on the light."

"What is it?" Komyagin asked in alarm.

"You might have won something. If you have, you can start living life correctly. But if you haven't, then you can lie down and die. There's no one else like you in the whole of the Soviet Union—how come you aren't ashamed of yourself?"

Komyagin made an effort to gather up the enfeebled thoughts there in his head. "The Soviet Union—why always the Soviet Union? Nowadays everyone's muttering about it, but I live in it as if in the bosom of warmth!"

"You've done enough living. Now die like a hero," Moscow proposed to him, insistently and with venom.

Komyagin thought about it. Really, nothing in particular would happen even if he were to die—thousands of billions of souls had already endured death and no one had come back to complain. But life evidently still fettered him with its bones, with its growth of flesh and its networks of veins—the mechanical stability of his own being was something too sure and habitual. He crawled on his knees into his own still uncompleted archives and began going through his bonds, while Moscow read out the list of winning numbers from a People's Commissariat of Finance booklet. One bond turned out to have won ten rubles, but Komyagin owned only a quarter of this successful bond and so his net profit was two and a half rubles; his life had been augmented only insignificantly, and it was still impossible to draw up the accounts without their showing a loss.

"So now what?" asked Moscow.

"I shall die," Komyagin agreed. "It's not my lot to go on living. Go to the police station tomorrow and hand in my book of fine receipts. There'll be a percentage of five rubles for you to collect. You can live on it when I'm gone."

He then lay down on something and fell silent.

Soon afterward Moscow whispered another question: "Well, Komyagin?" She was calling him by his surname, as if he were a stranger. "Gone back to sleep? And then you'll be waking up again, I suppose?"

"I'm not really asleep," Komyagin answered. "I've been doing some thinking. What if I were to do another ten years in the militia? Then I'd really learn how to instill discipline into the nation! I could become Genghis Khan!"

"Stop all your talk!" said Moscow angrily. "Opportunist cheat! You're stealing time from the State!"

"No, I'm not!" protested Komyagin. Then he said tenderly, "Do something sweet to me, Musya. Then I'll waste away more quickly. By morning I'll be an angel—I'll have died."

"I'll show you how sweet I can be!" Moscow responded threateningly. "If you don't peg out soon, I'll stamp you out myself with my wooden leg."

"All right, I'm done, I'm done! They say that, before dying, one should call to mind one's whole life. Don't be hard on me—I'll recall my life straightaway."

Silence set in as long years of existence passed one by one through Komyagin's mind.

"Well, have you done remembering?" said Moscow, hurrying him on.

"There's nothing to remember," said Komyagin. "All I can think of is the seasons: autumn, winter, spring, summer, and then again autumn, winter...In 1911 and 1921 there was a hot summer and a bare winter, without any snow. 1916 was the opposite—it poured with rain. And the autumn of 1917 was long, dry, and just right for a revolution. I can remember it as if it were yesterday."

"But you've loved a lot of women, Komyagin. That must have been your happiness."

"What happiness can there be for a man like me? It wasn't happiness—it was the poverty of mere lust! That's all love is—a bitter need."

"You know, Komyagin, you're not so very stupid after all!"

"Just average," agreed Komyagin.

"All right then," said Moscow in a clear voice. "That's enough!"

"All right," Komyagin repeated.

They fell silent again, and for a long time. Outside the door to where they were living, Sartorius waited with equanimity for Komyagin to die, so that he could enter the room himself. He felt his eyes beginning to ache, from the dark and from long torment of heart.

Eventually Komyagin asked Musya to cover his head up tight with a blanket, and to secure the blanket with a piece of string around his torso, so it wouldn't slip off. Using her wooden leg, Moscow got out of bed, covered Komyagin up as necessary, and then settled back down again, with sighs.

The night lengthened, as if standing still. Sartorius sat down on the ground in exhaustion: no one along the corridor had woken up yet, morning was still located somewhere over the mirror of the Pacific Ocean. But every sound had stopped, events had evidently gone deep into the center of the sleepers' bodies; only the pendulums of the wall clocks were knocking away for all to hear, as if some extremely important production mechanism were at work. And the work of the pendulums truly was of extreme importance; they were propelling forward the time that was accumulating, so that both heavy and happy feelings should pass through a human being without delay, without coming to a stop and ruining him once and for all.

No pendulum was knocking in Komyagin's room; all that could be heard from there was the pure, even breathing of Moscow, who had fallen asleep. There was no other breathing—none that Sartorius could detect. After waiting a little longer, he knocked at the door.

"Who's there?" Moscow asked at once.

"Me," said Sartorius.

Without getting up, Chestnova released the door hook with the big toe of her intact foot.

Sartorius went in. The light was on; it had not been turned off since the checking of the State bonds. Komyagin was lying on the floor, on some bedding, with a thick blanket wrapped tightly around his head; the blanket was held in place by a thin piece of string that cut into his chest. Moscow was alone on the bed, covered by a sheet; she smiled at Sartorius and began chatting to him. After a while Sartorius asked, "How is it you've ended up here, in the room of a stranger? And why?"

Moscow replied that she hadn't known what to do with herself. At first Sambikin had loved her, but then he had begun to puzzle over her, as if over some problem, and he had stayed silent without interruption. And she herself had begun to feel ashamed of living among her former friends, in the well-ordered city they all shared, now that she was lame, thin, and mentally not right in the head. So she had decided to hide away in the room of a poor acquaintance of hers, to wait out the time and then be merry again.

She was sitting on the bed; Sartorius was there beside her. After a while she lowered her now pale face; her long dark hair fell forward across her cheeks, and she began to weep in the thick of it. Sartorius tried to calm her by means of embraces, but to her it was all the same; she felt ashamed and hid her wooden leg deep beneath her skirt.

"Is he asleep?" Sartorius asked about Komyagin.

"I don't know," said Moscow. "Maybe he's died—it's what he wanted. Feel his feet."

Sartorius felt the ends of Komyagin's feet. The remains of his socks were like neckties—only the upper parts were whole, while his toes and the soles of his feet were bared naked. Komyagin's toes and heels proved cold right through to the bone, and his whole body was lying in a helpless position.

"He's probably died," said Sartorius.

"It's about time he did," Moscow pronounced quietly.

Sartorius silently rejoiced that there was no one alive in the room but himself and his former beloved Moscow, now sweeter and closer to his heart than ever, and that her happiness and fame had temporarily stopped, which meant that before her, once again, lay only what stretched out ahead. And he felt no pity at all for Komyagin. The night had been going on for a long time; Sartorius and Moscow were both exhausted and they lay down on the bed side by side.

Komyagin remained motionless on the distant floor. The evening before, so that the bedding would not get dirty, Moscow had spread out some old newspapers, *Izvestiya*s from 1927, and light was now falling on reports of past events. Sartorius embraced Moscow and began to feel happy.

Some two hours later people began to go up and down the corridor, getting ready for office and factory. Sartorius came to and sat up on the bed. Moscow was asleep beside him, and in her sleep her face was still and kind, like bread, not quite like her usual face. Komyagin was lying there as before; the electricity was burning brightly and illuminating the entire room, where everything was demanding to be refashioned or brought to an end. Sartorius understood that love originated due to the poverty of society, a universal poverty that had still not been eliminated and that meant people were unable to find any better, higher destiny and didn't know what to do with themselves. He turned out the light and lay down, to recover from the condition that had now set in. A weak light, like moonlight, began to spread along the wall above the door, penetrating through the window from the morning sky, and when it had lit up the whole room, it became even sadder and more cramped there than during the night, under the electric light.

Sartorius went up to the window. Outside it lay the smoky, wintry city; a routine dawn was making its way along the sagging belly of an indifferent cloud from which there was no chance of either wind or storm. But millions of people had already begun to stir on the streets, carrying diverse life within them. They were on their way amid the gray light to labor in workshops and to think inside offices and engineering bureaus; there were many of them, while Sartorius was sitting alone, never separable from himself. His mind and soul, along with his monotonous body, were structured the same until death.

The corpse Komyagin lay there, a witness to the events that had chanced in the room, but he did not move or feel envious. Moscow was asleep in alienation, her charming face turned to the wall.

Sartorius took fright: all that had been allotted to him, out of the entire world, was one warm drop stored in his breast, and he might never sense what remained but lie down soon in a corner like Komyagin. His heart seemed to turn dark but he comforted it with an ordinary understanding that came to his mind: that it was necessary to research the entire extent of current life through transformation of himself into others. Sartorius stroked the sides of his body, dooming it to suffer its way into another existence, something forbidden by the laws of nature and a person's habit of their own self. Sartorius was a researcher and was not preserving himself for a secret happiness; he intended to use events and circumstances to annihilate the resistance of his personality, so that the unknown feelings of others could enter him one by one. Since he had appeared in life, he must not miss this opportunity. It was essential to enter into every soul outside him. Otherwise, what he was he to do with himself? Alone with his own self, he would have nothing to live on. And if anyone did live like that, all they could do was turn goggle-eyed and stupefied from imbecility.

Sartorius put his face to the windowpane, observing the city he loved, and which was growing every minute into future time; agitated by work, renouncing its own self, it was thrusting itself forward with a face that was young and unrecognizable.

"What am I on my own? I must become like the city of Moscow."[71]

Komyagin stirred on the floor and took a breath of his already well-breathed air.

"Musya," he called out in uncertainty. "I've gone cold down here. Can I come and lie beside you?"

Moscow opened one eye and said, "Oh, all right then!"

Komyagin began to free himself from the blanket that was suffocating him, while Sartorius went out through the door and into the city, without farewell.

13

He became for some time as if lifeless. He stopped going to see Liza the typist because she was now firmly married to Viktor Vasilievich Bozhko. The weights and measures trust had been put to liquidation and laid waste, emptied of all its staff. Only one woman, the messenger, lived in the now cold and deserted premises; she had given birth to a child, and she nursed this child and made a home for it on a soft heap of outdated files.

Sartorius twice visited his old workplace, sat for a while at his bare desk, tried to sketch a project for weighing something weightless— and felt no sensation at all, neither sorrow nor pleasure. Everything had ended: the office family, which had unburdened people's souls, had been dispersed; the communal kettle was no longer put on to boil for twelve o'clock, and the glasses stood empty in the cupboard, where they were gradually being colonized by some kind of pale and papery petty insects. The messenger's baby cried or felt comforted, the pendulum clock went on its way forward above it, and the mother caressed her child with the usual love of mothers. She was awaiting with dread the arrival in the building of some new institute, since she had nowhere else to live, but on the eve of its move this new institute was also liquidated, so the space was turned over to the housing reserve and then allocated to tenants with families.

Sartorius's sight was continuing to worsen; his eyes were going blind. He lay in his room for a whole month before beginning to look a little again with painful vision. The messenger woman from the former trust came to visit him every other day, bringing him food and attending to the routine chores.

He was twice visited by Sambikin and an eye doctor, and they pronounced their medical conclusion: that the reason for his eye illness lay in the remote depth of his body, perhaps in his heart. Sambikin said that Sartorius's constitution was, on the whole, in process of indefinite transformation[72]—and he himself then felt preoccupied by this thought for many days.

Eventually, Sartorius went out of the building. He was gladdened by the crowds on the street. The energy of the rushing cars generated inspiration in his heart; uninterrupted sunlight shone on the uncovered hair of passing women and on the fresh leafy leaves of the trees, drenched in the moisture of their own birth.

Spring had set in once again; time was bearing Sartorius's life ever further away, making it ever more redundant. He was often blinking, blinded by light, and he would bump into people. He was pleased there were so many of them and that it was not, therefore, obligatory for him to exist—even without him, there were enough people to do everything that was essential and worthwhile.

A single heavy and dark feeling had taken hold of him. He carried his body as if it were a dead weight, something sad and tedious, now endured to its poor end. Sartorius gazed into the many oncoming faces; another person's life, hidden inside an unknown soul, was troubling him like some nearby delight. He stood aside and yearned.

In motion on Kalanchev Square were approximately ten thousand people.[73] As if he had never before seen such a spectacle, Sartorius stopped in astonishment beside the customs house.

"I'll hide away now, I'll disappear among them all," he said to himself, considering this intention of his lightly and indefinitely.

A misty figure came up to him, the kind of man you can't remember and will always forget.

"Comrade, you don't happen to know where Dominikov Lane begins, do you? Maybe you know it—I used to know it myself, but I've lost the thread."

"Yes," said Sartorius, "it's over there!" And he pointed out the direction, remembering this familiar voice and not remembering the face.

"And do you know if coffin production is still going on there—or has it already been transferred elsewhere in connection with construction and reorganization?" the passerby went on inquiring.

"There's no knowing. There may be something like that—wreaths and coffins," Sartorius explained.

"And transport?"

"Probably."

"Cars, I suppose, that go slowly and quietly?"

"Could be. They go in first gear and they carry the deceased."

"I see," the man agreed, not understanding the words "first gear."

They fell silent. The passerby glanced with passion at some people jumping up onto moving trams and clinging to them—and even made one indefinite movement of fury in their direction.

"I know you," said Sartorius. "I remember your voice."

"Quite likely," the man admitted with equanimity. "There are a lot of people I've had to fine for infringements, and when you do that, understandably, you shout."

"Maybe it'll come back to me. Tell me your name."

"First names don't matter," said the passerby. "What matters is the exact address and the surname—but even that's not enough. Documents must be presented."

He took out his passport,[74] and in it Sartorius read "Komyagin, pensioner," and the address. The man was unknown to him.[75]

"You and I are strangers," pronounced Komyagin, seeing Sartorius's disappointment. "You were just imagining. Often something seems serious—but then it turns out to be nothing. Well, you stay here, and I'll go and find out about a coffin."

"Has your wife died?" asked Sartorius.

"My wife's alive. She's left me. I'm predicting a coffin for myself."

"Why?"

"What do you mean—*why*? It's essential. I want to learn a deceased person's entire itinerary: where you get authorization for the digging of a grave, what factual data and documents are required, how you order the coffin, and then the means of transport, the burial, and how the balance sheet of life is finally drawn up: where and according to what formalities a man is once and for all excluded from the register of citizens.[76] I want to follow the entire itinerary in advance—from life to complete oblivion, to the liquidation beyond trace of every being. They say the performance of this itinerary is difficult. And it's true, dear comrade, people shouldn't die, citizens are needed. But look what's going on in the square! Citizens are rushing about, they just will not learn to walk normally. How often, in his time, did comrade Lunacharsky call for rhythmical movement on the part of the masses—and to this day they still have to be fined! How prosaic life is! Long live the heroic militia of the Republic!"[77]

Komyagin set off toward Dominikov Lane. As well as Sartorius, four bystanders and one vagrant child had been listening to him intently. This child, aged about twelve, set off briskly after Komyagin and declared in a mature voice, "Citizen, since you're about to go and die anyway, give me all the things you've got at home. I can come and walk off with them for you."

"All right," said Komyagin, "come along with me. You'll inherit my bits and pieces, but I'll take my share of fate a bit further with me. Farewell, my life—you have passed in organizational delights."

"It's kind of you to be dying," the sensible child pronounced benignly. "I need resources, you see, to further my career."

Sartorius's soul was experiencing a passion of curiosity. He stood there, conscious of the inescapable poverty of the separate human heart. He had long been astonished by the spectacle of living people and their diversity; now he wanted to live a life that belonged to a stranger and not to himself.

He was under no obligation to return: his room was empty, the trust had been liquidated, his family of colleagues had now moved to the well-lived-in rooms of other establishments, Moscow Chestnova was disappearing somewhere in the great space of this city and humanity—and these circumstances were making Sartorius feel merrier. Life's fundamental obligation—concern over one's personal fate, the sense of one's own body, constantly crying out with feelings—had disappeared. He could not go on being the same uninterrupted person; a yearning was beginning in him.

Sartorius made a movement with his hand—thus, according to universalist theories of the world, instigating an electromagnetic oscillation that would disturb even the most distant star. He smiled at such a poor and pitiful representation of the great world. No, the world was better and more mysterious: neither a movement of the hand nor the work of the human heart would disturb the stars—otherwise everything would have been shaken to pieces long ago by the trembling of this empty piffle.

Sartorius set off across the square through the oncoming people. He saw a metro construction worker in overalls, a woman with the same figure as Moscow Chestnova, and his eyes began to ache from the memory of love: life with immutable feelings was impossible. He tried to persuade this woman into a preliminary friendship, but she laughed and hurried away from him, dirty and beautiful.

Sartorius dried his failing eyes, and tried to persuade his heart, which had begun to ache for Moscow and all other beings, but he saw that his thinking was having no effect. But lack of respect for his own self made his suffering less difficult.

Wandering farther about the city, he often noticed happy, sad, or enigmatic faces, and he would begin to choose who to become. The imagination of another soul, of the unknown sensation of being in a new body, did not leave him. He thought about the thoughts in a stranger's head, walked with a gait that was not his own, and felt greedy joy in his empty and ready heart. Youth of torso was being transformed into a lust of Sartorius's mind; on squares and streets, a smiling, modest Stalin was standing guard over all the open roads of the fresh, unknown socialist world.[78] Life was stretching out into a distance from which there was no return.

Sartorius caught a tram to the Krestov market, to buy what was necessary for his own future existence. His own new life was a matter of the utmost concern to him.

The Krestov market was full of trading beggars and secret bourgeois, all of them trying, in dry passions and the risk-taking of despair, to procure their bread.[79] Unclean air hung over this packed gathering of standing and muttering people. Some were proffering meager goods, clasping them close to their breasts; others were rapaciously asking the price of these goods, touching them and falling into despondency, having counted on eternal acquisition. On sale here were old clothes cut in the style of the nineteenth century, impregnated with powder and kept intact through decades on a careful body. Here were fur coats that had passed through so many hands during the time of the Revolution that a meridian of the terrestrial globe would have been too short for the measurement of their journeys between people. And people were also trading in things that had lost their own meaning of life—housecoats from some extraordinary women, priests' cassocks, ornamented basins for the baptism of children, the frock coats of deceased gentlemen, charms on watch chains, and so on—but which still circulated among humanity as symbols of a strict evaluation of quality.[80] There were also many items of clothing worn by people who had died recently—death had not ceased to exist—as well as petty clothes prepared for infants who had been conceived, but then the mother must have thought twice about giving birth and had an abortion and now she was selling the tiny lamented-over garments of an unborn person along with a rattle purchased in advance.

One row of the market was set aside for original oil portraits and artistical reproductions. The portraits showed long-dead burghers, and brides and bridegrooms from provincial towns; each of them, judging by their faces, delighted in their own self and was expressing satisfaction with the life that was happening to them. Behind these figures could sometimes be seen a church, amid a landscape, and oak trees were growing in a happy summer that was always past.

Sartorius stood for a long time in front of these portraits of past people. Their gravestones were now being used for the pavements of new cities, and somewhere a third or fourth brief generation was trampling over the inscriptions: "Here is buried the body of Pyotr

Nikodimovich Samofalov, merchant of the second guild of the town of Zaraisk. The years of his life were...Remember me, O Lord, in thy kingdom." "Here lie the ashes of Anna Vasilievna Strizhevaya, spinster...We weep and suffer; but she beholdeth the Lord."

Rather than God, it was Sartorius who had now remembered the dead, and he shuddered from terror of living among them, in the time before the forests had been cut down, when a man's wretched heart was eternally faithful to solitary feeling, when his circle of acquaintances consisted entirely of relatives, when his vision of the world was magical and patient, and as for his mind—it languished and wept, by the light of a paraffin lamp in the evening, or during a radiant summer noon, amid a natural world that was spacious and full of noise; a time when a pathetic young woman, devoted and faithful, would embrace a tree in her yearning, a stupid, sweet girl who had now been forgotten without a sound. She was not Moscow Chestnova but one Ksenya Innokentievna Smirnova,[81] who no longer was and never would be again.

Farther on, there were sculptures for sale, along with cups, plates, trivets, forks, parts from some balustrade, and a twelve-pood weight. The last private traders in paints and oils were squatting on their haunches; demoralized out-of-work locksmiths were hawking hammers, home vises, axes for firewood, a handful of nails. Farther on stretched cobblers, doing jobs on the spot, and old women providers of nourishment: cold pancakes; pies stuffed with butchers' waste; suet buns kept warm in cast-iron pots beneath the padded jackets of the old men, now deceased, who had once been their husbands; slabs of cooked millet; anything, in short, that might relieve the hungry suffering of the local public—who were capable of swallowing any good thing, just as long as it could be swallowed.

Insignificant thieves were wandering about between those with needs and those with goods; they would snatch from someone's hands a length of cotton, a pair of old felt boots, some bread rolls, a single galosh, then run off into the jungle of stray bodies, earning fifty kopeks or a ruble from each act of plunder. In truth, they barely earned as much as a laborer, and exhausted themselves more.

Here and there amid the market towered wooden booths for policemen. Policemen were looking down from them into this shallow sea of raging petty imperialism, where laborers had been replaced but there were still layabouts.[82]

The cheap food made an audible noise as it was digested in people, and so each person felt burdened with heaviness, as if they were a complex enterprise, and unclean air rose upwards, like smoke over the Donbass.[83]

In the depths of the bazaar there sometimes resounded invocations of despair, but nobody ever rushed to help, and people went on buying and selling near to the calamity, because their own grief demanded urgent consolation. A woman selling bread rolls had attacked a weak man wearing a soldier's greatcoat from the old days; having driven him into a pool of urine beside the latrines, she was lashing him across the face with a rag. Now further weakened, the man collapsed beneath the latrine fence—and, springing to the woman's aid, a nomadic hooligan straightaway smashed him in the face till he bled. The man did not let out a cry and he did not touch his face, now awash with blood from his temples; hurriedly, struggling with rotten teeth, he was eating a plundered stale roll—a task he quickly completed. The hooligan gave him one more blow on the head, and the wounded eater, jumping up with the energy of a strength that was incomprehensible in view of his silent meekness, disappeared in the thick of the crowd, as if among ears of rye. He would find food for himself everywhere and would live for a long time without means and without happiness, but often eating his fill.

An elderly, demobilized-looking man was standing without motion in one place, just swaying a little from the nearby bustle. Sartorius had noticed him once before; he went up to him.

"Bread ration cards," said this motionless man, after a certain vigilance of observation of Sartorius.

"How much?" asked Sartorius.

"Twenty-five rubles, first category."[84]

"Give me one then," said Sartorius.

The trader cautiously took from a side pocket an envelope with the printed inscription: FULL PROGRAM OF THE INSTITUTE FOR THE PROCESSING OF MINERAL RESOURCES. Inside this program was a ration card.

The same trader also offered Sartorius a passport, should he need one, but Sartorius acquired a passport for himself later, from a man selling worms for fishing bait. The passport was in the name of Semyon Ivanovich Grunyakhin, a thirty-one-year-old native of the town of Novy Oskol, a worker in retailing and the commander of a reserve platoon. Sartorius paid only sixty-five rubles for the document, and in addition handed over his own passport, that of a twenty-seven-year-old man with a higher education, well known in his particular profession.[85]

Grunyakhin didn't know where to go from the market. He went by tram to a large square and sat on the iron rung of a ladder that went up to a booth for the regulation of traffic. The traffic lights changed their color, people rushed past in cars, trucks went by with girders and beams, the policeman moved his switch and strained his attention: many unknown people were standing to either side of the speeding traffic and forgetting their own solitary lives in observation of the lives of others. It seemed to Grunyakhin that his eyes were no longer aching and that he would never need Moscow Chestnova again, since there were many fine women crossing the road here—yet his heart was not inclined toward any of them.

Early that evening he was taken on by the provisions section of an insignificant factory in Sokolniki[86] that made some kind of auxiliary equipment, and a place was found for the new worker in the hostel, since the man's only possessions were his clothed body, which was not large, and a round face, which did not look intelligent, up above it.

Within a few days Grunyakhin had entered into the passion of his work. It was his job to apportion bread for lunch and put the allocated norm of vegetables into the pot, and also to calculate the meat so that each person should get a just piece. He liked feeding people; he worked with honesty and zeal; and his kitchen scales gleamed with cleanness and precision, like a diesel engine.

In the evenings, wearied by solitude and freedom, Grunyakhin wandered about the boulevards until the last trams. After one o'clock in the morning, when the tramcars were speeding to their depot, Semyon Grunyakhin would sit down in their deserted interiors and examine them with interest, as if the thousands of people who had been there during the day had left their own breath and best feelings on the empty seats. The conductress—sometimes an old woman, sometimes a woman who was young, sweet, and sleepy— would be sitting on her own, pulling the cord at the unfrequented stops to bring a quick end to the last journey.

Having become the second person of his own life, Grunyakhin would go up to the conductress and begin to talk about something unrelated, which had nothing to do with all the reality apparent around them—but the conductress would then begin to perceive something invisible inside herself. One conductress from a rear car yielded to Grunyakhin's words and he embraced her en route; they then moved to the back of the car, where it was harder to see, and they went on kissing and were carried away past three stops, until somebody on the boulevard noticed them and shouted, "Hurrah!"

After that, he tried now and again to repeat this friendship with a nighttime conductress—sometimes successfully but more often not. What interested him more and more, however, was not this private love that flowed by without trace, but Grunyakhin, the unknown human being whose fate was swallowing him up.

In the course of further work in the provisions section, he gradually got excited by his labor and surroundings and even began to feel intoxicated by life. He acquired a bookcase for himself, filled it with books, and began studying world philosophy, delighting in universal thought and the fact that good is inevitable in the world and that it is even impossible for anyone to hide from it. In the end, the laws of the golden rule of mechanics and the golden section acted across the globe always and everywhere. It was coming to seem that, thanks to the action of nature alone, a little work would always yield big successes and everyone would end up with a piece from the golden section—the hugest and most substantial piece of all. What determined the fate of mankind, therefore, was not so much labor as cunning, skill, and a soul ready to be intoxicated by happiness. Archimedes and Hero of Alexandria[87] had long ago rejoiced in the golden rules of science, which promised widespread bliss to humanity: using a one-gram weight and a lever with arms of unequal length, you could lift a whole ton—even the entire terrestrial globe, as Archimedes had calculated.[88] And Lunacharsky, for his part, had proposed lighting a new sun if the present one should prove inadequate, or simply tedious and ugly.[89]

Consoled by his reading, Semyon Grunyakhin worked well at the factory. In the course of a single month, on instructions from the head of the provisions section, he changed all the gloomy furnishings of the canteen for something luxurious and attractive. Grunyakhin signed a contract for one year with the Green Construction Trust, as well as with MoscFurniture and other organizations. He introduced potted plants and laid down strips of carpet. He then increased the circulation of air and himself repaired an electric motor for the second, damaged extractor fan, recalling his knowledge of electrical engineering with difficulty and no longer feeling any interest in it. On the walls of the canteen and the assembly workshop Grunyakhin hung large pictures showing episodes of ancient historical life: the Fall of Troy, the Voyage of the Argonauts, the Death of Alexander the Great. The factory manager praised him for his good taste. "We want things to be enigmatic and fine—almost unfeasible," he said to Grunyakhin. "Though of course these paintings are piffle in comparison with our own reality! But let them stay here—history was poor in the past and one shouldn't ask for too much from it."

Under the influence of this general orderliness and prosperity, Grunyakhin felt suddenly ashamed, and he began to acquire underwear, shoes, and fruit for his own personal use and even began to dream about a loving, single wife. Sometimes he remembered the poor, long-gone, weights and measures trust, when he was still Sartorius. There it had been sad and warm from his own heart, and there had been no need for a wife; but now, having become another person, Grunyakhin needed at least the artificial warming provided by a family and a woman.

In the workshop of new constructions there was a senior fitter, about thirty years old, called Konstantin Arabov; he was handsome, a member of the Dynamo Sports Club, and he knew Pushkin by heart. Duty engineer Semyon Ivanovich Grunyakhin[90] had come across him several times but had never paid attention to him. So it often happens—people whose fate will enter your heart can live unnoticeably for a long time ... Arabov got carried away by one of the team leaders, a French Komsomol member called Katya Bessonet-Favor,[91] an amusing and sensible young woman, and went off with her to live in love forever, leaving his wife and two sons—one was eleven years old and the other was eight. Arabov's wife, still young, but sad, used for some time to go along to the factory toward the end of the working day, so as to have a look at her husband; her heart, it seemed, couldn't immediately get out of the habit of him. Then she stopped going; her feeling of love had reached exhaustion and stopped. Soon afterward Grunyakhin learned from Katya Bessonet that Arabov's eleven-year-old son had shot himself with a neighbor's gun and had left a note just like a grown-up. Grieving and in tears, Katya told how somewhere in a room a child had lost heart and had died all by himself—at a time when she was being intoxicated by happiness with his father. Grunyakhin shuddered from fear and astonishment at such a death, as if, there in front of him, a weak howl had sounded amid universal silence. He regretted that he had not known the child before, that he had overlooked this being.

Tormented by her own consciousness, Katya Bessonet rejected Arabov, who wanted to calm his own despair by means of still more passionate love with her, as is usually the way. But being alone was also impossible for her, and so she went to the cinema with Grunyakhin and from there they set off together to visit Arabov's ex-wife. Katya knew that the dead boy's funeral had taken place that morning, and she wanted to help his mother in her eternal separation from the little person who for her had been the most faithful of all.

Arabov's wife greeted them with equanimity. She was clean and well dressed, as if for some modest celebration, and she was calm and not crying. She knew Katya Bessonet, of course, but she had seen Grunyakhin only once, at the factory, and did not understand why he had come.

Katya was quick to embrace her, but Arabov's wife stood there with her arms by her sides and did not respond; whatever happened now, it was all the same to her. She mechanically lit the primus and made some tea for these guests who were strangers to her. Grunyakhin liked this woman, with her face that was so ugly and absurd it called for pity. Her nose was large and thin, her lips were gray, and her eyes were colorless, muted by the solitary labor of housework; she was not yet old, but her body had already dried up and become like a man's, while her drooping breasts hung down as if they had nothing to do.

After drinking their tea, the guests got ready to leave. The meeting had not led to consolation, and Katya Bessonet herself was left with irritation inside her from the impotence of her own heart, which felt all too much but could not act. But as they left, Arabov's wife turned suddenly to the emptiness of her own room. Grunyakhin suddenly looked the same way himself, and every object at once seemed to him to become a likeness, or a distortion, of some kind of general, familiar human being that might even have been his own self; every object had turned its attention to the people present and was grinning sullenly at them all with unclear face and attitude. Arabov's former wife must have seen the same thing, because suddenly her eternal grief made her begin to cry and she turned away out of shame before these outsiders. She knew instinctively that there can be no help from others and that it's best to hide away on one's own.

Upset by such a life, Grunyakhin went out onto the street with Bessonet-Favor and said to her, "You've heard of the golden rule of mechanics. Some people have thought they can use this rule to cheat the whole of nature, the whole of life. Kostya Arabov too wanted to obtain with you, or out of you—how can I put it?—some kind of free gold. And he did get a little."

"A little—yes," Bessonet agreed.

"But how much? Not more than a gram. And to achieve equilibrium it was necessary to weigh down the other end of the lever with a whole ton of the graveyard earth that now lies on his child and crushes him."

Katya Bessonet frowned in bewilderment.

"Don't ever try to live by the golden rule," Grunyakhin went on. "That's an illiterate way to live, and an unhappy one. I'm an engineer, and so I know: nature's more serious. There's no tricking things out of nature. Well, goodbye now—here's your bus."

"Wait," said Katya Bessonet.

"I haven't got time," said Grunyakhin. "I'm not interested, I don't like it when people get intoxicated with themselves and then don't know what to do with themselves and want to go about with me. One should live correctly."

Bessonet-Favor laughed unexpectedly. "All right, all right," she said. "The way you come out with all these demands, anyone would think it was me who made me the way I am. I'm this way inadvertently—it isn't deliberate. But this won't happen again, I'm sorry…"

Grunyakhin went back to the room of Arabov's wife. She met him with her former equanimity, but he, as he crossed the threshold, suggested she marry him: he had nothing else to offer. The woman went pale, as if struck by a sudden illness, and said nothing. Semyon Ivanovich stayed there, sitting in the room till it was late at night and the traffic outside stopped. Then he involuntarily fell asleep; Arabov's wife arranged some bedding for him on the short settee and told him to lie down properly.

In the morning Grunyakhin went to work as usual, but in the evening he came back. Matryona Filippovna Cheburkova[92] (she had stopped using her husband's surname after his betrayal) neither greeted this new man nor drove him away. He gave her some money, putting it on the table; mechanically, she made him some tea and warmed up something to eat from the leftovers of her own food. A few days later the janitor came around in the evening and told Matryona Filippovna to get her new tenant registered: really, of course, it was up to her—she could marry him or she could send him packing—but no one could allow her to go on living like this. The janitor was a dispossessed kulak, and so he clung to the law with all precision: he had himself experienced and survived the power of the State.

"You watch out, citizen Cheburkova, or you'll get yourself fined. The State doesn't like to lose out!"

"All right then. In the past I wouldn't have got fined—but now that I'm weak and without a husband—"

"Well, get him registered!" The janitor pointed at Grunyakhin. "Don't go losing your norm as a married wife. Or else you'll lose your living space too, and you'll end up like Little Dumpling in the film[93]—except you're so skinny!"

"You can register him tomorrow—there's plenty of time," said Cheburkova. "Nowadays women need to think things over."

"So I see!" pronounced the janitor, and left. From the other side of the door he added, "In the past women didn't do any thinking at all, but they lived free of stupidity, the same as if they were clever."

Two days later Grunyakhin got himself registered for the time being, as a temporary tenant, but Cheburkova said he must register for a permanent life. "Who's going to believe that a man and a woman are living apart in the same room?" she said irritably. "And I'm not just a girl off the street—I'm a woman. Tomorrow you're going to the registry office with me—I swear by my life! Or else you can go back where you came from!"

Everything was done quickly and with due formalities, and Grunyakhin's life settled down in another person's room. He went out to work and Matryona Filippovna was mistress of the home, expressing various discontents and only rarely mentioning her son—most likely in order to experience, after her tears, the relief that is equivalent to delight of heart; she was not able to experience any other happiness, or perhaps the chance had never come her way. In secret from her own self, her son's death gradually became the reason for a quiet happiness of life—after brief tears, in slow, detailed recollections. And she would invite Semyon Ivanovich to take part in her poor feelings, where there was, nevertheless, the comforting warmth of a dark intoxication with her own sorrow and all the endurance of her soul. At such a time she always became kinder and meeker than her character required. Grunyakhin even liked it when Matryona Filippovna suddenly began to cry about her dead child—some kind of small privilege or tenderness from his wife would then come his way.

As a rule, Cheburkova did not allow her husband to go anywhere except to work, and she would watch the clock: Was he coming back home on time? She did not believe in official meetings, and she would begin weeping and cursing, saying that her second husband too was a scoundrel and was betraying her. If her husband still came back late, Matryona Filippovna would open the door to him and set about him, using an old felt boot, a coat stand along with its clothes, a flue from what had once been a samovar, a shoe off her own foot, or any other immediate thing—anything to exhaust her own irritation and unhappiness. During these minutes Semyon Ivanovich would look with surprise at Matryona Filippovna, while she herself cried plaintively—because one grief of hers had turned into another but had not disappeared completely. Grunyakhin, who had seen much of life, was not especially upset by her treatment of him.

Matryona Filippovna's second son would watch these quarrels between his mother and his new father with equanimity, since his mother always got the better of his father. But once, when Semyon Ivanovich seized his wife's hands because she had started tearing at his throat with her fingernails, the boy gave him this warning: "Comrade Grunyakhin, don't you hit my mama! Or I'll skewer you through the guts with an awl, you son of a bitch! You're not in your own home now—you'd better learn your place!"

Grunyakhin immediately came to his senses; it was only inadvertently, and because of severe pain, that he had forgotten himself. It was in the hot sweat of despair, in exhaustion, with the zeal of all her own heart that Matryona Filippovna was getting so agitated before him—she was defending her husband from vice and ensuring his fidelity to his family. Semyon Ivanovich listened, endured, and learned.[94]

At night, beside his wife, he thought that everything was as it should be; otherwise his greedy, light heart would quickly have exhausted itself and perished in fruitless attachment to a variety of women and friends, in a dangerous readiness to throw itself into the thick of all the luxury that ever happens on earth.

In the morning the second son—whose name was also Semyon— said to Semyon Ivanovich, "Why do you sleep with my mother? Do you think I enjoy watching you? Yes or no?"

Grunyakhin was abashed by the question. His wife was not there; she had gone to the bazaar for food. It was the beginning of a day off work, when people live by domestic feelings and shared thoughts and take their children to the cinema. Grunyakhin and Semyon went to the cinema too, to look at a Soviet comedy. Semyon was happy enough, although he criticized the film; to him such problems seemed petty—he had lived through more himself. At home Matryona Filippovna was sitting and crying in front of a picture of her past husband but, when she saw Semyon Ivanovich, she felt ashamed and stopped. Grunyakhin had no need of any greater love; he understood Matryona Filippovna's embarrassment as a sign of supreme tenderness and meek trust toward him. His sufferings at the hands of this woman were of no account: people had not yet attained the courage of uninterrupted happiness—they were only learning.

At night, after his wife and son had gone to sleep, Semyon Ivanovich would stand there, above Matryona Filippovna's face, and observe how entirely helpless she was, how pathetically her face had clenched in miserable exhaustion, while her eyes were closed like kind eyes, as if, while she lay unconscious, some ancient angel were resting in her. If all of humanity were lying still and sleeping, it would be impossible to judge its real character from its face and one could be deceived.[95]

Translated by Robert and Elizabeth Chandler
with Nadya Bourova, Angela Livingstone, and Eric Naiman

AROUND *HAPPY MOSCOW*

THE EARLY 1930s was a time of particular crisis for Platonov. In March 1931, he published "For Future Use," a satirical story about collectivization. This met with fierce criticism—Stalin himself referred to Platonov, in a letter to the editorial board of the literary journal *Krasnaya Nov'*, as "an agent of our enemies"[1]—and all Platonov's existing contracts with publishers were annulled. During 1932 and 1933 Platonov was unable to publish at all; in 1933 he wrote to Stalin, Maksim Gorky, and Leopold Averbakh (formerly the leader of the Russian Association of Proletarian Writers), asking for their help. In the second of the three letters that he wrote to Gorky, Platonov asked for a meeting "in order to receive an answer to the central question: 'Can I be a Soviet writer or is this objectively impossible?'" As far as we know, Gorky never answered this question.

Muteness is a common theme in Platonov's work of this period. Albert Lichtenberg, the hero of "Rubbish Wind" (1933), is beaten up and castrated by Nazi thugs; on recovering consciousness, he expresses surprise that "they had not removed his tongue; this was an oversight on the part of the State." And in "Immortality" (1936), the exhausted director of a railway station, overconscientious and over-concerned about the well-being of his subordinates, thinks that "in order to hear every voice, it is necessary almost to go mute oneself." It seems likely that these passages are autobiographical, that Platonov was afraid not only of being denied publication but also of losing even the ability to write.

Usually Platonov wrote fast, but he made only slow progress with *Happy Moscow*. After writing the first six chapters in the last four or five months of 1933, he seems to have spent well over two years working intermittently on the remaining seven chapters. Partly, no doubt, this was because of his two trips to Turkmenistan, in 1934 and 1935, and the works that these trips inspired. Probably, however, it was also because he was finding it difficult to resolve the novel's complex themes.

Platonov may well have genuinely hoped, as he began work on *Happy Moscow*, that he would be able to produce the kind of novel the authorities were calling for. In June 1933 *Literaturnaya gazeta* announced plans for an anthology about Moscow. And in July this same journal published an article, "Proletarian Moscow Is Waiting for Its Artist," the contents of which the Platonov scholar Natalya Kornienko has summarized as follows: "Photographs of inventors, designers of aircraft and balloons that have reached the stratosphere, of parachutists who have descended from record heights, of musicians and physicists—these photographs were printed together with the summons: 'We will write books about the splendid children of the heroic Komsomol—the builders of socialism.'"[2]

Platonov began work on *Happy Moscow* in the summer or autumn of 1933. His contract required him to complete the novel by January 15, 1934. Advance contracts with publishers were unusual in the early 1930s;[3] Platonov being granted one is an indication of the high regard in which he was still held—for all his difficulties with the authorities. The deadline for *Happy Moscow* was extended—first to October 1934, then to 1935, then to 1936. A different publisher included *Happy Moscow* in their schedule for 1937 but never published it; instead they published Platonov's finest collection of short stories, *The River Potudan*. By January 1937, Platonov seems finally to have abandoned work on *Happy Moscow* as a self-contained novel and decided, instead, to include it in a longer work. He crossed out the title on his manuscript and replaced it with the title of a new novel for which he had just received a contract: *A Journey from Leningrad to Moscow*. It is possible that Platonov wrote this novel but lost the text during the war; it is more likely, however, that he abandoned this too.[4]

It is hard to say what prevented Platonov from writing what was required of him. On the surface, he appears to have done everything right. He chose politically correct themes: parachuting, the construction of the Moscow metro, revolutionary medical discoveries, the joys of the new age of socialist abundance that, according to Stalin, had now set in. The novel's main characters seem equally well chosen. Sartorius, of peasant origin, represents a new, truly Soviet kind of engineer and inventor; Bozhko the Esperantist represents the lingering hope of world revolution, as conceived in the early 1930s; Sambikin embodies the early Soviet attempt to transform human nature and overcome death. Moscow herself represents both the Revolution and the riches and beauty of the Soviet capital, and her movement through the four elements—from fire and air to earth and then water—seems to bring the novel oddly close to the kind of "Shakespearean" screenplay that Sergey Eisenstein had publicly asked to be provided with, for a projected film called "Moscow Through Time."[5] Nearly all these themes, however, are resolved tragically. And of the main characters, only Bozhko survives relatively unscathed, though he seems to lose interest in both Esperanto and world revolution.

In many respects, it seems that Platonov knew very well what he was doing; the novel is carefully constructed and full of subtle parody of articles in the Soviet press and even statements by Stalin himself. Nevertheless, Platonov seems to have been deeply upset by the novel's rejection. A 1936 notebook entry, translated literally, reads: "The novel was not accepted—and arms and body came out in boils. It's easier for people to break a man than they think."[6] The Russian original contains no personal pronouns or possessive adjectives, and so we cannot be entirely certain that Platonov is writing about himself and *Happy Moscow*, but it is hard to imagine what else he could have had in mind. Platonov's apparent distress might lead one to think that he truly did not understand quite what he had written, that he genuinely could not imagine his agonized concern about the future of socialism being understood as an expression of a reactionary viewpoint. This is not impossible, but it too seems somewhat unlikely. Platonov was neither stupid nor naïve, and this is precisely what had happened, only a few years before, with regard to his earlier masterpieces *Chevengur* and *The Foundation Pit*.

Platonov's intentions may remain a mystery, but there is no doubt that he was searching during these years for a new way to write, for some way in which he could, as he had put it to Gorky, "be a Soviet writer." His breakthrough came with *Soul*, which he wrote in 1935, in the middle of his work on *Happy Moscow*. *Soul* too was never published in Platonov's lifetime,[7] but it nonetheless marks the beginning of a new phase in his work. It is in *Soul* that Platonov first discovered the apparent simplicity of style, and patient acceptance of life, that characterize his later work, much of which he did manage to publish. *Soul* and *Happy Moscow* are mirror images of each other. *Happy Moscow* begins with a promise of paradise and ends in despair; much of the first half of *Soul* takes place in what Platonov calls "the hell of the whole world," but the novel ends with the establishment of something close to an earthly paradise. The profoundly different tone of *Soul* is apparent even from its first chapter, which is set in Moscow: "He put his arms around her, and they fell asleep in the bright time of day. The noise of Moscow being constructed, of machines drilling into her depths, of citizens quarrelling in the city's trams and trolley-buses—everything fell silent in their ears. They just held each other in their arms, and each heard through sleep the meek, muffled breathing of the other." The imagery is similar to that of *Happy Moscow*—for a moment we may imagine that we have got muddled and are in fact reading a passage from *Happy Moscow*—but *Happy Moscow* contains no moments of such tender peace; even its most joyful scenes are imbued with a certain tension and angst.

Happy Moscow and the works around it are, perhaps, less coherent than *Soul*, but they show Platonov at his most brilliantly original. Platonov wrote more unfinished works between 1930 and 1936 than at any other time in his life, and this allows us to see him experimenting with his material, taking up particular themes and images and presenting them to us from different perspectives, in different genres. Komyagin, with "his own still uncompleted archives" under his bed, is in some respects a self-portrait; the lines of verse he reads aloud are from a poem Platonov wrote in 1920–1921. Komyagin's inability to complete anything is probably evidence of a real anxiety on Platonov's part. On the other hand, Platonov was at this time attracted by the idea of open-endedness. One of his 1936 notes for *Happy Moscow* includes these sentences: "At the end, there must remain a great tension and plot potential—as abrupt as at the beginning of the novel. The plot mustn't be over at the end, it mustn't come to an end."[8] And in his 1937 essay "Pushkin—Our Comrade," Platonov wrote, "Pushkin never managed to exhaust himself even through the very greatest of his works—and this remaining inspiration, not transformed in any direct way into the given work yet still sensible to the reader, works on us irresistibly. A true poet does not fall dead after the final period but stands once again by the beginning of his work. The endings of Pushkin's works are like sea horizons; reaching them, you again see before you an infinite space, limited only by an imaginary line."[9] It seems possible, in the light of these two statements, that *Happy Moscow* may be almost complete as it stands. It is clear from question marks in the margins of the manuscript that Platonov wanted to do more work on some passages—above all on several of Sambikin's speeches—but he may have decided that there was no need to extend the novel. As we have already seen, it has an entirely logical structure as it stands.

The works in this second half of the book are linked to one another and to *Happy Moscow* by shared images, themes, and characters: a couple kissing in a tram, love triangles, trios of portraits on the wall of an apartment, a lonely violinist, a sparrow, catastrophic accidents of all kinds, attempted suicides, images of levers and balances. This creates a strange effect—almost as if these characters truly exist and we are being granted unexpected glimpses of them from different vantage points.

"The Moscow Violin" (1934) is one of the most enigmatic of all

Platonov's works; it is not surprising that Platonov should have carried on developing many of its images, which are far from transparent. It is clear, though, that there is much of Platonov himself in the story's hero. Both Platonov and Wiseman are from the provinces; both go to Moscow, intending to devote their lives to art. Both love sparrows; Wiseman plays a "favorite composition" about a sparrow, and Platonov himself went on to write "The Sparrow's Journey"— the last story in this volume. Most important of all, Wiseman plays on a violin, made from waste material, that sings with extraordinary resonance; this makes him very similar indeed to Platonov, who not only often wrote about people and things whom society has rejected as "waste" but who was also an adept recycler of "waste" from his own unfinished or unpublished work.

"On the First Socialist Tragedy"—probably written around the same time as "The Moscow Violin"—deserves to be recognized as one of the earliest and greatest of classic ecological texts. It is vivid and forceful. Platonov's central point—that nature gives us nothing for free—has seldom been put more clearly. The article is also of interest for the light it sheds on *Happy Moscow* and on Platonov's thinking as a whole. The insistence on the importance of exploiting "favorable side winds," rather than confronting nature head-on, is reminiscent of Emily Dickinson's "Tell all the Truth but tell it slant." Nevertheless, Platonov's treatment of a famous statement by Stalin, though not overtly confrontational, is astonishingly bold. Rather than questioning whether Stalin is right to declare that "Technology decides everything," Platonov simply agrees with this statement— and then adds that this is why man's condition is now so profoundly tragic: technology has developed, but our souls have not.[10]

Platonov's screenplays have received far less attention than his other work. Not one has yet been made into a film, even though several films have been made from his stories. To Platonov, however, the cinema was important and he carried on writing screenplays throughout his career. His views on the cinema were characteristically uncompromising. In a 1930 article, he wrote:

Because of a temporary technological inadequacy, the cinema was once called "great and mute."... it would now be more appropriate to call our cinema "The Great Blind One": our cinema simply does not see where the camera lens should be focused. Our cinema is blind, like a newborn being; most films have nothing at all to say to the tense consciousness of contemporary man—their muteness is absolute, not a matter of mere technology.[11]

Platonov's "Father" (his earlier title was "Father-Mother") is a short, occasionally surreal parable about a theme central to all his work: orphanhood. Its more particular theme—that of a child in search of its mother and father—appears in several other works from 1936 and 1937. The story line is often comic, with its plethora of love triangles, but it includes references to Pushkin, Freud, and Plato. What is perhaps the most striking motif of all is so extraordinary that its meaning and importance can easily escape the reader: one of the many love triangles is constituted by the figures of Stalin, Pushkin, and a woman who represents the Russian people.[12] Platonov wrote this script at a time when both Stalin and Pushkin were being deified: Stalin, in connection with the new Soviet Constitution of December 5, 1936; Pushkin, in connection with the massive official celebrations of the centenary of his death on February 10, 1937. After appearing, in his characteristic way, to accept all this at face value, Platonov poses an extraordinary question: Should the Russian people choose Pushkin or Stalin to father her children? As always, Platonov's humor is bold and offbeat.

Platonov often took material from one genre and continued to explore its themes in another. He first outlined the themes of *The Foundation Pit* in a 1929 screenplay, *The Engineer*, and he wrote his greatest short story, "The Return," only after completing a far longer screenplay on the same theme. "The Sparrow's Journey"—the one entirely finished work in the present collection—is expanded from a few lines in "The Moscow Violin," about how the fiddler-hero plays "his favorite composition about a sparrow—about how a sparrow flew somewhere not far away in search of simple grain and ate his fill there amid numerous animals. But the fiddle played away almost of its own accord, and the fiddler followed cautiously as its melody grew more complex; the musical theme broadened and the sparrow's fate changed."

"The Sparrow's Journey" has often been included in collections of Platonov's work intended for Russian children. The subtitle is "A Fairy-Tale Happening" and the language seems, at least at first glance, to be simple. Nevertheless, the themes are indeed "complex" and "broad"—and this is all the more apparent if the tale is read in the context of the other works in this volume. The sparrow learning how best to move through the wind, "the way to move almost athwart a storm," is Platonov the scientist and engineer, learning to make use of nature's "favorable side winds," and it is also Platonov the writer, learning how to "tell it slant" as he lives through the storms of the Soviet 1930s.

Though set in central Moscow, the tale is imbued with much of the tenderness and the concern for the nonhuman world of *Soul*, the Central Asian novel he had written a year earlier. In one of his Central Asian notebooks, Platonov writes that "Humanity—if it is not ennobled by animals and plants—will perish, grow impoverished, fall into the rage of despair, alone in its loneliness."[13] And in *Soul* he declares, "Otherwise one would have to assume that true enthusiasm lies only in the human heart—and such an assumption is worthless and empty, since the blackthorn is imbued with a scent, and the eyes of a tortoise with a thoughtfulness, that signify the great inner worth of their existence, a dignity complete in itself and needing no supplement from the soul of a human being." The meek, attentive, music-loving tortoise of "The Sparrow's Journey" has come from the pages of *Soul*.

As for sparrows, they are important throughout Platonov's work. In *Chevengur*, he calls the sparrow "a true proletarian bird, pecking up its bitter grain." And he continues: "All tender creations can perish on earth as a result of long and gloomy adversity, but such life-bearing creatures as the peasant and the sparrow will remain and endure until a warmer day." And the hero of "A Clay House in a Provincial Garden" (1935) says to himself, "Even nightingales can live in cages and eagles can be tamed. But a sparrow has his shelter almost beneath your feet—so why does he die as soon as he is made captive? What does he need freedom for, when he never flies farther than a few feet and he lives the whole of his life within the yards of two peasant huts? Whereas someone who can fly across the sea turns out to go on singing even in a cage!"[14]

The sparrow is a traditional Slavic symbol for the soul; for Platonov, it seems emblematic of freedom. It also seems emblematic of Platonov himself. Like a sparrow, he was far from showy—either in his work or in his behavior. Like a sparrow, he was alert to the importance of small things. Even the once widely believed myth that Platonov spent his last years working as a janitor, sweeping up litter from the yard of the House of Writers, makes him seem sparrowlike.

Seven years after writing the tale, which like all the works in this collection was published only posthumously, Platonov extended the final sentence. The original ending is simple: "Then he put the fiddle down and began to weep." The revised version is more complex: "Then he put the fiddle down and began to weep, because not everything can be expressed by music and the final means of life and suffering remains poor man himself."[15] Even in this admission of art's ultimate powerlessness, Platonov's voice remains distinctive and eloquent. And, as always, he is saying something unexpected. Life and suffering—he appears to imply—exist almost independently of humanity; humanity's role is simply to provide a way for them to express themselves.

—ROBERT CHANDLER

THE MOSCOW VIOLIN[1]

I

WALKING toward the city of Moscow was an itinerant worker; he was from the Victor collective farm and his name was Semyon Wiseman. He was not a tall man, and he had a broad, inexact face like some place or other in the country. On it lay an ambiguous expression: a smile by his mouth and gloomy concentration within his unclear eyes. His father's surname was not Wiseman but Chewbeard, and his peasant mother had once carried him in her innards beside warm, well-chewed rye bread. Instead of an ordinary little box and some carpenter's tools, Wiseman was carrying in his hands a violin case, but there was nothing inside this case except some cold pancakes and a piece of meat.

The collective farm was located almost a hundred kilometers from Moscow and close to a railway line, but Wiseman, after waiting for a train to arrive, did not board it. There were a lot of people, quarrels were happening beside the ticket office, and he had no wish to spoil his or any stranger's heart; there had been more than enough of all that in the millennia that had already passed by.

He set off on foot amid surrounding nature. Ahead of him lay a lot of time—forty years of uninterrupted life; it was June and all over the country it was good weather out of doors. What a lot of thought you can think through, what a lot of forgotten things you can recall, what a lot of unknown things can be lived in the course of your own empty road. Wind and the movement of legs always tune consciousness in your head and develop strength in your heart.

In Moscow Wiseman appeared at the conservatory office and presented his letter of secondment. In it was written that the Tishan village soviet, along with the management board of the Victor collective farm, were sending comrade Semyon Yakovlevich Wiseman to study. The collective farm would pay, if necessary, for his right to study, taking all responsibility for his funding; at the same time, it would not leave Wiseman himself in need—that is, it would feed him with products from the earth for as long as necessary, as well as sending him money for equipment and for current cultural pleasures. The village soviet presidium and the management board of the collective farm requested that Wiseman be looked on as someone dear to them, who had often resolved on his fiddle difficult life questions that were impossible to recount and that, if you did recount them, it would not be convincing. His fiddle, however, had been plundered by an unknown enemy and was not to be found in his hands; all that remained was its case, and money had been given to Wiseman for an appropriate acquisition. Should Wiseman's convictions or character happen to spoil—because of the influences of external life—they requested to be informed of this, in order that social funds should not contribute to the downfall of a good man.

In the conservatory Wiseman was told that it was summer, and that the next intake of students would be in the autumn; all that could be done now was to offer him a place in the student hostel.

"But life goes on every minute!" said Wiseman. "When's there to wait?"

"As you please," said the clerk. "Shall I make you out a written authorization for the communal living quarters—or what?"

"But how do I know what I please?" retorted Wiseman, dissatisfied. "My living quarters are the entire USSR, not just a written authorization. I'll be back here by autumn, then we'll see . . ."

Having left the conservatory, Wiseman began going around shops to find himself a new violin. He tried the violins for sound and for a sense of their constituent material, but for some reason he didn't like them; the notes sounded, but they did not emerge from the wood and out into space.

Wandering farther about the city, Wiseman noticed happy, anxious, or enigmatic faces everywhere, and to him they seemed splendid because of an assumption of their soul. He thought that the task of music was the expression of the varied life of strangers, not just of one's own life—one's own life was not enough, a personal body was too narrow to contain an object of eternal and universal interest, while not to live eternally was pointless. And Wiseman tried to choose among the people he encountered: Who among them should he become, in order to learn the mystery of a stranger for the sake of music?

This imagination of another soul, of the unknown sensation of wearing a new body, would not let him be. He thought about the thoughts in another head, walked with someone else's gait, and felt greedy delight with his emptied and ready heart. His torso's youth was being transformed into a greedy lust of mind.

On squares and streets, a smiling, modest Stalin was standing guard over all the open roads of the fresh, socialist world; life was stretching out into a distance from which there was no return.

One pretty girl, with whom you could live half your life, advised Wiseman to get a tram to the Krestov market. Sometimes people dealt in musical instruments there; she went to a music college herself, although she did not study the violin. Semyon Wiseman wanted for a few minutes to turn into her husband, but first he set off for a violin.[2]

2

The Krestov market was full of traders: conscious beggars and secret bourgeois, all of them trying, in dry passions and the risk-taking of despair, to procure their bread. Unclean air hung over this crowded gathering of standing and muttering people. Some were proffering meager goods, clasping them close to their breasts; others were rapaciously asking the price of these goods, touching them and falling into despondency, having counted on eternal acquisition. On sale here were old clothes, cut in the nineteenth century, impregnated with a special powder and kept intact through decades on a careful body. Here were fur coats that had passed through so many hands during the time of the Revolution that a meridian of the terrestrial globe would have been too short for the measurement of their journeys between people. And people were also trading things that had forever lost application—housecoats from some extraordinary women, ornaments from small basins for the baptism of children, the frock coats of now deceased gentlemen, charms on watch chains, chamber pots from the days before the appearance of a sewage system, and so on; but these things still circulated among local humanity, not as necessities but as a currency of strict value.[3] There were also items of clothing from people who had died recently—death had not ceased to exist—as well as petty clothes prepared for infants who had been conceived, but then the mother must have thought twice about giving birth and had an abortion and now she was selling the tiny lamented-over garments of an unborn person along with a rattle purchased in advance.

One row of the market was set aside for original oil portraits and artistical reproductions. The portraits showed long-dead burghers, and brides and bridegrooms from Moscow's encirclement of small towns; each of them, judging by their faces, delighted in their own self and was expressing satisfaction with the life that was happening to them, taking pride in it as if in a well-deserved medal. Behind these figures could sometimes be seen a church, standing amid nature, and oak trees were growing in a long-past summer. One picture was especially large and hung on two poles that had been stuck into the earth. The picture showed a peasant or merchant—a man who was not poor, yet unclean and barefoot. He was standing on a broken wooden porch and, from this height, was peeing downward. His shirt was billowing in the wind, litter and straw could be found in his petty little beard, which was dense with life, and he was looking with equanimity into a desolate world where a pale sun was either rising or setting. Behind the man was a large forlorn-looking house; inside it, most likely, were stored pots of jam and a hundredweight or so of mushroom pies—and there was a wooden bed, equipped almost for eternal sleep. An aging peasant woman was sitting in a glass-covered balcony—all that could be seen was her head—and looking, with the expression of a fool, into an empty place in the yard. Her man had just woken from sleep, and now he had gone out to relieve himself and check whether anything in particular had chanced to happen—but everything remained constant, the wind was blowing from across ragged, unloved fields, and in a moment the man would return to his rest, to sleep and dream no dreams, so as to live through life quickly and without memory.

Wiseman stood for a long time in observation of these past people. Their gravestones were now being used for the pavements of new cities, and somewhere a third or fourth generation was trampling over the inscriptions: "Here is buried the body of Pyotr Nikodimovich Samofalov, merchant of the second guild of the town of Zaraisk. The years of his life were . . . Remember me, O Lord, in thy kingdom." "Here lie the ashes of Anna Vasilievna Strizheva, spinster . . . We must weep and suffer; but she beholdeth the Lord."

Rather than God, it was Semyon Wiseman who had now remembered the dead, and he shuddered from terror of living among them, in the time before the dark forests had been cut down, when a man's wretched heart was eternally faithful to a single feeling, when his circle of acquaintances consisted only of relatives, when his vision of the world was magical and patient—and as for his mind, it languished and the man would weep by the light of a paraffin lamp or, just the same, during a radiant summer noon, amid a spacious nature full of the noise of wind and grass; a time when a pathetic young woman, devoted and faithful, would embrace a tree in her yearning, a silly and sweet girl who had now been forgotten without a sound— and she no longer was and never would be again, nor ought she to be.

Farther on, there were sculptures for sale, along with cups, plates, trivets, details from some balustrade, a weight that weighed twelve old poods, and an iron block that had been dug up in this very spot, so that only the edge of it was visible and the rest of it was underground and unknown. The last private traders in paints and oils were squatting down nearby; demoralized out-of-work locksmiths were hawking hammers, home vises, axes for firewood, a handful of nails. Farther on stretched cobblers, doing jobs on the spot, and old women providers of nourishment: cold pancakes; pies stuffed with butchers' waste; suet buns kept warm in cast-iron pots beneath the padded jackets of the old men, now deceased, who had once been their husbands; slabs of cooked millet; anything, in short, that might relieve the hungry suffering of the local public—who were capable of swallowing any good thing, just as long as it could be swallowed.

Insignificant thieves were wandering about between those with needs and those with goods; they would snatch from your hands a length of cotton, a pair of old felt boots, some bread rolls, a single galosh, then run off into the jungle of stray bodies, earning fifty kopeks or a ruble from each act of plunder. In truth, they barely earned as much as a laborer, while exhausting themselves more.

Here and there amid the market towered wooden booths for policemen. Policemen were looking down from them into this shallow sea of raging, petty imperialism, where there were almost no laborers but where layabouts still remained. The cheap food made an audible noise as it was digested in people, and so each person felt burdened with heaviness, as if they were a complex enterprise, and unclean air rose upwards, like smoke over an ancient village.

In the depth of the market there sometimes resounded invocations of despair, but nobody ever rushed to help, and people went on buying and selling close to a stranger's calamity, because their own grief demanded urgent consolation. A woman selling bread rolls had attacked a weak man wearing a soldier's greatcoat from the old days; having driven him into a pool of urine beside the latrines, she was lashing him across the face with a rag. Now further weakened, the man collapsed beneath the latrine fence—and, springing to the woman's aid, a nomadic hooligan straightaway smashed him in the face till he bled. The man did not let out a cry and did not touch his damaged face; he was hurriedly eating a plundered stale roll, his rotten teeth working hard to grind their way through it, and it did not take him long to complete this task. The hooligan gave him one more blow on the head, and the wounded eater, jumping up with the energy of a strength that was incomprehensible in view of his silent meekness, disappeared in the thick of the crowd, as if among ears of rye. He would find food for himself everywhere and would live for a long time without means and without happiness, yet often eating his fill.

An elderly, unclear-looking man was standing almost motionless in one place, just swaying a little from the bustle. Wiseman had noticed him once before; he went up to him.

"Ration cards for bread," the motionless man pronounced to himself.

"How much?" asked Wiseman.

"Twenty-five rubles for first category."

"Give me one then," said Wiseman, wanting to spend his money on something.

The trader cautiously took from a side pocket an envelope with the printed inscription: FULL PROGRAM OF THE INSTITUTE FOR THE PROCESSING OF MINERAL RESOURCES. Inside this program was a ration card. The same trader also offered to look for a fiddle for him, but Wiseman acquired a fiddle for himself later, from a man who was selling his instrument in order to buy worms for fishing bait and who grumbled at every passerby, as if they were enemies of the State.

Before making his purchase, the musician had wanted to try out the fiddle, but tightly packed people were all the time hindering him. Then he had climbed up into the policeman's box, and the policeman had moved aside to make room for the musician. From the height of this superstructure Wiseman had begun to play. No one down below had listened to him. People here had long ago got used to all human facts; music could not penetrate every clamoring heart already encumbered by cares of its own. But this chance violin played well. It looked coarse—it was made from a dark material heavier than wood—and it made by itself a sound that was nobler and more heartfelt than a musician could. Semyon Wiseman listened to its singing as if he himself were listening from the outside and felt surprised that all the vast, surrounding air was shaking from the weak friction of the bow yet people were paying no attention. He consulted the policeman about this, and the latter explained, "What do you expect? This is where the last bourgeois element is wandering about. He's been allotted a place in this enclosure, and now he's alone with his yearning."

"He's perishing," said Wiseman.

"What do you expect? Some thieve, some beg, some trade . . . The bourgeois has a soul of his own; he'll live his life out, then he'll die."

"But why don't they work?" asked the fiddler.

"What can I say?" The policeman looked deep into the crowd. "There's one sort of man you can get to change with a word and there's another sort who'll change if you punish him—those two sorts are all right, they've been living like people for a long time now. But there are other men—like this bunch here—who won't listen to anything except death. If they're to become people, they need to live two lives, one after the other. This is a boring place, citizen. Get on now with whatever you have to do—don't hinder me in my external observation."

Hunched from despondency, Wiseman left the Krestov market forever. This place too would soon cease to exist, as the spinster, Anna Vasilievna Strizhevaya, no longer existed, and as that unclean, barefoot merchant who had pissed from his porch into an unwelcoming, weather-blown world had also died.

3

Since then Semyon Wiseman had been living in Moscow. The very crowds woke strength in his heart; he walked among people as if in enchantment, and he sensed their body and the warmth it gave off. He used to walk until evening; under socialism it is possible to become a happy tramp, if there is a melody in one's heart that is fitting for everyone.

The musician did not think about shelter until late at night, and he walked about with his fiddle, parallel to people's common movement, amid light, cleanliness, and warmth. He felt that it was impossible to perish here, to remain without attention, food, and care, if there was no hostility within him toward people. And he truly did not remain unnoticed. Wiseman ended up spending his first Moscow night in the room of a tram conductress.

He made her acquaintance by chance. After one o'clock in the morning, when the trams were speeding back to their depots, Wiseman had got on board one of them and begun to examine its deserted interior with interest, as if the thousands of people who had been there during the day had left their breath and the best of their feeling on the empty seats. Wiseman had repeated his journey and traveled in various directions in a number of tramcars. The conductress—sometimes an old woman, sometimes a woman who was young, sweet, and sleepy—would be sitting alone in the car at this hour, pulling the cord at the unfrequented stops so that this last journey would soon be over. Wiseman had gone up to these conductresses and begun to talk about something unrelated, that had nothing to do with all the reality apparent around them—but the conductress would then begin to perceive something invisible inside herself. One conductress from a rear car had yielded to the musician's words and he had embraced her en route; they then moved to the back of the car, where it was harder to see, and they went on kissing and were carried away past three stops, until a man on the boulevard noticed them and called out: "Hurrah!"

After that, he tried now and again to repeat this friendship with a nighttime conductress—sometimes successfully but more often not. The first night's conductress had invited him back when he had said he wanted to sleep, and she had put him beside her grandmother on a wide bed from the old days, where he had slept well.

Another evening Semyon Wiseman went out onto the boulevard where the Pushkin monument stands. He left his violin case below and entered—up to the foot of the monument, onto the height of all its steps.[4] From there, imagining himself before the whole of Moscow, he played his favorite composition about a sparrow—about how a sparrow flew somewhere not far away in search of simple grain and ate his fill there amid numerous animals. But the fiddle played away almost of its own accord, and the fiddler followed cautiously as its melody grew more complex; the musical theme broadened and the sparrow's fate changed. The sparrow failed to reach the nearby food; the element of wind snatched him up and carried him far away, into terror, and the speed of his own flight made him numb—but he met night, and the darkness hid space and height from him. The sparrow grew warm, fell asleep, huddled in his sleep into a little ball and fell downwards, into a thicket, onto a small, soft branch; he awoke in silence, in the dawn of an unknown day, amid exultant and unfamiliar birds. The passersby listened spellbound to the musician, and into his violin case on the ground flowed almost uninterrupted earnings. Ashamed that people should think he was a beggar, Wiseman did not know what to do with the money.

A young metro worker, with a forlorn look and with her feet wide apart like a peasant woman, was standing not far away and listening to Wiseman. She was wearing a man's overalls, which only laid bare her woman's nature. There was charm and intelligence in her face, which was framed by dark hair; clarity of heart shone in her eyes, and the traces of clay and machine oil from underground work did not spoil her body so much as adorn it—a mark of honor and immaculate purity.

While he was playing, the musician looked at the young metro worker with equanimity and without attention, not attracted by any of her charm—as an artist, he always felt within his own soul some still better and more manly charm that drew his will on ahead, past ordinary delight. Toward the end of his play, tears came from Wiseman's eyes. He himself liked the music, and he was moved—but many of his listeners were smiling, while the metro worker was laughing out loud.

Wiseman came down from the monument and turned angrily to this metro worker. "Shame on you, you public! You don't know how to think yet, but you have a good laugh at feeling. You nonentity of a nobody!"

"It's not you playing—you don't know how to play like that," said the metro worker. "I know that violin. Even I can play on that violin."

"And what does a silly little girl know? A silly little girl with nothing to show for herself but a pretty face?" After this appraisal, Wiseman went on: "And as for me, maybe the entire Soviet Union is stirring inside my mind."

"Like that, is it?" the metro worker pronounced enigmatically. "You think you're a famous musician—which means you're a boring fool."

She left him and went about her business, but he followed her all the way back to her dwelling, until she disappeared inside. After committing to memory the place of this metro worker's life, Wiseman got into some tram or other and rode a long way on it, far outside the city. There he wandered about in anguish, sat down beside a field of rye, played his fiddle in wordless solitude, and remained unable to understand its method of construction: Why did his play make this fiddle play away of its own accord without fully listening to him and obeying him? He did not know physics or technology; he could only feel the passions of the soul and the anxious, tense movement of the human heart. The human heart, though, was not a solid body, whereas the fiddle was something entirely hard and evident. Far-removed Moscow was humming tenderly, like a large orchestra; the sky just above the horizon reflected the city's electrical glow onto the earth, and the poorest of lights already reached as far as the fields, lying on the ears of rye like a false, early dawn. But it was still late night. Semyon Wiseman listened to faraway Moscow with lust, looked at the sky's electrical dawn, and thought how all this was secret music—and once again he set his fiddle in motion and listened as everything apparently wild and mute gathered around it and accompanied his inexpert play through virginal, parched lips.

4

Metro construction worker Lida Osipova, who had been listening to the fiddler's play by the Pushkin monument, lived on the fourth floor of a new building, in two small rooms. This building was a home to pilots, aircraft designers, engineers of all kinds, philosophers, economic theorists, and other professions. The windows of her apartment looked out over the neighboring Moscow roofs and sometimes, after she had come back from her shift and had a wash, Lida would lean out of the window with her stomach against the sill. Her hair would hang down and she would listen to the noise of the universal city in all its triumphant energy, and to the occasional laughing human voice that rose up from the dense and sonorous mass of mechanisms in motion. Raising her head, Lida would see an empty, destitute moon climb into the extinguished sky, and she would feel inside her a warming current of life. Her imagination was continually at work and had never yet tired—in her mind she could sense the origin of matters of every kind and she took part mentally in their existence; in her solitude she filled the whole world with her attention, watching over the flames of streetlamps so they would go on shining, thinking about the machines that exerted their power day and night so light would burn in the darkness, so books would go on being read, so rye could be milled by electric motors in time for the early-morning bake, and so water could be pumped through pipes into the warm showers of dance halls and the conception of a better life could take place in people's ardent and firm embraces, in the dark, in privacy, without sight of faces, in the pure emotion of a conjoined happiness—so that, in a word, the city of her youth, the world capital of human labor, intelligence, and true human kindness should shine with fire and gleam with joy. What Lida Osipova wanted was not so much to experience and delight in this life as to safeguard its success; she wanted to stand night and day by the brake lever of the locomotive that was taking people to meet one another; she wanted to repair water mains, to ride on a steam roller compacting new asphalt, to weigh out medicines for patients on pharmaceutical scales, to be a lamp that goes out just at the right moment, as others kiss, taking into itself the warmth that a moment before had been light. She was not, however, denying her own needs—she too wanted somewhere to put her large body; she was simply postponing these needs to a more distant future, since she was patient and able to wait.

When Lida hung out of her window during these evenings of solitude, passersby would shout greetings to her from below, calling her to come out and share the summer dusk with them, promising to show her all the attractions of the Park of Culture and Rest and to buy her flowers and two gateaux. Lida laughed in reply, but said nothing and did not go.

Later, from above, Lida would see the roofs of the old houses in the neighborhood begin to be populated; whole families would make their way through attics onto these metal roofs, spreading out blankets and then lying down to sleep in the fresh air, mothers and fathers placing their children between them; courting couples would go off on their own into the ravines between roofs, somewhere between the chimney and the fire escape, and, located below the stars yet above the multitude of humanity, would not close their eyes until morning.

After midnight almost all the windows in sight would stop shining—the day's shock labor required deep oblivion in sleep—and late cars would whisper by, not disturbing anyone with superfluous signals. Only occasionally would these extinguished windows briefly light up again; night-shift workers were coming home, having something to eat without waking the sleepers, and then going straight to bed, while workers who had already had their fill of sleep—turbine operators and engine drivers, radio technicians, scientific researchers, aircraft mechanics manning early flights, and others who were now rested—were getting up to leave for work.

Lida Osipova would often forget to close the door into her apartment. Once she found a stranger asleep on the floor, lying facedown on his coat. Lida waited for him to turn over and at once recognized in him the musician who had been playing beside Pushkin. Wiseman had come in without asking; he had put his fiddle away in the toilet. On waking, he said he wanted to live with her for a while—it was spacious and he liked it here. Lida Osipova could not bring herself to push communism away into the distance because of the paucity of housing and her own right to additional living space; she said nothing and gave her lodger a pillow and a blanket. Semyon Wiseman began his life there; at night he would get up, then tiptoe over to the sleeping Lida and pull her blanket back over her—because she used to toss and turn, throwing the bedclothes off and getting chilled. In the morning he never used the toilet in the apartment, not wanting to burden it with his own filth and make a noise with the water; he would go instead to the public toilet in the yard below. After a few days of life in Osipova's apartment, the fiddler was reinforcing the heels on Lida's worn-down best shoes, secretly brushing off bits of dirt that had stuck to her autumn coat, and heating water for tea in joyous anticipation of his landlady's awakening. At first Lida scolded the fiddler for his servility, but after a while, to put an end to such slavery, she introduced a regime of socialist self-sufficiency, darning her lodger's socks and even shaving his stubble with a safety razor.

When Lida went out to work, Wiseman quietly began to play the fiddle, trying to divine the secret of its magical construction. But the fiddle looked ordinary and cheap—and yet windowpanes, walls, furniture, ceiling lights, and empty air all responded to its sounds, singing together like an orchestra. But when Lida was at home, Wiseman was afraid to play.

Not once did Wiseman dare to ask her about the secret of his instrument or the meaning of her mocking words beside the monument. Nevertheless, Wiseman understood that there was no one else he could turn to: only from this black-haired girl could he learn the truth of the new music that sang, in any dead substance, like a living feeling. And so he had appeared, to live with her and to try and love her in everything.

Soon Wiseman found out that Lida Osipova worked as a drilling technician, and this encouraged him to remain with her further, since she was an educated person.

One night, when he was covering her up in his usual way as she slept, he heard her happy laughter, and she whispered the unclear words: "I'm bored, my darling. I miss you."

Semyon Wiseman asked her straightaway, "Whose is this fiddle, my darling?"

Lida opened her eyes.

"Why?"

"Well, I need to—" But Wiseman was afraid to embrace her straightaway.

"What do you need?" said Lida as she came to herself. "I'll tell you tomorrow—it's hardly an urgent matter." And she slept on further.

In the morning she told Wiseman that there would be a ball in the evening. He should go there together with his fiddle—he didn't really want to carry on idling away until autumn, did he?

"But whose is this fiddle, my darling?" asked Wiseman. "Please tell me!"

Lida looked slowly up and down the whole of the fiddler's torso.

"*My darling*? What's all this about? This fiddle is made out of waste from the laboratory of my fiancé. And it's he who calls me darling. Understand?"

"Yes," said Wiseman. "I'm not such a philistine as all that. I'm someone special."

"So I see!" said Lida, without attention and without offense.

5

That evening, in the district Komsomol Club, there was a gathering of young scientists, engineers, pilots, doctors, teachers, performing artists, and famous workers from the new factories. No one was over the age of twenty-seven or thirty, yet each was already known throughout the new world of their motherland—and this early fame made them all feel a slight shame, which hindered their lives and covered their faces with an excessive excitement. The men and women who worked at the club, who were older and who had wasted their lives and talent during the unfortunate bourgeois time, let out secret sighs of inner impoverishment as they arranged the furnishings in the two halls, setting up one for a formal meeting and the other for conversation and dining. Among the first to arrive were Poluvarov, a twenty-four-year-old engineer, and Kuzmina, a pianist and Komsomol member who was constantly lost in thought from the imagination of music.

"Let's go fill our faces!" said Poluvarov.

"Yes, let's!" Kuzmina agreed.

They went over to the bar. Poluvarov, a pink-cheeked and powerful eater, immediately consumed eight pieces of bread and sausage, while Kuzmina took only two pastries; what she lived for was play, not the digestion of food.

"Poluvarov, why do you eat such a lot?" asked Kuzmina. "Maybe it's good, but looking at you makes me ashamed!"

Poluvarov ate with indignation; he chewed as he had plowed, with insistent labor, with zeal in both of his trusty jaws.

After a while, ten more people arrived together: Golovach the explorer; Gausman the mechanical engineer; two girls who were friends, both of them hydraulic engineers from the Moscow-Volga canal; Vechkin the aviation meteorologist; Muldbauer the designer of high-altitude aircraft engines; and the electrical engineer Gunkin, with his wife. Then came the sound of other voices, and some more people arrived; among them were Lida Osipova and Wiseman the fiddler.

Last of all appeared the surgeon Sambikin; he had come straight from the clinic, where he had been performing a trepanation on a small boy. He arrived crushed by the sorrow of the construction of the human body, which squeezes between its own bones far more suffering, exhaustion, and death than life and movement. And Sambikin found it strange to be feeling well now, in the tension of his own concern and responsibility for the improvement of every thin and tormented human body. His whole mind was filled with thought, his heart was beating calmly and truly, he had no need of any better happiness than to be in charge of another person's heartbeat—and yet, at the same time, consciousness of his secret delight was beginning to make him feel ashamed. He was about to go up and read his paper, because the bell had already rung, but he suddenly caught sight of a young woman he did not know, standing beside a violinist and chatting to him. The unclear charm of her outward appearance surprised Sambikin; concealed behind the modesty and even timidity of her face, he could see power and luminous inspiration. Trembling from an unexpected, mysterious feeling, Sambikin went out for a moment onto the open balcony.

The Moscow night shone in the darkness outside, sustained by the tension of distant machines; the excited air, warmed by millions of people, was penetrating Sambikin's heart in the form of anguish. He glanced at the stars, into the magical space of the dark, and whispered old words he had heard and remembered: "My God!"

Then Sambikin went into the hall, where his comrades and colleagues had already gathered. He was going to read a paper about the most recent developments in the institute where he worked. The subject of his paper was human immortality.

The young woman with the attractive face was in the second row; the violinist was still beside her, sitting there with his instrument. The smile of youth, and a senseless charm, made her beautiful, but she herself did not notice this... Sambikin and his comrades in the institute wanted to obtain a long power of life, maybe an eternity of it, from the corpses of beings who had fallen. A few years back, while digging about in people's dead bodies, Sambikin had found faint traces, in the region of their heart, of some unknown substance, and he had been perplexed by it. He had studied it and discovered that this substance was endowed with the power to stimulate a weakening life—as if at the moment of death some kind of mysterious sluice opens in the human body, and from it there flows around the organism a special moisture that has been carefully preserved all through life, up until the supreme danger. The role of this moisture is to wash away all the dust and pus of exhaustion.

But where in the darkness, in the bodily ravines of a human being, is this sluice that faithfully and miserlily preserves the last charge of life? Only death, when it rushes through the body like an indifferent wave, can break the seal on that reserve of clenched life—and then, like an unsuccessful shot, this life resounds inside a person for the last time and leaves unclear traces on his dead heart...

The wandering beam of a distant searchlight stopped by chance on the club's huge windows. Through an ensuing moment of silence came the sound of pile drivers on the Moscow River, letting off steam and hammering down their piles. Lida Osipova began to seem anxious, glancing around whenever anyone came into the hall. She went several times to the telephone, to ring whomever she was expecting, but she received no answer from there; probably the apparatus was out of order, and she came back, keeping her sorrow to herself.

Then the guests all moved to the other room, where the table had been laid for a shared supper, and they returned to an argument about immortality; how it had been the one-eyed, prehistoric Cyclopes—the very first proletarians—who had built Greece and the hills of Olympus; how Zeus himself had been no more than a convict with a gouged-out eye, a convict who had then been deified by the clever aristocracy in honor of his labor that had formed an entire country; and about many other things. Semyon Wiseman sat there, filling with knowledge, like an empty sack, in which, somewhere imperceptible, lived only the ghosts and scents of light feelings.

Every half meter there were flowers, looking pensive because of their delayed death and giving off a posthumous fragrance. The wives of the designers—and the young women who worked as engineers, philosophers, brigade leaders, and supervisors—were dressed in the finest silk of the Republic; the government liked to adorn its best people. Lida Osipova was wearing a deep blue dress, which weighed only around ten grams and had been so skillfully sewn that even the pulsing of her blood vessels and anxiety of her heart was revealed by the rippling of the silk. All the men, even the careless Sambikin and Vechkin, the unkempt meteorologist, had come in suits that were simple but precious, made from first-class material; to dress badly and dirtily would have been to reproach with poverty the country that had nourished everyone present and dressed them with her choicest goods, herself thriving on this youth's strength and compression, on its labor and talent.

Sambikin asked Wiseman to play something: Why, after all, did he never part from his fiddle?

Wiseman stood up and with a transparent, happy strength began to play his music—in the midst of young Moscow, into her noisy night, over the heads of now silent people who were beautiful from nature or from inspired animation and unfinished youth. The whole world around him suddenly became abrupt and intransigent—it was composed entirely of hard heavy objects, and a coarse, harsh force was acting with such fury that it was itself falling into despair and crying with a human, emaciated voice on the edge of its own silence. And once again this force was rising up out of its own iron arena and, with the speed of a howl, was routing some cold, stone enemy of its own that occupied with its dead torso the whole of infinity. This music was losing all melody and turning into a strident howl of attack, yet it still had the rhythm of an ordinary human heart and was as simple as labor beyond one's strength performed out of vital need.

But as he played, Wiseman was again unable to understand his own instrument: Why did the fiddle play better than he himself could? Why did the fiddle's dead and pathetic substance produce from itself additional living sounds that played not on the theme but deeper than the theme and more skillfully than the hand of the fiddler? Semyon Wiseman's hand merely troubled the fiddle; it was the fiddle itself that sang and led the melody forward, drawing to its aid the hidden harmony of the surrounding space—and the whole sky then served as a screen for the music, waking in nature's dark essence a response in kind to the agitation of the human heart.

Lida covered her face with her hands and began to cry, unable to conceal her grief. Leaving their places, everyone present went up to her. Wiseman put down his fiddle in bewilderment. The meeting's universal joy was cut short.

"Listen," Lida Osipova said to her neighboring comrades. "Has anyone got a car? I need to leave."

"In a moment," said Sambikin.

He called for a car by telephone. Ten minutes later Lida Osipova, Sambikin, and Wiseman set off, following Lida's directions.

Not far from Kalanchev Square the car turned into a narrow alley and stopped. It was impossible to go any farther. Fire engines were standing there, even though there was no sign of fire anywhere and all that could be heard was some kind of tender and threatening melody.

In the remoteness of the alley was located a small one-story building with a sign stating that this was the V. I. Grubov factory for the production of measuring weights and new heavy masses.[5] An ambulance was standing right by the factory gates. The beam of the fire engine's searchlight was illuminating one window of the main building; behind this window, inside the building, an independent violet light was shining statically. Ready for anything, the firemen were standing in a chain opposite the window and undertaking no measures; a man was lying inside the little factory and it was not known if he was alive or dead.

With a cold heart Lida Osipova sized up the situation, but suddenly, without action of mind or heart, she cried out in her high, naïve voice and rushed at the factory—through the line of firemen, who were too slow to seize her.

For a few minutes they waited for her, but she fell silent there and did not come back. The chief fireman ordered the building's outside wall to be dismantled and the people inside to be extricated with the help of some long devices.

The tender, threatening singing continued, spreading out onto the entire alley and rising toward the electrical glow of nighttime Moscow.

Wiseman recognized this voice of space and wild surrounding substance that until then had always been dead and mute; it was the voice of his fiddle, which was now lying in its case in his hands. He raised the case to his ear and listened: all the instrument's material was singing something and, changing the melody, was following an unknown and touching theme, but the external hum and bustle of people made it difficult to catch the thought of the music.

"That fiddle's mine, comrade. You must have been saying thank you for it—except that you had no one to say it to."

Wiseman recognized the man who had been trading fishing worms at the Krestov market and from whom he chanced to have bought his fiddle. He was a man of some years, and he turned out to be working as a watchman outside this weights factory; before that he had been a woodworker and, out of love for nature, had used to go fishing.

"What's going on here?" asked Wiseman. "Some chance emergency?"

"It'll soon be over…Vladimir Ivanovich has collapsed in the laboratory again. He's gone rigid."[6]

"Who's he?"

"Who's he! Read the signboard—that's who he is! But he'll come around, he'll get over it."

"Get over what?"

"Who…what…who…what," grumbled the old man. "Get over whatever it was…Come to from his task…Next thing we know the woman will be lying rigid in there beside him."

"What woman?"

"There you go again! She was standing with you just now. Vladimir Ivanovich's woman—his fiancée."

The strange deep sound stopped; the sad light in the laboratory window faded. Lida Osipova appeared in the doorway of the office by the factory gate and said to the firemen, "Quick, come here now, stop spoiling the building! There's no danger anymore. The current's off."

The firemen went inside the building and carried out a silent man, dressed in the rags of former clothing. He was taken to the ambulance.

"No, I want to go home," said engineer Grubov. "Where's Lida?"

"Bring him over here!" Sambikin opened the door of his car. "We'll go to the institute," he said to the driver.

The exhausted man was carried to the car. In places his body was visible, and it was covered with the dense moisture of sweat, as if he had struggled beyond his strength, but his face was healthy and his eyes were declining into sleep.

"Hello there!" Sambikin said to Grubov.

"Hello!" replied the sick engineer.

"We're going to our institute. I can help you," Sambikin said as the firemen got Grubov into the car.

"I don't want that," said Grubov.

"But it's very interesting indeed. I'll infuse you with something I've obtained from a corpse. It's a most intriguing experiment. I advise you to experience it."

"All right then, let's go," Grubov immediately agreed.

"Wait!" The night watchman, the author of Wiseman's fiddle, put his head through the car window. "Vladimir Ivanovich, what happened in there? Did you collapse?"

"Yes, Sidor Petrovich, I went rigid."

"I wanted to go in after you, you know. But something was pushing at me, pushing me back."

"You mustn't, Sidor Petrovich. It'll kill you."

"Then I won't. But can I take the waste products? I want to make two more fiddles. They'll be the last ones."

"All right, Sidor Petrovich, take them . . . Go and sleep now. I'm worn out too."

They drove off. The alley emptied. Only Sidor Petrovich and Wiseman were left.

6

Living, in his customary way, wherever life took him, and even by means of the life of a stranger, Semyon Wiseman stayed in the weights factory. He was appointed as a manual worker, and he began to live with Sidor Petrovich in his room in the factory yard. Soon the watchman had taught Wiseman to make fiddles. The watchman made them in an ordinary way, and he did not know any ancient art—it was simply that what he took for his work was dark, shining material from Grubov's laboratory; this material was no longer precise enough for the engineer and was being thrown out. All the same, Wiseman was still unable to understand why natural substance should play inside itself almost of its own accord and more intelligently than the fiddler's art. Sidor Petrovich did not know this either, and he was not even interested.

For two whole months Wiseman languished, unable to find anything out, until the factory moved over to the production of new weights. There was a shortage of weights in the collective farms; the collective farmers' bread, the recording of their workdays, the storage of the harvest—that most precious shared good of all—depended on the presence of accurate weights. It was important to produce them quickly, and many workers were being sent on short courses to upgrade their qualifications. Wiseman too was sent off to learn this new work. Then small electric machines appeared in the factory, similar to radio receivers. These machines emitted an abrupt, atomizing, invisible force, which made the material being processed first sing sadly and then fall silent, ready for fabrication. The materials for the weights were clay, plastic, plain earth, and everything cheap and accessible. After being worked over by electricity, this substance became hard and stable, like metal.

Engineer Grubov explained to the workers that the world, especially those of its places that have been worked over by man, is constructed from infirm material, since every petty molecular part of it has been beaten out by fire, labor, machines, and other events from the best place of its birth and is now suffering anguish as it wanders about within substance. High-frequency electric current and ultrasonic oscillation quickly return molecules to their ancient places; nature becomes healthy and stable, molecules come to life, they begin to give out a harmonic resonance, that is, they respond to any irritation by means of sound, warmth, and electricity and even continue to sing of their own accord when the irritation has ceased, letting it be known in their distant voice that they are suffering and resisting. And this sound has turned out to be comprehensible to humanity—a human heart, when it bears the tension of art, sings in almost the same way, only less precisely and more unclearly.

"The truth of all this has been proved correct by Sidor Petrovich's violins," Grubov once said at a production meeting. "These violins are made from material of a quality too poor for measurement weights. Out of our waste he has received music ... But now I think we need to make a few fiddles out of real material ..."

Grubov smiled and his face, darkened by long labor, turned meek and young. This man had lived many times through deathly sufferings brought about by the cruel, wild forces of electricity; only on the edge of his own grave had he learned the fate of dead substance and changed it as much as he could.

Semyon Wiseman worked at the weights factory until September, but then he disappeared—no one knew where. Big Moscow drew him in, the crowds acted on him like an inspiration, and the heart of a stranger was more interesting than his own. He wanted to test his soul in all the multifarious fate of the new world—not only in the capacity of a fiddler, not only within the narrow limits of his own torso and talent.

Comrades from his collective farm searched for him that autumn all over Moscow, but they found only faint signs of Wiseman in the form of documents about where he had been living. But nowhere could they find the living Wiseman; he had lost himself among people and had, perhaps, changed his face, surname, and character. His country was great and good.[7]

*Translated by Robert and Elizabeth Chandler
and Olga Meerson*

ON THE FIRST
SOCIALIST TRAGEDY[1]

IT IS ESSENTIAL not to thrust oneself forward and not to get drunk on life; our time is both better and more serious than blissful delight. Everyone who gets drunk is sure to be caught, sure to perish like a little mouse that messes with a mousetrap in order to "get drunk" on the fat on the bait. All around us lies fat, but every piece of this fat is bait. It is necessary to stand in the ranks of the ordinary people doing patient socialist work—that is all we can do.

> No, you must carry out your obstinate,
> Difficult duty, the tasks your fate demands
> Of you, then suffer quietly and die.
> —Alfred de Vigny

But it is, of course, a matter not of death but of victory.[2]

The actual arrangement of nature corresponds to this consciousness. Nature is not great and is not abundant.[3] Or—to be more precise—her design is so rigid that she has never yet yielded her greatness and abundance to anyone. And this is a good thing; otherwise—in historical time—we would long ago have looted and squandered all nature; we would have got drunk on her right through to her very bones. We would always have had appetite enough. Had the physical world been without what is, admittedly, its most fundamental law—the law of the dialectic—it would have taken people only a few centuries to destroy the world completely and to no purpose. More than that, in the absence of this law, nature would have annihilated herself to smithereens even without any people. The dialectic is probably an expression of miserliness, of the almost insuperable rigidity of nature's construction—and it is only thanks to all this that humanity's historical development has been possible. Otherwise everything would long ago have come to an end on this earth—like a game played by a child with sweets that melt in his hands before he has even had time to eat them.

Where lies the essence of the contemporary historical tragedy? It lies, in my view, in the fact that "technology decides everything."[4] The relationship between nature and technology is, in principle, tragic. The class struggle, the question of the defense of the USSR and victory over imperialism, is now also, above all, a matter of technology.

Technology's aim is "Give me a fulcrum and I shall overturn the world."[5] But nature's construction is such that she does not allow herself to be outmaneuvered. With the right moment of force it is possible to overturn the world, but so much will be lost in the journey and in the travel time of the lever that in practical terms the victory will be useless. This is an elementary episode of the dialectic. Let us look now at a fact from our own time: the splitting of the atomic nucleus. There is no direct gain in power; that is, it is still impossible to expend n quantity of energy and receive $n + 1$. But the genius of technology lies on oblique paths. What is required for the destruction of the atom are "favorable" powers of nature—a "following wind," let us say, of cosmic rays; only then will the overall balance turn out positive.

Nature herself, if we look straight at her, stays aloof; a quid pro quo—or even a trade with a markup in her own favor—is the only way she can work. Technology, however, strains to achieve the opposite. The external world is defended against us by its own dialectic. The entire art of technology depends on the favorable side winds of nature, who herself acts for the sake of her own concentrated interests.

In sociology, in love, in the depth of a human being, the dialectic is no less immutable and invincible if one confronts it directly. A man with a ten-year-old son left the boy with the boy's mother—and married a young beauty. The boy began to long for his father and patiently, clumsily hanged himself. A gram of delight on one end of the lever is balanced by a ton of graveyard earth on the other.

The father took the rope from the boy's neck and soon followed him into the grave. What he wanted was to get drunk on an innocent beauty; he wanted to bear love not as a duty, not as an obligation with a single wife, but as pleasure. *Don't get drunk—or it will be the end of you.*[6] *The world you find yourself in is difficult and wretchedly poor.*

Ideology is located not on some external height, not in the "superstructure," but in the very heart of man and of his social feeling.

History as a universal tragedy began along with mankind, but it is technology that serves as its final act. In the West this tragedy is moving not toward a resolution but toward destruction, toward the cancellation of the theme by means of fascism and war. It is only in our country that the theme given to us is being resolved.

I want art to be not merely a "reflection" but a precise prophecy of new cyclopic works—for the sake of changing the life that exists everywhere, which is like the copulation of the blind in nettles.

Technology—originally a form of self-defense on the part of the slaves of slaves, and then the working class's way of defending itself against mortal exploitation—is still to some degree a means of class struggle. But in the USSR it is already taking on another quality and another purpose. The working class, having spent an entire century working on the sheer substance of nature, has acquired such a creative technological potential that now, ennobled by socialism, it is constructing a technology capable, in the course of one or two decades, of making this class into the mind of nature, with absolute power in practical dimensions.

But man himself changes more slowly than he changes the world. This is the center of the tragedy. This is why we need creative engineers of human souls. They must prevent the danger of the human soul being left far behind by technology. Even now man is no longer on the same level as history.

In the optimal conditions for technical progress that exist in our country, we live on the eve of a substantive conquest of the world—on the eve of the regulation of all the world's processes, until now spontaneous, that are of practical importance to us. Yes, but contemporary man, even his very best representatives, is inadequate. He is not armed with the kind of soul, the kind of heart and consciousness that will one day allow him, finding himself at the head of nature, to fulfill his duty and heroic deed to the end and not destroy, for the sake of some psychological game, the entire construction of the world and his own self. Here the dramatic situation has a purely Soviet content, a content that is purely "ours." Socialism can be seen as the tragedy of the soul under tension, trying to overcome its own wretched poverty, in order that the most distant future should be insured against catastrophe.

In the formula about the engineers of human souls is hidden the theme of the first purely socialist drama. In a few years this problem will become more important than metallurgy; all science, technology, and metallurgy—all our weapons of power over nature—will be of no use if they are inherited by an unworthy society. More than this, an imperfect Man will then create out of history such a tragedy without end and without resolution that his own heart will grow tired.

But this will not happen if we work now. If we become real engineers and inventors of human souls—rather than their foremen.[7]

To carry out this task, we must first of all create a socialist soul within our own selves.

I once saw, amid the Soviet intelligentsia, how a young woman had been made to feel sad. She was an extraordinarily gifted chemist, but she was plain. Everyone was having a merry time in a summer garden, but no one was paying attention to her as a woman and comrade. Everyone was throwing summer flowers and confetti around, but she was sitting awkwardly to one side, alien and alone. The celebration continued further into the evening. Then this young woman secretly gathered up flowers and scraps of paper that had fallen near her neighbors, went away with them into the darkness, behind the trees, scattered them over her own hair and neck, and came back smiling, her eyes shining through tears. When she was still at a distance, a handsome and brilliant engineer rose to his feet to meet her and, red with shame, began to dance with her, and to spend all that remained of the evening with her.

None of this is good. A man of socialist soul would have noticed this woman before she went into the garden to weep and scatter scraps of paper over herself.

Translated by Robert and Elizabeth Chandler
and Olga Meerson, with Jonathan Platt

FATHER[1]

(A Screenplay)

MAIN CHARACTERS
ZHENYA, age 22–24, assistant locomotive driver
KATYA BESSONET-FAVOR, age 20–22
CONDUCTRESS, age 25–30
STEPAN, age 8–10, but looks younger
IVAN (VANYA) BEZGADOV, age 26–28, manager of a cinema
KONSTANTIN NEVERKIN, age 22–23
POSTMAN, around 40
LUCIEN, a Negro, a locomotive driver
BLIND OLD MAN
BOY, age 5–6, the old man's guide
HAPPY REGISTRY OFFICE OFFICIAL

NOTES FOR THE PRODUCER

The film should be directed and acted in a dry, severe, economical fashion, without the least sentimentality. Chaplin's *A Woman of Paris* exemplifies the style most appropriate for the theme of this screenplay.

The role of the boy Stepan must be played not unconsciously—as so often happens when children act in films—but with artistic skill and, once again, without the least sentimentality or childlike "charm." The screenplay relies, above all, on the performances of the actors.

The central melodic theme for the soundtrack should, I think, be Beethoven's "Marmotte."

—The author

Late night. A Moscow boulevard (the "A" ring, for example).[2] Occasional human figures.

An empty tram moves along the roadway behind the trees of the boulevard.

The only person in the rear car is a CONDUCTRESS.

The tram stops.

A single passenger enters the rear car.

The tram moves on.

Fleeting strips of light from its windows illuminate the almost empty boulevard: trees, benches, footpaths, soft-drink kiosks, Eskimo ice-cream signs, a few figures walking in pairs.

On the end platform of the fast-moving rear car stands a couple: a POSTMAN and a conductress.

The postman gently places his hand on the conductress's shoulder.

With his other hand he strokes her bag of money.

The light from the windows races across the boulevard fence: the tram speeds along.

A dimly lit spot on the boulevard: a man and a woman are standing there.

The man kisses the woman.

(Increasingly loud noise of the approaching tram.)

The man stays close to the woman.

Strips of light from the tram race across them, across their clothes and faces.

The tram stops on the other side of the fence—opposite the kissing couple on the boulevard.

On the platform of the rear car the postman kisses the conductress.

From outside—from a different point of view—the stationary tram.

The driver looks out—and back down the empty street.

The driver disappears back to his place.

The boulevard with the figures of the man and woman, as before, standing in an embrace.

Opposite them is the tram.

End platform of the rear car: pressing up to the conductress, the postman raises his left hand.

He pulls the signal rope.

The tram moves.

The man on the boulevard leans away from the woman.

Hurrah!—he shouts and waves in the direction of the tram as it moves off.

The platform with the two figures quickly vanishes into the distance. The tram rings its bells.

The boulevard. The same two figures.

Hurrah, comrade!—the man shouts from the boulevard.

WOMAN: Behave yourself, Vanya! You should shave more often, if you want to kiss. You're scratchy.

MAN: Learn to be patient. You're going to be a wife.

He takes her arm.

WOMAN: If you don't shave, I'll paint my lips. You'll be poisoned.

MAN: No I won't: I'll spit myself free.

They set off along the boulevard, receding into the distance.

They walk along the pavement, past buildings.

The long, guttural cry of a man in torment, like a child's lament.

Signs: VENEREAL CLINIC, NIGHT CLINIC.

The façade of a large building. A small garden.

The first floor. Windows are open, and light from the windows falls on the virginal green of the bushes in the garden. It is from these windows that the suffering voice comes.

The man (BEZGADOV) and the woman (ZHENYA) stop by the wall with the sign.

The suffering voice in the window of the clinic quietens a little.

ANOTHER, CALM VOICE *(the doctor's)*: Shout, shout again…
Come on! Why aren't you shouting?

THE SUFFERER'S VOICE: In a moment… But don't you have any
painkilling medicine? It's hurting, it's hurting again! *(Cries out as
before.)*

THE DOCTOR'S VOICE: But loving, and kissing—that felt good,
didn't it? Now sing, sing! That's it, that's it.

> *Zhenya and Bezgadov in a square.*[3]
> *Ripped-up roadway. A trench. Floodlights shining over it.*
> *Trucks. Workers.*

ZHENYA: What was he yelling about? Was he having something
like an abortion?[4]

BEZGADOV: Something like that.

ZHENYA: Did you ever have one?

BEZGADOV: No. I'm a baby maker.

ZHENYA: They're tearing our building in half.

BEZGADOV: Where are we going to live when we're married?

ZHENYA: We can stay where we are. Our half of the building will
still be here. It's a shame: the people who're being evicted are getting apartments in new buildings. I even cried because we're not
being evicted.

> *Half a building. The other half lies in ruins.*
> *Zhenya and Bezgadov can be seen in the distance on the*
> *pavement.*
> *A child emerges from the remaining entrance of the half*
> *building: he looks about six or seven. (He's wearing galoshes*
> *on bare feet, trousers hanging from only one button, a shirt.)*
> *The boy looks down the street in the direction opposite to*
> *that from which Bezgadov and Zhenya are coming.*
> *There is no one there. Streetlights shine. Cleanliness*
> *sparkles.*

BOY: They've filled their faces. Now they'll be sleeping till tomorrow
afternoon.

He looks in the direction of Bezgadov and Zhenya.

BOY: Two people are coming. Let them. The wrong kind of people are walking around.

>*Zhenya and Bezgadov keep walking; they are seen from behind. Beyond them—in front of them—is the figure of the boy.*

ZHENYA: Look at that boy standing there. So late, and he's not asleep, poor little devil.

BEZGADOV: He's waiting for his mother... So Zhenya, does this mean I'll have to shave tomorrow?

ZHENYA: I'm afraid you must! After all, what is it we're doing tomorrow?

BEZGADOV: Tomorrow you and I are having our wedding, tomorrow we're going to the Registry Office.

ZHENYA: So we are!

>*Bezgadov kisses her as they walk.*

ZHENYA: What are you doing? You'll give me eczema.

>*The boy takes a police whistle out of his trousers. Whistles.*
>*Bezgadov and Zhenya walk up to the boy.*
>*Bezgadov takes out his wallet and three rubles.*

BEZGADOV: Here, *brigadmil*,[5] get yourself some candies.

BOY: Move along, citizens. I'm not begging, I'm an orphan.

>*And he turns away.*
>*Zhenya squats down in front of the boy.*

ZHENYA: It's very late. How come you aren't asleep?

BOY (*not looking at her*): I've got things to do.

ZHENYA (*standing up*): What a wonderful boy! I must have one just like him.

>*Bezgadov and Zhenya disappear into the building's entrance.*

BOY: Go ahead and have one. All well and good for you to kiss, but I'm the one who has to live afterward.

A big corridor. At its end burns a night-light. Silence. Emptiness.

The interior of a clean, orderly room: on the wall—near a large window—hang portraits of Stalin and Pushkin; between them is a photo of Zhenya.

A nightstand with a telephone. Cupboards. Other furniture.

A large bed. Zhenya is sleeping alone in the bed, her face peeping out above the blankets, her half-childish mouth open.

The door leading from this room into the kitchen.

The kitchen; a gas stove; on top of this stove, on a complex structure of bedding, Bezgadov is sleeping.

On the wall by the stove hangs a pendulum clock. The clock says 3:00 a.m.

Half dark. Silence. The clock ticks.

A distant, timid knock.

A pause.

The knock is repeated in a different place.

Bezgadov is sleeping.

Zhenya is sleeping.

Someone is taking small steps somewhere in the corridor, galoshes are slapping against the floor.

A pause.

A knock on the door of Zhenya's room.

Zhenya slightly opens one eye, but this eye is unconscious and sleeping.

Another knock on the door—quite loud.

Zhenya slightly opens her other eye but doesn't wake up.

A pause.

The same steps in the corridor, their sound receding into the distance.

The empty corridor. The boy is walking away, his galoshes slapping the floor.

Zhenya laughs in her sleep; she whispers something inaudibly.

She says aloud:

ZHENYA: You are my boy from the chopped-off building... That's enough. I feel bad, ashamed ... Shave, all of you, your bristles are scratching me.

> *The telephone on the nightstand rings.*
> *Zhenya opens her eyes and closes them again.*
> *The telephone rings again.*
> *Bezgadov wakes up.*
> *He touches the hands of the pendulum clock with his fingers.*

BEZGADOV: It's after three o'clock. What wandering angel can be calling us?

> *The telephone rings.*
> *Zhenya jumps out from beneath the blankets, sleepy and uncomprehending.*
> *She picks up the receiver.*

ZHENYA: Huh? What is it? Vanya, is that you? I said, tomorrow. I'm sleeping, I'm tired.

> *On the stove in the kitchen, Bezgadov smiles.*
> *Zhenya is silent, her ear pressed to the phone.*

ZHENYA: I don't understand you ... *(Pause.)* This is Zhenya. But who are you? *(Pause.)* I am not Mama. *(Pause. Zhenya smiles.)* I remember. I remember ... Hurry up, you must be frozen—come and warm up in bed with me ... Apartment twenty-seven. Twenty-seven, on the second floor. Just don't make a noise ...

> *Zhenya puts down the receiver.*
> *She turns the key and slightly opens the door into the corridor.*
> *Hides beneath the blanket.*
> *Bezgadov keeps first sitting up, then lying back down on the kitchen stove; his face is sad.*
> *With his finger he stops the clock's pendulum.*
> *He turns the stove gas on and off.*
> *Finds the belt from his trousers.*
> *Makes a noose with it. Measures the noose against his neck.*

The foyer of the same building. A public telephone. The boy hangs up.

BOY: At last, I got through.

The same apartment.
Morning. Light in the window.
Zhenya's bed. Zhenya and the boy are sleeping beneath a single blanket.
The boy's galoshes lie by the bed.
His trousers and shirt are on the chair.
Bezgadov, already dressed, is making breakfast on the stove, now clear of bed linen. He is frying a sausage in a skillet.
He chuckles a little, clears his throat, and spits.
Pats his stomach.
His stomach rumbles; Bezgadov bends over a little and says to himself, into his stomach:

BEZGADOV: Just a moment, you Fascist. You'll be eating your fill in just a moment. Don't hinder the mind when it's thinking.

Pats his stomach.

ZHENYA *(from the other room)*: Vanya! Good morning!

BEZGADOV: Ah, my bride! Well, good morning to you!

ZHENYA: Don't shave now, or you'll be bristly again by evening. Wait till later.

BEZGADOV: I'll shave twice—I am, after all, full of zeal.

Zhenya's room. Zhenya, Bezgadov, and the boy are eating breakfast at the table.
The boy eats carefully and with respect for the food. He takes only a little sausage, a lot of bread.

ZHENYA: But how did you know my telephone number?

BOY: I read it on the door. First of all, I knocked on your door. You sleep soundly—I could hear your breathing.

BEZGADOV: And who do you belong to?

BOY: I don't belong to anyone. I'm walking around looking for father-mother.

BEZGADOV: A homeless little crook, is that it?

BOY: No ... My aunt was nagging me to death: I eat too much bread, I wear holes in my trousers. So I keep walking and walking, asking and talking, but no one knows them.

BEZGADOV: No one knows who?

BOY: No one knows my father or mother. My auntie thinks it's all my fault, and she hits me across the face with her bony hand.

ZHENYA: But do this father and mother of yours live somewhere?

BOY: No one says. I'll go now and ask. Maybe they do—there are a lot of kids in the world, after all, so they've just gone and forgotten one of them.

BEZGADOV: But why aren't you living in a kindergarten?

BOY: I've told you, I'm walking around looking for father-mother. There are plenty of kindergartens—there'll be time enough for that later.

ZHENYA: Well, live with us for the time being. I'll find you a father and mother.

BOY: We can be patient.

> *Zhenya looks at her wristwatch.*

ZHENYA: I've got to go.

> *She gets up. Puts on her raincoat, adjusts her cap. On it is an engineer's badge, the profile of a locomotive. She picks up her case—a little iron trunk.*

BEZGADOV: Zhenya, it's our wedding this evening.

Zhenya *says goodbye to the boy, gives her hand to* Bezgadov.

ZHENYA: No, let me think a bit more.

> *Leaves.*

> *Evening on Gorky Street. Bezgadov, in his holiday best, is walking along with his purchases.*
>
> *Beside him walks the boy, in new clothes, with a bouquet of flowers wrapped up in paper. Bezgadov squats down next to the boy.*

BEZGADOV: Tell me—how's the mug?

> *The boy checks Bezgadov's cheeks and chin.*

BOY: Smooth.

BEZGADOV: Ask the policeman where the nearest Registry Office is. I do know, but it's best to check.

> *Bezgadov stops on the pavement.*
> *The boy steps out into the street.*
> *A policewoman in the middle of the street.*
> *The boy goes up to her.*
> *The policewoman salutes him.*
> *The boy speaks.*
> *The policewoman can't hear.*
> *She squats down to his level.*

BOY: Where do they register marriages around here?

> *The policewoman replies, giving directions with her*
> *hands: straight, turn right, turn left, turn right...*

BOY: I'll find it. Look, people are crossing the street: hurry up and whistle! You're not attending![6]

> *The policewoman jumps to her feet.*
> *Bezgadov and the boy are once more walking side by side*
> *down the pavement.*
> *Zhenya's apartment.*
> *She is alone, dressed as a bride.*
> *A knock at the door.*
> *Enter Bezgadov and the boy.*

ZHENYA: I'm ready.

BEZGADOV: Let's hurry up and go. Why do we always have to go on being patient?

ZHENYA: Wait a moment. First he and I must go on our own. You can come along in an hour's time.

> *Bezgadov is surprised: a sound bursts from him, some-*
> *thing like a short hiccup.*
> *Zhenya takes the boy by the hand.*
> *She walks with him to the exit.*
> *Turns and sticks her tongue out.*
> *Leaves.*
> *Bezgadov throws open the window onto the street.*

Walks away from it to the opposite end of the room.
Charges around.
Runs up to the windowsill,
leaps up onto it,
and stands there on the windowsill, using his arms to help keep his balance.
Returns to the other end of the room.
Charges around again, and,
as he runs past the table, grabs a piece of sausage, sits down on the windowsill,
and eats the sausage.

The registry office. A tidy and well-ordered interior. A
HAPPY OFFICIAL *behind a desk.*
Zhenya and the boy walk up to the desk.
The Happy Official stands to greet them (he is happy from imagining the love of others, seemingly being organized by him by means of a document).
Zhenya and the boy in front of the desk.

ZHENYA: I want to adopt this child.
The Happy Official shakes her hand.
He gives his hand to the boy, too.

HAPPY OFFICIAL: Very glad. The Soviet land is kind! Your document, please.
Zhenya gives him her passport.
The Happy Official takes the passport, sits down, sticks out a moist tongue, delighting in the execution of official duties (as he writes, his tongue makes roughly the same movements as his pen).

HAPPY OFFICIAL: Child's name? Age?
Zhenya doesn't know what to say.
She looks at the boy.
The boy sits down in the armchair.

BOY: If father and mother were here, they'd know. They'd know what to call me, too. I've forgotten everything.

The official hides his tongue.

HAPPY OFFICIAL: But do you agree to be adopted?

    Pause.

BOY: I have to agree.

OFFICIAL: How do you wish to be registered?

BOY: Write me down as Styopka.

OFFICIAL *(sticking out his tongue)*: Stepan?! Does it have a good resonance to it? What do you think?

ZHENYA: I think it does.[7]

    The Official writes with passion, working his protruding
    tongue at the same tempo.

OFFICIAL: And how old are you?

BOY: Put down that I'm in my eleventh year. Then I can join the Red Army earlier.

    Everyone stands.
    The Happy Official bids Stepan farewell.

ZHENYA *(to* Stepan*)*: Run home and get Father. I'll wait here.

    Stepan *leaves.*

OFFICIAL: So he has a father too?

ZHENYA: He will in a minute.

    Sits down in a chair.
    The official gets up from behind his desk and walks away.
    Returns with a small bouquet of flowers.
    Gives the flowers to Zhenya.

OFFICIAL: For you, from our State.

    Zhenya's empty room.
    A table. An abundant spread.
    Voices and the sound of steps outside the door, in the
  corridor.
    Enter Zhenya.
    Enter Bezgadov, with Stepan in his arms.

ZHENYA *(removing her deep blue raincoat)*: Look what we've got—a ready-made son, we can move straight from the era of construction to the era of assimilation and adjustment.[8]

Bezgadov makes a hiccupping sound.
Puts Stepan down.
Brushes the dust off his clothes.

BEZGADOV: We'd have done better to start with construction activity—and only then move on to assimilation.

STEPAN: Mama! That's enough silly talk! Stop now, or I'll leave you.

Zhenya grabs Stepan in her arms,
hugs him close,
and kisses him.
Bezgadov makes a hiccupping exclamation and moves his
arms about in the air, around Zhenya.

BEZGADOV: There's nowhere to put my arms.

The telephone rings.

ZHENYA: Wait. The wedding guests are coming.

She puts Stepan down
and bustles around the table.

STEPAN: Huh, you're certainly making a big deal of this wedding of yours. Show-offs!

Stepan takes a pillow from the bed.
Walks with the pillow into the kitchen.
Puts the pillow on the gas stove.
Clears away the pots and frying pans from the top of the
stove.
Zhenya's room.
Zhenya and Bezgadov.
Voices outside the door.
The knocking of several hands.
Fade to black.

Silence. Half dark.
Zhenya's room.
The table with scraps of food, empty wine bottles, the
usual disorder after guests.
Zhenya's bed: on it three people are sleeping close

together—Zhenya, Stepan, and Bezgadov, the boy in the
middle, husband and wife on either side.

In the window—the dawn of the clear day to come.

Bezgadov stirs in his sleep,

falls out from under the blankets and onto the floor.

Lies in his underwear on the floor without waking.

Sleeps.

Fade to black.

Stepan is sleeping alone in the bed. By the bed stands a
small table: on it is a breakfast prepared for a child: a roll,
some butter, a bottle of milk, a glass of coffee. On the glass
lies a sheet of paper—a note.

A knock at the door.

Stepan sleeps.

A second knock.

The door opens a little.

The postman looks inside.

Enters cautiously.

Puts the newspaper on the table.

Sees the sleeping child.

Walks over to the bed.

Carefully runs his hand over the boy's head.

Takes the note off the glass.

Reads.

In block letters: DEAR STYOPKA! BE SURE TO EAT
EVERYTHING. IF YOU WANT MORE, LOOK IN THE
CUPBOARD. WE'RE AT WORK. I WILL BRING YOU
BOOKS AND TOYS. GO OUT AND PLAY A LITTLE. YOUR
MOTHER ZHENYA.

Puts the note back.

Takes the bottle of milk.

Drinks half the bottle.

Puts it back.

POSTMAN: They leave an awful lot for the child. People overfeed their children.

> *Takes some old, canceled stamps from the depths of his bag. Puts them on the table beside the breakfast.*

POSTMAN: Let him play with them and develop his mind. There's nothing you can't learn from stamps: where there's fascism, where there's communism, where things are in-between.

> *Leaves.*

> *A cinema foyer: ticket windows, people in line, film posters, a door into the director's office, the little window of the duty manager.*
> *A group of people:* KATYA BESSONET-FAVOR,[9] KONSTANTIN NEVERKIN,[10] *and three other comrades of theirs: two young men and a young woman.*
> *They are having some kind of disagreement.*
> *Katya Bessonet and Neverkin are arguing, even quarreling.*
> *Katya walks away from Neverkin.*
> *She goes up to the manager's window and stands with her back to the viewers.*
> *She talks into the window.*
> *Walks away.*
> *Knocks on the director's door.*
> *Walks into his office.*
> *The interior of the office of the director of the cinema.*
> *Behind the director's desk—Bezgadov.*
> *Katya Bessonet walks up to this desk.*

KATYA: Hello! Please give me a ticket.

BEZGADOV *(distractedly)*: Purchase tickets from the ticket window... And who might you be?

KATYA: I was only asking. I'm no one—just a young woman.

BEZGADOV: A young woman! What kind of young woman—a distinguished one?

KATYA *(sadly)*: No: I'm ordinary.

BEZGADOV: An ordinary young woman? How come—by now you should be distinguished.

KATYA: I wanted to be, but they won't let me. I wanted to jump from ten thousand meters, but my heart aches. It didn't use to.

> *Pause.*
>
> *Bezgadov is working with concentration, even with deep thought.*
>
> *Katya is standing—*
>
> *then she picks up some blank forms from his desk,*
>
> *absentmindedly rips one off,*
>
> *holds it in her hand.*

BEZGADOV (*remembering his visitor*): Your heart aches? Get it to stop and then it won't ache anymore.

KATYA: It can't. It loves and has become weak.

BEZGADOV (*hiccupping briefly*): Loves? No point in that. Loves whom?

KATYA: Just someone. But he inadvertently went and fell out of love with me.

> *She sits down by the desk.*
>
> *Afraid she may start crying, she frowns fiercely, in order to preserve an expression of equanimity.*
>
> *Bezgadov extends his hand to her across the desk: he can't reach her.*
>
> *He picks up a ruler.*
>
> *He reaches her with the ruler and strokes her hair with it.*
>
> *A knock at the door.*

BEZGADOV (*absentmindedly*): Come in, come in!

> *Discards the ruler.*
>
> *Konstantin Neverkin appears.*
>
> *Presents himself at the desk.*

NEVERKIN: Comrade director! All the tickets have been sold, the only places left are the fold-down seats. Please tell them to sell these seats.

KATYA (*meekly*): Kostya! Here's a pass for you.

She hands him the sheet of paper.

NEVERKIN *(taking the pass)*: But I need four.

KATYA: Five! Five counting me!

BEZGADOV: Feeling like a good cry, are you? Go along and cry then. What else are cinemas for?

Tears are pouring down Katya's face,
but she looks bravely at Bezgadov, her eyes open exaggeratedly wide, as if nothing had happened.
Neverkin stands there like a stranger, with a look of equanimity.

KATYA: Comrade director! This is Kostya: he doesn't love me.

NEVERKIN: No, not at all!

BEZGADOV: And why not?

NEVERKIN: What a question! Our worldviews were incompatible.

BEZGADOV: Give me the pass. I'll put you down for two seats.

KATYA: For me and Kostya? Thank you!

Neverkin gives him the sheet of paper. Bezgadov takes it and writes.

BEZGADOV: No, not for you and Kostya, but for you and Vanya— you and me! I like your worldview.

Hands the pass to Katya.
She takes it.

BEZGADOV: Go on into the cinema. I'll be there in a second. Don't do too much crying.

Katya stands up,
moves uncertainly toward the door,
quickly powders her little face,
leaves.
Bezgadov locks his desk.
Neverkin stands there perplexed, tensing his face and forehead for the sake of thought.
Bezgadov gets up, walks away from his desk,
and reaches for the light switch.

NEVERKIN: And me?

BEZGADOV: And you—come along tomorrow, for the matinee.

> *Turns out the light.*
> *Leaves.*
> Neverkin's *silhouette remains.*

NEVERKIN: What a snake! And it's quite something—a real thriller!

> *Fade to black.*

> *Night. A stream of people leaving a Moscow cinema.*
> *Bezgadov and Katya, arm in arm, separate from the* stream.
> *They walk away down the pavement.*
> *Bezgadov bends down toward Katya's face.*
> *Out of the entrance to the Bezgadovs' building walks* Stepan, a little suitcase in his hands.
> *He looks down the street, right and left.*
> *Sets off down the pavement, past hundreds of hurrying* people.
> *He walks slowly.*
> *Stops.*
> *Looks attentively at the faces of all the older people—* men and women.

STEPAN: All these people are strangers: no father-mother here. What a miserable business.

> *Walks uncertainly a little farther.*

ZHENYA'S VOICE: Styopka!

> *She runs across the road.*
> *Stepan stops.*
> *Police whistles.*
> *Two policemen run toward Zhenya.*
> *Zhenya grabs Stepan in her arms.*
> *The policemen reach the mother and son.*
> *Zhenya stands there, holding Stepan in her arms.*
> *The policemen stop beside her,*
> *smile, and salute.*

Zhenya carries Stepan in her arms.

ZHENYA: Where were you going?

STEPAN: I've got things to do.

ZHENYA: What kind of things?

STEPAN: Looking for my father-mother.

ZHENYA: Why? I am your mama.

STEPAN *(silent, then asks)*: But where's father? A mother alone isn't enough.

ZHENYA: He's at work, he'll be here soon. What's wrong? Did you miss me, were you crying for me?

STEPAN: No one was crying. I got my suitcase ready... I packed some grub.

Zhenya's building.
Outside the entrance, standing alone, is Katya Bessonet.
Zhenya puts her son down on the pavement.
Stepan looks at the upper floors of the building.
A light is burning in a window on the second floor.

STEPAN: Father's here. I turned the light out, but now it's on again.

Stepan walks into the entrance.
Zhenya follows him.
A light in the second-floor window.
The light goes out.
Katya walks back and forth on the pavement.
Out of the entrance rushes Bezgadov, while Zhenya's
hand tries to hold him back.
For an instant a laughing Zhenya herself appears
and then vanishes again inside the entrance.
Bezgadov walks next to Katya, breathing heavily, and
says to her:

BEZGADOV: I had to tell Mama I'd be out a bit longer.

KATYA *(taking his arm)*: Are you sure you don't mean your children?

BEZGADOV: There's no need to be cheap!

They walk arm in arm. Bezgadov suddenly frees his arm
from Katya's. Shoves his hands in his pockets.

BEZGADOV: I think I forgot my matches.

> *A dark window on the second floor.*
> *The light flares.*
> *Katya and Bezgadov.*

KATYA: But you don't smoke.

BEZGADOV: Oh, right! I quit, didn't I.

> *The second-floor window, now illuminated.*
> *In the window appears Stepan's face.*
> *Stepan surveys the street.*
> *Zhenya's figure appears in the window.*
> *Zhenya opens the window.*
> *Zhenya and Stepan, now lying on the windowsill, look down the street in the direction of Bezgadov and Katya.*
> *Stepan shouts (as can be seen from the movement of his mouth) the inaudible words "Papa, come home, you bastard!"*
> *Close-up of Bezgadov and Katya.*
> *Bezgadov hears the words falling down on him out of the air as "Papa ... bastard!"*
> *Katya doesn't hear or doesn't understand these words.*[11]
> *In the distance—behind the couple on the street—can be seen two heads: Zhenya and Stepan, watching Katya and Bezgadov from the second floor.*

BEZGADOV *(freeing his arm)*: I'm going back for matches. I feel like smoking again.

KATYA: It's bad for you. Wait a bit, wait till you've walked me home. Is it really that difficult?

BEZGADOV *(bravely)*: No, it's easy.

> *They walk on, not turning back.*

> *A new building.*
> *A flower bed lit from somewhere by electric light.*
> *Katya and Bezgadov stand there.*
> *He is holding her hands in his.*

KATYA: So you just fell in love with me instantaneously?

BEZGADOV *(with conviction)*: Yes, instantaneously.

KATYA: All right then, love me, and don't forget me. Good night.

> *Pulls her hands away.*
> *Runs into the entrance.*

BEZGADOV: Wait a minute. When are we going to meet? Katya!

KATYA *(looking back)*: Sometime...When I next go to the cinema.

> *Disappears into the entrance.*

BEZGADOV *(alone)*: Life's not so bad after all. Yes, we can learn a little patience.

> *A tram stop late at night.*
> *A few passengers stand there—among them Bezgadov and the postman with a thin, empty bag.*
> *An empty tram approaches.*
> *The passengers, except for Bezgadov and the postman, board the first car.*
> *Bezgadov enters the rear car, where there is only the conductress.*
> *The postman follows.*
> *The tram starts.*
> *Bezgadov takes out five rubles, hands them to the conductress.*

POSTMAN: No one's got any change here, citizen. Move into the front car at the next stop.

CONDUCTRESS: No one's got any change here, citizen.

> *Bezgadov looks at them both,*
> *and they—innocently—look at him: it is their faces that Bezgadov saw from the boulevard, when he was kissing Zhenya.*

BEZGADOV: Actually, I think I *have* got some change myself.

> *Searches in his pockets.*
> *Hands some money to the conductress.*

POSTMAN: Damn it—it seems it's not our night! *(Takes the coins from* Bezgadov's *hand. Counts them.)* There are only nine kopeks here! Move into the front car, citizen—you're making difficulties for both yourself and the conductor.

> *The tram stops.*
>
> *The postman hands the coins back to Bezgadov.*

BEZGADOV *(to the postman)*: Come here to cheat on your wife, have you?

POSTMAN: Fool! This is love, not cheating.

> *Carefully embraces the conductress.*
>
> *The tram driver comes in from the front car.*

TRAM DRIVER: What's up? Are we going to be staying here till morning?

POSTMAN: Let's go!

> *And he pulls the signal cord.*
>
> *The tram driver leaves.*
>
> *The postman takes a coin from his pocket*
> *and gives it to Bezgadov.*

POSTMAN: Here—take this kopek. Get yourself a ticket. You're a nobody—a matter of total indifference to us!

> *The tram starts.*
>
> *Bezgadov rushes to the rear platform and jumps off the*
> *moving tram.*

> *Zhenya's dark room.*
>
> *The door opens.*
>
> *Bezgadov enters on tiptoe.*
>
> *Turns on the light.*
>
> *Asleep in the bed are Zhenya and her son, embracing,*
> *helpless, and unconscious.*
>
> *On the table, on a clean towel, are a rissole, a slice of*
> *bread and butter, and a glass of milk—the dinner left for*
> *Bezgadov.*
>
> *A chair has been placed next to the short settee and a bed*
> *has been made up there.*

Bezgadov takes the rissole
and guzzles it down
and turns out the light: darkness.

Morning. Bezgadov is lying on the short settee. Zhenya is standing next to him.

ZHENYA: Who were you with yesterday?

BEZGADOV *(wearily)*: Ah … a girl cousin of mine suddenly turned up.

ZHENYA *(with a happy smile)*: And there was I thinking … something else. Bring her along to see us.

BEZGADOV *(yawning)*: Okay … but you'll soon get sick of her.

Zhenya puts on her coat and cap,
picks up her case, the little iron trunk,
and kisses the sleeping Stepan.
Kisses Bezgadov.
Makes a farewell gesture with her hand,
leaves.
Bezgadov closes his eyes.
A knock at the door.
Bezgadov is asleep or dozing.
The door opens slightly.
The postman's face appears.
He puts the newspaper on the chair nearest the door.
Looks at Bezgadov, recognizing him.
Bezgadov opens his eyes,
sees the postman,
cries out.

BEZGADOV: But you're meant to be a dream, you devil!

The postman's head disappears.
Bezgadov sits up on the settee.

BEZGADOV: Or maybe you aren't!

He looks over at the sleeping Stepan.
Stepan sleeps.
Bezgadov stands,

> *walks over to Stepan's bed,*
> *kneels beside the bed,*
> *observes the sleeping child,*
> *then carefully kisses his cheek.*
> *Stepan stirs.*

STEPAN: Papa, wake me up...

> *Bezgadov shakes Stepan.*
> *Stepan opens his eyes, wakes up,*
> *looks at his father, takes things in.*

STEPAN: Papa! You're here? And I've just been watching a terrible dream! Again—no one, no father, no mother—I'm living alone, and then there's that auntie...

> *Bezgadov strokes the child through the blanket.*
> *Stepan calms down.*
> *Bezgadov sits next to him on the bed, pulls him out from under the blankets, places him on his knees.*

BEZGADOV: You must forget about all those aunties now!

STEPAN (*running his fingers over his father's shirt*): Yes... but yesterday you were walking arm in arm with some other auntie... You must love only Mama, there's no need for any aunties.

> *Pause.*

BEZGADOV (*after a brief hiccup*): I won't anymore...

> *Stepan gets down from Bezgadov's knees.*
> *Puts on his trousers, then his shirt.*
> *Bezgadov helps him.*

STEPAN (*slowly*): Let's live in peace together... Let's you and I labor, we'll wait for Mama...

> *Bezgadov begins to make the bed and fusses about the room with housekeeperly zeal.*
> *Stepan eats a bread roll, drinks milk at the table,*
> *looks at his father.*

STEPAN: Make an effort, make an effort. Don't play around so much...

> *Fade to black.*

The distant melody of an engine working under pressure,
then this melody comes closer and—
bursts from the screen.

A large freight locomotive enters the screen at high speed.

The right-hand side of the locomotive's cabin: a black
driver is looking ahead out of the cab window.

The left-hand side of the engine: from the window the
driver's assistant, a dirt-smeared Zhenya, observes the
operation of the valve mechanism.

The left-hand drive is working under full pressure.

With her hand Zhenya adjusts the controls inside the
cabin—turning the control rod for the cylinder drain cocks.

The locomotive begins energetically releasing steam.[12]

Inside the locomotive's cabin: the driver on the right,
Zhenya on the left, and between them the controls.

The driver is quietly humming.

The locomotive is moving ahead.

DRIVER *(to Zhenya)*: Dzhena![13] The valve!

Zhenya opens the drain valve to empty the cylinders.

Steam from outside pours into the cabin and envelops the
human figures.

Zhenya closes the valve; the steam disperses.

DRIVER *(looking ahead, anxiously)*: Dzhena! Dzhena!

The driver abruptly closes the regulator with his left
hand.

With his right hand he gives three blasts of the whistle,
puts the brake into emergency position,
and turns the reverse lever.

Zhenya leans a long way out of the window
and looks ahead.

The track, rushing to meet the locomotive.

In the distance—a tall figure with a long cane, standing
at the edge of the sandy track bed, is poking uncertainly with
the cane at one of the rails.

A very small boy, who looks only about three or four years old, tugs at this person's long canvas coat and pulls him forward across the track.

The figure with the cane follows his small guide onto the track and again pokes about with the cane.

The locomotive gives three whistles.

The guide looks in the direction of the locomotive,
leaves the tall person alone between the rails,
runs across the track,
and hides in the grass growing in the drainage ditch alongside.

The long, drawn-out whistle of the locomotive.

The tall person, still poking about with the cane, turns in circles.

On the screen this figure becomes larger and larger—as the camera tracks toward him, the point of view being that of the locomotive moving toward him.

The tall person—an old man with a beard and dark glasses. He is blind. With his cane he finds the open space between the rails.

The locomotive whistles.

The blind man breaks into a run, away from the locomotive, but staying between the rails.

He is running over the crossties.

As he runs he feels for the rails with his cane, first the right, then the left.

The locomotive whistles.

The locomotive cabin.

DRIVER: The drain valve!

Zhenya opens the drain cocks again to empty the cylinders.

ZHENYA (*shouts at the driver*): Full reverse!

The driver moves the regulator to the middle of its arc.

The locomotive engine: howling whirls of steam burst from the valves below the cylinders.

Fire glistens and spurts from beneath the brake shoes.

The locomotive cabin. Zhenya pushes the regulator as far along its arc as it will go.[14]

The locomotive engine: still more violent whirls of steam burst from beneath the cylinders.

From under the brake shoes: fire.

The locomotive whistles.

The blind man rushes on between the rails, away from the locomotive.

The locomotive cabin.

ZHENYA: We're not stopping. We must close the drain cocks.[15]

DRIVER: That's too dangerous. It'll wreck the engine.[16]

ZHENYA *looks out of the window at the track.*

The running blind man is very near.

To one side, parallel to him, the little boy guide is running as fast as he can.

Zhenya reaches for the draincock control.

DRIVER: Dzhena! Don't!

Zhenya closes the valve.

ZHENYA: There!

The locomotive engine: gusts of steam from beneath the cylinder.

The steam stops at once.

Simultaneously: the coupling rods stop turning the wheels, they freeze,

but the locomotive continues to move ahead as before. It is skidding along the track.

The buffer coupling between the locomotive tender and the train: the pads in the buffers between the locomotive and the first truck have compressed their springs to snapping point: the momentum of the cars behind is overwhelming.

The locomotive cabin.

ZHENYA: Release sand!

The driver opens the sand chute.

Zhenya, leaning out of the window, tilts her head toward the engine.

ZHENYA: Nothing's coming out!

The locomotive engine as before: the end of a pipe near a wheel rim—nothing is coming out of it.

The locomotive cabin. Zhenya grabs a large wrench.

She opens the door from the cabin onto the running plate alongside the boiler.

Jumps out onto this running plate.

From the sandbox a pipe runs across the firebox and down to the wheels below.

Zhenya pounds on this pipe with the wrench.

The blind man keeps on running.

To one side the little-boy guide is running as fast as he can along a parallel path.

The locomotive whistles.

The guide dashes onto the tracks—towards the blind man.

The footplate alongside the engine. Zhenya is hammering on the sand pipe with the wrench.

The locomotive cabin. The dripping black driver is moving the regulator lever.

The blind man is running.

The little boy-guide runs straight after him, now in between the two rails, the same as the blind man.

The train's whistle is now very close.

The guide takes a flying leap onto the blind man's back,
grabs his shoulders,
pulls himself up
and sits on top of his shoulders (around his neck).

The old blind man staggers,
slows his pace,
drops his cane.

The locomotive is almost at his back.

The guide grabs the blind man by the ears
and turns his head to the left.

Zhenya on the footplate, beside the firebox.

The locomotive engine in the same dead condition, while the locomotive continues to skid.

The sand pipe by the wheel rim.

Sand starts to flow from it.

The locomotive's coupling rods, which had been hanging motionless, start to move in reverse.

They spin the driving wheels in a direction opposite to that of the locomotive itself.

The wheels turn faster

and fire spurts from beneath their rims as they grind against the rails.

The little boy on the shoulders of the blind man, who is now hardly running.

Still holding the old man's ears, the boy turns his head to the left.

The blind man turns left.

He trips over the rail.

Along with his guide, he falls beyond the edge of the trackbed, and they both roll into the drainage ditch, which is overgrown with grass.

The locomotive from outside: it is stationary. Drops of water, oil and thin sludge are running down the firebox. The driver and Zhenya are standing nearby. They run their hands over the locomotive, stroke the wheel rims, check the various parts.

The blind man lies on the slope of the ditch, breathing heavily; from beneath his dark glasses streams of tears and dirty sweat are running down his face.

The face of the child guide peers out from the tall weeds: his black eyes are watching with extreme curiosity.

Zhenya is squatting down opposite the guide, who is hidden in the weeds.

A pause.

Zhenya and the boy study each other.

ZHENYA: Well, hello there, person!

GUIDE: Hello.

> *Zhenya extends her hand to the guide.*
>
> *The locomotive from outside.*
>
> *The boy takes hold of one of the blind man's coattails and leads him to the ladder going into the locomotive's cabin.*
>
> *Zhenya follows them.*
>
> *She helps the new passengers up the ladder.*

ZHENYA: It'll be quicker if you come with us.

> *All three of them climb the ladder into the locomotive and vanish inside it.*

> *A freight station in Moscow.*
>
> *The locomotive is stationary.*
>
> *Next to the locomotive—Zhenya, the blind man with his guide, the driver, and the station shift supervisor in a red cap. The driver is writing in a book that the shift supervisor is holding. Zhenya is writing in her own little notebook. She tears out a sheet of paper and gives it to the little boy guide.*

ZHENYA: Here . . . this is where I live. You really must come and see me.

> *The boy takes the sheet of paper.*
>
> *Leads the blind man away.*
>
> *The station supervisor's book closes.*
>
> *The supervisor and the driver salute each other.*
>
> *The supervisor leaves.*
>
> *Water is pouring from the tap on the tender;*
>
> *beside it, Zhenya is wiping her face with a towel—she is now white and clean.*
>
> *She passes the soap to the driver.*
>
> *The soot-covered driver is washing under the tap. Dirt pours off him, but he remains black. He is a Negro.*
>
> *Zhenya gives him the towel, smiling.*

ZHENYA: You're still just as black as before!

DRIVER: Dzhena, you're a chauvinist—you're against the Negro.

ZHENYA: And who are you for?

DRIVER: I am for thee. For you.

ZHENYA: Lucien! I have a son at home. Take the engine into the depot yourself—I'll be off.

DRIVER LUCIEN: O-okay, Dzhena! I'll do it just for you.

ZHENYA: Thank you, Lucien.

> *They say goodbye.*
> *Zhenya walks away carrying her little trunk case.*
> *Lucien is alone: he watches Zhenya walking away.*
> *Bows his head,*
> *looks at his chest.*

LUCIEN: My heart wanted to love Dzhena!

> *(Strikes himself on the chest.)* No! Stop it! Love the locomotive. O-okay!

> *Moscow. Early evening. The façade of the building where Katya Bessonet lives.*
> *Neverkin walks past,*
> *glances up at the building, whistles three times.*
> *On the third floor, a small pane opens in the top of the window*
> *and a hand reaches out,*
> *waves a greeting,*
> *and then closes into a fist,*
> *making the "fig" sign.*[17]
> *Neverkin looks at it,*
> *sings very quietly.*

NEVERKIN: "Here's how my own dear mother…"[18]

> *Then, looking up toward the window, belts out the last words.*

NEVERKIN: "The Bolsheviks will get by just fine without you!"

> *Katya sticks her head out through the window. Standing on the windowsill behind the glass, she shouts.*

KATYA: And you, will you also get by just fine without me?

NEVERKIN: Of course! What's the difference?

KATYA: Wait a minute, please don't go getting by without me! I'll be down straightaway!

NEVERKIN (*smugly*): That's more like it!

> *Katya and Neverkin are sitting on a bench, beside a flower bed.*
>
> *The evening sun shines in the sky and lights up Katya's cheek and ear, from which dangles a small golden earring with a blue stone.*
>
> *Katya is sad.*
>
> *Neverkin is holding one of her hands.*

KATYA: So you really need them badly, do you?

NEVERKIN: What a question! I really do—I've had it up to here with patience.

KATYA: Then take them...

> *Brings her face close to Neverkin.*
>
> *Neverkin takes from her ears the small golden earrings.*

KATYA (*slowly to* Neverkin): But they were a gift from you...I loved them.

NEVERKIN: You'll get by just fine without them! You can love me spiritually...

> *Puts the earrings safely in his jacket pocket, after wrapping them in paper.*
>
> *Katya observes him silently.*

KATYA: You're going to give them to another fiancée!

NEVERKIN (*standing up*): What a question! And even if I were...
Well, I'm off now!

> *He leaves, without shaking hands.*
>
> *Katya remains, sitting alone on the bench.*
>
> *With empty eyes, she watches Neverkin walk away.*
>
> *Tears well up in her eyes: she struggles with them, wrinkling her face.*
>
> *The postman and the conductress appear on a nearby path, without their bags. They are out for a stroll, walking arm in arm.*
>
> *They pass the bench where Katya is sitting.*

The postman studies Katya vigilantly.

POSTMAN: There is grief in this world: we need to undertake measures . . .

> *They pass on by.*
> *Katya is alone.*
> *She is as if sleeping with her eyes open.*
> *She touches the lobes of her ears where the earrings had hung.*
> *She stands up,*
> *looks at the sky—*
> *white mountains of clouds lit up by the evening sun,*
> *a simple light-blue space.*
> *Katya walks along the path.*
> *Near the exit from the gardens is a small stall.*
> *The postman and the conductress are riffling through the sweets on sale.*
> *Katya appears.*
> *The postman sees her.*
> *Katya draws level with them.*

POSTMAN *(to Katya)*: Dry your tears, little daughter . . .

> *Katya stops and looks at the postman.*

POSTMAN: Come to the cinema with us so you can smile . . .

KATYA *(with equanimity)*: All right.

> *The three walk along together: the postman in the middle, arm in arm with the two ladies.*

> *The cinema foyer: crowds, a ticket window, and a sign that reads: ONLY 4 RUBLE TICKETS LEFT.*
> *Standing together: the postman, the conductress, Katya.*
> *The postman riffles through his wallet, counts his money.*

POSTMAN: I haven't got enough.

KATYA: I'll be right back . . .

> *She walks quickly away from them.*
> *Bezgadov's office. Bezgadov at his desk.*

A knock at the door.

BEZGADOV: Come in.

    Katya enters.

    Bezgadov stands up.

BEZGADOV: You again? You've already seen this picture.

    Katya stands there silently.

    Occasional tears escape from her eyes and run down her face.

KATYA: It interests me . . .

BEZGADOV: Here you are.

    Writes out a pass.

    Hands it to her.

    Tears pour down Katya's face.

BEZGADOV: What's the matter?

    Katya covers her face with her hands.

    Bezgadov rushes towards her.

KATYA: Someone took the earrings from my ears . . .

    Bezgadov strokes her head, comforts her.

BEZGADOV: I'll buy you another pair.

    Embraces her.

    Katya, still covering her face with her hands, opens her fingers so that she can see.

    Her eyes are now visible: she looks at Bezgadov.

KATYA: Is it true you fell in love with me instantly?

    He pushes her hands a little apart and kisses her on the lips.

KATYA: But I can't fall in love instantly, only gradually . . .

    Quietly, the door opens a little.

    Stepan appears and behind him is the postman, who lingers in the doorway as an observer.

    Bezgadov and Katya stand there embracing each other.

STEPAN: Papa! Who does this auntie belong to?

BEZGADOV (*remembering himself, moving away from* Katya): What's brought you here?

STEPAN: I've come to watch films for free. Give me a ticket I don't
have to pay for.

> *Bezgadov writes out a pass for him.*
> *Katya tries to stroke Stepan on the head.*
> *Stepan pushes her hand away.*

POSTMAN: Well I never ... how strange!

> *Bezgadov looks at the postman in horror.*

BEZGADOV: Who are you?

POSTMAN: I work in a certain insignificant commissariat. I'm a
communications worker, a union member ...[19]

> *He disappears through the door.*
> *Stepan takes the pass and leaves.*

KATYA: Was that ... your son?

BEZGADOV: No, just a little devil, a strange little devil! *I* didn't
make him.

> *Katya sits down.*

KATYA: I'm sick and tired ... Something's missing ... I want ...

> *Bezgadov walks over to her, puts his hand on her shoulder.*

BEZGADOV: What do you want?

> *Katya, instantly pressing against him, hiding her face.*

KATYA: Eternal love ...

> *Bezgadov, caressing her inattentively.*

BEZGADOV: No problem, I can do that.

> *Zhenya's empty room.*
> *The sound of a key in the door.*
> *The door opens. Zhenya enters—carrying the same little
> trunk case as when she left the locomotive.*
> *Zhenya puts the case on a chair,*
> *picks up a note from the table,*
> *reads it.*
> *In childish writing: MAMA I GONE SEE FATHER TO
> WATCH A FILM FOR FREE AND ENNIWAY GOODBY
> STEPAN*

Zhenya smiles,
tucks the note away,
picks up her handbag,
takes out a little mirror,
powders her face,
puts on a different little hat,
and leaves.

Evening outside the brightly lit cinema.
A crowd of people. The cinema entrance.
Zhenya appears and walks inside.
The foyer. The door of the director's office.
Out of the office walk Bezgadov and Katya.
Bezgadov locks the office door.
Zhenya in the foyer; she sees them.
Bezgadov takes Katya by the arm.
Zhenya turns to face the wall;
in confusion, she runs the palm of one hand over the wall.
People look at her.
Bezgadov and Katya walk to the exit.
They leave.
A pitiful, sad Zhenya timidly makes her way through the
crowd to the exit.

The window of a jewelry store.
Bezgadov and Katya are looking at the things on display.
Zhenya stands in a dark corner—near this window, a
few steps away from Katya and Bezgadov. Close-up of
Bezgadov and Katya.

KATYA (*pointing at a pair of earrings in the window*): That's the kind
    I had—nothing so very special.

BEZGADOV: You shall have better ones. I'll buy some for you
    tomorrow.

A Moscow night. The shine of the newly washed asphalt of an almost empty street. A couple walking in the distance: Bezgadov and Katya.

Closer to the viewer walks Zhenya, cautiously following the receding couple.

The façade of the building where Katya Bessonet lives.

The main door from the street.

Bezgadov and Katya appear.

They go through this door.

On screen: the door as seen from the street. Pause. No one there.

Zhenya runs up to the door.

She opens it and disappears inside.

The dim, murky space inside this door.

The figure of Zhenya, hiding in this dim space; from a distance—a conversation between Katya and Bezgadov. Their voices can be made out, but not their words.

The voices fall silent. Pause. Zhenya stands there without saying anything.

The sound of two distinct kisses.

A brief howl from Zhenya.

An empty night street, shining with artificial light.

Zhenya is running, alone, in her coat, without her little hat, her hair in disarray.

A black screen. The sound of a key in a lock.

Light. After entering her room, Zhenya has turned on the electricity.

Stepan is sleeping, fully dressed, on the bed.

Zhenya carefully removes his shoes, undoes his buttons, covers him with a blanket.

Turns out the light.

Morning in Zhenya's room: Zhenya and Stepan are sleeping on the bed.

>*The sound of a key in the lock.*
>
>*Cautiously, frightenedly, Bezgadov enters the room.*
>
>*Zhenya opens her eyes, gets up, and sits on the bed.*

ZHENYA: Go away, leave us alone.

BEZGADOV: What's the matter?

>*Zhenya gets out of bed and walks in her nightgown to the cupboard, opens it, rummages around, pulls out a little box, and opens it: inside are some large earrings.*

ZHENYA *(to Bezgadov)*: Give them to her.

>*Hands him the little box.*
>
>*Bezgadov takes the little box, looks at the earrings, puts the little box on the table.*

BEZGADOV: I'm leaving…

>*Pulls a suitcase from beneath the settee, opens it, throws in socks, ties, books, etc.*
>
>*Zhenya is sitting on the bed.*
>
>*She wakes Stepan.*
>
>*He wakes up, looks attentively at his mother and father.*

ZHENYA: Get up, Stepan: Father is leaving us.

>*Stepan sits up in bed.*

STEPAN: Papa, where are you going? To that auntie in the cinema?

BEZGADOV *(packing his things)*: Yes, Stepan. Goodbye now.

STEPAN: But why do you hug that auntie of yours? You'd be better off loving just Mama.

BEZGADOV: You'll understand when you grow up, Stepan.

>*Stepan is pensive and sad.*

STEPAN: I'm just waiting to grow up… and then I'll give you what for. I'll cripple you!

BEZGADOV *(tensely)*: Why?

STEPAN: Then I'll start having children and I shall live with them until death… They'll have a father, even if I don't…

>*Pause.*
>
>*Bezgadov turns, looks at Zhenya and Stepan.*

BEZGADOV *(quietly)*: Zhenya, maybe I should stay?

ZHENYA: Don't forget your other suitcase ... Shall I help you pack so you can leave sooner?

BEZGADOV *(gloomily)*: Don't bother. I can manage.

> *A knock at the door.*
> *The door opens.*
> *The postman. He holds out a newspaper.*

BEZGADOV *(looking at the postman)*: Yet another devil! Wait here a minute, then we can leave together.

> *The postman has walked into the room and taken out his watch.*

POSTMAN: I am overfulfilling the plan: I can wait.

> *Stepan, sitting on the bed next to Zhenya, turns his face to the headboard.*
> *Bezgadov closes both suitcases. Gives one to the postman.*

BEZGADOV: Help me carry it out!

> *The postman takes the suitcase.*
> *Bezgadov picks up the other suitcase*
> *and walks silently out of the door.*
> *The postman follows Bezgadov, then turns around at the door.*
> *Stepan lifts his face from the headboard: it is streaked with tears.*
> *The postman puts down the suitcase, goes back into the room, takes a stamp from the depths of his bag, and hands it to the boy.*

POSTMAN: It's African. The country of Abyssinia: imagine it in your mind—and you'll stop crying.[20]

> *Stepan takes the stamp.*
> *The postman leaves, taking Bezgadov's suitcase.*
> *Zhenya dries the tears from Stepan's face with a towel.*

ZHENYA: What's all this? Don't cry, you mustn't ...

STEPAN: "Don't cry, don't cry"—but I've got no father again!

ZHENYA *(caressing him)*: You have a mama ...

STEPAN: Yes, Mama ... but there are meant to be two: a father and a mother. A mother alone is just half ...[21]

> *Stepan again rests his face on the headboard of the bed.*
> *Zhenya gets up from the bed, quickly puts on a dressing gown,*
> *and goes through to the kitchen.*
> *On top of the gas stove lies a pair of men's braces that Bezgadov has forgotten.*
> *Zhenya picks them up, holds them in her hands, and examines them.*
> *Lying on the floor is a dirty photograph.*
> *Zhenya picks it up.*
> *It shows Zhenya and Bezgadov, in the tender pose of a couple in love.*
> *Zhenya wipes the photograph with the sleeve of her gown, examines it with the look of someone recalling a distant time.*
> *She takes a clean sheet of paper and wraps it around the braces and the photograph.*
> *Zhenya's room. Stepan is lying on the bed, the blanket pulled up over his head.*
> *Zhenya walks up to him,*
> *bends down, and pulls back the top of the blanket.*

ZHENYA: I'm about to go off to work. Get up now!

STEPAN (*from under the blanket*): I'm not going to get up.

ZHENYA: Tomorrow I'll find you a nanny; then you'll be going to kindergarten, and then to school ...

STEPAN: Who knows?

> *Zhenya is dressed for work: in her coat and the little cap with the locomotive badge. She is holding the little iron trunk. Breakfast is on the table and the room has been tidied up. Stepan is still lying in bed with his head beneath the blanket.*

ZHENYA: So you really aren't going to get up today until I come back?

STEPAN: Who knows?

> *Zhenya walks over to him, pulls back the blanket, and kisses her son three times on the forehead.*

ZHENYA: All right, stay there! But don't grieve.

> *The room is empty. Only Stepan, lying in bed. From outside the window: the sound of cars, the singing of their horns, the banging of hammers, and the whine of saws on a construction site very nearby. In the distance a locomotive gives a long, anxious whistle.*
>
> *Stepan sits up in bed (he is wearing a child's long nightshirt.)*
>
> *He looks slowly around the entire surrounding world of the room,*
>
> > *then gets up from the bed.*
>
> *The portraits of Stalin and Pushkin on the wall.*
>
> *Stepan glances for a moment at the portraits of Stalin and Pushkin. (Between them is the photograph of Zhenya).*
>
> *From outside the closed window comes the muffled sound of a Young Pioneer band, with drums. It is approaching the building.*
>
> *Stepan opens the cupboard, takes out a sheet of paper, an inkwell, and a pen,*
>
> > *then sits down at the table and writes.*
>
> *It is clear from the rattling of the windowpanes that the Young Pioneer band is now passing right by the building.*
>
> *Stepan gets up from the table, goes over to the window, stands up on the sill, unfastens the latches,*
>
> > *gets down from the sill,*
> >
> > *and opens both windows wide, to the outside.*
>
> *The band is loud, but it is clear all the same that it is now moving away; the music is getting quieter.*
>
> *From under the bed Stepan pulls out a small suitcase— the one he was carrying when he went away before, when Zhenya met him on the street.*
>
> *He opens the case,*

*packs his street clothes, which are lying on the chair by the
bed, and some old galoshes from behind the wardrobe—but
he remains, as before, in his nightshirt.*

He closes the suitcase,

carries it to the wardrobe,

and hides it inside, carefully closing the wardrobe door.

*By now the Pioneer band has fallen completely silent in
the distance.*

Stepan walks through the open door into the kitchen;

he comes back with a small ladder

*and leans it against the wall beside the large photograph
of Zhenya (on either side of this photograph are the large
portraits of Stalin and Pushkin).*

*He pulls back the bedding, plumps up the pillows, and
neatly pulls a blanket over the bed;*

he takes a broom from behind the wardrobe,

sweeps the floor,

and puts the broom back;

*he takes the candy from the breakfast that his mother has
left for him on the table,*

takes off the wrapper,

puts the candy into his mouth,

but immediately takes it out again and puts it on a saucer.

He examines the paper wrapper, then discards this too.

STEPAN: It's a boring wrapper.

He takes a book off the nightstand,

opens it, leafs through it,

discards it.

STEPAN: Boring old alphabet letters . . .

He picks up the telephone receiver.

A brief pause.

STEPAN: Why doesn't anyone ever call us? . . .

A brief pause.

STEPAN: I am a boy . . . Why doesn't anyone ever talk to us on the
phone? Someone really ought to call soon—I'm waiting.

Puts down the receiver.

Sits by the nightstand, his legs pulled up on the chair.

Waits.

A pause.

Jumps down from the chair.

Climbs up the ladder toward the photograph of Zhenya.

Reaches the photograph and kisses it.

Climbs down two rungs.

Climbs back up again.

Kisses Stalin's portrait (to the left of Zhenya's).

Kisses Pushkin's portrait (to the right of Zhenya's).[22]

Climbs down several rungs.

From one of the rungs he steps onto the sill of the wide-open window.

Stands for a moment on the sill, his back to the viewer.

Takes a step—toward the street.

Takes a second step and disappears: he falls into the street.

The usual polyphonic din of the street, that has been audible all the time through the open window, falls suddenly silent for several seconds, then begins again.

The room is empty. On the floor: the candy wrapper, the discarded book, litter swept into the corner.

A knock at the door.

A second knock.

The postman slightly opens the door, glances inside.

POSTMAN: Second delivery. A registered letter.

Holds out the letter.

Walks into the room.

Puts the letter on the table.

POSTMAN: No one to sign for it. I'll sign for it myself.

He opens his delivery book.

Signs with the same pen that Stepan has just been using.

Picks up Stepan's note. Reads it.

The telephone rings. The postman picks up the receiver.

POSTMAN: Hello! It's me! No, not Styopka... Just a moment, just a moment...

> *Dries his eyes.*

POSTMAN: I brought you a registered letter... It's from me: from the postman! I delivered it from myself, without a stamp...

> *A brief pause. The postman listens to the phone.*

POSTMAN: Are you his mother? Then come back home: he's deceased now...

> *Puts down the receiver.*

> *Stepan's letter: DEAR MAMA ZHENYA YOU ARE NOT MAMA AND INNT IT TRUE FATHER LEFT US AND LUVS A STRANGER WOMAN IM BORED LIVING BUT DINT WANT TO BE BORN DINT ASK NO ONE TO HAVE ME I KNOW HOW TO DIE I JUST GONE AND DIED SO ENNIWAY IM GONE NOW AND GOODBY STEPAN.*

> *The postman stands alone in the room.*
> *He sits down on the bed.*
> *Abrupt knocks at the door.*
> *The postman doesn't stir.*
> *Fade to black.*

> *Morning. Light plays across the walls of a stairwell.*
> *Katya and Bezgadov are going down the stairs.*

KATYA: You lied! You knew everything. You bastard!

BEZGADOV (*turning vicious*): Oh shut up, you lousy bitch!

> *Katya stands still, slaps Bezgadov in the face.*

KATYA: Take that, you snake!

> *Bezgadov covers his face and turns away in pain and for self-preservation.*

KATYA: Don't gamble with the lives of children—and don't tell lies in bed. Your children are dying—and you carry on with another woman, you carry on kissing me!

> *Katya presses her face against the wall.*

Bezgadov runs quickly downstairs and away.
Fade to black.

A hospital from outside.
The entrance.
Zhenya and the Negro Lucien appear. Lucien is holding Zhenya by the hand. In his other hand he is carrying a small bouquet of flowers and a box of presents.
They walk up the steps to the entrance.
The hospital door opens: out come the postman and the conductress.
They all greet one another.

ZHENYA *(anxiously)*: Have you just been with him? How's he doing?

POSTMAN: Wonderful! He'll be missing one leg, that's all. But technology's on the move now: they'll make one for him all right! A leg's nothing![23]

CONDUCTRESS: He's filled out a little, and he's lying there so good and clever...

POSTMAN: Can you imagine it? From the second floor! He wouldn't have jumped from our place...

ZHENYA *(not understanding)*: What?

POSTMAN *(severely)*: A fine job you did. You let the child slip through your fingers! Well, anyway, goodbye!

Bows and leaves with the conductress.
Zhenya stands there, at a loss. Lucien supports her carefully.
They enter the hospital.
Fade to black.

Zhenya's room.
Zhenya and Lucien are sitting there, fully clothed.
Pause.

LUCIEN *(timidly)*: Dzhena...

ZHENYA: What is it?

> *Lucien reaches out to touch her hand but then pulls his hand back in confusion.*

LUCIEN: You ... aren't reading any letters or newspapers ...

> *On the nightstand with the telephone, lies a stack of newspapers and several sealed envelopes.*

LUCIEN: The postman is asking for an answer ... He's been waiting two months now ...

ZHENYA: I know ... He told me. He's asking me to let him adopt the boy. He's got married, and his wife wants the boy too.

> *Lucien gives Zhenya a tender and inquiring look.*
> *Zhenya takes Lucien's hand.*

ZHENYA: I'll probably agree. All that's happened to the boy is my own fault.

LUCIEN: You are not at fault. You are noble and good.

ZHENYA: No, I didn't know how he needed to be loved ... Probably I should have had children first myself.

> *Lucien strokes Zhenya's hands.*

LUCIEN: To love, you have to give birth ...

> *Zhenya pulls her hands away.*

ZHENYA: What do you mean? I want to love all children, not only my own.

LUCIEN (*kissing* Zhenya's *hand*): We will ... all children ...

> *With a sad smile Zhenya touches Lucien's hair with her free hand.*
> *A knock at the door.*

ZHENYA (*freeing herself from* Lucien): Yes?

> *Katya Bessonet comes in quickly.*

KATYA: Forgive me ... Are you Zhenya?

ZHENYA: Yes.

> *Katya embraces Zhenya, kisses her on the cheeks and neck. Zhenya is embarrassed and tries to free herself.*

KATYA: Forgive me ... I was the wife of your husband, Vanya Bezgadov.

> *Zhenya frees herself from Katya.*

KATYA: Don't hold it against me: I found out what happened to your boy and I divorced Bezgadov.

LUCIEN *(standing up)*: Getting divorced—that's not good.

KATYA *(studying Lucien)*: I slapped him in the face and left him.

ZHENYA *(smiling)*: You're very sweet...

KATYA: Not at all. I've come to ask your forgiveness. But where's the boy—has he recovered yet?

ZHENYA: No. Come around again tomorrow. Tomorrow he's being released from the hospital.

KATYA: Good, I'll come. Let's you and me become friends.

> *Kisses Zhenya.*
> *Zhenya kisses Katya.*
> *They say goodbye.*
> *Katya leaves.*
> *A pause.*

LUCIEN: Dzhena!

ZHENYA: What is it, Lucien?

LUCIEN: You're not going to love Vanya Bezgadov again, are you?

ZHENYA *(laughing)*: Not likely...

> *And she places her hand on Lucien's shoulder.*

LUCIEN *(sadly, not noticing* Zhenya's *hand on his shoulder)*: I am a black person...

ZHENYA *(keeping her hand on* Lucien's *shoulder)*: Really?...That's something I inadvertently forgot.

LUCIEN *(smiling and taking both of* Zhenya's *hands in his own)*: I'm truly grateful to you.

> *The door opens without a knock.*
> *Zhenya and Lucien separate.*
> *The postman walks in.*

POSTMAN *(immediately)*: Well, how about it, missus, have you thought it over? Are you going to give the orphan up?

ZHENYA: Come around tomorrow, we can talk then.

POSTMAN *(displeased)*: Yet another tomorrow—a post office worker wants to be sitting down, not always walking around!

He leaves.
A pause.
Lucien carefully brushes some invisible dust from
Zhenya's sleeve.
Zhenya turns around in front of him and
Lucien brushes dust from her back too.
Fade to black.

Autumn trees and bushes in the hospital garden. A path.
At the end of it—a porch and the entrance to the hospital.
The hospital door opens.
Zhenya walks out first; she is leading Stepan carefully by
the hand. The boy is walking, supporting himself with a
crutch. His right leg hangs uselessly.
Zhenya supports Stepan under his left elbow as they go
down the steps.
They walk along a path. Stepan is paler than before, and
his head is bandaged.
They are large on the screen.

ZHENYA: Did you get bored lying in bed?

STEPAN: It was all right. Living was even more boring.

ZHENYA: But do you feel better now?

STEPAN: Little by little, I've learned to be patient. *(surveys the entire world around him)*: Mama, buy me a bird in a cage. I'll think it's a little person ... Look—there's a lame dog walking along the path too.

> *He tries to point ahead with his crutch (a little dog is*
> *stumbling along the path on three legs, dragging the fourth),*
> *loses his balance and falls,*
> *but his mother stops him,*
> *picks him up in her arms,*
> *and carries him (Stepan lays his crutch on his mother's*
> *shoulder).*

Zhenya's room. On the table: a cake, candy, flowers, a
box of Meccano. Sitting expectantly in the room: the postman
in his holiday best; the conductress, obviously pregnant;
Lucien, now all spruced up; an elegant Katya Bessonet-Favor.

THE POSTMAN (*stands up and begins to walk about the room*): Existence has become interesting now: every day you meet with some kind of happiness. Yesterday the price of food was lowered, today I'm receiving a son, and tomorrow—just wait—a manned balloon will fly up into the stratosphere.[24]

A timid knock at the door. Everyone falls tensely silent.
The door opens.
In comes a boy—the guide of the old blind man, who
follows him in.
They stop in confusion, not going any further inside.

THE BOY GUIDE (*shows a note*): An auntie told us to come and visit...

LUCIEN (*takes the note from the* boy *and holds out his hand*): Hello, hello, please sit yourself down.

Lucien seats the boy guide at the table, seats the old blind
man beside him,
and offers the boy some candy.
From far down the corridor comes a repeated knocking
sound. The sound of steps and of a harsh indefinite knocking.
No one in the room speaks.
The strange steps—as if of three feet—come closer. There
is the regular, harsh knock of wood on wood.
The steps stop by the door.
The door opens.
Stepan enters, tapping the floor with his crutch.
Zhenya walks in after him.
Stepan looks around at everyone,
looks at the portraits of Stalin, Pushkin, and Zhenya on
the wall,
says nothing.

POSTMAN: Well then, citizens, let's all rejoice...

> *A pause. Everyone is silent. Zhenya squats down before the boy guide and says hello to him.*

POSTMAN: All right then, we won't... Stepan, let's collect your things: I'm your father now... *(To* Zhenya.*)* And you, citizen, don't forget your document—we must go to the Registry Office together, to have your son struck out.

> *Pause.*

STEPAN: I don't need a father anymore.

KATYA *(bending down toward* Stepan*)*: Do you want a mother?

STEPAN: No, I don't—I've got out of the habit.

> *Zhenya, not listening to anyone and indifferent to her guests, takes Stepan on her knees and starts to unwind the bandage around his head.*

POSTMAN: What's going on? What sort of behavior is this? I've already bought him a little bed and a goldfinch in a cage.

> *Throughout this scene Stepan submits to Zhenya, but as if he does not feel or notice her; Zhenya seems equally unconcerned by Stepan's words and conduct: she does as she likes with him, replaces his bandages, examines his nails, looks in his ears, and wipes his eyes. Surrendering to her unconsciously, he does not resist.*

STEPAN: Get yourself another boy—look, there's one sitting right there. *(Points at the guide.)*

> *The postman vigilantly examines the guide.*
> *So does the conductress.*

CONDUCTRESS *(to the postman)*: He's got a clever little face.

POSTMAN: Yes, he's not a nutcase. He's not going to start jumping out of windows.

STEPAN: Who's a nutcase?

POSTMAN: You. But that fellow over there *(points at the guide)* is not a nutcase, he's a good citizen.

> *Stepan throws a cake at the postman; it lands on his face, just by his mouth. The postman licks up the custard close to*

his lips, swallows it down, then wipes his face with a corner
of the tablecloth.

The postman lifts the guide up from his chair and takes
him in his arms.

POSTMAN: Let's get out of here.

CONDUCTRESS: Yes, you're right. What does it matter? One little
boy's the same as another.

She wipes the guide's eyes with the corner of her scarf,
then wipes the whole of his face.

GUIDE: But who's going to guide grandfather?

KATYA *(smiling)*: *I* will. I've got four cats at home, but now I'm going to send them packing and I shall live with your grandfather.

THE BLIND MAN: Where are you, little daughter?

Katya walks up to the blind man
and he begins to run his fingers over her face and hair,
then squeezes her cheeks between his palms and kisses her.
The postman carries the guide out in his arms,
followed by the preoccupied conductress.
Katya agrees about something with the blind man,
says goodbye to Lucien,
says goodbye to Zhenya. Zhenya is still busy with Stepan.
By now she has finished changing the bandage on his head
and taken care of everything else. She has sat him on the bed
and is now changing his clothes.

ZHENYA: Are you serious about taking in the old man?

KATYA: Of course I am. I'm used to having another human being
with me. At first I had my fiancé—he left me. Then your husband—I sent him packing myself ... And now I'm all alone, with
cats ... I've got nowhere to put my heart.

Katya takes the blind man by the arm;
the blind man bows into empty space;
they leave.
Stepan is dozing.
Zhenya carefully places his head on a pillow.

Lucien stands by the bed.
Zhenya and Lucien observe Stepan. A pause.
The boy sleeps.

LUCIEN: Dzhena ... I want to be his father.

Zhenya is silent.
Quickly, without a sound, the door opens.
Bezgadov appears with two suitcases;
for a moment he observes everything,
then puts his suitcases down on the floor.

BEZGADOV *(meekly)*: Zhenya ... I've come back ...

ZHENYA: Come back where? Our building's being torn down. We're moving ...

BEZGADOV: Who's moving?

ZHENYA: We are, all three of us ...

She embraces Lucien and gives him a resonant kiss.
Bezgadov hiccups briefly, bends down to his suitcases and
picks them up.

BEZGADOV: So you've gone over to black bread, have you?

He turns, kicks the door open, leaves.
A pause.

STEPAN *(in his sleep)*: Mama ... Let Stalin be father, and nobody else.

ZHENYA: All right, all right ...

STEPAN *(in his sleep)*: Go and get married.

ZHENYA: Yes, all right, I will in a minute ...

Zhenya lies down beside Stepan.
A happy Lucien stands silently over their bed.[25]

A view of a beautiful Moscow street. A few pedestrians.
The postman is walking along fast, with the child guide
in his arms; the conductress is hurrying along beside them.
They have moved into the distance but are still visible.
Katya Bessonet is leading the blind old man by the hand;
they move slowly into the distance.

*In the foreground Bezgadov—on the far side of the
street—is rushing along with his two suitcases.*

BEZGADOV: A whole sixth of the world's dry land—and nowhere
for me to go!
(Grabs his suitcases.) Some mother of a mess!

Translated by Robert and Elizabeth Chandler

LOVE FOR THE MOTHERLAND

OR, THE SPARROW'S JOURNEY[1]

A Fairy-Tale Happening

THE OLD fiddler-musician liked to play by the foot of the Pushkin monument. This monument is in Moscow, at the beginning of the Tverskoy Boulevard; verses are written on it and there are marble steps climbing up to it from all four sides. After climbing these steps right up to the pedestal, the old musician would turn to face the boulevard, looking toward the distant Nikita Gates, and put his bow to the strings of his fiddle. A group of people would at once begin to gather beside the monument—children, passersby, readers of newspapers from the nearby kiosk—all falling silent in expectation of the music, because music consoles people, promising them happiness and glorious life. The musician would put the case from his fiddle on the ground, opposite the monument. The case would be shut; inside it would be lying a piece of black bread and an apple, so there would be something for him to eat when he felt like it.

Usually the old man went out to play toward evening, at first twilight. It was better for his music if it was quieter and darker in the world. His old age did not bring him hardship, because he received a pension from the State and was adequately nourished. But the thought of not bringing any good to people made the old man feel dismal, and so he went out of his own goodwill to play for the boulevard. There the sounds of his fiddle resounded in the air, in the twilight, and occasionally at least they reached into the depth of a human heart, touching it with tender and courageous strength, drawing it on to live a higher, splendid life. Some of the listeners took out money to give to the old man, but they did not know where to put it; the case from the fiddle was shut and the musician himself was high up by the foot of the monument, almost beside Pushkin. Then people put one-kopek and ten-kopek coins on top of the case. But the old man did not want to cover his need at the expense of the art of music; putting his fiddle back in its case, he would scatter the coins on the ground, paying no attention to their value. Only when it was late would he set off home; sometimes it was already midnight. People would be few and far between, and only some chance lonely man or other would be listening to his music. But the old man could play even for just one person, and he would carry on playing a piece to the end, until the listener left, having begun to weep to himself in the darkness. Maybe this listener had some grief of his own, now stirred up by the song of art, or maybe he had begun to feel ashamed of living incorrectly, or he had simply been drinking.

In late autumn the old man noticed a sparrow; the sparrow had settled on his case, which was lying, as usual, some way away on the ground. The musician was surprised that this little bird was not yet sleeping and that it was occupied, even in the dark of evening, with work for its own sustenance. True, it was difficult now to get enough food in the course of a single day. All the trees had already gone to sleep for the winter; the insects had died; the earth in the city was bare and hungry because horses came by only seldom and the yard-men immediately cleared up the dung they left. Where indeed is a sparrow to find food in autumn and winter? In the city, after all, even the wind is weak and meager between the buildings—it does not hold a sparrow when he spreads his exhausted wings, and so the sparrow has to flap them all the time and keep laboring.

The sparrow inspected the whole lid of the case and found nothing there that was of any good to him. Then, with his little feet, he edged the coins of money about, picked from them with his beak the very meanest bronze kopek, and flew off somewhere or other with it.

He had not, then, come in vain—what he had taken was nothing much, but nothing much is better than nothing! Let him live and do what he needed to do—he too had to exist.

The next evening the old fiddler opened the case. Maybe yesterday's sparrow would come—then he could nourish himself with the soft crumbs lying on the bottom of the case. But the sparrow did not appear; probably he had eaten his fill in some other place—and had failed to find any use for the kopek.

Nevertheless, the old man patiently awaited the sparrow, and on the fourth evening he saw him again. The sparrow settled without hindrance on the bread inside the case and, in a businesslike way, began pecking the ready-prepared food. The musician came down from the monument, went up close to the case, and quietly studied the little bird. The sparrow was disheveled; he had a large head and many of his feathers had turned gray. From time to time he looked vigilantly around about him, in order to see enemy and friend with precision, and the musician was surprised by his calm, sensible eyes. This sparrow must have been very old or unhappy because he had already managed to acquire a large mind through grief, hardship, and long years of life.

For several days the sparrow did not appear on the boulevard; clean snow had been falling, and there had been a touch of frost. Every evening, before going out to the boulevard, the old man had crumbled some soft warm bread into the case of his fiddle. Up by the foot of the monument, playing a tender melody, he had kept a constant eye on his open case, and on the small paths nearby and the now dead bushes of flowers on the summer flower bed. The musician was waiting for the sparrow and longing for him: Where was the sparrow sitting and warming himself now? What was he eating on the cold snow? Around the Pushkin monument the streetlamps burned quietly and brightly; splendid, clean people, illuminated by electricity and snow, were walking softly past the monument, furthering happy and important affairs of their own. The old man played on further, keeping to himself a pitiful feeling of sorrow for the diligent little bird, which was now living somewhere or other and failing in strength.

But another five days went by, and the sparrow still did not come to visit the Pushkin monument. The old fiddler continued, as before, to leave his case open for him, with bread crumbled inside it, but expectation was tiring the musician's heart and he began to forget the sparrow. During his life the old man had had to forget many things beyond return. And the fiddler stopped crumbling the bread; what lay in the case was now a whole, unbroken slice, though the musician went on leaving the lid open.

In the depth of winter, near midnight, a blizzard began. The old man was playing his last piece—Schubert's *Winterreise*—and then he intended to go off to rest.[2] Just then, from the middle of the wind and snow, appeared the familiar, graying sparrow. With his delicate, insignificant little feet he settled on the frosty snow; then he walked a little around the case, fearless and indifferent to the whirls of wind buffeting him over his entire body—and then he flew right inside the case. There the sparrow began pecking the bread, almost burying himself in its warm softness. He ate and ate, probably for a whole half hour of time. Because of the blizzard, snow had almost entirely covered his accommodation, but the sparrow was still moving about within the snow, working away at his food. Evidently, he was able to eat enough to fill him for a long time. The old man went up to the case with his fiddle and bow and stood for a long time amid the whirling snow, waiting for the sparrow to free his case. At last the sparrow made his way outside, cleaned himself in a small snowy drift, briefly said something, and ran away on foot to his sleeping quarters, not wanting to fly in the cold wind, so as not to expend his strength in vain.

The following evening the same sparrow came again to the Pushkin monument; he flew straight down into the case and began to peck the ready-crumbled bread. The old man looked at the sparrow from high up by the foot of the monument, played music from there on his fiddle, and felt that there was good in his own heart. That evening the weather was quiet, as if tired after the biting blizzard of the previous day. After eating his fill, the sparrow soared high out of the case and murmured in the air the whole of a small song.

In the morning it did not get light for a long time. Waking at home in his room, the pensioner-musician heard outside his window the singing of a blizzard. Harsh, frosty snow was being carried along the alley, obscuring the light of day. During the night, while it was still dark, the frozen forests and flowers of an unknown magical country had pressed themselves against the glass of the window. The old man began to wonder at this inspired play of Nature, as if Nature too—like man and music—were pining for a better happiness.

There would be no going to play for the Tverskoy Boulevard that evening. Today the blizzard was singing, and the sounds of the fiddle would be too weak. Nevertheless, toward evening the old man put on his coat, wrapped a shawl around his head and neck, crumbled some bread into his pocket, and went outside. With difficulty, choking from the hardened cold and wind, the musician walked along his alley toward the Tverskoy Boulevard. On the boulevard the iced branches of the trees rasped desertedly, and the monument itself was rustling mournfully from the flying snow chafing against it. The old man wanted to put the little balls of bread on one of the steps below the monument, but he saw that this was no use; the storm would immediately carry the bread away, and snow would cover it over. All the same, the musician left his bread on the step and saw it disappear in the half dark of the storm.

That evening the musician sat at home on his own. He played his fiddle, but there was no one to listen to him and in the emptiness of the room the melody did not sound right; it touched only the single soul of the fiddler—and that was not enough, or perhaps his soul had become poor from old age. He stopped playing. Outside streamed the hurricane: yes, it must be hard for sparrows at a time like this. The old man went up to the window and listened to the power of the storm through the frozen glass. Was it possible that even now the graying sparrow would not be afraid to fly to the Pushkin monument, to eat bread from the fiddle case?

The graying sparrow did not fear the snowy hurricane. Only he did not fly to the Tverskoy Boulevard but went on foot, because it was a little quieter down below and it was possible to shelter here and there behind snowy drifts and other objects on the way.

The sparrow conscientiously scrutinized the entire vicinity around the Pushkin monument and even dug with his little feet in the snow, in the place where the open case with bread usually stood. He tried several times to fly up from the downwind side onto the steps of the monument that had been blown bare, so that he could look and see: Had the hurricane brought any crumbs or old grains there? Then he could catch them and swallow them. But the storm would immediately seize the sparrow, as soon as he took off from the snow, and carry him away until he hit against a tree trunk or a tramway pole, and then the sparrow would quickly drop down and bury himself in the snow, in order to warm himself and rest. After a while, the sparrow gave up hoping for food. He dug the pit in the snow a little deeper, huddled into it, and dozed off. All that mattered was not to freeze and die; as for the storm—it would come to an end some time. All the same, the sparrow slept carefully, sensitively, attending in his sleep to the action of the hurricane. Amid sleep and night, the sparrow noticed that the snowy mound inside which he was sleeping had begun to move along the ground with him—and then all the snow around him collapsed and scattered, and the sparrow remained alone in the hurricane.

The sparrow was carried far away, at a great empty height. Here there was not even snow—only a bare, clean wind, hard from its own clenched strength. The sparrow thought a little, curled his body up tighter, and fell asleep in this hurricane.

After he had slept all he needed, he awoke, but the storm was still carrying him. The sparrow had already learned a little about how to live in the hurricane; it had become easier, even, for him to exist, because he did not feel the weight of his own body and there was no need to walk or fly or bother about anything at all. The sparrow looked around in the gloom of the storm; he wanted to understand what time it was—day or night. But he was unable to make out either light or dark through this gloom, and he huddled himself up again and fell asleep, trying to preserve some warmth at least inside himself; it did not matter if his feathers and skin got cold.

When the sparrow awoke a second time, he was still being carried by the storm. He was already getting used to it, only he was concerned about food. The sparrow did not feel the cold anymore, but there was no warmth either; he just trembled in this gloom and current of empty air. The sparrow huddled up again, trying not to be conscious of anything until the hurricane was over.

The sparrow awoke on the ground, in a clean and warm silence. He was lying on leaves of big green grass. Unknown and unseen birds were singing long musical songs; the sparrow felt surprised and listened to them for some time. Then he tidied and cleaned his feathers after the whirlwind and went off to find nourishment.

Here, probably, summer was eternal, and so there was a lot of food. Almost every grass had fruits on it. On the stems, in between the leaves, hung ears of grain or soft pods with little spicy flat cakes—or else there were big juicy berries growing quite openly. The sparrow pecked all day, until he began to feel ashamed and revolted; he remembered himself and stopped eating, although he could have eaten a little more.

After sleeping all night on a grassy stem, the sparrow began feeding again in the morning. Now, however, he ate only a little. Yesterday, powerful hunger had stopped him from noticing the taste of the food, but today he felt that all the fruits of the grasses and bushes were either too sweet or, on the contrary, too bitter. Nevertheless, the fruits contained a lot of nourishment, in the form of thick, almost intoxicating oil, and as this second day began the sparrow was already a little plumper and glossier. During the night, however, he was troubled by heartburn, and then the sparrow began to yearn for the customary sourness of plain black bread; the memory of the bread's soft dark warmth inside the violin case of the musician by the Pushkin monument made his little intestines and stomach begin to whimper.

Soon the sparrow became completely sad on this summery, peaceful earth. The sweetness and abundance of the food, the light of the air, and the fragrance of the flowers held no attraction for him. Wandering in the shade of thickets, the sparrow met not a single acquaintance or relative: sparrows did not live here. The fat local birds had fine, many-colored feathers; usually they sat high on the branches of trees and sang splendid songs from up there, as if it were light itself that was issuing from their throats. These birds ate seldom, because pecking one succulent berry from the grass was enough to sate them for an entire day and night.

The sparrow began to live in solitude. Gradually he was exploring the whole of this country, flying a little higher than the bushes, and everywhere he observed dense thickets of grasses and flowers, squat low trees, proud singing birds, and a deep blue, windless sky. Even the rains here fell only at night, when everyone was asleep, so that bad weather would not spoil anyone's mood.

After some time the sparrow found himself a constant place for life. It was the bank of a stream, covered by small stones; nothing grew there and the earth lay scant and uncomfortable.

There was also a snake living in a crevice in the bank, but she had no poison and no teeth. She fed herself by swallowing moist soil, like a worm; little earthy animals would remain inside her, while the chewed earth would come back out again. The sparrow made friends with this snake. He would often appear before her and look into her dark, welcoming eyes, and the snake would look at the sparrow too. Then the sparrow would go away, and living in solitude would be easier for him after his meeting with the snake.[3]

Downstream the sparrow once caught sight of a high, naked cliff. He flew up onto it and decided to sleep here, every night, on this elevated stone. The sparrow was hoping that one night a storm would set in and that it would snatch him up from the stone while he was asleep and carry him back home, to the Tverskoy Boulevard. The first night he slept on the cool cliff was uncomfortable, but by the second night he had got used to it and he slept soundly on the stone, as if in a nest, warmed by his hope of a storm.

The old musician understood that the graying, familiar sparrow had perished forever in the winter hurricane. Falling snow, cold days, and blizzards did not often allow the old man out onto the Tverskoy Boulevard to play his fiddle.

On days like these the musician sat at home and his only consolation was watching the frosted glass of the window, where a picture of an overgrown, magical country—a country probably inhabited only by singing birds—was silently taking shape and being destroyed. The old man could not imagine that his sparrow was now living in a warm, flowering country and sleeping at night on a high stone, placing himself in the path of the wind. In the month of February the musician bought himself a small tortoise from a zoological shop in the Arbat. He had once read that tortoises live for a long time, and the old man did not want his heart to grow accustomed to a being that would perish sooner than he did. In old age the soul does not heal; it torments itself for a long time with memory—so let the tortoise outlive him.

Living together with the tortoise, the musician began going only very seldom to the Pushkin monument. He stayed at home every evening and played on the fiddle, and the tortoise would slowly come out into the middle of the room, extend her thin, long neck, and listen to the music. She would turn her head a little aside from the man, as if to hear better, and one of her black eyes would look at the musician with a meek expression. The tortoise was probably afraid that the musician would stop playing and that living alone on the bare floor would become boring for her again. But the musician played for the tortoise until late night, until the tortoise laid her little head on the floor in tiredness and sleep. After waiting for her eyes to be shut by the wrinkles of eyelids, the old man would put the fiddle away in its case and then lie down to rest too. But the musician slept poorly. Now there would be a shooting pain somewhere in his body, now there would be an ache, now his heart would start racing, and often he would suddenly awake in terror that he was dying. Usually it turned out that he was alive and that, outside the window, in the Moscow alley, a calm night was still continuing. In the month of March, waking up from faintness of heart, the old man heard a mighty wind; the glass in the window had thawed; the wind was probably blowing from the south, from the direction of spring. And the old man remembered about the sparrow and pitied him for having died. Soon it would be summer, the trees on the Tverskoy Boulevard would be reborn again, and the sparrow could have lived a little longer in the world. And come winter the musician would have taken him into his room; the sparrow would have made friends with the tortoise and would have freely got through the winter in warmth, as if on a pension ... The old man went back to sleep, calming himself with the thought that he had a living tortoise and that this was enough.

The sparrow was also sleeping that night, even though he was flying in a hurricane wind from the south. Only for one moment had he awoken, when he was torn from the elevated stone by the sudden force of the hurricane, but, overjoyed, he had gone straight back to sleep, huddling his body more warmly. When the sparrow woke again, it was already light; the wind was carrying him with mighty strength to somewhere far distant. The sparrow was not afraid of flight or height; he stirred about a little inside the hurricane, as if in a heavy, viscous dough, said something or other for his own self, and began to feel that he wanted to eat. Cautiously the sparrow looked around him and noticed various extraneous objects. He studied them with care and saw what they were: seeds, pods, whole ears of grain, and separate plump little berries from the warm country; and there were even whole bushes and branches of trees, flying along a little farther away from the sparrow. It was evidently not only he himself who had been snatched away by the wind. A small grain was hurtling along right beside him, but thanks to the heaviness of the wind it was difficult to seize it. The sparrow thrust out his beak several times but he was unable to reach the grain; against his beak, the storm wind was like stone. Then the sparrow began to rotate around his own self; when he was upside down, with his little legs up above him, he put out one wing and the wind at once carried him to that side. First it took him to the nearby grain—and the sparrow pecked it up at once—and then the sparrow made his way to more distant berries and ears of grain. He ate his fill and, as well as nourishing himself, learned the way to move almost athwart a storm. Having eaten, the sparrow decided to go to sleep. He felt good now; plentiful nourishment was flying beside him—while, as for cold or warmth, amid the hurricane he felt neither. The sparrow kept on sleeping and waking up again and, on waking, would lie down along with the wind, his little legs in the air, in order to doze in peace. In the intervals between one sleep and another, he would feed himself from the surrounding air until he was full; sometimes some berry or pod with a sweet filling would knock up against his body, and all he had to do then was peck up this nourishment and swallow it. The sparrow, however, was a little afraid that at some point the wind would stop blowing—and he had got used now to living in the storm and getting plentiful nourishment from it. He had had enough of trying to obtain food for himself on the boulevards through constant predation, of getting chilled in winter and wandering on foot over empty asphalt so as not to expend his strength on flight against the wind. His only regret was that amid all this mighty wind there were no crumbs of sour black bread; flying beside him there was only sweetness or bitterness. Fortunately for the sparrow, the storm went on for a long time; whenever he woke up, he felt himself to be weightless and he tried to sing himself a song out of satisfaction with life.

In spring the old fiddler went out almost every evening to play by the Pushkin monument. He took the tortoise with him and set her down beside him on her little feet. Throughout the time of the music the tortoise listened to the fiddle without moving, and during intervals in the play she waited patiently for a continuation. As before, the case from the fiddle lay on the ground opposite the monument, but the lid was now always closed, because the old man was no longer expecting a visit from the graying sparrow.

One fine evening the wind picked up and snow began to fall. The musician tucked the tortoise against his chest, put the fiddle in its case, and set off back home. When he was in his room, he fed the tortoise as usual and then put her to rest in her box lined with cotton wool. After that the old man wanted to make some tea, so as to warm his stomach and to lengthen the time of evening. But there turned out to be no kerosene in the primus stove—and the bottle was empty too. The musician went out to Bronnaya Street to buy some kerosene. The wind had stopped; thin, wet snow was falling. On Bronnaya the kerosene shop was closed for stocktaking, and so the old man had to go to the Nikita Gates.

After he had bought the kerosene, the fiddler set off back home through the fresh, melting snow. Two boys were standing in the gateway of an old house, and one of them said to the musician, "Buy this bird from us, granddad. We need money to go to the cinema!"

The fiddler stopped. "All right," he said. "But where did you get it?"

"It fell onto these stones, it fell by itself from the sky," the boy answered, and held it out to the musician in his cupped hands.

The bird was probably dead. The old man put it in his pocket, paid the boy twenty kopeks, and went on farther.

Back home the musician took the little bird out of his pocket and into the light. There in his hand lay the graying sparrow, his eyes closed, his little legs tucked up helplessly beneath him, and one wing hanging feebly down. There was no knowing whether the sparrow had gone dead for a short time or forever. Just in case, the old man tucked the sparrow under his nightshirt and against his chest; either the sparrow would warm up again by morning or he would never awake again.

After drinking his fill of tea, the old man lay carefully down on one side, not wanting to harm the sparrow.

After a while the old man dozed off, but he woke up again at once; the sparrow had stirred beneath his shirt and pecked him on his body. "He's alive!" thought the old man. "His heart must have stepped back from death!" And he took the sparrow out from the warmth beneath his shirt.

Now that the little bird had come to life again, the musician put him with the tortoise for the night. The tortoise slept in a little box with cotton wool: it would be soft for the sparrow.

At dawn the old man woke up properly and had a look: How was the sparrow? How was he doing in the little box with the tortoise?

The sparrow was lying on the cotton wool with his thin little legs pointing up; the tortoise had extended her neck and was looking at him with kind, patient eyes. The sparrow had died and had forgotten forever that he had been in the world.

That evening the old musician did not go to the Tverskoy Boulevard. He took his fiddle out of the case and began to play tender, happy music. The tortoise came out into the middle of the room and began meekly listening to him on her own. But something was lacking in the music; it was not enough for the full consolation of the grieving heart of the old man. Then he put the fiddle down and began to weep, because not everything can be expressed by music and the final means of life and suffering remains poor man himself.[4]

Translated by Robert and Elizabeth Chandler
and Olga Meerson

THE TEXT AND THE TRANSLATION

FOR MANY years the existence of *Happy Moscow* was unknown; none of the earlier Platonov scholars so much as mention it. Natalya Kornienko, who has been editing Platonov's texts for the last twenty-five years, had read a typescript of the first few chapters in the main Russian State literary archive but had assumed that this was all Platonov had written. In the late 1980s, however, Kornienko was helping Platonov's daughter Maria Andreyevna to sort through files and envelopes containing her father's papers. Someone—probably Platonov's widow—had evidently ordered these papers neither by date nor by literary genre but simply according to the size of the pages Platonov had used and whether they were plain, lined, or squared. It eventually dawned on Kornienko that, split up between six different files, written in pencil on at least six different kinds of paper (some sheets had been torn from school exercise books—others were blank pages from manuscripts of his early poems), were the thirteen chapters of *Happy Moscow* as we now know it.[1] Her task was made somewhat easier by the fact that the pages were clearly numbered. Kornienko published the novel for the first time in 1991, the year of the demise of the Soviet Union. We have translated the text as published in *Strana Filosofov*, 3 (Moscow: IMLI, 1999). This publication indicates all of Platonov's deletions and changes; we have translated some of the most interesting of the deleted passages in our endnotes. There are a few occasions where Platonov never made a final choice between his different variants; here we have made our own choice. We have not indicated the points at which he left question marks in the margins or other small notes to himself.

In May 2011 I took part in a seminar at Ghent University for translators of Platonov. During one session we focused on a small number of sentences from *Happy Moscow*; one at a time, each sentence was projected onto a screen, along with translations into Dutch, English, French, German, and Serbian. Some of the translations had already been published, others had been prepared specially for this seminar; there were two different French translations. We then commented on our own translations or asked questions of the other translators. Interesting though the discussion was, what struck me most of all—and not, of course, for the first time—was the extraordinary power of Platonov's words. Even though these were sentences I already knew very well, almost by heart, seeing them singled out on a large screen made me sense them afresh. They seemed stark, shocking, endowed with an almost physical presence. Robert Hodel, a German scholar who has been writing about Platonov for many years, wrote to me afterward:

> It is as if the idiosyncratic language, which (as if inadvertently) undermines the usual idiomatic nature of linguistic behaviour, at the same time destroys the armour of convention that usually defends a person against penetrating looks from outside. Regardless of whether readers approve of a particular character's views or actions, they find themselves sympathizing—*feeling with*—him or her. It is as if, within each of Platonov's characters, one senses the seed that will one day be transformed into their death.

It is probably impossible to reproduce what is most extraordinary in a writer's style unless one understands why he or she has chosen to write in this particular way. We were all of us still far from a perfect understanding of Platonov, but we had all come to understand him at least a little better over the years. All of us found ourselves apologizing for ways in which we had inadvertently toned down his starkness; all of us wanted to revise our translations, to reproduce more faithfully details of syntax or vocabulary choices that we had previously thought unimportant or even failed to notice. I was fascinated to learn that Kees Verheul, the Dutch translator of *The Foundation Pit*, had done the same as I myself have done:[2] fifteen years after publishing his first translation of *The Foundation Pit*, he had translated the novel again, entirely afresh. I know of no other instance of the same translator doing two separate translations of a work of prose—let alone of two translators independently choosing to retranslate the same book.

Our first translation of *Happy Moscow* was done with more understanding, and more scholarly help, than our first version of *The Foundation Pit*. It has not, therefore, seemed necessary to translate the novel entirely afresh. Nevertheless, we have made many changes, always trying to reproduce Platonov's unique language more precisely. None of Platonov's deviations from standard usage are willful or random; there is always a reason for them, even if this is not always obvious.

In 1940 Platonov wrote an article about the Futurist poet Vladimir Mayakovsky. He may well have realized that his words are applicable not only to Mayakovsky but also to his own work:

If we read Mayakovsky's poems accurately, thoughtfully, and without preconceived ideas, then we will notice that their idiosyncratic form—a form unlike that of any previous poetry—does not hinder us. On the contrary, this form better complies with the rhythm of our own inner life; it complies more naturally with it than the symmetrical form of, say, the iambus. Mayakovsky answers the law of—let us say—our own pulsing blood circulation and our own complex movement of consciousness more precisely than his predecessors. Evidently, our consciousness and our feelings work not according to a simple harmonic curve, like a sine wave, but in a way that is more lively and less "correct," in a more complex rhythm. Mayakovsky may have discovered this intuitively; nevertheless, he discovered a truth, and his struggle for a new poetic rhythm had a much deeper meaning and touched on deeper principles than was first apparent. Let us remember, in order to shed more light on all this, that what Copernicus first discovered was only a simple movement of the Earth around the Sun and on its own axis—a very harmonious rhythm. Now it is apparent that the Earth has several dozen modes of movement; this has not caused the harmony to vanish, but it has been transformed from a single line of melody into a symphony....[Mayakovsky's] achievement was to battle with the inertia of human beings and force them to understand themselves, force them not through violence but through teaching them a new relationship to the world, a new sense of what is beautiful in the new reality; battling with the inertia in their souls always occasions people pain, and so they resist the person leading them forward and they struggle against him. This struggle is far from painless for the innovator—he lives the ordinary lot of a human being, his poetic gift does not separate him from society, does not protect him with armor plating against anyone or anything. [...] "A master of life," Mayakovsky taught the living to understand their own voice and he "crafted" for them a poetry worthy of the creators of a new world. Being a "master of life," however, does not mean that the poet was the master of his own personal happiness; he was a master of a bigger life, of life as a whole, and he expended his own heart on its construction.[3]

For Platonov, the technical, the personal, and the social are inseparable. The role of his translators is to enter as deeply as they can, using all the scholarly help available, into Platonov's unique vision of the world and to reproduce this vision as faithfully as possible. I am deeply grateful to my co-translators: my wife, Elizabeth, with her unique sensitivity to rhythm, idiom, and tone; to Nadya Bourova, Angela Livingstone, and Eric Naiman, all of whom worked with us on our earlier version of this novel; to Katia Grigoruk and Kevin Windle, both of whom have checked the entire translation against the original; and to Olga Meerson, who has not, unfortunately, been able to collaborate as closely with us on *Happy Moscow* as she did on *Soul* and *The Foundation Pit* but who has nevertheless been of incalculable help. I have drawn many understandings from Heli Kostov's excellent book about *Happy Moscow*, *Mifopoetika Andreya Platonova v Romane* Schastlivaya Moskva, and from Clint Walker's equally fine PhD thesis, *Transformation Metaphors in the "Soviet Moscow Text" of the 1920s and 1930s*.

There is probably no twentieth-century writer of Platonov's stature who is so little known in the English-speaking world. Those who do know his works, however, tend to be passionately enthusiastic, and many others have been generous with their time and knowledge. All of the following have made important contributions: Ruth Ahmedzai, Lena Antonova, Anne Berkeley, Keith Blasing, Scott Brodie, Philip Bullock, Penny Burt, Lucy Chandler, Olive Classe, Ben Dhooge, Musya Dmitrovskaya, Evgeny Dobrenko, Boris Dralyuk, Natalya Duzhina, Gareth Evans, Kobi Freund, Flora and Igor Golomstock, Katharine Holt, Alina Israeli, Olga Kerziouk, David King, Lena Kolesnikova, Natalya Kornienko, Olga Kouznetsova, Susan Larsen, Nick Lera, Lars Lih, Nina Malygina, Mikhail Mikheyev, Mark Miller, Artem Oganov, Jonathan Platt, Kevin Platt, Natalya Poltavtseva, Margo Rosen, Gerald Skinner, Avril Sokolov, Lyudmila Surovova, David Tugwell, Valery Vyugin, Clint Walker, Tony Wood, Yevgeny Yablokov, Roman Zhvansky, and many other participants in the SEELANGS e-mail forum—always a source of informed and generous help.

—ROBERT CHANDLER

NOTES

INTRODUCTION TO *HAPPY MOSCOW*

1. *Child of the Revolution* (Chicago: Henry Regnery, 1957), 21–22. Eric Naiman quotes this passage in his introduction to our earlier translation of *Happy Moscow* (Harvill, 2001), xix.

2. Paperno's observation is quoted by Katerina Clark in *Moscow, the Fourth Rome*, 128. One could, of course, add that the impossibility of anyone actually living there is probably a necessary condition for a city to be considered "utopian."

3. Ibid., 135.

4. Fyodorov was an important influence on—among others—Maksim Gorky; the poets Vladimir Mayakovsky, Nikolay Zabolotsky, and Boris Pasternak; and the rocket scientist Konstantin Tsiolkovsky.

5. Platonov, *Fabrika literatury* (Vremya, 2011, vol. 8 of Collected Works), 77. The Admiralty spire, often visible from a great distance, is the most ethereally beautiful of all St. Petersburg's landmarks.

6. Ibid., 78.

7. See Clint Walker, *Transformation Metaphors in the "Soviet Moscow Text" of the 1920s and 1930s*, 376–389; and "Unmasking the Myths and Metaphors of the Stalinist Utopia," *Essays in Poetics* 26 (2001): 149–151.

8. This paragraph is condensed from Maria Dmitrovskaya's "Ognennaya Maria" in *Strana filosofov*, vol. 5 (Moscow: IMLI RAN, 2003), 108–141.

HAPPY MOSCOW

1. Olga Meerson has suggested that one of the inspirations for *Happy Moscow* may have been Velimir Khlebnikov's "Moscow, Who Are You?," a poem first published in 1933, the year Platonov began work on his novel. The poem is addressed to the city of Moscow, seen as a woman; the novel is about a woman, seen as representing the city. ["Moskva, kto ty?," in *Tvorchestvo Andreya Platonova* (St. Petersburg: Nauka, 2004), 205–214.] Khlebnikov's poem begins, in English:

    > Moscow, who are you?
    > Enchantress or enchanted?
    > Forger of freedom
    > or fettered lady?
    > What thought furrows your brow
    > as you plot your worldwide plot?
    > Are you a shining window
    > into another age?
    > O Moscow, are you femme fatale
    > or fetter-fated,
    > fated or fêted?

    (tr. R.C.)

2. Chestnova—Moscow's last name—is derived from the adjective *chestny*, which means "honest." In an early draft, her name was to have been Yavnaya—"clear." See N. V. Kornienko, "Na krayu sobstvennogo bezmolviya," *Novy mir* 9 (1991): 60.

3. Aleksey Vasilievich Koltsov (1809–1843), a poet born in Platonov's native city of Voronezh, was best known for his pastiche folk songs.

4. An early story by Chekhov, "The Holiday Work of Schoolgirl Nadenka," includes by way of a grammatical exercise the sentence: "Beef is made from bulls and cows, mutton from sheep and lambs." Platonov returned to this story several times. A 1931 notebook entry reads: "A Little Girl's Story about a Cow: A cow has legs at its four corners. Beef patties are made from a cow, but potatoes grow separately. A cow gives milk herself; a turkey tries, but it can't." See *Zapisnye knizhki* (Moscow: IMLI, 2000), 115.

    The first version, in *Happy Moscow* itself, of Moscow Chestnova's composition reads: "Story of a Little Girl with no Father or Mother about a Cow: There are few cows, since they get eaten. A cow has legs at its four corners. Beef patties are made from a cow, everybody gets one patty, but potatoes grow separately. A cow gives milk herself; other animals try, but they can't. It's a pity they can't, it would be better if they could. The girls are full of meat patty; they've gone to bed by themselves and they smell. I'm bored." See *Strana filosofov*, vol. 3 (Moscow: IMLI RAN, 1999), 10.

5. A 1933 notebook entry reads: "She, Moscow, lived independently, paying no attention to the current, the fate, and the persecution of the world, to all the rubbish, to everything—as if she were some kind of plant, alive with an inner warmth, under wind, storm, rain, and snow. It detached itself for the sake of uniting with the future." See *Zapisnye knizhki*, 119.

6. Bozhko is based on a real figure, Andrey Gavrilovich Bozhko-Bozhinsky, whom Platonov had known in Voronezh as a senior Party official. His surname evokes the word *bozhok*, which means "a small god," "a small idol," "a person worthy of adoration."

7. Esperanto—The Soviet Esperanto Union (SEU) was founded in 1921. Proponents claimed that the language was an ideal way of informing foreign workers about Soviet achievements. In 1933—the year Platonov began work on *Happy Moscow*—members of the SEU sent abroad 20,000 copies of the four-page question-and-answer pamphlet *La Vero pri Sovetunio* (*The Truth About the Soviet Union*). Membership of the SEU peaked in 1935 at more than 14,000, but in 1937 the Moscow center of the IPE (International of Proletarian Esperantists) was closed and many Esperantists were executed or sent to the Gulag. Membership of the SEU was reduced to 5,286. A slightly adapted version of this second chapter of *Happy Moscow* was published in a journal in February 1934, under the title "Love for What Is Distant." As a young man, Platonov had studied Esperanto. See Peter G. Forster, *The Esperanto Movement* (New York: Mouton de Gruyter, 1982); Oleg Krasnikov, *Istoriya soyuza esperantistov sovetskikh respublik* / Detlev Blanke, *Istoriya rabochego esperanto-dvizheniya* (Moscow: Impeto, 2008); *Esperanto en Ruslando: Historia skizo de Halina Gorecka kaj Aleksandr Korjenkov* (Ekaterinburg: Sezonoj, 2000); and www.irishdemocrat.co.uk/about-connolly/connolly-and-esperanto/.

8. The Soviet authorities were fond of pointing out that the Soviet Union constituted "one-sixth of the world."

9. The Soviet Union was a highly militarized society and military metaphors were prevalent in most areas of life. By analogy with "shock troops," it was common to speak of "shock work" and "shock workers."

10. Every institute, factory, etc., would produce its own "wall newspaper" —a propaganda-filled newsletter, posted regularly on a wall.

11. The Society for the Promotion of Defense, Aviation, and Chemistry (Obshchestvo sodeistviya oborone i aviatsionno-khimicheskomu stroitel'stvu) was a "voluntary" civil defense organization that promoted patriotism, marksmanship, and aviation skills. Founded in 1927, it was described by Stalin as vital to "keeping the entire population in a state of mobilized readiness against the danger of military attack, so that no 'accident' and no tricks of our external enemies can catch us unawares." The society sponsored clubs and organized contests throughout the USSR; by 1929, there were around 12 million members.

12. Founded by the Comintern in 1922, the International Organization of Aid for Revolutionaries (often referred to by its acronym, MOPR) collected funds to publicize the plight of political prisoners in capitalist countries and to provide their families with material help. In 1932 MOPR had 9.7 million members.

13. An earlier version of this paragraph continued: "He now understood that in Moscow was being born a new flying being—a further development of the human body—this being was capable of flying without breath over the abyss and not perishing."

14. In the 1930s the profession of parachutist was extremely glamorous. Parachute jumping—mainly from "parachute towers" in city parks— was also widely practiced by amateurs, both as a sport and as a form of civil defense training. The December 1935 issue of the prestigious journal *USSR under Construction* was entirely devoted to parachuting. One of the most famous parachutists was Lyubov Berlin, the first woman, according to *Pravda*, to parachute from a glider. She and her friend Tamara Ivanova were killed on March 26, 1936, during a jump with special late-opening parachutes. Their pictures were published in

Pravda and their bodies lay in state in the Moscow Press House; they were hailed as "young, energetic, fearless daughters of the Lenin Komsomol" (*Pravda*, March 28, 1936: 4). Lyubov Berlin, born in 1915, became known as the country's youngest female parachutist when she made her first jump at the age of seventeen. The title *Happy Moscow* appears in Platonov's notebooks in 1933, so it is not impossible that Lyubov Berlin provided part of the inspiration for his choice of title.

15. The "parachute issue" of *USSR under Construction* includes this account of a jump: "And then you must drag your body out [of the airplane], pressing your chest, shoulders and head against a mad wind. The airplane, which until now has seemed frail and unsteady, has now become for you a symbol of everything steady and material. It is now so dear, so firm. It is your last stronghold in the sky. But you must abandon the sky and jump headfirst."

16. Another account in this same issue of *USSR under Construction* includes the sentence: "Flying through a storm-cloud that is altogether superfluous at such a place and time, you try not to step on a snake of lightning." Platonov had completed the chapters about Chestnova's parachuting exploits before this was written. Nevertheless, the casualness with which this parachutist refers to "a snake of lightning" shows the tenacity, in the popular imagination, of the mythical link between lightning and snakes. See page 5 of introduction.

17. As well as being the wife of the Thunder God, Moscow Chestnova is a Soviet embodiment of Sophia, the Divine Wisdom. The religious philosopher Pavel Florensky, to whose work Platonov often alludes, refers to the divine Sophia as Chistaya Chestneishaya, "The Pure and Most Honest." And he writes that "Her face and hands are the colour of fire, and behind her back are two large wings like fire." Quoted by N. Drubek-Mayer in "Rossiya—'pustota v kishkakh' mira," *Novoe literaturnoe obozrenie* 9 (1994): 255.

18. This was originally followed by two more sentences, which Platonov deleted: "He was called 'the gift of God.' Arkanov, for his part, responded by calling his comrades 'organizers of their own coffins,' secretly pointing out their insensitivity to machines and the element of air—an insensitivity that leads to a brief and fatal execution."

19. An earlier version of this sentence ended: "on the grounds that the air force does not need organizers of their own coffins."

20. The September 1934 issue of *USSR under Construction* was devoted to the Maksim Gorky Park of Culture and Rest in central Moscow. As its name implies, the park was meant to be both recreational and educational. Its attractions included not only an avenue "decorated with reproductions of the best works of classical sculpture" but also a "parachute tower," described as "the most attractive entertainment in the park." The English version of this journal, which was published simultaneously in four languages, continues: "Very numerous are the people who take an 'air stroll' from the top of the tower and are safely delivered to the ground by the multicoloured parachute." The promotion of "merriment" was also seen as important: "Here and there in the park are 'Glee Parties' in costumes and masks. Their duty is to turn up in any place where people are getting bored and begin to make them merry.... Everyone feels the urge to dance.... On various merry pretexts they entice the 'learners' into the circle." For the opening of the winter season in 1935, a banner with the slogan "Life has become better, life has become merrier" was hung across the gates. More than 10,000 people arrived in the first three hours. See Sheila Fitzpatrick, *Everyday Stalinism*, 94.

21. The Communist Union of Youth.

22. The Russian word *vnevoiskovik* literally means someone "outside the army." Here it probably means someone who is "outside the struggle," not fighting to further the cause. During 1931 and 1932 Platonov made notes for a story with this title (*Zapisnye knizhki*, 81 and 350, note 47), but no such story survives. It seems likely that whatever he wrote was eventually incorporated into *Happy Moscow*.

23. See note 11.

24. Many apartment houses in large cities were, from 1931 to 1937, formally referred to as *zhakty* or "rental cooperatives."

25. That is, he received the minimum State pension.

26. An earlier version of this paragraph ended: "and his mind lived with the intensity of electricity working on a short circuit. The rhythm of life conditioned by the flow of the human heart was Sambikin's scien-

tific subject. He penetrated with particular vigilance of consciousness and anxiety of heart into all the facts of the contemporary creative history of socialism and, because he was taking part in the general advance on them, he felt constantly happy from the great tasks standing like mountains on the horizon of the future."

27. From March 1928 until the late 1930s, the charge of "wrecking" or "sabotage" was an extremely common one. The least slip, accident, or failure to meet a production target could lead to a worker or engineer being imprisoned or shot.

28. Platonov's young son underwent an operation to remove a brain tumor, probably in 1929 or 1930. See Kostov, *Mifopoetika Andreya Platonova v Romane* Schastlivaya Moskva (Helsinki: Slavica Helsingiensia, 2000), 110.

29. Platonov himself worked on at least one project the aim of which was to use the power of an electric arc as the equivalent of a saw. One article in his archive is titled "Let us master the technology of the voltaic arc!" See Elena Antonova, "A. Platonov—Inzhener Tresta 'Rosmetroves,'" in *Strana filosofov*, vol. 4 (Moscow: IMLI RAN, 2000), 790.

30. This German name could be translated as "garbage builder." This evokes "Rubbish Wind," Platonov's 1934 story set in Nazi Germany.

31. "In the mid-1930s, articles in journals exhorted composers to turn to the symphony (as well as opera) as the form most appropriate to the heroism of the age; Beethoven's famous revolutionary work with its choral finale hymning universal brotherhood was held up as the ideal. . . . The high point of its influence came in December 1936 when it was performed (along with Georgian folksongs and extracts from Georgian operas, all in honor of Stalin) at the Bolshoy Theatre as part of the celebrations marking the signing of the Soviet Constitution." See Philip Bullock, "The Musical Imagination of Andrei Platonov," *Slavonica* 10, 1 (April 2004): 55.

32. Newspaper articles about the All-Union Institute of Experimental Medicine repeatedly asserted that the human being would be studied there "from every angle" (*vsestoronne*). Both Lunacharsky and Gorky attached great importance to this institution, and the name "Gorky" was added to the institute's official title. See Walker, *Transformation*, 290, note 424; and Kostov, *Mifopoetika*, 198, note 451.

33. In 1870 Florenz Sartorius, of Göttingen University, founded Fein-mechanische Werkstatt F. Sartorius and began the production of analytical balances. The company soon became known throughout the world and remains important to this day. Sartorius was evidently one of the many people who, after the Revolution, chose a new surname with a scientific or political resonance. Platonov had himself changed his surname, which was Klimentov. His choice was probably in homage to Plato—"Platon" in Russian.

34. An allusion to the Mycenaean period of Greek history (1600–1100 BCE). The stone blocks used for the Mycenae acropolis are so massive that it was later thought to have been built by the one-eyed giants known as Cyclopes. See Walker, *Transformation*, 285–286.

35. The poet Nikolay Mikhailovich Yazykov (1803–1847) was a contemporary of Pushkin. In this 1829 poem "The Sailor," he promises sailors that if they remain "strong in soul" they will survive the coming storm.

36. According to traditional Russian lore, crumbs falling out of your mouth is a sign that you are going to die soon. If a crumb of bread falls to the ground, you must—in order to escape death—pick it up, kiss it, and either eat it or throw it into the fire. See *Slavyanskaya mifologiya: Entsiklopedichesky slovar'* (Moscow, 1995), 385.

37. Through the word "sluice" (*shlyuz*) Platonov is alluding to his earlier story "The Locks of Epifan" ("Epifanskie shlyuzy"). Walker writes: "In 'The Locks of Epifan' Peter the Great intends to control the flow of water, and hence subject nature to his will, by constructing a series of locks along the river. In *Happy Moscow* Platonov transfers this metaphor to the human body.... If Peter meant to harness the 'elemental forces' of nature by directing the flow of the water in rivers, the Stalinist utopian project aims to harness the elements inside the human body itself, uncovering the key to immortality in the process!" See *Transformation*, 330.

38. In January 1935, an article was published in the "Science and Technology" column of *Izvestiya*, entitled "Necrobiotic Rays" and detailing the discovery of "an emanation released by living organisms at the moment of death and called necrobiotic rays." See ibid., 331.

39. In a 1932 notebook entry, Platonov wrote: "N.B. There does exist such a version: The new world really does exist, insofar as there is a generation that is sincerely thinking and acting in the plane of orthodoxy, in the plane of an animated 'poster,' but it is local, this world, it is provincial, like a geographical country beside other countries, other worlds. Worldwide and universally historical this new world will not be, and cannot be. But the living human beings making up this new, this fundamentally new and serious world, already exist and it is necessary to work among them and for them." *Happy Moscow* as a whole, and this chapter in particular, can be seen as a development of these thoughts. The following page includes the consecutive, entries: "A dark figure with a burning torch" and "About a world protected from reality by its own delight, its own complacency, its own superiority—forever; only when reality takes on a velocity of n is it able to enter this blessed world. The world of socialism is an isolated world!" See *Zapisnye knizhki*, 112 and 113–114.

40. During the 1930s, many self-contained commercial and industrial organizations were known as "trusts."

41. In prerevolutionary Russia, boundaries between estates were often indicated by a plowed strip. At regular intervals along this strip, and at points where the boundary line changed direction, there were deep pits.

42. Bozhko-Bozhinsky (see note 6) was appointed director of the Republic Trust for the Production and Repair of Scales and Measures (Rosmetroves) in the spring of 1932, and he immediately took both Platonov and his younger brother Pyotr onto the staff. Platonov began work on May 29, 1932 (Antonova, "A. Platonov," 787–804). Platonov describes the trust with almost documentary accuracy; the address is real, and the trust was indeed under threat of "liquidation" for five years, until it was finally closed in 1937. Platonov was considering resigning at least as early as July 1935; he resigned in February 1936.

43. A 1934 notebook contains the entry: "And then they meet, but they are already quite different. Sartorius is blind; Moscow has had many children, but she is invincible." Natalya Kornienko suggests that Platonov at one time intended this scene as a conclusion to the novel, but that he then incorporated part of it into the picture held out here by

Sartorius's "unclear imagination" See *Zapisnye knizhki*, 139 and 375, note 44.

44. This sentence is unfinished in the manuscript.

45. During the 1930s, before closing down for the night, State radio would broadcast the bells of this famous Kremlin tower chiming midnight and then playing "The Internationale."

46. This was originally followed by twelve lines that Platonov deleted. One sentence is particularly striking: "Like a worm that, by means of its own body, processes harsh dead ground into living softness—with the same patient passion, [Sambikin] was penetrating into the dark distance of the unresolved world."

47. The Imperial Institute of Experimental Medicine was founded in Petersburg in 1890, reorganized into the All-Union Institute of Experimental Medicine in 1932, and transferred to Moscow in 1934. Gorky played a crucial role in establishing the institute in Moscow; his hope was that research conducted there would slow the aging process and eventually make immortality possible. This theme was also much discussed by writers. Platonov's frequent use of the word "irrevocable" (more literally: "unreturnable") is, in part, a reply to Mikhail Zoshchenko's *Youth Returned* (1933)—a book about a depressed intellectual who hopes that having an affair with a younger woman will prevent him from aging. See also notes 32 and 38.

48. The Institute of Experimental Medicine is associated, above all, with Ivan Pavlov (1849–1936), head of physiological research there for several decades. Pavlov believed that all psychic activity can be explained on a physiological basis. He is best known for his research into digestion and—above all—"conditioned reflexes." Noticing that dogs expecting food began to salivate before the food was actually delivered to them, he referred to this saliva as a "psychic secretion." See Loren Graham, *Science in Russia and the Soviet Union*, 239.

49. A distorted echo of the claim made in *The Brothers Karamazov* that reformers who seek to feed the poor will never accomplish anything if they do not believe in God.

50. In 1934, restaurants were opened to whoever could afford them. For four years they had been open only to foreigners.

51. Though often frowned on by the authorities, jazz was surprisingly popular in the Soviet Union, and it enjoyed something of a golden age during the years 1932–1936. Why Platonov refers to jazz as European is unclear. He may be using "European" as a synonym for "Western," or he may have chosen the word because several jazz bands from European countries did play regularly in Moscow at this time.

52. Throughout the first chapters, Moscow was repeatedly identified with fire and electricity. At this point, something of her original fiery nature evidently still remains. See page 5 of the introduction.

53. The construction of the Moscow metro began in 1932, and 1933 saw a massive campaign to bring more workers to the construction sites. An article published in *Izvestiya* on March 8, 1935 (International Women's Day) relates how a group of female Komsomol members volunteered for work in the metro: "At first they were turned away at the gates with the words 'Women aren't allowed!' But the zealous young women refused to take no for an answer: 'We've already been on the surface, comrades. And I've already jumped three times with a parachute—how can I go any higher? Now let me go below, underground.'" The women are taken on, and one of them is then praised for being able to keep her hair perfectly clean and neatly curled. See Walker, *Transformation*, 334–335.

54. Platonov and his brother invented some "electrical scales," and Platonov received a prize for them on July 4, 1933 (Antonova, "A. Platonov," 790). Sartorius's device is entirely feasible, and Platonov may well be describing the scales that he and his brother invented. When subjected to strain, quartz becomes electrically polarized, and the degree of polarization is proportional to the strain. By measuring electrical polarization one can, therefore, determine the strain and load that has caused it. The only problem is that this method would, in fact, be extremely expensive. (Thanks to Artem Oganov, of Stony Brook University, for his help with this note.)

55. This remarkable passage is foreshadowed by a notebook entry from 1931: "In order to destroy entire countries, it is not necessary to wage war; it is necessary only to have so great a fear of one's neighbors, to construct so great a military-industrial complex, to ill-treat the population to such a degree, to assign such importance to the manufacture

of military stores and equipment that the entire population will perish as a result of economically unproductive labor, while mountains of food products, clothes, machines, and artillery shells are left in the place of humanity, in place of a grave mound and headstone." See *Zapisnye knizhki*, 103.

56. Walker has pointed out that *vozhdelenie* (lust) appears to include the word *vozhd'* (leader) and that Stalin was commonly referred to as *vozhd'*. Walker continues: "The popular mythology surrounding Stalin in the 1930s was that he never slept. At one point Sartorius says, '... only the scum probably isn't sleeping, it is lusting (*vozhdeleyet*) and pining away.' Stalin allegedly wrote 'scum' on the edges of Platonov's story 'For Future Use' (*Vprok*). Perhaps Platonov was subtly paying Stalin in kind with his own form of 'marginal notes.'" See *Transformation*, 340, note 510.

57. This was originally followed by four paragraphs, most of which Platonov deleted:

> "The soul should be destroyed, that's what I think," Sartorius pronounced sullenly. "It works against people, against nature. She comes between people and brings about separation. Because of her, nothing works out."
>
> "What do you mean?" asked Bozhko in surprise. "And what is the soul? Does it exist?"
>
> "She does exist," Sartorius confirmed. "She acts, she breathes and moves about. She torments me. She's senseless and more powerful than everyone."
>
> [...] "This accursed soul is everywhere."

58. An allusion to Stalin's call, in his February 1931 speech "On the Tasks of Managers," for maximal intervention in economic production: "It is time to finish with that rotten policy of non-intervention in production. It is time to master a new policy that corresponds to the situation of today: 'Intervene in Everything.'" See Stalin, *Collected Works*, vol. 13, 410, available at www.hrono.ru/libris/stalin/13-18.php.

59. In 1934, at the First Congress of the Union of Soviet Writers, Stalin said, "There are also engineer-metallurgists, engineer-builders, engineer-

electricians, who are quite necessary to socialist construction. We need engineers who build automobiles, tractors. But no less than this we need engineers who build human souls; you, writers, are engineers building human souls." [*Literaturnaya gazeta* (August 17, 1934): 1.] These sentences were projected on a screen throughout the Congress. (Walker, *Transformation*, 309.)

60. Sartorius's feelings toward Moscow reflect Platonov's feelings for his own wife. In a letter (June 1935) to Maria Aleksandrovna, then on holiday in the Crimea, Platonov wrote, "But how can I work faster with such a heart, when it is thinking only one thing? Everyone can see I'm ill, but they don't know the reason. Admittedly, people sometimes make correct guesses, but it is hard to say aloud to everyone, 'Comrades, I'm ill because I love my own wife too much and she isn't here with me.' And this illness is harder, more excruciating than the plague." (*Arkhiv A. P. Platonova* (IMLI, 2009), 522.) In another letter to Maria Aleksandrovna from 1935–36, he wrote, now perhaps sounding more like Sambikin: "I am writing about our love. This is supremely difficult. I am simply tearing the peel off my heart and then examining my heart, in order to note down how it suffers. In general, a writer is both a victim and an experimenter, in one person." (Platonov, *Gosudarstvenny zhitel'* (Minsk: 1990), 680.)

61. A famous Soviet pilot; one of Stalin's "three falcons into the stratosphere" who died in a crash on January 30, 1934, while the XVII Party Congress (then referred to as "The Congress of Victors") was in session; Fedoseyenko and his crew of two had taken the stratosphere balloon Osoaviakhim-1 to a record height, but they lost control during the descent. The crash was all the more shocking because of the excitement then being generated about the country's technological successes; newspapers had been full of such headlines as "During the Second Five-Year Plan the Soviet Union will be the most technologically advanced state in Europe." Fedoseyenko and his colleagues were buried in Red Square on February 2, 1934; Stalin, Molotov, and Voroshilov carried the urns containing the ashes of the three dead pilots.

62. Literally "into a blind passage" (*slepoy prokhod*); this fuses the terms for "anal duct" (*zadny prokhod*) and "large intestine" (*slepaya kishka*). The image of the metro as representing the city's bowels was common.

The writer Lev Kassil, for example, noted the contrast between the now palatial stations and the "raw, dank and uninviting bowels" they had once been. See Keith Livers, "Scatology and Eschatology," *Slavic Review* 59 (2000): 154–182.

63. Compare Jesus's words in Matthew 8:22: "Let the dead bury their dead."

64. Compare the words of a contemporary Soviet journalist: "We still sometimes hear timid voices complaining about the undue severity of surgical methods.…We cannot reconstruct a city like Moscow without a surgeon's scalpel." [L. Perchik, "Moskva na stroike," cited in Timothy J. Colton, *Moscow*, 269.] The two surgical operations in the novel hint at the violence inflicted on the city of Moscow, and on Soviet society as a whole, with the supposed aim of preserving socialism from possible damage or infection.

65. The novel contains many references to both mythology and music. This dream may be a version of the death of Orpheus.

66. That is, representatives of the Party, the trade union, and management.

67. Not only an indication of Moscow's growing sense of self-disgust but also a sarcastic allusion to the description in *Izvestiya* of a female metro worker with immaculate hair. See note 53.

68. An old measure of weight, the equivalent of forty pounds.

69. There may be something of Stalin in this "mountain man." Born in 1878, Stalin was in his late fifties as Platonov was working on *Happy Moscow*. He was from the mountainous Caucasus and the name of his birthplace, Gori, is the Georgian word for "mountain," as well as being very similar to the Russian word. As "father of the Soviet nation," Stalin could well have called Chestnova his "Russian daughter." The first sentence of this paragraph originally read, "'Take it, my Russian daughter,' the old *Caucasian* [my emphasis—R.C.] peasant explained." The mountain man's ability to conjure up grapes in winter is intended as a travesty of Stalin's "miracle-working." See Walker, *Transformation*, 354–362; and "Unmasking the Myths," 144–149.

70. We have taken the words "electing a constituent assembly" from an early draft; their omission from the final draft may have been an act of

self-censorship. The Constituent Assembly was elected in late 1917; the Bolsheviks won less than a quarter of the votes. Rather than remain a minority in this first democratically elected Russian parliament, the Bolsheviks used the Red Guards to disband the delegates. Platonov's final draft contains what may be a more veiled—and certainly untranslatable—allusion to the Constituent Assembly. The word *golos* means both "voice" and "vote"; Moscow's previous question could have been translated: "But who fired that shot and all that shouting of votes began in the prison?"

71. A 1935 notebook entry reads: "Sartorius at the end of his reincarnations becomes convinced that, for the completion of his life task and for satisfaction through love, he himself must become Moscow—and with his reincarnation into her, into a woman who is the savior of the world, he comes to an end and so does the novel." See *Zapisnye knizhk*i, 162.

72. Platonov first wrote "destruction," then "transformation," and never chose between these variants. "Constitution" earlier in the sentence translates *konstitutsiya*. Like its English equivalent, this can be used in both a medical and a political sense, and it is clear that both senses are intended here. It had been announced in the summer of 1935 that a more liberal and democratic constitution was to be drawn up. See Leonhard, *Child of the Revolution*, 22.

73. Three major railway termini are located on this square. In a 1935–1936 notebook entry, Platonov wrote: "The Best Place: He, Sartorius, especially loved Kalanchev Square. These people, about to disappear irrevocably in a train—it is the last half hour they are with him." See *Zapisnye knizhki*, 176.

74. Internal passports were introduced by law in December 1932; until then they had been seen as a symbol of the authoritarian old regime. See Fitzpatrick, *Everyday Stalinism*, 120.

75. Sartorius's failure to recognize Komyagin's surname or address may perhaps indicate the degree to which his past life is already slipping away from him.

76. See notes 18 and 19. This is a striking example of Platonov making literal what he had first intended as a metaphor.

77. Anatoly Lunacharsky (1875–1933) was the first Bolshevik Commissar for Enlightenment, that is, education and the arts. Walker describes Lunacharsky as one of the most influential advocates of "a practical, technical culture" that would transform not only the external environment but also the souls of the Soviet people. Walker's view is that Lunacharsky was a crucial "ideological filter through which avant-garde theories of art passed into Stalinist culture," that it was by appropriating Lunacharsky's thinking that Stalin was able to make a political reality out of the avant-garde's dream of reshaping the world. Walker points out that Komyagin uses the same word (*mechutsya*) for "rushing about" as Lunacharsky uses in a passage from his *Bringing Up the New Man* (1928): "human society represents something like a gaseous substance in which each molecule-human knocks around on all sides, bumping into all his neighbors and chaotically *rushing about without any order.* To organize these molecules, to give them a unified direction, to give them a unified aim and goal, order—this is the key to the affair." (*Transformation*, 296–317.) Walker sees Platonov as sympathetic to the Platonic ideal of "tuning" or "harmonizing" society but critical of Lunacharsky's superficial understanding of this ideal. The Russian for "to tune" (*nastraivat'*) is cognate with the word for "mood" (*nastroenie*) as well as with many other words to do with order and disorder; Platonov plays a great deal on all these words not only in *Happy Moscow* but also in *The Foundation Pit* and indeed throughout his work.

78. Walker suggests that Platonov is punning on the words for "leader" (*vozhd'*) and for "lust" (*vozhdelenie*): "Thus Sartorius experiences 'leader-lust of the mind' (*vozhdelenie uma*) while standing in front of the Stalin monument.... Platonov's use of 'leader-lust of the mind' is most likely... a response to Maksim Gorky's speech at the First Writers' Congress in 1934. In this speech Gorky discusses the 'sickness of the epoch,' which he calls 'leaderism' (*vozhdizm*). He labels this a sickness of capitalist countries ... 'the individualistic striving of a petty bourgeois to stand a head taller than his comrade, which is accomplished rather easily when one possesses mechanical cunning, an empty head and an empty heart.'" After noting how the phrase "empty and ready heart" echoes Gorky's words and how Platonov juxtaposes "leader-lust" with a mention of Stalin, Walker concludes that Pla-

tonov is implying that the Soviet Union is also, like Germany, suffering from "leaderism." For more on these and other associations, see ibid., 364–371. It is worth adding that, after what seems to be only a brief glance at the statue of Stalin, Sartorius moves at once—in the next paragraph—to a concern with his own future existence and his own new life. See also note 56.

79. The legal status of such markets was ambiguous. A May 1932 central government decree granted peasants and rural craftsmen—but not town dwellers—the right to trade in them. Fitzpatrick writes that "In practice, Soviet authorities never succeeded in keeping 'resellers and speculators' out of the kolkhoz markets, which became a major focus of black-market activity and shady dealings of all kinds." See *Everyday Stalinism*, 57. The Krestov market evidently changed little during the following decades; a recent memoirist recalls it during his own childhood, in the 1970s: "The market was dirty and stinking, there was always something flowing beneath one's feet...there were a lot of nondescript people selling something 'from under their coats,' whispering mysteriously to the adults.... By the entrance to the market there was always a terrible crush, probably specially staged by the pickpockets, who stole mercilessly and cut pockets with razors." Available at www.dostovalov.ru/Ch1.html.

80. Fitzpatrick writes of Ivy Litvinov, the English wife of the first Bolshevik Commissar for Foreign Affairs: "She had supposed, she wrote to a friend in England, that in revolutionary Russia 'ideas' would be everything and that 'things' would hardly count 'because everyone would have what they wanted without superfluities.' But 'when I walked about the streets of Moscow peering into ground-floor windows I saw the things of Moscow huggermuggering in all the corners and realized they had never been so important.' That insight is crucial...Things mattered enormously in the Soviet Union in the 1930s for the simple reason that they were so hard to get." See *Everyday Stalinism*, 40.

81. Her surname is derived from the adjective *smirny*, meaning "humble."

82. The wordplay here is complex. The word *krest* means "cross," but the name of this market also evokes a once well-known writer: Vsevolod Krestovsky (1840–1895), the author of the popular novel *The Slums of Saint Petersburg: A Book About the Well-fed and the Hungry*. The

novel's original title is *Peterburgskie trushchoby*. In his January 26, 1934, speech to the Seventeenth Party Congress ("The Improvement of the Material Position and Culture of Laborers"), Stalin claimed that dark, damp slums (*trushchoby*) have been replaced (*zameneny*) in Soviet cities by good-quality, newly constructed, bright blocks of workers' apartments." Punningly reversing Stalin's words, Platonov writes: *gde trudyashchikhsya zamenili* ("where laborers had been replaced"), *no byli trushchiesya* ("but there were still layabouts"). See Walker, *Transformation*, 371–372; and also Clark, *Moscow*, 100.

83. The Donetsk Basin, the center of the Soviet Union's coal, iron, and steel production.

84. There were three categories of ration cards. First category was for members of the Party and the Soviet government, Red Army soldiers, and manual workers. (Fitzpatrick, *Everyday Stalinism*, 90.) Since bread rationing was abolished in early 1935 (this was proclaimed to be heralding a new age of plenty), it seems that the novel is set in 1933–1934.

85. Fitzpatrick writes that "all sorts of things" were traded in kolkhoz markets: "agricultural produce bought from peasants by middlemen, manufactured goods stolen or bought from state stores, second-hand clothing, even ration cards and forged passports." (Ibid., 61.) She also tells how Soviet citizens with a dubious past—for example, former priests and kulaks—took on new identities in a similar way to Sartorius, though, of course, for very different reasons. (Ibid., 132–137.) This is Sartorius's second change of name; see note 33.

86. A suburb of Moscow.

87. Hero of Alexandria (c. AD 10–70), a Greek mathematician and engineer, is considered the greatest experimenter of antiquity. His inventions include the first-recorded steam engine and a force pump.

88. Archimedes (c. 287–c. 212 BCE) lived in Syracuse, Sicily. His "golden rule" of mechanics explains the functioning of a lever: the less force at your disposal, the more distance you need. With pulleys and ramps, we can lift weights too heavy for muscle alone. Curiously, Trotsky referred to Archimedes several times during the time that Platonov was working on *Happy Moscow*. In 1934, he wrote, "That highest form

which the Yankees gave to the law of the productivity of labour is called conveyor, standard, or mass production. It would seem that the spot from which the lever of Archimedes was to turn the world over had been found. But the old planet refuses to be turned over." See "Nationalism and Economic Life," available at www.marxists.org/archive/trotsky/1934/xx/nationalism.htm.

89. *The City of the Sun*, by Tommaso Campanella (1568–1639), twice published in Russian in 1918, is one of several classic utopian works that were republished in the Soviet Union in 1934–1935. Anatoly Lunacharsky wrote a play about Campanella in 1920. And on July 14, 1935, Nikolay Bukharin, in an article for *Izvestiya* about the "General Plan for the Reconstruction of the City of Moscow," wrote, "We have built giant factories, powerful electric power stations, the Kaganovich metro, a structure which even our enemies admire. And now we are initiating a plan to build a new Moscow in a decade, two times as large, immeasurably better, a joyous, green, beautiful, clean, healthy and sparkling capital of the socialist world, a real City of the Sun!" See Walker, *Transformation*, 275–276.

90. Platonov hesitated over Sartorius's new name and patronymic. He began by calling him "Ivan Stepanovich," then switched for several pages to "Ivan Mikhailovich," and then replaced this by "Semyon Ivanovich." We have consistently called him "Semyon Ivanovich."

91. Platonov mentions a hydraulic pump called "Bessonet-Favor" in his article "Goryachaya Arktika" [*Chutyo pravdy* (Moscow: Sovetskaya Rossiya, 1990), 335–340]. In *Happy Moscow* this name is a pun. It recalls the achievements of world technology, and it is erotically charged. Bessonet is reminiscent of the French *besogne*, meaning "need" or even "sexual intercourse"; Favor sounds like *faveur*, meaning "favor," also often in a sexual context.

92. Her first name includes the Russian for "mother": *mat'*.

93. A reference to *Pyshka*, Mikhail Romm's 1934 film of Maupassant's "Boule de suif" ("Ball of Fat"). "Boule de suif"—in Russian she was given the more attractive name of Pyshka or Little Dumpling—is the name of a plump, kindhearted, and patriotic French prostitute.

94. Sartorius has something in common with the title character of

Thomas Carlyle's philosophical novel *Sartor Resartus* (*The Tailor Retailored*), which was translated into Russian in 1902. Both Sartorius and Carlyle's narrator renounce their own selves, along with all striving toward personal happiness. In his new personality, Sartorius learns to fulfill Carlyle's injunction to "do the duty which lies nearest thee." Carlyle's narrator progresses from the "Everlasting No" to the "Everlasting Yea," but only after learning almost Buddhistic detachment while passing through "The Centre of Indifference." See Walker, *Transformation*, 365–366, n. 536. That Platonov had at least glanced at *Sartor Resartus* is confirmed by a striking similarity between the first sentences of the two novels; each contains a prominent mention of a torch—in Carlyle's novel, "the Torch of Science."

95. So the novel ends. During 1936, however, Platonov made a small number of additional notes. These include: "Perhaps Sartorius eventually turns into the type, the character of Moscow herself and takes possession of her soul for free, without the efforts Moscow expended on her great education. At the end, there must remain a great tension and plot potential—as abrupt as at the beginning of the novel. The plot mustn't be over at the end, it mustn't come to an end." (See *Zapisnye knizhki*, 181 and 104.) "He, Sartorius, perhaps himself imagined all the souls he moved into. In this way a beggar enriched and populated a whole world." (Ibid., 182.) "When Sartorius was many people, he had unusual success. He had power over groups of people. Without knowing how or why, he charmed people—because, in practice, he possessed their soul." (Ibid., 183.) "For Sartorius there are as many 'sexes' as people. He feels for each of them the curiosity a young man feels about a young woman. There is something other, something 'not me,' in every man and woman." (Ibid., 187.) "And my body, my bones, squeeze my life like tight-fitting, dried-up, hard shoes." (Ibid.) All these seem to be developments of an idea first noted down in 1934, during Platonov's first visit to Turkmenistan: "Sartorius is a researcher, a one-way seeker of facts who has never returned anywhere, either in path or wish, who has penetrated into life through all the thick of reality and been overgrown by it. This is a new world type. A new state of life—irreversibility of soul. There are no such people, but such is everyone." (Ibid., 144.) The very last notebook entry relating to *Happy Moscow* is from 1938: "He, Sartorius, from time to time remembers

himself as he was before, unchanged, long ago, and he secretly wants to return to that, albeit poor, yet 'natural' state." (Ibid., 209.)

AROUND *HAPPY MOSCOW*

1. Benedikt Sarnov, *Stalin i pisateli*, vol. 3 (Moscow: Eksmo, 2009), 727.

2. *Schastlivaya Moskva*, vol. 4 of Collected Works (Moscow: Vremya, 2010), 586.

3. Kostov, *Mifopoetika*, 19, note 40.

4. Platonov's title alludes to two earlier works of Russian literature: Aleksandr Radishchev's *A Journey from St. Petersburg to Moscow* (1790), a critique of serfdom and the autocracy for which Radishchev was exiled to Siberia, and Aleksandr Pushkin's *Journey from Moscow to St. Petersburg* (1836). We know that in February 1937 Platonov began a journey by post-horse between the two capitals as research for the novel. It is unclear whether he completed this journey. According to one memoir, he soon sold the horses and gave away to people in need all the money he had been allocated for the trip; this may, however, be a myth. See ibid., 25, note 67.

5. Ibid., 80.

6. *Zapisnye knizhki*, 176.

7. Apart from two pages that were published in a journal in 1947.

8. *Zapisnye knizhki*, 181. See also *Happy Moscow,* note 95.

9. *Fabrika literatury*, 81.

10. Platonov's insistence on the importance of what we might now call "the human factor" anticipates an important speech given by Stalin on May 4, 1935, probably around six months after Platonov had completed his article. In his "Address to the Graduates of the Red Army Academies," Stalin said, "Without people who have assimilated technology, technology is dead. In the charge of people who have assimilated technology, technology can and should perform miracles. . . . That is why emphasis must now be laid on people, on cadres, on workers who have assimilated technology. That is why the old slogan, 'Technology decides everything,' . . . must now be replaced by a new slogan, the slogan

'Cadres decide everything.'" (Available at www.duel.ru/publish/ kurs/kr_kurs12.htm.) This is only one of many instances where Platonov's sensitivity to political change seems almost uncanny.

11. "Velikaya glukhaya" (The Great Deaf One) in *Fabrika literatury*, 583.

12. Yevgeny Yablokov sees Yevgenia (Zhenya) as a feminine equivalent of one of the classic embodiments of the little man in Russian literature: Yevgeny in Pushkin's "The Bronze Horseman." See "Gorod platonovskikh polovinok," in *Nereguliruemye perekryostki* (Moscow: Pyataya strana, 2005).

13. *Zapisnye knizhki*, 155.

14. Ibid., 381, note 92.

15. *Schastlivaya Moskva*, 617.

THE MOSCOW VIOLIN

1. We have translated the complete text, as published in *Tvorchestvo Andreya Platonova*, vol. 2 (Petersburg: Nauka, 2000), 287–305. Platonov left two slightly different typescripts of this story. In the version published in the Collected Works, vol. 4, the hero is called not Wiseman but Semyon Sartorius, as in *Happy Moscow*. Platonov submitted the story in late 1934 to *30 Dney*—where, in February of that year, he had published his "Love for What Is Distant." (According to an e-mail from Kornienko, December 12, 2011.)

2. In April 1934, during his first trip to Turkmenistan, Platonov wrote down in his notebook his own, greatly abbreviated, version of Nikolay Gumilyov's poem "The Magic Violin":

> Dear boy, you are so merry,
>   your smile is so bright.
> Don't ask about this happiness
>   that poisons worlds.
> You don't know, you don't know
>   what this violin really is,
> Or what is the dark horror
>   of the initiators of play.

Whoever has once taken a violin
    into his imperious hands—
He has lost forever
    the calm light
        of his eyes.
The spirits of hell like to listen
    to these imperious sounds.
Maddened wolves wander about
    on the path of fiddlers.

    . . . .

And die a glorious
    death,
the terrible death
    of a fiddler.

3. See *Happy Moscow*, note 79. "Wiseman" is our translation of the Russian *Veshchy*. The phrases most immediately conjured up by this adjective are *veshchy son* (prophetic dream) and *Veshchy Oleg* (Oleg the Prophetic, a tenth-century Russian prince). The noun *veshch'*, however, means "thing"—and things play a central role in this story.

4. Walker points out that Platonov sees Pushkin both as the high point of Russian culture and as its foundation, an entrance into Russian culture that is, paradoxically, "at the height of all its steps." See *Transformation*, 395–396.

5. "Grubov" is derived from the adjective *gruby*, which means coarse. Walker points out that Grubov's initials—V.I.—are the same as Vladimir Ilyich Lenin's, and that they are also the same as Iosif Vissarionovich Stalin's—but in reverse order. He goes on to suggest that Grubov embodies "what has become of the Leninist impulse under Stalin's leadership." Grubov's strange experiments parody Lenin's pledge to electrify the entire country. The term "heavy masses" "subtly links human masses with material for production"; the whole Soviet nation has been turned into material to be experimented on and refashioned. See ibid., 391.

6. Here Platonov is drawing an analogy between Grubov and the dead Lenin. Grubov is both the experimenter and the one experimented

on; Lenin wanted to electrify the entire Soviet Union but is now lying rigid in his mausoleum—the embodiment of a utopian revolutionary impulse that has now gone dead. See ibid., 389–392.

7. Here Platonov is alluding to the account in *The Primary Chronicle* (the most important early work of Russian history) of how the Slavs invited the Varangian Rus (a people from the Baltic region who from the ninth to the eleventh centuries traveled east and south along the rivers of what is now Russia, Belarus, and Ukraine) to come and rule over them. The Slavs supposedly said to the Varangians, "Our whole land is great and abundant, but there is no order in it. Come to rule and reign over us." [Adapted from Serge Zenkovsky, *Medieval Russia's Epics, Chronicles, and Tales* (New York: Penguin, 1974), 50]. The last line of "The Moscow Violin" thus places the reigns of Lenin and Stalin in the broader context of the enduring longing of the Russian people for a ruler who will bring order to their vast land. Interestingly, Platonov has changed "great and abundant" (*velika i obil'na*) to "great and good" (*velika i dobra*). Russia's wealth seems, in Platonov's view, to lie in the goodness or kindness of her people. (With thanks to Walker for pointing all this out in e-mail correspondence.)

ON THE FIRST SOCIALIST TRAGEDY

1. Platonov wrote this article in the spring of 1934 and submitted it to G. Korabelnikov, who was editing an anthology to be titled *Two Five-Year Plans* (*Dve pyatiletki*). Korabelnikov forwarded the article to Gorky, who was in overall charge of this project. In his accompanying letter, Korabelnikov wrote, "I think that what Platonov has written, while being more sincere, more direct, and more profound than Zelinsky's article, is even more politically alien, philosophically hostile, and melancholy. That writers like Platonov are still obstinately raising such questions shows what a hold these questions still have over literary figures. The collective cannot and should not ignore them…. Please advise as to how I should proceed." Gorky advised against publication, but said that the article should be kept "for the future." See *Fabrika literatury*, 710; see also V. V. Perkhin in his commentary to the typescript in *Russkaya literatura* 2 (1993): 200–206. The article exists in two forms: the shorter, manuscript version, our translation of

which was published in the *Times Literary Supplement*, August 23, 2011; and the longer typescript version, which we translate here.

2. The poem quoted is one of de Vigny's most famous: "La Mort du Loup." The poet watches the wolf die heroically and imagines the wolf advising him, with his last look, not to moan, weep, or pray but to carry out his duty and die as he must, in stoic silence.

3. Here Platonov again alludes to the account in *The Primary Chronicle* (see *The Moscow Violin*, note 7) of how the Slavs supposedly said to the Varangians, "Our whole land is great and abundant, but there is no order in it. Come to rule and reign over us." Platonov is evidently polemicizing with Gorky, who quoted these same words in a triumphalist article (1932) about "how our earth is more and more generously revealing its countless treasures." (*Russkaya literatura*, 2 (1993): 204, note 2.) Platonov also quotes these words in his earlier story "The Locks of Epifan."

4. The words are from a speech by Stalin on February 4, 1931, at the First All-Union Conference of Workers in Socialist Industry. The main thrust of this important speech was the need for rapid industrialization. See Stalin, *Sobranie sochinenii*, vol. 13, 41.

5. This famous statement is ascribed to Archimedes.

6. The manuscript version of the article concluded with these two paragraphs, following "or it will be the end of you":

> Some naïve people may retort that the contemporary crisis of production overturns this point of view. It does not overturn anything. Imagine the extremely complex technical equipment of the society of contemporary imperialism and fascism, the grinding exhaustion and destruction of the people of these societies—and it will become only too clear at what price this increase in the forces of production has been achieved. Self-destruction in fascism, war between states—these are the losses entailed by increased production, these are nature's revenge for it. The tragic knot is cut—but without being resolved. What results cannot—in the classical sense of the word—even be called tragedy. Without the USSR, the world would be certain to destroy itself in the course of no more than a century.

> The tragedy of man, armed with machine and heart, and with the dialectic of nature, must in our country be resolved by way of socialism. But it must be understood that this task is an extremely serious one. Ancient life on the "surface" of nature was able to obtain what was essential to it from the waste products and excretions of elemental forces and substances. But we mess about deep inside the world, and in return the world crushes us with an equivalent strength. [*Novy Mir* 1 (1991): 146.]

7. Walker writes, "With that one final phrase, 'and not their foremen,' Platonov rejects with characteristically economical bluntness the entire Stalinist bureaucratic system of the 1930s, driving a deep ideological wedge between his use of the term 'engineers of human souls' and its usage within the Stalinist cultural model." See *Transformation*, 318.

FATHER

1. Our translation is based on Platonov's final typescript (1936), as published in Platonov, *Duraki na periferii* (Moscow: Vremya, 2011). A previous translation, by Susan Larsen [*New Left Review* 53 (September–October 2008)], is based on Platonov's manuscript, titled "Father-Mother." This screenplay was first published in *Iskusstvo kino* 3 (1967): 118–139; like most publications of Platonov's work between the early 1960s and the late 1980s, it omitted all references to Stalin. Platonov first used the title "Father-Mother" in a notebook in 1934: "'Settlement' begins with an orphaned child being driven out into the world by the relatives he has been living with since the death of his father-mother, his life made a hell by their reproaches about his eating their bread. Or should I call the novel Father-Mother?" See *Zapisnye knizhki*, 147.

2. The "Boulevard" (or "A") Ring circles Moscow's historic center. A wide grassy strip, with trees and frequent benches, and bordered by wrought-iron fences, separates two roadways. Trams used to run along the edge of each roadway, next to the central strip.

3. "Bezgadov" means "without reptiles" or "without vileness." But this name makes one expect that the man *will* be vile.

4. In May 1936 the government put out a draft law intended to strengthen

the family. This included a ban on abortions and large cash payments for mothers with seven or more children. After much officially sponsored public discussion, the draft was made law on June 27, 1936. See Fitzpatrick, *Everyday Stalinism*, 152–153.

5. "Volunteer policeman": a typical early Soviet portmanteau word, made up from *brigada* and *militsioner*.

6. Platonov had written several screenplays for the silent cinema, though none was ever actually filmed. He wrote "Father" when the Soviet "talking" cinema was still in its infancy. He was clearly aware of the difficulties occasioned by the poor quality of microphones and the resulting constrictions on actors' movement; his choice of locations—an empty tram, a room or office with only a few people in it, an empty nighttime street—was evidently designed to minimize these difficulties. But Platonov also, on occasion, enjoys pitting the old and the new cinematic languages against each other. Here, for example, the boy first fails to hear the policewoman's words, then understands her complex gestures perfectly, and lastly reproaches her for neglecting her whistle—that is, her official responsibility to the world of sound. Oleg Aleinikov—to whom I owe these insights—sees this scene as "profoundly allegorical." He continues: "on a noisy street, without so much as a word, a policewoman lets a boy know how difficult it is to find the way to the new, state-regulated family.... Mutual understanding is achieved, on this occasion, thanks to the 'forgetfulness' of a character from the world of official words, her failure to fulfill her prescribed 'sound role.'" See "Stsenary 'Otets,'" in *Strana filosofov*, vol. 7 (Moscow: IMLI RAN, 2011), 392.

7. Styopka is the standard diminutive form of Stepan. By having the official call attention to its "resonance," Platonov probably intends to make the reader think of the first rhymed story in Heinrich Hoffmann's famous children's book *Der Struwwelpeter* (usually translated as *Shockheaded Peter* or *Slovenly Peter*); the story's Russian title is *Styopka-Rasstryopka* ("Disheveled Styopka"). This and all subsequent notes about literary and political allusions in this screenplay are drawn from Yevgeny Yablokov's "Gorod platonovskikh polovinok." See "Around *Happy Moscow*," note 12.

8. It was common to refer to the years after the Civil War as the "era of

reconstruction." And the word "assimilation" (*osvoenie*) was also a standard part of Stalinist rhetoric. But this term is Zhenya's humorous invention; there was no period officially known as "the era of assimilation." The joke is subtler in Russian, since the etymological meaning of *osvoenie* is "making one's own." Having acquired a "ready-made" son, Zhenya and her husband can now go on to make him "one of the family."

9. The names of Platonov's characters often have multiple resonances, but this name is especially complex. The young woman with this name in *Happy Moscow* is French, and the name's French associations are explained in note 91. But the name also conjures up associations in Russian, all of them religious. Mount Tabor, the site of Christ's Transfiguration, is—in Russian—Mount Favor. The Tabor Light, the light revealed during the Transfiguration, is *favorsky svet*. Bessonet is close to the Russian adjective *bessonny* ("sleepless"), and this too may evoke an Orthodox image: that of the icon of Christ known as "The Unsleeping Eye": even in sleep, Christ is looking after the world.

10. This name could be translated as "Don't trust him," "Unfaithful," or even "Unbeliever."

11. Images of words evidently "fall on" Bezgadov in the way they might have done in a silent film. Here again, Platonov is exploiting both the old and the new cinematic languages. See note 6.

12. That is, steam is shooting out sideways from between the front wheels —a standard procedure to scare away animals or people likely to stray into a train's path.

13. The driver, not a native speaker of Russian, mispronounces Zhenya's name. This brings it closer both to the Russian for wife (*zhena*) and to *dzhan*, the Persian word for "soul" or "dear" that Platonov chose as the title of his short novel set in Central Asia (our English translation is titled *Soul*).

14. That is, to fully open, thus sending maximum steam to the cylinders and out through the open drain cocks, in a further attempt to scare away the blind man.

15. The drain cocks would need to be closed in order for the reversing valves to work.

16. The driver correctly wants to allow a time lag (at least half a minute) in order for the forward steam flow to cease.

17. An insulting gesture. After making a fist, you thrust your thumb between the index and middle fingers, so that it protrudes.

18. A Red Army song, written in 1918. The next line is "saw me off to join the Army."

19. Here the manuscript and the typescripts differ. In the manuscript, the postman begins not with "I work in a certain insignificant commissariat" but with "I work for Aleksey Ivanovich." From 1924 to 1930 Aleksey Ivanovich Rykov (1881–1938) was the Soviet Premier, but he was then edged out of power. In 1931 he was appointed People's Commissar of Communications, but on September 26, 1936, he was dismissed from this post. He was arrested in February 1937 and executed in March 1938. That Platonov chose to omit Rykov's name is unsurprising; apart from anything else, he wanted to keep his work up-to-date. What is interesting is the wry humor of the substitute translation, with its implicit acknowledgment that only someone already on their way out would be put in charge of such a commissariat.

20. Originally the stamp was not Abyssinian but Liberian; Platonov was probably attracted by the symbolism of the country's name. But Mussolini invaded Abyssinia in October 1935 and the Italo-Abyssinian war was widely reported in the Soviet press between February and May 1936, and it was probably during these months that Platonov introduced this change—no doubt, in the interests of topicality.

21. Platonov's work of the mid-1930s contains many references to Plato, and the various mentions of "halves" in this script are allusions to Plato's myth of the androgynes—beings endowed with both male and female sexual organs. Alarmed by the growing power of these beings, Zeus eventually cuts them in half, since when each half—that is, Man and Woman—has been seeking the other. The more surreal moments in Platonov's script, such as the precisely half-demolished building and the man undergoing "something like an abortion," allude more parodically to this myth.

22. "Father" is full of love triangles. Two are obvious: Bezgadov, Zhenya, and Lucien; and Bezgadov, Katya, and Zhenya. A third is revealed

only in part: Neverkin, Katya, and the woman to whom Neverkin wishes to give Katya's earrings. There is, very likely, a fourth: the postman, the conductress, and one of their spouses. Briefly, as they walk to the cinema, the postman, the conductress, and Katya form a fifth. And then, unexpectedly, there is the triangle formed by Zhenya and two potential fathers of the Russian nation: Pushkin and Stalin. See page 125.

23. Freud's *Introduction to Psychoanalysis* was first published in Russia in the early 1920s. In it Freud refers to *Straw Peter* (see note 6) and interprets Little Suck-a-Thumb's loss of his thumb as a symbolic castration. Platonov was interested in Freud and it seems likely that Stepan's loss of a leg is also intended as a symbolic castration. Since the break-up of families seems inevitable, and orphanhood so unbearable, Stepan appears to have decided not to inflict this pain on still more children.

24. See *Happy Moscow*, note 61.

25. Lucien's name derives from the Latin *lux*, meaning "light." He is a positive figure, and Platonov almost certainly associates him with Pushkin, who had some negroid features and one of whose great-grandfathers was African. In spite of Stepan's "Let Stalin be father," it seems that Zhenya will marry Lucien and thus—symbolically—marry Pushkin rather than Stalin. Platonov saw Pushkin as a spokesman for the common people (in Russian, often called *cherny lyud*—"black people"). Platonov may be suggesting that the Russian people should look on Pushkin—rather than Stalin—as their father.

LOVE FOR THE MOTHERLAND

1. Platonov submitted this story to the journal *Znamya* in late 1936, but it was not accepted.

2. Philip Bullock writes, "*Winterreise* is the archetypal romantic song-cycle, with a tormented and lovelorn hero articulating the melancholic disillusion of generations of outsiders: Platonov's violinist is as incongruous a figure in Stalin's Moscow as Schubert's lyric hero is in Metternich's Vienna." See "The Musical Imagination of Andrei Platonov," *Slavonica* 10, 1 (April 2004): 54–55.

3. Through this snake Platonov is probably alluding to Boris Pilnyak's story "Moist Mother Earth." Platonov lived with Pilnyak in Moscow in 1927–1928, and during the late 1920s the two writers collaborated on the travel sketch "Che-Che-O" and the play *Fools on the Periphery*. See Walker, *Transformation*, 397, note 580.

4. See page 127.

THE TEXT AND THE TRANSLATION

1. See N.V. Kornienko, "Arkhiv A. Platonova v IMLI," in *Teksto-logichesky vremennik*, vol. 1 (Moscow: IMLI, 2009), 71–73; see also Kostov, *Mifopoetika*, 18.

2. I first translated *The Foundation Pit*, in collaboration with Geoffrey Smith, for Harvill (1996); and second, in collaboration with Olga Meerson and my wife, Elizabeth Chandler, for NYRB Classics (2009) and Vintage Classics (2011).

3. *Fabrika literatury*, 432–433. See also Walker, "Platonov's Revisiting of Pushkin's Sculptural Myth," *Essays in Poetics* 27 (2002): 91–92, note 47.

THE HISTORY OF VINTAGE

The famous American publisher Alfred A. Knopf (1892–1984) founded Vintage Books in the United States in 1954 as a paperback home for the authors published by his company. Vintage was launched in the United Kingdom in 1990 and works independently from the American imprint although both are part of the international publishing group, Random House.

Vintage in the United Kingdom was initially created to publish paperback editions of books bought by the prestigious literary hardback imprints in the Random House Group such as Jonathan Cape, Chatto & Windus, Hutchinson and later William Heinemann, Secker & Warburg and The Harvill Press. There are many Booker and Nobel Prize-winning authors on the Vintage list and the imprint publishes a huge variety of fiction and non-fiction. Over the years Vintage has expanded and the list now includes great authors of the past – who are published under the Vintage Classics imprint – as well as many of the most influential authors of the present. In 2012 Vintage Children's Classics was launched to include the much-loved authors of our youth.

For a full list of the books Vintage publishes,
please visit our website
www.vintage-books.co.uk

For book details and other information about the classic authors we publish, please visit the Vintage Classics website
www.vintage-classics.info

www.vintage-classics.info

Visit www.worldofstories.co.uk for all your
favourite children's classics